Wind

Dunbar Campbell

White Bird Publications
P.O. Box 90145
Austin, Texas 78709
http://www.whitebirdpublications.com

This is a work of fiction based on true events.

ISBN: 978-1-63363-382-7
LCCN: 2019934606

This book is dedicated to the thousands of African slaves who died in Grenada during the Fédon Rebellion of 1795-1796. We will never know your names, and we can only imagine your pain. But I hope this story gives us a glimpse into your humanity so that we never forget how much of you still lives in us today.

Acknowledgement

I am thankful to many, whose ideas and inspiration contributed to this novel. However, I am especially grateful to my critiquing partners Sylvia Dickey Smith and Joy Nord for their long hours of generous discussions and thoughtful editing. Sylvia did double duty as my agent and successfully guided its publication with White Bird Publications, a truly professional and supportive organization.

Insightful conversations with Ashley Steele and valuable scholarly research by Dr. Curtis Jacobs helped shape this story. I also had the good fortune to meet Grenada people whose passion for their history implanted in me a constant reminder that Grenada had a story which had to be told. Jerry Hagins, those early discussions reaffirmed that the story was worth telling.

Finally, my appreciation goes to my wife, Susie, and daughters Malia and Crystal for their boundless encouragement and patience, especially during the many hours I spent alone with my computer, 'Betsy'.

Winds of Fédon

White Bird

Publications, LLC

Chapter One

10 April 1793
Half past ten in the morning
St. George's Bay, Grenada

"I would rather split that mongrel's skull like a coconut before I shake his hand like a gentleman."

Father's biting words under furious St. George's sunshine reminded Malcolm how far his father had come. Twelve years past, Father had limped off the ship in Liverpool, a defeated soldier wrapped in cold winds.

"I have yet to meet this man." Malcolm raised his voice as squawking seagulls drifted overhead. "But I already detest him."

They addressed each other in the bustling St. George's Bay, waiting for a moored galleon to take Father back to England for six months of military and business matters.

Along rows of warehouses facing the bay, gang leaders cracked whips and barked orders at African slaves. Estate gentlemen in waistcoats and breeches huddled over sales contracts, waving their hats in exuberant negotiations.

Father stood dressed in full Red-Coat military regalia, energized with a pride Malcolm had thought his father lost when he returned to Liverpool from the American Revolutionary War in the early winter of 1781.

The Yorktown humiliation at the hands of the ragtag American mobs, aided by the treacherous French, left Father with gaunt cheeks, boney limbs, and burdened posture. His tortured demeanor inspired no hope he could recover his will to fight again. He withdrew into his study in their Duke Street house with only his pipe and a bottle, taking brief moments for food or latrine relief.

For hours each day, months on end, eleven-year-old Malcolm sat on the polished floor outside the study, waiting for Father's spirited words to ignite his adventurous imagination with stories about virgin shores and unconquered lands. Malcolm ached for Father to grip him by the shoulders again, to encourage the notion that Malcolm's fortune and happiness awaited him in the new world, in glorious service to His Majesty, King George III.

But all Malcolm received during those gray months were rum fumes and tobacco smoke escaping under the door from Father's self-imposed confinement. Father's absence felt like death, a death Malcolm could not yet bring himself to grieve. As long as there was hope.

And when hope did arrive—in a dispatch of new military orders from His Majesty— Father rose from the dead to all the jubilation young Malcolm could exert without exploding like gunpowder. On that memorable day, a grateful Malcolm promised his life in loyal service to King George III and promised to never let his father go into battle again for King and Country without Malcolm at his side.

Father and son, they would be, until death.

That promise took Malcolm to the Royal Military Academy at Woolwich Common, a commission with His Majesty's Army, and an assignment to Grenada six months ago as a second lieutenant in the Sixty-Seventh Regiment under the command of his father, Colonel Hector McDonald. By age twenty-one, Malcolm had earned Father's total trust and confidence in military matters, as well as property and business affairs. Hence the reason for Father's parting instructions in the humid St. George's Bay today.

"This man I want you to meet is a mixed breed with no loyalty to black or white," Father said. "I will send you his papers as soon as I arrive in England. When you receive them, go and get his signature. But leave promptly and watch your back."

"Yes, sir."

A donkey cart hauling bales of raw tobacco creaked past and stopped next to the ship's cargo ramp. This was probably the last shipment of tobacco from Grenada, given the sugar, cocoa, and coffee plantations gobbling up the island.

Tobacco scents no longer revived Malcolm's tormented memories of Father's pipe-smoking hermitage back in England. Those days seemed far away and so long ago now.

Today, the aroma of crops stirred ambitions for wealth and raised hope, the kind that restored Father's robust physique and pride. Five feet ten inches, he stood tall in his red coat, buttons glittering in the sunshine. His blue eyes focused with such steadfastness, Malcolm got the sense they penetrated the present and saw into the future.

Family and friends thought that the clean-shaved father and son bore a striking resemblance, even with Father's hair as white and immaculate as the white belts crossing his barrel chest. His only blemishes, a chipped tooth from the American War and tobacco stains on his fingertips from years of stuffing his pipe.

Across the roadway, the British slave galleon groaned against the ropes that restrained her to the wooden docks, as if impatient to embark on the transatlantic journey that would take Father back to Liverpool. A nauseating odor oozed from the ship, escaping from under the rich fragrance of raw crops baking in the sunlight.

Malcolm smelled the ship even before he saw it pull into the port a week ago to disgorge a fresh supply of Africans. After seven weeks across the Middle Passage, from Africa to the West Indies, the exhausted slave ship exhaled its decaying breath over St. George's Bay. The pungent blend of puke, human excrement, and unwashed bodies still turned Malcolm's stomach upside down even though it had not been his first exposure to the ships.

And, he acknowledged to himself with a tinge of regret, it would not be his last.

In his early weeks on the island, he had also seen slaves carry off the bloated rot of their unfortunate brethren. Those who perished during the journey but remained undiscovered in the bowels of the ships until their arrival in port.

Malcolm wondered how many more might have been discarded overboard along the way.

During subsequent ship arrivals, he would seek refuge from the stench in his hilltop Fort George barracks, on the spine of the western peninsula. But it hardly mattered. The winds racing down the green mountains to the bay would inhale the ships' foul vapors and roar up the two-hundred-foot ridge to the fort. Then, they would blow their sickening contents over the thick stone walls and into Malcolm's room.

This matter of slaves, Father always reminded him, even with its unpleasant hiccups, was a necessary fixture in the otherwise efficient mercantile traffic that helped to build and protect the expanding British Empire. Should King George just sit idly by and watch the French, Dutch, Spanish, and Portuguese reap the rewards of unlimited

African labor? These countries were amassing wealth from their own vast slave plantations in the New World. Their burgeoning accounts financed armies and navies to threaten Great Britain and her subjects on every continent. Even Africans captured their own to do God's work for His Majesty.

Who was Malcolm to question the morality of extracting their industrious energies or losing a few dearly-departed souls along the way?

He dismissed the temptation to dwell on it much further. Father battled for and helped build the British Empire. Today, as the highest-ranking officer in Grenada, he stood at the crest of opportunity to share in Grenada's agricultural wealth, sailing back to Mother England to draft the documents for the lucrative sale of a large Grenada estate. Father had never occupied the estate but leased it to the buyer until a London company agreed to finance the sale.

"I shall send you the documents on the first vessel departing London," Father said. "Should take about two months. Once he signs, seek your leave immediately. Expect me back in six months."

Malcolm felt a touch of puzzlement that Father would sell an estate of such magnitude to a free colored man—and a slave-owning French mulatto at that. But he knew better than to question his father. The colonel's frequent consultations with the governor in recent weeks probably erased any impropriety in the sale. All Malcolm had to do was await the delivery of documents authorizing the sale of Belvidere Estate, 450 acres of bountiful land, along with eighty slaves, sixteen head of horned cattle and five horses.

Later that day, Malcolm stood on the Fort George heights watching the immense white sails drag the ship away from Grenada's shores and into the blood-red sunset. He recalled Father's words.

This man I want you to meet is a mixed breed with no loyalty to black or white.

5

Despite the warning, he considered Father's request simple, given the size of the transaction. All Malcolm had to do was saddle his horse and ride up the mountains to get a signature from a mixed-breed, free-colored mongrel named Julien Fédon.

"Mail Call!" Three months after Father departed for England, the announcement from the Sergeant of the Guard bounced off Fort George's stone-walled corridors to Malcolm's barracks. Just as Father promised, a package awaited Malcolm when he marched into the mailroom ahead of the echoing footsteps of other excited soldiers.

He hurried back to his room and ripped open the paper-wrapped bundle. Much to his delight, in addition to Father's formal documents, it contained a book and letters from his brothers and Mother. He read her letter first.

> *My Dearest Malcolm,*
>
> *My heart misses you daily, but the proud service you render King George at such a tender age excites my deepest admiration. Father speaks glowingly of your courage, your intelligence, your maturity. We beg that you soon plan to share your success with a young lady of fine class and enduring qualities...*

Of course, Mother meant the daughter of that Lord from Cheshire, the retired general who groomed Father's rise in military ranks during the American war. Malcolm met the girl two years ago, a shy flower with pink cheeks and impeccable etiquette, but she hardly sparked his curiosity.

The most remarkable memory of that visit with his parents to the Lord's elegant country house came when a black man opened the door for them. Malcolm stood bewildered by the man's wide nose, soft eyes, and the sheen of his color. He must have sensed Malcolm's wonder, for his amused smile burst forth with an unrestrained breeze of humanity. His flawless British accent floated on a cushion of humility as he motioned them into the waiting room with his white-gloved hands.

"England always had blacks," Father reminded Malcolm later. "Mainly in London and ports bustling with the transatlantic trade, such as Bristol and Liverpool. But we have many more of them now, especially after slavery was abolished here in England in 1772."

Malcolm had known about Africans before that day. Mother used to wear an enamel gold-trimmed pendant showing a black girl serving at a tea party, and Malcolm's English Literature teacher taught that black musicians entertained Britain's aristocrats as early as the fifth century. Malcolm had also seen black men driving carriages at a distance in Liverpool.

Yet, even now in St. George's, where blacks outnumbered whites ten to one, he never forgot this first greeting from a black man. Perhaps because it struck him then that, had Malcolm been blindfolded, he would have assumed the man a white Englishman. So why would the skin color matter? The question lingered in Malcolm's mind, and so did the memory of the Lord's doorman, more so than the Lord's daughter.

Despite their best efforts, Malcolm's parents failed to plant seeds of romance for their son during that visit, or since, but Mother never gave up. With her letters and gifts, she intended to keep him wrapped in his English customs and in her dreams of marital bliss for him. She included in his mail, a packet of Chinese green tea and a pair of porcelain tea cups along with matching saucers.

He turned his attention to his brothers' letters, which told of neighborhood cricket games and more troubling news crossing the English Channel. Four years after mobs stormed the Bastille Fortress, France still quaked with revolutionary tribulations. They installed guillotines, executed King Louis XVI, and now Queen Marie Antoinette languished under house arrest.

Malcolm reached into the package and paged through a book on Edmund Burke. Then he retrieved Father's papers. They comprised the Belvidere documents for Monsieur Fédon and a letter for Mr. Turnbull, the owner of Beauséjour Estate, halfway up the west coast to Gouyave.

As Father instructed, Malcolm later hired a rider to notify Mr. Turnbull of Malcolm's plan to stop by on his way to Belvidere Estate. Thereafter, the rider delivered a note to Monsieur Julien Fédon, stating Malcolm's intention to arrive with the sale papers for signatures later that same day, a week hence

The rider returned to Fort George the next morning with verbal regards from Mr. Turnbull and a written response from Monsieur Fédon.

> *Dear Lieutenant McDonald,*
>
> *I look forward to seeing you next week Monday, 15 July 1793 at or around two o'clock in the afternoon. Present also will be my barrister and witnesses to complete the sale documents.*
>
> *Best wishes for a safe journey to Belvidere Estate.*
>
> *Your most humble servant,*
>
> *Julien Fédon*

In *Italiante* style, with graceful twirls throughout, the note had an attractive feminine flair. Either a woman had written it, or Monsieur Fédon did not deserve the harsh attributes Father had assigned to him.

Chapter Two

Malcolm rolled out of his bed before the fifers and drummers awakened the fort. He read a Psalms passage from the King James Holy Bible that Mother tucked into his baggage the day he embarked on his voyage to Grenada.

Later, he washed and changed into a loose cotton shirt, light waistcoat, and dark breeches. He struggled into his riding boots, tossed on a wool cocked hat, and hurried down the stone walkway to the mess hall. He consumed a hearty meal of buttered bread, cheese, saltfish, and eggs, followed by a leisurely cup of steaming tea.

He then met with his company commander, a captain who briefed him on security concerns in Gouyave, twelve coastal miles north of St. George's and separated from Belvidere by three mountainous miles.

The captain handed him dispatches to deliver to the Gouyave Militia post, headed by a Dr. John Hay. "Dr. Hay will apprise you of the state of his militia. So, grant him a

1

few hours."

"How does he manage his patients and the militia at the same time?"

"He is quite a patriot. You will see him in action. Loved by all. But be careful in Gouyave. We have a few British subjects there, but most of the residents still think they are French."

"I notice our maps call it Charlotte Town," Malcolm said.

The captain could barely contain his aggravation. "Yes, but they much rather name it after a bloody fruit than after Her Majesty, Queen Charlotte."

Lest he offended anyone he encountered there, Malcolm reminded himself to pronounce the town correctly, guava—minus the last 'a.' He too wondered with amusement what kind of people would hate the British so intensely, that they preferred to name their town after a fruit than after a British queen.

Malcolm thanked the captain and headed to the stables to prepare Father's horse for the ride to Belvidere Estate. Father had claimed the brown and white Quarter Horse from a Frenchman who fled to Trinidad to escape bad debts. Quick and hardy, the horse would surely enjoy the ride now that Father's absence meant long hours of inactivity at the Fort George stables. Malcolm's horse, one he shared with other junior officers, never lacked for exercise, given their daily patrols around the bustling town.

For extra padding on the long ride, he folded a thick saddle blanket, discretely without regimental emblem, and buckled the saddle in place. He also decided against carrying his Army single-bladed saber. Such a British signature might make him a tempting and unnecessary military target in the staunchly French countryside. But with Father's words ringing in his ears, he slid his short-barreled flintlock carbine into the bearskin bucket.

"A soldier is always ready for battle," Father repeatedly lectured.

The warnings rang especially true in Grenada, where slaves and hostile French residents vastly outnumbered Englishmen. The French angrily resisted British rule, complaining that even though the British landed first in 1609, it was French blood that succeeded in driving the indigenous Indian savages to their suicidal demise off Leapers Hill in Sauteurs in 1650. French and slave sweat had developed Grenada's soil for more than a century before Commodore Swanton captured it without a shot in 1762.

One night a few months ago, soon after Malcolm had arrived in Grenada, a drunken Frenchman with rancid breath had attempted to explain the ensuing years to Malcolm in a tavern along St. George's Bay.

"When *L'Anglais* stole our...beloved *L'Isle de la Grenade*, Devine Providence intervened," the man mumbled under lantern shadows. "Earthquake...in 1766. Next year, slave rebellion. In 1771, fire burned down Royal, what you...you people call St. George's today. Then again...in 1775, Royal burned flat. Four years later, we finally defeated *L'Anglais* and chased them from our shores."

"But," Malcolm reminded the man, "the British flag was planted here first, in 1609, forty years before the first Frenchman landed on the island. Your own country returned it to us under the Treaty of Versailles in 1783, ten years ago."

The man persisted, his rotten teeth emitting a nauseating odor and his jagged filthy fingernails almost at Malcolm's nose. "That treaty will be...washed away with blood. Divine Providence will return soon. Fire and rebellion will be the curse of *L'Anglais*."

Malcolm worried the man might be right. The last bastion of civilized governance on the island remained His Majesty's Sixty-Seventh Regiment under Colonel McDonald, heavily concentrated in St. George's. The remaining ninety-five percent of the island balanced precariously on a tightrope between entrenched French loyalties and nervous British control, held in place only by an unpopular treaty.

After listening to the Frenchman's ramblings, Malcolm now felt that the British hold on the French and slave population was as rational as holding an angry wolf by its ears.

It was just a matter of time.

The tavern conversation weltered on Malcolm's mind as he swung a pouch of bullets and a powder horn over his shoulder in preparation for his ride to Belvidere. He stuffed extra pouches of the same next to his carbine in the bearskin bucket. The stack of bound documents fitted snuggly into his leather saddlebag, along with the Edmund Burke book and Father's letter to his friend, Mr. Turnbull of Beauséjour Estate.

Malcolm mounted the horse and galloped down the hill from the fort to the coast. He crossed the guarded bridge and headed north in a light trot on the meandering carriage trail—his first time outside the secure limits of St. George's.

The smell of cooking smoke, which typically smothered the town, faded behind him, and the lush countryside beckoned him with aromas of sweet fruit and wildflowers. To his left, sharp midmorning sunlight glittered off the blue Caribbean as far as the eye could see. Waves whispered up sandy beaches and sprayed the air with salt-scented mists. To his right, luxuriant greenery rolled all the way up cloud-capped mountains.

Just ahead, the road broke to the right and disappeared into sugarcane fields. The scent of molasses thickened the air and drenched his taste buds. At the base of the foothill, the white sails of a windmill rotated in a steady breeze. On a lower slope, a boiler house belched dense smoke against unblemished skies. Slaves sang amidst the cane stalks, their battered straw hats peeking above swaying sheets of green.

Malcolm wondered if they sang to nourish their

despondent spirits, or in gratitude to be in productive labor for His Majesty. Surely, they would be none the better in the hostile African jungles, living in fear of kidnappings and attacks from their own kind.

He kept in the shadows of the big mahoganies to avoid the biting sun, but within an hour of his departure from the fort, the rising heat and humidity had soaked his shirt. He took a heavy gulp of water from his canteen. He would welcome Liverpool's perpetually gray skies and cool winds right about now.

At a wooden bridge spanning a shallow crystal-clear river, he entered the running water instead, pausing in midstream to cool the horse's hoofs. The horse blew a low rumble with a joyous shake of his head. The stream sang past them, meandering through clusters of sun-bleached rocks and down the ridge to the sea.

He dismounted at the far bank and refilled his canteen with river water. When he stood to pluck a yellow mango from a low-lying branch, frantic rustling disturbed the reeds. He grabbed his carbine just as a flock of waterfowl scattered into the tree line. He resisted the temptation to collect a few, lest his gunshots attracted undesirable attention. With such unclaimed abundance of wildlife, fruits, and beauty on the island, he could now understand the French reluctance to surrender it.

But treaties had to be respected.

Grenada belonged to the British.

He trotted the horse back onto the mud-caked roadway and continued north. A donkey-drawn cart, laden with bulging bags and ridden by a slave, headed in the opposite direction, towards St. George's.

The slave pulled over to the side and nodded without eye contact. "Marning, Sah." A toothy smile lit his face.

"Good morning," Malcolm answered. "Do you know how much farther to Mr. Turnbull's Beauséjour Estate?"

"Not far, *oui*." He pointed in the direction Malcolm headed. "Two hills, one river, Sah."

"Thank you." Malcolm rode off a few horse lengths and glanced back.

The slave had not moved. He just kept staring at Malcolm.

Chapter Three

"Welcome to Beauséjour Estate, Lieutenant McDonald."
Mr. Turnbull, in his mid-fifties, bounced down the balcony
steps of his sprawling two-storied brick house, his scuffed
buckle shoes cowering under his rotund weight. Despite a
steady breeze, the man sweated profusely in his stretched
waistcoat and soaked white shirt. He carried a knotted
leather thong—thicker than a horsewhip—coiled at one
side of his red breeches and a holstered pistol on the other.
He posed an intimidating sight, but when he removed his
wide hat, his dimpled smile and British mannerisms
disarmed Malcolm's concerns.

The man stepped onto an immaculate front lawn,
which embraced the full length of the white house. Flowers
graced the open verandah with a brilliance of colors that
Malcolm had until then, never seen. The lawn cascaded to
the right side of the house, fading to where a horse trail
stretched from thick hillside woods down to the seashore.

Adjacent to the trail, a muddy flat rested in the sun-spotted shade of a luxuriant mahogany tree. Wavering spears of light pierced the leafy canopy to a basket-sized hole in the ground. Nearby, a pole stood erect with a rope dangling from its summit.

Mr. Turnbull's voice boomed. "I can see the resemblance to Colonel McDonald immediately."

Malcolm dismounted and retrieved Father's letter from the saddle bag.

He handed Mr. Turnbull the letter and shook his hand. "I am pleased to make your acquaintance."

The handshake vibrated around the man's chin, rolls of fat that made it difficult for Malcolm to distinguish where the neck started or ended. Mr. Turnbull directed a slave to take the horse to a nearby tree shade.

A curvaceous woman with red hair and glowing smile stepped out of the doorway and floated down the verandah steps towards them. She emitted a pleasant disposition, heightened by an appealing scent of fresh soap-washed linen hung out to dry. Mr. Turnbull's presence discouraged Malcolm's temptation to expand his visual exploration from the woman's freckled face and brown eyes to the generous breasts that bulged in her thin white top.

Probably twenty years Mr. Turnbull's junior, he introduced her as his wife.

Mrs. Turnbull stood at her husband's side and shook Malcolm's hand. "You are every bit the English gentleman as your father," she said with a conspicuously crisp accent. "And might I add in confidence, more handsome."

"Thank you, Ma'am. I promise to keep it a secret from him."

Malcolm's surprise at her accent must have shown on his face.

Mr. Turnbull quickly explained, scratching his bushy sideburns. "Mrs. Turnbull spent her youth in Boston. Convincing her to leave the crumbling American colonies for a future here in the Indies was an easy task."

"I am lucky," she said. "The view from here takes me back home to where I overlooked Boston Harbor." She gazed over the sea. "And not to mention, I have the most charming husband on the island."

Malcolm obligingly joined Mr. Turnbull in a hearty laugh.

Mrs. Turnbull did not.

Located on a wind-swept hill, the great house held an imposing view of the vast sugarcane greenery that waved in the breeze from the edge of the house grounds all the way down to the shoreline. An occasional voice lifted in song from the fields but soon died in the blistering heat. A gust, drenched with a smoky blend of sweet molasses and sea salt, blew up the hill with a flurry of ash flakes.

Mr. Turnbull removed his hat and fanned his face. "We get ashes for a couple days after burning some of the fields. The burning removes all the leaves and kills pests before harvesting but keeps the stalks in good processing shape. It also reduces manual labor and replenishes the soil in one stroke. So, you see, even nature is a friendly participant in this enterprise."

A lull in the winds gave way to a mouth-watering aroma that reminded Malcolm of his mother's cooking.

Mrs. Turnbull glanced back at the house. "I must return to the kitchen now. God knows what mischief the servants get into when I am not around to supervise."

Malcolm lowered his head and tipped his wool cocked-hat. "It was a pleasure meeting you, Mrs. Turnbull."

"I do hope you plan to join us for lunch."

"You're very kind, Ma'am. The temptation is overwhelming, but I must leave soon to keep a business appointment in Belvidere."

"So sorry."

"I am the one sorry to miss your Boston flavors, Ma'am."

"Maybe next time." She smiled with a nod, and

gracefully crossed the lawn to the steps, her long red hair flowing behind her.

As she climbed the steps to the verandah, the wind blew Mrs. Turnbull's loose flowered skirt around pale-white legs. Too soon, she vanished into the house. Malcolm hoped his brief but satisfying gaze on Mrs. Turnbull did not betray any appearance of impropriety to her husband.

Mr. Turnbull cleared his throat with obvious exaggeration. "Off to meet Monsieur Fédon?"

"Yes, sir. He is to sign the agreement of sale for Belvidere Estate."

Mr. Turnbull tugged open Father's letter with his beefy fingers and read the pages as they flapped in the wind.

Mrs. Turnbull emerged on a second-floor balcony and dealt a servant a Bostonian tongue lashing, but her tone lacked the fierce edge Malcolm had heard from other women accosting their slaves in St. George's. He wondered if she was simply vying for Malcolm's attention while her husband read the letter.

Fearful his untamed desire to examine her feminine gifts might embarrass him a second time, Malcolm shifted his focus to the bustling activities around the sugarcane field. Donkey-drawn carts, laden with sugarcane, crept along trails towards the windmill on the north perimeter of the estate. Smoke rose unimpeded into the clear sky from the nearby boiler house, a long building with a chimney at one end. Horsemen with whips patrolled the work areas. And across the rolling field of green, the sun glistened off sweating black skin and sharpened machetes.

Malcolm glanced at the ridge top overlooking the boiler house, where a little girl stood watching. She wore rags and leaned on a walking stick. She did not share the same dark complexion as the slaves. Dark, but more dark-brown.

She must have noticed him staring at her. She turned and hobbled away, tilting on her stick as she vanished into the tree line at the edge of the field.

One leg seemed horribly mangled.

Mr. Turnbull finished reading the letter and inserted it in his vest pocket.

"I have at length warned Colonel McDonald about Fédon. That man embodies the cunning of the French and the deceit of the Negroes."

Malcolm restrained his impulse to defend Father's business decision with more vigor. "Father thinks Grenada must embrace all the King's subjects, as distasteful as some of this might be."

"You do not know Fédon as I do." Mr. Turnbull paused as if to choose his next words with care. "Some of our British gentlemen are gambling that most of the French residents will eventually pack their bags and join their comrades in friendlier islands like Guadalupe and Trinidad. Men like your father will profit exceedingly well if they reclaim defaulted estates from departing French owners or repurchase them at very low prices."

"But why would they leave Grenada? Did not Fédon and others recently sign the Declaration of Loyalty to Great Britain?"

"Yes, thirty-four of the French and their mulatto estate owners signed it. But they are all wolves in sheep's clothing." Mr. Turnbull's smile engaged only one side of his big face. "I do not think they plan to leave Grenada or to live in a British Grenada either."

"Are you suggesting they will break the treaty?"

"Me boy, treaties only last until the next cannon is fired. Remember, we captured Grenada from them in 1762 during the Seven Years' War and sealed it under the Treaty of Paris. But then they recaptured it in 1779 during the American War of Independence. It took another four years and another treaty for us to get it back in 1783. The American War brought France to her financial knees. But they will soon become belligerent again, especially with their bizarre revolution. If they would behead their own king, they surely would have no friendly overtures for King George."

Malcolm wondered if Father arranged this meeting for Mr. Turnbull to share his intimate knowledge about the island's history and future. If so, did Father know the man would paint such bleak a picture of times to come?

Men like Mr. Turnbull in Grenada were like British fish outnumbered in a sea of French sharks. Nine out of ten in the population spoke French. Even the slaves spoke their own kind of French patois. Every estate, every town, and every village, except maybe St. George, had a French name, Marquis, Petite Anse, La Baye. Mr. Turnbull's own estate maintained its distinctively French name, Beauséjour Estate. What indignities did he suffer each night going to sleep on an estate with such a reminder?

Malcolm continued. "Would not a good place to start sinking British roots here be to change the names around the island to English names?"

"That is swimming upstream, me boy." Double wrinkles stretched across his sweaty forehead. "They had the island for one hundred and twenty years. We have had it for only twenty-five. Even the French Roman Catholic Church in St. George's is older and larger than our Anglican Church. The largest symbol of King George on the island is the Union Jack. But it only continues to fly because brave men like you and your father awake each day to defend it."

"I do admit I have much to learn."

"We do not need to argue on our first meeting. Allow me to show you something." Mr. Turnbull led Malcolm away from the house to the edge of the front yard.

"Dealing with all of His Majesty's subjects is not that simple," Mr. Turnbull said. "You only have to understand what happened to the King's American Colonies to assess the magnitude of our challenges."

Malcolm recalled all that Father told him about Mr. Turnbull, and it helped him to understand the man's dismal temperament. Having lost a lifetime of earnings in Boston during the American Revolutionary War and disgusted by the disloyal mobs that overran the King's former colonies, Mr. Turnbull arrived in Grenada in 1783, while the ink on the Treaty of Versailles was still wet. When the British governor offered him Beauséjour Estate, one of several large holdings abandoned by French owners too proud to live under the Union Jack, he readily accepted. By Father's account, Mr. Turnbull's industry and combative nature made him an ideal candidate for the British to establish loyal footholds on the island's lucrative sugar trade.

But his prosperity had done little to lift his contentment.

"You feel those winds blowing down these hills?" Mr. Turnbull asked. "They also blow strange ideas about freedom from places like Paris, Saint Dominique, and Guadalupe."

"My brothers just wrote me of more turmoil in Paris."

"Let the French destroy each other." Mr. Turnbull pointed his finger at his busy sugar plantation. "Sugar is king. Just in this century, the average English family has quadrupled their consumption of sugar. Every supper table in Europe needs it. You see these acres and acres of cane flourishing here? They build empires. Our taxes build His Majesty's Navy and arm his soldiers like you, to spread civilization around the world. French ideas do not build empires. My stock of Negroes eats better here than in the African chaos from which we rescued them. What you are looking at here is a happy formula for progress. French ideas about liberty and equality will poison this. Freedom will kill these slaves."

"Do you think—"

A shout echoed from the tree-clogged hills overlooking the house. A big black man on horseback rode out of the jungle canopy and onto the trail, a musket held aloft.

A barefooted woman shuffled behind the horse, her

hands tied to a length of rope that trailed from the saddle. Dogs barked from behind the house.

Mrs. Turnbull yelled from the second-floor balcony, shading her eyes with her hand as she scanned the sunny hillside. "Is that Kojo? Did he find her?"

"Haha." Mr. Turnbull bellowed. "Looks like Kojo has done a most commendable job again, my dear."

"Is she a runaway?" Malcolm asked him.

"Yes, four months gone. Stay right here, me boy," Mr. Turnbull said. "You now have the best seat to an important lesson in plantation management."

Mr. Turnbull wobbled his way across the lawn towards the trail and shouted at a young slave sweeping the verandah. "Ring the bell."

The boy began to hit an iron rod against the insides of a triangular metal frame. The clanging drifted over the fields. Several horsemen armed with carbines cracked their whips and barked orders. On cue, multitudes of slaves hurried barefoot from the fields. They headed up the hill to the mud flat beneath the mahogany tree.

Mrs. Turnbull raced down the verandah steps and hurried towards Malcolm. "I detest this sort of thing." Her voice quivered. "But Mr. Turnbull believes masters who do not discipline their slaves eventually lose their heads."

"Did you know her?"

"One of my best kitchen helps. Pretty young girl. Seventeen, maybe eighteen. She keeps running away to join other runaways, maroons who prefer a wretched existence in the wild interior than a free full plate on the plantation. This is her third time."

"Mrs. Turnbull—"

Her voice softened. "I prefer you call me Charlotte. Like Queen Charlotte, but Mr. Turnbull reminds me every day I am no queen."

He wondered why she had not told him her first name when Mr. Turnbull made the introduction earlier. "What is going to happen with her?"

"'Tis not only what will happen to her." She fixed her sight on his face and lips, her bosom heaving with the rising anxiety in her voice. "'Tis also what will happen to you."

He turned away and gazed up at the hillside. Kojo guided the horse down the trail from the woods, with the barefoot girl stumbling behind. Now closer to the house, she looked pregnant.

"She is full with child." Charlotte shouted at her husband.

"Then I shall have a little mercy since she is adding a little pickaninny to the flock," he yelled back. "I shall let her keep her leg."

"Oh Jesus," Charlotte moaned. "He uses that hole under the tree to protect the babies when he punishes women heavy with child. Does he not know the baby feels it too?"

When he reached the tree, Kojo dismounted his horse and grabbed the rope that led to the girl.

Mr. Turnbull marched up to her.

Her eyes bled tears down her dusty face. "No Massa, please."

Kojo tugged the rope tied to the girl's wrists. "Hush up." He turned to Mr. Turnbull. "Please, let me do it, Massa."

Mr. Turnbull glanced at Kojo and nodded.

With one drag of his black muscular arms, Kojo ripped off her thin, soiled dress.

She tried in vain to cover her swollen breasts and belly. "The baby, Massa. Please, the baby."

About a hundred slaves, in work rags and straw hats, shuffled in silent despondency around the tree.

"Everyone better be watching," Mr. Turnbull shouted at them. "I shall no longer spare the rod."

The slaves looked on with blank expressions and glassy eyes.

Malcolm's heart raced.

Kojo grabbed the girl by the neck and shoved her to her knees. He called over two other slaves. They lifted her by her struggling arms and legs and positioned her face down, the hole in the ground accommodating her protruding stomach. Kojo stood over her with a barefoot firmly on her lower back. The other men roped her restrained hands to the pole and tied her ankles to two wooden stakes hammered into the ground.

"Massa, please no," she cried. "Ah never run again."

Kojo's helpers stepped out of the way and returned to the crowd.

Mr. Turnbull handed his platted and knotted leather thong to Kojo. "Give her twenty of your best."

Kojo stepped forward, shaking the whip. The muscles on his arms and back bulged as if snakes crawled beneath his black skin. He shifted his bare feet in the dirt and eyed the girl. His hand shot up and then down, dragging the whip on a slashing rage through the air.

The whip clapped against the girl's exposed back and bounced off.

She recoiled. A prolonged screech, the likes of which Malcolm had never heard from a mortal being, rose over the hillside.

A long strip of her black skin turned white, and then red as it swelled with blood.

Malcolm bit his lip.

Tears flowed down Charlotte's cheeks. She turned and fled up the steps to the house, her hands covering her ears.

Mr. Turnbull looked on, his big arms folded and a strangely contented glee on his face.

Another slash through the air.

Another clap.

Another scream.

Malcolm lost count of the number of times the whip collided with the girl's bloodied back before the word roared from deep inside him. "Stop."

More screams filled the air.

He rushed passed Mr. Turnbull and plowed into the downcast gathering. Sweaty bodies cleared a hurried path, dense with fear and stale human odor. Dark eyes stared back at him.

Behind him, Mr. Turnbull barked. "Lieutenant McDonald. Do not dare."

Malcolm raced towards Kojo just as the man's muscular arm rose to deliver another strike of the whip.

Malcolm grabbed Kojo's arm. "That is enough."

Kojo turned. His watery eyes blazed a fury that could only have meant one thing.

Malcolm had just made a deadly mistake.

Chapter Four

"Rosette," Her father's shout thundered through the hilltop Belvidere Estate great house with such ferocity, Rosette wondered if he would one day shake their new home off its foundation.

"*Oui*, Papa." She preferred calling him *Papa*, rather than the stuffier *Père* that some of her friends called their fathers. Her early morning calm now rattled, Rosette shut the book she had been reading and rolled off her bed. The polished wood floor cooled the naked soles of her feet as she raced through the narrow hallway. She hurried down the stairs and sprinted through the living room to where Papa's robust frame filled the verandah doorway.

Unruly hair dangled out from beneath his tattered straw hat and crawled along the sides of his sweaty coffee-brown face. His intense dark eyes burned in a manner as threatening as the leather whip looped at his side. She hoped he changed his soaked black shirt, soiled britches, and muddy boots before the English visitors arrived, but she dared not venture to express such sentiments to him. Few dared ever to lecture Monsieur Julien Fédon.

"The sun is already up, and you still in your bed clothes?" he bellowed.

"*Pardon,* Papa."

"Have you forgotten we have visitors this afternoon and *Saraka* tonight?"

Of course, she would never forget the *Saraka*, the African tradition of food, song, and dance planned for tonight to celebrate their ancestors and to give thanks for the future. Tonight's celebration carried even deeper sentiments now that Papa's purchase of Belvidere was just hours away. "I was just selecting a book to read to Grandmère—"

"There is no time for reading." He growled. "Go make yourself available to your Maman in the kitchen."

He turned and vanished into the cool hazy morning.

Papa's carriage had always been abrupt and anxious, but even more so in recent months. She understood, given his pressing business plans for Belvidere Estate. But he was not the man to welcome words of compassion, and especially not so when his seventeen-year-old-daughter delivered them.

Words meant little to Papa, neither written nor spoken. He lived in a world of deeds. Words were lazy bystanders, idle observers of the heights accomplished by inspired men and women of action. When written words became necessary, for a shipment contract or to purchase an African, he turned to people who squandered time on books and papers.

People like Rosette.

Her grandmother had planted the earliest seeds, paying for her tutoring, and embracing the times Rosette could sit and read to her. Grandmère's favorites were passages from the Bible and books that her now departed husband had left behind. Rosette used to believe that Grandmère's fading eyesight was the reason the old woman never read, until she discovered that illiteracy was a silent plague afflicting the family.

Rosette still nursed the embarrassment that stung her when she discovered her parents' marriage certificate in their Grand Pauvre home, when she was almost eleven. The French words sprung at her like a coiled snake.

Les parties contractantes ont declarés ne savoir signer. "The contracting parties have declared that they cannot sign."

Rosette's parents, Papa and Maman, both mulatto descendants of slaves and slave owners. And now about to own a lush slave plantation in the middle of the island, were as unread as their slaves. So close was Papa to some of his slaves, in manner and fellowship, Rosette often wondered if illiteracy created its own bond between men. Maybe so, but the workers' familiarity with Papa, rarely invited contempt. Only the most insolent of the enslaved ever tested Papa's role as undisputed master. Those who gambled with disobedience wore scars as silent testimony to their bad judgement.

But even more damning were his threats to sell those slaves to feared British masters.

Papa always delivered on his threats when pushed.

And it did not take much to push Papa.

His aspirations for his family and Belvidere Estate were paramount to any bond crafted from skin color and illiteracy.

Dated in 1780, a year after the glorious French reclaimed Grenada, the certificate also revealed that Papa and Maman had previously married under the rule of the *L'Anglais* in 1774, two years before Rosette was born. It referred to Maman as 'Mestive,' which explained the native Amerindian features that Rosette inherited from her mother: high cheekbones and coarse black hair that, when braided, stretched down the length of her back.

But given the British scorn of anything French,

Rosette often pondered if they would one day claim that her parents' French Roman Catholic marriage had nullified their earlier British Protestant marriage, and therefore none existed. The Grenada legislative council, which banned French and Catholic members, had already passed legislation decreeing that only marriages, baptisms, and funerals performed by Protestant clergymen were recognized.

Would a man long dead and buried be considered alive unless a Protestant clergyman said otherwise?

Such British madness.

She was too young to remember her Grandpère before his passing, but another of the certificates she discovered acknowledged him and his wife as *'Pierre Foedon Européén, et de Brigitte negresse libre créole de 'isle Martinique.* "A Frenchman married to a free negress from Martinique.

Discovering her parents' illiteracy was hardly the only ache in Rosette's chest. Growing up, it seemed, was about accumulating bitterness. And nothing fired her angst like the rage *L'Anglais* inspired in her father. Papa would be so much a warmer father to her, and less antagonized, but for the British and their tyrannical rule over the French on the island.

Nonetheless, just as Papa had begun to learn from Rosette the value of reading and writing, Rosette also learned his clever ways of disarming the British with smiles, humility, and sworn loyalties.

She had never met this Lieutenant McDonald, to whom she had written the note for her father. But when he showed up this afternoon, she would ensure he had not the slightest suspicion of her hatred for him and his kind.

Rosette ran downstairs to the porch when the first English visitor galloped up to the great house just before two o'clock on the sun-beaten afternoon. Her heart raced with heightened expectation, but not for the visitors. Today would be blessed with good fortune for Papa, his family, and the Belvidere enslaved. If the British colonel and his son upheld their word, Papa would move from leaseholder to owner of one of the largest estates on the island, after a modest down payment of ten shillings. Then the Saraka would begin. She tapped her toes to the drum rhythms she would be dancing to in just hours.

She had already spent the full morning helping to prepare lavish piles of plantains, yams, fish, and beef for tonight's Saraka. While large outdoor pots bubbled on raging wood fires behind the kitchen, she accompanied Maman and servants into the fields to cut stacks of banana leaves from which the feast would be served. Surely, the anticipation and enticing aromas must have also reached the coffee and cocoa workers in the breezy afternoon, for their merry songs chorused unceasingly from the vast rolling greenery that hugged Belvidere. Later, Rosette soaked in her tub, filled with cool river water, and bathed her taste buds with the cooking flavors that drifted through her window.

Papa also surrendered to the contagious spirit blowing through Belvidere that day. After a well-deserved scrubbing, he let Maman select his wardrobe for the events. Over a short waistcoat of white cotton, he wore a blue open jacket with gold buttons. His matching blue breeches reached the top of his favorite black boots, shiny from many hours of polishing, but still frayed from the demanding terrain Papa roamed every day.

Maman wore a red head scarf and a simple white dress that highlighted her glistening dark complexion. She adjusted Papa's red ruffles at his chest as he headed out the door to await his visitors. "No Englishman on Grenada looks more handsome than my Monsieur Fédon," she said.

His laughter boomed throughout the house and echoed down the hill.

Rosette wondered if birds over Belvidere might even

pause in flight at the sound of such rare but welcomed exuberance coming from Monsieur Fédon.

Papa walked down the porch steps to the man Rosette recognized as Dr. Hay from Gouyave, three winding, hilly miles down to the coast. A slender man with flushed cheeks and more gray hair than his youthful face suggested, Dr. Hay dismounted and fidgeted to get his spectacles on his narrow face.

A slave took the reins and led the horse towards the stables, a stone's throw from the house.

"Thank you for coming, my dear friend." Papa's smile exposed his missing side tooth, but his eyes glowed with open delight at seeing the only Englishman he ever referred to as his dear friend.

"Always happy to visit with you, Monsieur Fédon, especially on such a momentous occasion. I am honored that you invited me to witness it."

"*Mon plaisir*." Papa glanced past Dr. Hay at the empty road leading up to the house. "I thought Lieutenant McDonald might also be riding with you."

"I expected him to reach Gouyave by noon, so I saved him a plate." Dr. Hay reached into his vest and pulled out a chained silver watch. "When he had not arrived by one o'clock, I took my leave. But I paid a guide in Gouyave to ensure he gets here without any hindrance. If he is anything like his father, I am sure he will be here shortly."

"I hope so." Papa's jaws tightened. "Please come inside from the sun."

Maman greeted Dr. Hay at the front door and led him into the drawing room where a servant served tall glasses of freshly squeezed passion fruit juice.

Papa waved Rosette over and turned to Dr. Hay. "My daughter will sit with us today."

"Is she old enough to sign for you?" Dr. Hay asked, a touch of puzzlement on his face.

"No more X's." Papa grinned. "This time Madame Fédon and I sign our own names. Thanks to Rosette."

Dr. Hay leaned forward in his chair and shook Papa's hand. "Congratulations to you all. This indeed is a special day."

Rosette basked in the fleeting moment of recognition, but held her silence, as Papa always insisted she did in the presence of adults. She did not mind. So much conversation amongst men seemed so forbidding, walled off by harsh tones and short-lived laughs, dictated more by their demanding circumstances than their humanity.

'Tis probably why she enjoyed reading so much. Books served as her gateway to people and circumstances that she could relate to without strain or regret. If not for today's activities, she would be upstairs, either reading to herself, or to her ailing grandmother.

The wall clock chimed half-past-two. Papa sulked again. He glared at the floor and clasped his hands in an unyielding hold. Rosette had seen his rage explode in an instant. Nothing raised his fury higher and faster than disrespect, especially when it came from the hated and oppressive *L'Anglais.* Purchasing Belvidere most surely would be his crowning achievement. But every passing minute on the clock probably felt like another British stab in the back.

Dr. Hay cleared his throat and pulled out his watch. "I am sure he has a good explanation for his delay."

She hoped Lieutenant McDonald showed up very soon. She was yet to meet the lieutenant, but already she had begun to collect a pool of resentment towards him.

The sound of a galloping horse broke the silence and lifted her hopes. Papa rose from his chair and dashed to the front door. Rosette followed.

A tall, muscular black man pulled up his horse at the foot of the porch steps and dismounted in haste. The horse, shining in profuse lather, flared its nostrils and puffed. The man dripped with sweat like he had just climbed out of the river.

Papa stomped down the steps and snarled. "Why are

you here?"

"Madame Turnbull send...send me talk something to you, Sah."

"Madame Turnbull? I want no dealings with the sorry wife of that devil." Papa glanced back at Rosette. "Get back inside."

She retreated into the doorway, where she could still see the men but could no longer hear their lowered voices. She remembered the man well enough. His huge build, tattered clothing, and bitter scowl tarnished his otherwise handsome features. He frequented Gouyave with the Turnbulls on shopping days at the bustling market square.

Rosette recalled the discomfort she felt when, on those occasions with her parents, Papa's jaws would constrict around his cigar, and his face would harden in the presence of the Turnbulls. Madame Turnbull, always wearing a wide-brimmed hat, would politely smile her freckled face at Rosette, but her round husband would roll pass without the slightest pretense of civility. Most assuredly, he regarded the Fédons as mere slaves, no higher in social standing than the giant who followed them around like a loyal pet.

Earlier, the servants in the kitchen rumored about how Mr. Turnbull and other Englishmen treated their workers worse than Frenchmen on the island treated theirs. No wonder Mr. Turnbull's slaves ran away so often, they said.

One woman whispered news she had heard in the Gouyave market, from where she had just returned. She talked about a young girl who had abandoned the Turnbulls to join an encampment of maroons in the forested mountains behind Belvidere, about six miles from Mr. Turnbull's Beauséjour Estate. The woman said she heard the girl was caught before sunrise that morning.

The other women did not believe the girl would let herself get caught alive to be returned to Mr. Turnbull's cruelty. Another said the girl did not have the agility to escape because she was with child.

Whatever the reason behind the unannounced visit

from Mr. Turnbull's slave, he arrived with such agitating news as to push Papa closer to his brink than she had seen in years. Papa roared his disgruntlement, his clenched fist dangerously close to the man's nose.

This day, so rich in high expectations just hours ago, appeared to be speeding towards catastrophe before her very eyes.

Yet again, Englishmen stirred turmoil in the Fédons.

Lieutenant McDonald, disrespectfully late. Mr. Turnbull's estate, the source of some yet unknown dreadful news for Papa.

Whatever happened, Papa's fury explained the consequences. His aspirations would pay the price again. How many more reminders Papa needed to conclude that a French mulatto would never achieve prosperity and happiness in Grenada as long as *L'Anglais* controlled their destiny?

She turned and hurried past the drawing room where her mother sat in low conversation with Dr. Hay. She raced up to her room and collapsed on the bed.

Then the realization swept over her. If she felt so oppressed as a mulatto, what deeper agony must the enslaved endure? How did they labor under the hot sun from daybreak to sundown, the daily threats of punishment, torture, and death hanging over their heads, with no hope for freedom? Unless they ran away into the mountains like Mr. Turnbull's young slave. And not get caught.

Then she remembered the name of Mr. Turnbull's slave outside. One of the servants had mentioned it in the kitchen.

Kojo.

Chapter Five

Malcolm opened his eyes to the glaring sun beating off a paned window above him. A sofa and pillow accommodated him with some comfort, but his head ached as if thunder drummed inside his skull. A black woman, humming a song to herself, sat next to him and held a damp cloth to his forehead. At the touch of the cloth, his forehead burned, but he could neither move nor utter his displeasure higher than a feeble wince.

"Madame Turnbull." The woman's shouts banged against his head. "Him wake up."

A freckle-faced woman rushed up to where he lay flat on the couch, her familiar voice floating with the softness of an ocean breeze. "Lieutenant McDonald, can you hear me?"

He blinked and nodded, but confusion marred any recognition of her.

She dismissed the woman with the wave of her hand and pulled the chair closer to the couch. She leaned over him, her endowed breasts barely contained in her thin laced bodice. "'Tis me, Charlotte. Do you remember what happened?"

Charlotte? He had seen her before. But where, and what was she asking him to remember?

He allowed his gaze to wander around the room in search of anything or anyone else who might rekindle his faded memory. A regency cut-glass chandelier he had never seen before, hung from a high ceiling beam over a drawing room of elegant light blue velvet chairs and sofas he had never sat in before. In the far corner, past a sprawling Persian floor rug, a longcase mahogany clock stood watch, ticking seconds aloud. A large canvas painting on the main wall, embraced in floral-carved frames, portrayed a scantily dressed woman lounging in a flower garden, with adoring black girls seated at her pale feet. The aroma of rich food filled the room—in a house that obviously belonged to someone of enviable financial means, maybe an estate owner.

Perhaps this woman's husband? Charlotte's husband... Mr. Turnbull.

It all flooded back. The girl on the ground, her back shredded and bloody. Her screams. Malcolm dashing into the crowd towards her, the odor of unwashed bodies enveloping him.

Mr. Turnbull yelling behind him. "Do not dare."

Malcolm, grabbing Kojo by the arms.

Kojo's rage, piercing through teary eyes, shifted to alarm when he looked past Malcolm.

Malcolm glanced back just in time to see the pistol butt about to collide with his forehead, like a hammer about to smash a rock.

Then nothing.

Until now.

"What happened to the girl?" he asked.

"Her people will care for her. I was worried about you when my smelling salts could not revive you. We had to use it on her too."

"Can I see her?" If he ended up with a knot on his head protecting the girl, he figured he deserved to examine her condition, as heart-wrenching as it might be.

"'Tis too painful and embarrassing for her. I will let her know of your concern."

"How did I end up in here?"

"I had Kojo carry you. Mr. Turnbull disappeared."

Malcolm inhaled deeply. "Wished I had talked Mr. Turnbull out of it."

"Do not blame yourself." She shook her head. "That was a brave thing you did, but I should have warned you about my husband."

"You tried." He recalled her words. *'Tis not only what will happen to her. 'Tis also what will happen to you.*

She sat back and twisted her red hair over her shoulder. "Something about this whole odious slave affair devastates the insides of masters to the same degree as the punishment they inflict on the skin of the enslaved. Not a natural thing."

His head throbbed. "Where is Mr. Turnbull?"

"Whenever anything like this happens, he goes away for a few days. He packs his rum bottles like medicine and rides off to heal himself. I believe he stays at the estate of his good friend, Ninian Home, the Speaker of the House of Assembly. Mr. Home owns an estate up north. When Mr. Turnbull rides back up this hill in a few days, he will be purified for another round, like nothing happened."

"How does a Boston lady fit into all this?"

"I do not." She reached out and held his cheek, the warmth of her palm soothing even his head. "I just endure, daydreaming that someone like you would show up once in a while, if only for a minute."

Charlotte could not have been quite thirty-years-old. Yet, her sentiments resonated with his growing desire for companionship with the fair sex since arriving in Grenada. As an officer and son of the commanding officer in

Grenada, he refrained from venturing into the ramshackle taverns along the port, especially those known for loud, aggressive women of ill-repute—and diseases. He preferred to listen to the intoxicated ramblings of his fellow officers after their nights of reckless release.

Occasionally, he would re-read his brothers' letters to remind him about admiring English maidens back home, but this daydreaming lacked the sensual awakening he felt in Charlotte's presence. The fact she was married to one of Father's friends seemed of little consequence.

While he debated in his mind whether military honor demanded he seek retribution against Mr. Turnbull, just lying here on the couch receiving his wife's exclusive attention felt wickedly gratifying. Revenge for the blow to Malcolm's head—and for ordering the pregnant girl whipped.

Yet, a part of him also wanted to ease the loneliness that dulled Charlotte's brown eyes.

The clock chimed half-past the hour.

"I am sorry I cannot stay longer." He tried to raise himself to his elbows. "I do not want to be late for Monsieur Fédon." From where he lay, his hazy eyesight could not identify the clock numbers.

"You are already late." She pointed at the wall clock. "'Tis half-past two."

Panic seized him. "What?" He sat up—too quickly. Dizziness and pain sapped his energy, and he collapsed back onto the couch.

"Do not worry," she said with confidence. "I sent Kojo over the mountains to let Monsieur Fédon know you are delayed. He is probably already there. He knows the mountains better than anyone else."

"Dr. Hay was also going to be there as a witness." He remembered. "We were supposed to ride together from Gouyave."

"Fear not. If Dr. Hay is unable to wait for the signing, I am sure Monsieur Fédon will find another witness if necessary. Kojo's message will give them time."

The mention of Kojo's name reminded Malcolm of the tears he saw in the African man's eyes before Mr. Turnbull swung the pistol. "Kojo was crying while he whipped the girl."

"The servants believe he wanted to make her his wife. But Mr. Turnbull is very reluctant to accept marriage here."

Malcolm groaned. "Father will be disappointed if he knows of all that occurred today."

"I do not know if Mr. Turnbull will tell. But you can be assured any secrets you and I share will *never* be divulged by me." She smiled for the first time. "Stand slowly and come with me. You and I will break bread together yet, Lieutenant McDonald."

"You can call me Malcolm."

She lowered her voice. "Only when we are alone. In the company of others, you will be Lieutenant McDonald."

Charlotte dismissed her house servants, who hurried out of the house in apparent relief for the unexpected free time. "You shocked them. No one ever stood up to Mr. Turnbull like you did."

"I hope the girl and the baby are well."

Charlotte sighed. "Time will tell."

She led him to a long table decorated with crystal glasses, chinaware, and sterling silverware on a red tablecloth. She showed him to the head of the table, and she sat on the next chair. Their knees touched.

After a glass of Spanish wine, she served him a hefty dinner plate of meat pie containing fruits and island spices, along with a stack of pancakes and fritters. An array of side dishes held sauces and pickles. When he thought he could eat no more, she returned with an assortment of dried fruits, custards, and tarts. Malcolm wondered if Mr. Turnbull was a lean man before he married Charlotte.

She filled their glasses again. "Would you be so kind as to deliver a gift to Dr. Hay for me?"

"But of course," Malcolm said.

She disappeared into the kitchen and returned with a glass jar. "The best honey. Imported from Spain through Trinidad. Please tell him it is not to heal patients. It is for his tea."

He chuckled. "We are surrounded by sugar, but you buy him honey for his tea?"

"I do not use sugar either." She paused and stared at him. "Next time you come back, I will take you on a tour of the estate, so you will know why."

She wrapped the jar in cloth and placed it on the table in front of him.

The clock chimed three times.

"Your horse is well watered and fed," she said. "You could get there by half-past-four."

"I am much obliged for all that you did. Thank—"

"Do not thank me," she whispered. "I wish you did not have to leave me here alone."

"I wish I could stay with you too." The words came too fast for his thoughts to put a stop to his rising desires.

She stretched over and placed her finger to his lips. "You can visit me on your way back to St. George's tonight."

"I plan to stay at the Gouyave...I mean Charlotte Town militia post tonight. I have a full day of militia business there tomorrow. Maybe before sunset tomorrow."

"Then please come have supper with me. We can watch the sunset together. It is painted by God."

He thought for a moment. "Mr. Turnbull may not take too kindly to me returning in his absence. How would I know if he is back?"

Her smile added a mischievous twinkle to her eyes. "If he returns, I will hang my red sweater on my bedroom balcony. You will see it from the bottom of the hill."

She showed him to the washroom where he washed his hands, rinsed his mouth, and examined the discolored knot on his forehead. He tried on the hat, but it was too tight and painful around the swelling. He would just have to show up at Monsieur Fédon's house with an exposed bump and hope the questions were at a minimum.

He exited the washroom and found Charlotte waiting for him in the narrow hallway. Their mouths met in a heated sensation of moist lips and heavy breathing flavored with wine. He wrapped his arms around her full body and braced her against the wall, her firm curves rousing to his touch. She squeezed her hips against his. His enlargement responded, and she moaned, grabbing him around her neck and guiding his face to her chest. He loosened the strings on her bodice and took one of her breasts in his mouth, slurping a delightful taste of sweat off her nipple. She sank her fingernails into his neck, her moans and gyrations building his desire.

She whispered in his ear. "Come upstairs with me to my chamber."

Along with his headache, any concerns about being tardy for Monsieur Fédon's meeting, or any guilt he expected from enjoying the passions of another man's wife, all vanished at that moment. "Lead the way."

She held his hand and squeezed it.

Just then, rapid knocking at a back door brought a rude end to their privacy.

"Madame Turnbull?" A woman's voice called out. "Madame Turnbull?"

"Oh darn," Charlotte stepped back from him with a sigh, restoring her bodice and fixing her hair, as red as the blush on her freckled face. "The servants are returning."

"Go send them away." He would not be denied now. "I will wait here for you."

She shook her head. "Sorry, we have to be careful. You must leave. Promise you shall return tomorrow."

"I shall."

With strained reluctance, Malcolm kissed her a hasty farewell, retrieved his horse, and galloped down the hill. He glanced up at the ridge to see if the little girl with the bad limp might be back. But there was no one there. Workers in the sugarcane fields paused to gaze up at him, but no one sang. One hand went up in a slow wave. The vicious lashing they witnessed just hours ago most likely crushed any enthusiasm a slave could pluck from his being in a hot field.

Malcolm tried in vain to hold on to the memory of Charlotte's lonely lips on his. But the agonizing screams of the runaway girl followed him all the way down to the coastal roadway—and found an uneasy resting place in his conscience.

Malcolm galloped his horse along the mud-hard roadway to Gouyave, meandering between sugarcane fields and jungle-covered mountains on the right, and vertical drop-offs to the blue sea on the left. Flocks of quarrelling seagulls patrolled against bright skies, their squawks cutting the air with sharp echoes. Waves pounded the rocky shores below, leaving in their wake blankets of foamy whitewash that lingered just long enough for the next wave to come crashing in. On occasion, the rugged shoreline submitted to crescent bays, which invited calm turquoise water to unfurl gentle rollers up their white sand.

He paused on a ridge overlooking a bay. Hugged by steep green hillsides, the sandy bay looked black. Sure enough, less than twenty yards ahead, a small hand-painted sign labeled Black Bay pointed down a trail to the bay.

Several times along the narrow road north, he reined in his horse to allow donkey-drawn carts the space to rattle pass in the opposite direction. The African cart drivers appeared surprised when he gave way to them and proceeded only when he expressed his insistence with the firm wave of his hand. The wheels crunched on the gravel road under the weight of the cargo, filled burlap bags exhaling a rich aroma of spice and sugar. The drivers nodded appreciation from the shadows of battered hats covering their heads, and made haste past him, on the winding journey to awaiting ships moored along the busy St. George's port.

Malcolm gazed up at the hills to his right. Solitary great houses held watchtower positions over green plantations bustling with workers swinging machetes, donkeys pulling laden carts, and boiler house chimneys burping thick smoke. Except for a small hamlet called Grand Roy, most of the dwellings along the way congregated in messy clusters of beaten-down shacks, pushed off to the edge of the fields like discarded boxes. Scrawny chickens scratched around in dusty patches, and laundered rags swung on ropes stretched between trees. Barefoot women, one with a screaming baby on her back, fanned crackling fires under meager pots. Thin smoke from the cooking sites rose in lazy swirls over patched roofs. When the wind blew in Malcolm's direction, the unappealing aroma of wild game from the pots did little to suffocate the stench of human waste.

He wondered if the pregnant girl and her unborn baby could recover from wounds in the same grungy conditions on Monsieur Turnbull's estate. And how could Charlotte's femininity thrive under the same roof with a brute like Mr. Turnbull?

Her words floated like dark storm clouds across his mind. *Something about this whole odious slave affair devastates the insides of masters to the same degree as the punishment they inflict on the skin of the enslaved—not a natural thing.*

But would King George consent to any practice other than those that conditioned untamed African souls for productive labor, civilizing them under the Union Jack, and preparing them for Christian deliverance? Surely, any personal aggravation one felt from the close encounter with slavery's jagged edges paled in contrast to its immense power to spread the mighty British civilization to every continent on God's planet.

Men like Mr. Turnbull were but petty annoyances in a

mercantile system serving God, King, and country. And Father's sale of Belvidere Estate to Monsieur Fédon was but one small transaction in the multitude of daily business agreements conducted in the furtherance of such a noble purpose.

A burst of pride filled Malcolm's chest, reminding him of his delayed trek to seal the Belvidere contract. Father's trust and confidence in him held more currency than gold itself, and certainly worth more than any retribution Malcolm could gain from a physical confrontation with Mr. Turnbull.

Malcolm would reveal nothing to Father about what occurred on Beauséjour Estate today, if it meant preserving the friendship between Father and Mr. Turnbull. Damaging their friendship over such an incident could fracture the bond between father and son.

But Malcolm knew it would be a lot easier to avoid Mr. Turnbull than it would be to avoid the man's wife.

He pressed his heels against the horse and picked up speed towards Gouyave.

Gouyave finally came into view, from where the road squeezed between a sheer cliff on the right and a precipitous drop to the sea on the left. Malcolm slowed the horse to enjoy the sight, a lone church-steeple piercing the skyline above shingle rooftops and waving coconut trees.

The road curved down and met the shoreline at a bridge that spanned a rushing river. The horse's shoes clapped upon the wooden bridge, alerting dark women who washed clothes on huge bleached rocks along the river banks. The women, in white garb and head wraps, gazed at Malcolm without a pause in their vigorous scrubbing.

Offshore, fishing boats bobbed on a sea brilliant with sunlit slivers while rowdy seagulls circled overhead. Sea mist drenched the air with a fishy odor, tempered by a floral breeze, whispering down from cloud-capped mountains.

He considered dismounting to savor the strangely inviting experience but thought better of it when he imagined Monsieur Fédon's displeasure at Malcolm's delay.

Instead, he settled for an unhurried ride through the town. Dull stone-walled houses lined both sides of the road. Narrow doorways and louvered windows looked out at him, beckoning him with cooking aromas of fish and beef. He recalled his conversation with the drunk Frenchman in the St. George's tavern, when the man described how fires easily ravaged the wooden houses in the port town. Thereafter, many residents moved to Gouyave where most of the houses were built from the generous supply of gray stones along the shoreline.

A horse-drawn cart rattled towards him on the pebble-strewn road. The white driver, in hat and glove, frowned at him, probably reacting to the discolored bump on his forehead. A skinny dog lying on a doorstep barked without rising. Malcolm's horse ignored the uninspired threat and held a steady pace. Children screamed in playful skirmishes on the roadsides and in narrow alleys, yelling in a French dialect that sounded different from the sparse French he learned at school in Liverpool.

He stopped at an open market square. Two British soldiers, sweating in thick redcoats, white pantaloons, and black high boots, guarded the entrance. Behind them, workers swept the grounds with straw brooms and wiped stalls with rags. Others collected garbage, banana leaves, coconut shells, and fruit skins strewn about after what must have been a busy market day. The lingering raw aroma of slaughtered cattle thickened the air.

"Excuse me," Malcolm called to the soldiers. "Would you please point me to the militia post?"

"By what reason you ask, stranger?" one of the soldiers asked with a glare laced with suspicion. "Better yet, tell us how you received that bump on your head, and we will tell you how to get to the post."

The soldiers laughed.

"How dare you." Malcolm barked. "I am an officer in King George's Army, soldier. I suggest I get an answer from you forthwith!"

The other soldier elbowed his companion and pointed at Father's horse. They must have recognized it as belonging to the commanding officer of the Grenada Regiment, for they immediately snapped to attention.

"Pardon me, sir." The first soldier pointed to an intersection ahead. "Take a right there. 'Tis on the hill half-a-mile to the right. You will see the Union Jack flying high, sir."

"Thank you." Malcolm galloped off.

He rode up the steep hill to the post, a square enclosure protected by thick stone walls. Three cannons protruded from high in the walls, with unimpeded ballistic range to the town and the sea below. He identified himself to the guard at the gate and walked the horse into the post. Ahead, a dusty drill yard, just long enough to accommodate a platoon, stretched between two narrow wooden barracks. A food store, armory, officers' mess adjoining the adjutant office, and an occupied stable completed the remaining structures within the enclosure.

He tied his horse in front of the adjutant office, intending to stay just long enough to deliver the dispatches from Fort George and to find a guide to take him to Belvidere.

But as he approached the shut door, loud shouting gave him pause.

"That young scoundrel is an imposter, I tell you!" a man said. "He should be forbidden from selling that estate to that colored snake in Belvidere. If you do not stop him when he comes here, then by the authority given to me by King George, I shall!"

Mr. Turnbull sounded like he had already started on his rum medicine.

Chapter Six

Dr. Hay fumbled to return his chained silver watch to his vest pocket, avoiding eye contact with Monsieur Fédon who sat across from him in the modest Belvidere House drawing room. For two uncomfortable hours, the doctor had occupied a creaky chair with rough armrests, wringing his hands, cleaning his glasses, and removing his watch to check the time. But nothing seemed to relieve the tension thickening the air between him and the coarse man facing him. Not even the delicious snacks of coconut cake and custard tarts that Madame Fédon served along with a perfect cup of tea, sweetened with honey as he requested.

Throughout the afternoon, Monsieur Fédon kept insisting in a booming voice, from behind clouds of cigar smoke, that the British had no rights to his island. "Tell me, Dr. Hay. Would you rather live in a British Grenada or a French Grenada?"

"Remember, Monsieur Fédon, I have lived in both.

And both can be lacking."

He ignored Dr. Hay's answer and struck a match to rekindle his cigar. "This is my tobacco, you know. Grown and cured in the hills behind us. But my brother Jean-Pierre tells me the cool misty air does not leave it dry enough for his satisfaction. Needs too many re-firings." He touched the lit match to his cigar, and, with rapid puffs, sent a finger of flame shooting upwards. "That is more like it."

As far as Dr. Hay was concerned, even free people of color, or as the French called them, *gens de couleur libres*, deserved an enterprising role as subjects in His Majesty's colony. At age forty-five, he had spent most of his adult years in the Indies after becoming a doctor in England twenty years ago. He had travelled and worked between Barbados and St. Kitts before deciding to settle in Grenada in 1778, a year before the French invaded Grenada.

In their attempts to reverse seventeen years of British heavy-handedness, new French laws allowed the seizure of property and bank accounts from Englishmen. By 1783, the Treaty of Versailles, which ended European hostilities over the American Revolution, also returned Grenada to Great Britain. But peace treaty notwithstanding, British vexations came roaring back to avenge four miserable years of French haughtiness.

Dr. Hay always managed to walk the tightrope on an island so divided. His medical practice opened the doors into grand estate homes and inhuman slave huts across the island, French and British, Catholic and Anglican, for whites, blacks, and browns. He made friends from all sides of the odious divisions slashing across the island. And in his capacity as a Justice of the Peace, Dr. Hay gladly witnessed official documents for all upstanding subjects of His Majesty's colony. His signature lent credence to documents for free coloreds like Monsieur Fédon and his family, including Fédon's brother Jean-Pierre, who lived on a nearby estate.

But the sale of Belvidere Estate agitated ominous

misgivings in Dr. Hay's gut.

Monsieur Fédon puffed on his cigar again, and smoke shrouded him. "The British treat us like dogs. Some of my family and friends gave up and moved to Trinidad. If all of *L'Anglais* were like you, Dr. Hay, Grenada would be tranquil."

Dr. Hay wondered then, why would this free man of color, continue to dig in his heels on an island Monsieur Fédon deemed inhospitable to all things French, Catholic, and free colored?

Yes, it was well known he signed the Declaration of Loyalty to Great Britain three years ago.

But this document would not be the first to disguise the true motives of the signatories.

The very conditions Monsieur Fédon protested so vigorously led many other French landowners to pack their goods and slaves and sail away to the Spanish island of Trinidad, just ninety miles away. Certainly, if Fédon departed Grenada, few Englishmen on the island would miss him.

So why remain, and why invest in the four hundred and fifty-acre Belvidere Estate? Dr. Hay's medical experience taught that when an infection took over a living being, in time either the patient or the infection would die.

The peaceful coexistence of both defied God's design.

Did Monsieur Fédon have hidden motives for purchasing the estate and remaining under the hostile British? Dr. Hay felt a growing discomfort, questioning Monsieur Fédon's sincerity while a welcomed guest in the man's home. Dr. Hay's abdominals tightened and hastened his decision to delay no further his ride back to Gouyave.

"I am sorry that I must take my leave now." Dr. Hay stood, hoping his words conveyed more regret than the true sentiment he felt, relief. Lieutenant McDonald's tardiness had unknowingly gifted the British doctor with the perfect escape from his promise to witness the sale. "I have patients in Gouyave awaiting my return before nightfall."

Monsieur Fédon seemed oddly relaxed after Kojo's disappointing news of Lieutenant McDonald's late arrival. He puffed on his cigar and blew a cloud of smoke towards the high ceiling. "Much obliged that you traveled this hilly distance for me." His voice filled the room. "You always treat my family with respect and dignity. I want to return the favor one day."

"I am sorry that I will not be here for such an esteemed signing," Dr. Hay said. "I hope your family understands, but I know Mr. Webster will gladly sign in my place."

"I will send one of my riders to fetch him," Monsieur Fédon said. "His estate is a brief ride away."

Just days earlier, in Gouyave, Dr. Hay had discussed the signing with his good friend, Ben Webster, assistant justice of His Majesty's Court of Common Pleas and Registrar of the Grenada Supreme Court. When Dr. Hay disclosed his belief that the forthcoming sale might be tainted with bad omen, the bearded Webster dismissed his concerns.

"Doctors should not harbor such superstitions." Webster chuckled. "Maybe you spend too much time with the Africans."

Dr. Hay persisted. "Even Mr. Turnbull is expressing deep reservation about a free colored Frenchman in possession of such a lofty estate in the middle of King George's colony. It can be the source of much wrath and division between us Englishmen."

"But Governor Home gave his blessings to Colonel McDonald," Mr. Webster said. "If you do not desire to witness the deed, I have no qualms in doing so myself. You know where to find me."

Assured now that Mr. Webster would soon arrive to witness the signing, Dr. Hay bade farewell to Monsieur Fédon and his gracious wife. He galloped his horse down the hill and into the green canopy towards Gouyave. A half-mile away, he slowed at a stream to gather his thoughts and to calm his stomach.

Despite the soothing music of the running water, his abdominal stresses boiled.

And he knew why.

Monsieur Fédon's purchase of Belvidere Estate meant one thing: he planned to stick around—in hope for another French invasion.

The memories of that July night fourteen years ago came flooding back. Dr. Hay received his first taste of war as a doctor with the militia in St. George's. Dispirited after failed attempts to execute decisive victories for the Americans in their revolutionary war, Admiral D'Estaing arrived off Grenada with a French fleet on July 2nd, 1779. Two nights later, French troops came over the northern hills of St. George's by the thousands. With bayonets drawn and rifles blasting, they attacked.

Deafening explosions. Walls shattered in eruptions of fire, smoke, and merciless shrapnel. Flesh ripped like old cloth and bones broke like snapping twigs. The raw stench of open bowels, entrails pulsating out of living men. Bodies mangled into unrecognizable shapes. Blood trickled off upper walls and splattered onto stone paths like black rain in the night.

Dying men screaming for God, like hungry babies shrieking for milk.

Strangers killing strangers.

More than three hundred of the King's soldiers died that night, fourteen years ago.

Today, Grenada had accumulated fourteen more years of anger and distrust between the British and French. Between master and slave. Between Anglican and Catholic. Another conflict on the island could lead to an even worse bloodbath. Between people who knew each other.

Did Monsieur Fédon know something that no Englishman on the island suspected?

Dr. Hay hurried into the bushes and relieved himself.

Chapter Seven

Rosette peered through her thin bedroom curtains with fury burning her chest. She watched Dr. Hay gallop with haste away from Belvidere House, taking with him another slice of Papa's struggling hope. Another British promise dashed. Contrary to his highest aspirations, Papa would not own Belvidere. His nagging doubts had come to fruition. The authorities would ever allow a *gens de couleur libre* like him to own such a lavish estate, Even after owning a small tobacco estate in Grand Pauvre before their move here to Belvidere, Papa would now rise no higher than a lessor of someone else's land, working for someone else's prosperity.

Hardly more than a slave.

She had laid on her bed listening to the drumbeat of his voice slip under her door with the potent fragrance of his burning cigar—like drum and smoke signals of approaching calamities. The signals must have blown over all of Belvidere Estate as well. The cooking, hammering, and sweeping in preparation for the night's *Saraka* continued, but the festive exertions and singing from the fields dimmed.

When the master's mood soured, the slaves trembled.

Rosette often wondered how the slaves knew things no one told them, as if they had ears on walls everywhere. So little she knew. So little she understood. In moments like this, her Grandmère, Papa's mother, always provided wise counsel for Rosette's troubled sentiments.

Rosette grabbed the book she had selected that morning and hurried down the hallway to Grandmère's bedroom.

She tapped on the door. "'Tis me, Rosette."

"Come in, *Pitit cheri mwen*." Grandmère's soft Creole-French endearment, *my dear child*, welcomed Rosette into the room and lifted her spirit like it always did, even on the cloudiest days.

Grandmère, Brigitte Fédon, sat at the sunny window in her favorite armchair, a chair one of her slaves made her before she left Martinique with her French husband many years ago. A young servant stood behind the chair, brushing Grandmère's long silver hair in the sunlight. Despite sunken cheeks and missing teeth, Grandmère's aging face emitted a happy glow when Rosette walked into the sparsely furnished room. Her smile gathered deep wrinkles on the outer sides of her eyes and lips. Dark splotches blended with lighter complexion on her face, like maps of unknown places with unknown futures.

Grandmère and the room smelled like fresh laundry, with a sprinkling of fruit-scented perfume.

Rosette kissed Grandmère on her moist face. "You look beautiful."

"'Tis Anna's hard work." Grandmère reached over her shoulder and tapped the servant's hand. "She wants me to look the best tonight in case someone my age shows up."

Anna smiled timidly and continued brushing

Grandmère's hair.

Rosette stepped over to the vanity and helped herself to a handful of sweetened coconut snacks she had helped prepare in the kitchen earlier. "Hmmm. Lovely!" She smacked her lips.

"Did you bring me another book?" Grandmère asked.

"I selected it since this morning. *The Life and Strange Surprising Adventures of Robinson Crusoe.*"

"*Oui, oui!*" Grandmère's approval warmed Rosette. "Your Grandpère loved that book. He used to read parts of it to me, even before you were born."

"*Oui*, written seventy years ago. About a white man who became friends with a black runaway slave on an island. It might bring back good memories of Grandpère."

"At my age, all I want are good memories."

Anna rolled Grandmère's hair into a bun, and, around her head, tightened a white headscarf that matched the long dress covering her to the ankles. Grandmère thanked Anna and dismissed her with a wave of her hand and a smile. "Now you go get ready for tonight."

Rosette decided against telling Grandmère that tonight's celebration might be premature, especially since Lieutenant McDonald had not yet arrived.

Alone now with her, Rosette retrieved the oval mirror from the wood vanity and held it for Grandmère to view herself. Rosette wondered if her grandmother's fading vision, behind misty curtains which stole the sparkle she once had in her eyes, could appreciate what the mirror reflected. The full beauty of her being blossomed on her face and filled Rosette with love.

"I am happy to be the granddaughter of such a beautiful woman," Rosette said.

Grandmère smiled. "Your words give me life."

Rosette wished Papa could say the same thing to her, especially on days like this. She knew that keeping her silence and remaining aloof allowed Papa the space he needed to tame his own tribulations. Even Maman tiptoed around him, giving full attention to his requirements with little regard to her own, or to Rosette's.

Grandmère had become Rosette's lifeline to sanity.

Her grandmother broke the silence. "*Pitit cheri mwen*, what troubles you today?"

Rosette marveled at her grandmother's perception, even more so with fading eyesight. She dwelled on the question a moment, returned the mirror to the vanity, and sat on the side of the bed facing Grandmère.

"Do you think we can live happily in Grenada?" Rosette asked.

"Your happiness needs just two ingredients, my dear. You and family."

"We have you here and Uncle Jean-Pierre just across the valley where we can see him on a clear day. But the British are making it more and more difficult, even to keep family together. We have uncles and aunties who moved to Trinidad and never returned."

Grandmère sighed. "Your grandfather missed his family in France too, that is why he worked so hard to keep us together. Our children tried to do the same thing. They lived close together, purchased and sold land together. Your Papa, and two of his brothers even married three sisters from the Cavelan family. Your Maman and her two sisters. Etienne married Elizabeth, and Jean married Margaret. Your Uncle Jean-Pierre's wife is Margueritte, who was a free black woman from Gouyave. Difficulties come and go, but families must remain."

"Papa talks sometimes about your mother too, with such awe," Rosette said.

"Your great-grandmother was a special woman."

Grandmère walked Rosette's imagination back across the unforgiving Atlantic slave passages to where it all began on the West Coast of Africa. There, Papa's Yoruba grandmother and her twin sister had mastered the powers of manifest destiny from the ancestral spirits that resided in the sacred jungles. Grandmère explained that the Yoruba people believed twins were born with supernatural powers to create health and happiness. That changed for Papa's grandmother when gunshots, ropes, and a long march in chains ripped her apart from her twin sister. But deep in the decomposing bowels of the slave ship, the Yoruba powers throbbed in her heart until Martinique's virgin streams, lakes, and Silk Cotton trees welcomed her in an ecstatic embrace.

When her French master unleashed his lust on the young African girl, she mothered Grandmère, to whom she passed along the ways of the ancestors. Now a *negresse libre creole*, Grandmère married a Frenchman and moved to Grenada, where she raised her family, including Papa, and made a home for them in Grand Pauvre. At the same time, she made a home for her Yoruba traditions in the lush mountains around Grand Étang Lake.

Rosette recalled her first encounter with those powers at the lake one night. With Papa away in St. George's on business, she had accompanied Grandmère and a Shango priestess named Josephina on the long trek to a lakeshore landing decorated with colorful flags. Against a moon-lit sky, Mount Qua Qua stood guard over them. Rosette watched enthralled from the shadows as Grandmère and other women danced and sang to drums and rattles in blazing torchlight. They danced faster and faster, harder and harder, until the spirits overtook their bodies in orgasmic spasms. Strange voices gushed from their mouths, and their eyes rolled white in the moonlight.

Rosette knew not how Papa discovered his mother had taken her to the ceremony, but he rumbled his displeasure throughout the house for days, especially, as he complained, it was forbidden by the British.

Grandmère cleared her throat. "If you understand my mother, you understand your papa. The Yoruba people believe that if twins are separated, their supernatural powers become angry and vengeful. Your papa might have some of his grandmother's anger."

"His temper worries me sometimes."

"Fear not, my child. His father also nourished his enterprising side. Said he has a keen eye for commerce, that he has a white brain in a brown body."

Rosette collapsed on Grandmère's pillow. "He complains that the British think him a black slave, like his grandmother was."

Grandmère glanced out the window, but not in time to hide the teardrop that rolled down her cheek. "'Tis a most suffering thing to live like him."

Rosette tried to imagine the fires raging in Papa. A brown man with a white brain. A mulatto detested by whites. A slave master, himself the grandson of a slave. A Frenchman under the oppressive British. A Catholic under offensive Anglican rules.

Her sadness for Papa simmered into fury. "Grandmère, I am finding it so easy to hate. I do not think I would flinch if I see an Englishman bleed—"

Grandmère spun around from the window and hissed. "Stop it." Tears rolled down both cheeks, and her chin trembled. "There is enough of that hatred in your papa. It will kill you long before it kills your enemy!"

Chapter Eight

Malcolm backed away from the adjutant's office and the shouts coming from behind the shut door. It would be ill-timed to confront Mr. Turnbull, especially now that Belvidere seemed so close. Father's friend sounded rather displeased about the Belvidere sale to Monsieur Fédon. Not about Malcolm's intrusion into the flogging of the pregnant girl.

Why?

From all accounts, the sale document held full legal weight. Amongst the sale documents Father sent, was a formal declaration called *Abstract of sundry Securities and Transactions to and by William Lushington and James Law Esqrs., and Lists of the Deeds in their possession*. The law firm enjoyed the prestige of prominent Englishmen, both in England and in Grenada. Men such as Benjamin Webster, Assemblyman Alexander Campbell, and his good friend, Grenada Speaker of the House of Assembly, Ninian Home.

Something felt strangely incomplete.

Malcolm walked the horse back to the gate with the afternoon sun in his face and approached the guard. "Soldier, I need to get to Belvidere promptly. Do you know if Dr. Hay arranged a guide for me?"

"He is a Monsieur...I forget his name...some sort of whiskey. Strange fellow, rides all over the island on a skinny horse. Not sure how the bloody thing—"

"Where is he?"

The soldier led him out the gate and pointed down to a small red-roofed church on a path off the main road. "You will find him asleep under that huge mango tree before you get to the church. That is where he belongs but..."

The soldier's last words faded as Malcolm mounted his horse and sped off down the hill, away from the militia post and Mr. Turnbull.

Even in the shade of the mango tree, Malcolm immediately recognized the man dozing with his head on a saddle. He snored through his open mouth. An empty bottle sat nearby, dangerously close to the stomping hoofs of his gaunt horse. Malcolm had seen the man a few months ago, in a tavern along St. George's Bay. The Frenchman with discolored teeth, rancid breath, and a downpour of revulsion for everything British.

"Good afternoon," Malcolm called out.

The man opened bloodshot eyes and moaned. "*Oui*?"

"You are to take me to Belvidere."

"*Oui, oui*, Monsieur." The man struggled to his feet.

"I am late. We should get going."

In minutes, the man sobered up and buckled the saddle on his lethargic horse. Malcolm worried that the horse might not make it up to Belvidere, but remembered the soldier saying the man rode the horse all over the island.

They were about to ride off when a round man in black clerical attire stepped out of the side door of a small house facing the brick church. He hurried towards them with a small bag in his hand and a hanging cross bouncing off his chest.

"*Excusez moi s'il vous plait.*" Almost gasping for breath, he extended his hand to Malcolm. "Father Père Pascal Mardel...at your service, sir."

"Pleased to meet you, Father."

"Everyone around Gouyave calls me Father Pascal. When Bourbon told me he would be guiding you to Belvidere...I asked him to come get me before you leave. He must have forgotten."

Malcolm chuckled to himself at the guide's name. It was clear Bourbon had no recollection of Malcolm and their intense conversation in the tavern. And Malcolm was quite pleased that he would not have to endure a brutal continuation of the discussion.

"Would you be so kind as to do me a favor?" Father Pascal handed the bag to Malcolm. "Two bags in there with sugar cakes and tarts from worshippers. One for you and Bourbon to share. The other for Monsieur Fédon's daughter, Rosette. She is rather fond of the sweets."

"Thank you, Father Pascal," Malcolm said. "We will enjoy the snack. Equally happy to make the delivery."

Father Pascal frowned at him. "How is that headwound feeling?"

"Just an accident. Slight headache, but it will go away once I get off my horse."

"If you have a minute, a prayer and some Holy water would help." He gazed sadly at the church. "Your laws forbade me from using my own church, so you have to come to my little house."

Malcolm made a mental note to mention the conversation in his next letter to his mother. As an Anglican, and deeply anti-Catholic, she would find the conversation most ironic. "I appreciate the offer, but I must be on my way."

"One last thing. Please tell Monsieur Fédon I will say a special prayer for your transactions to go smoothly."

"I shall." Malcolm wondered how many people knew

of the Belvidere sale. Some wanted to pray for its success, others wanted to use soldiers to stop it.

Strange indeed.

Malcolm followed Bourbon on the uphill ride, across shallow streams, narrow bridges, and muddy trails. A pleasant blend of spice and guava scented the air that got steadily cooler the higher they climbed into the welcoming greenery. Rolling hills of fiery flowers waved from a sea of lush vegetation. On cultivated land, barefoot workers carried filled baskets of crops balanced on their heads. Several times, men led donkeys downhill, laden with filled burlap bags, most likely to the Gouyave port, where sloops waited to sail the goods to St. George's for overseas shipment.

Malcolm took a couple of pieces of the snacks from Father Pascal's bag and passed the rest to Bourbon. In silence, the Frenchman took turns between snacking the treats and sipping from a small bottle he pulled from his saddle bag. When he offered his bottle to him, Malcolm refused with a wave of his hand.

At a point where the trail flattened, Bourbon suddenly halted his horse.

"Why are we stopping?" Malcolm asked.

"We are almost there, but I need to get paid."

"Did not Dr. Hay pay you?"

"He said you will pay me."

"Very well. How much?"

Bourbon named a price. Malcolm thought it high, but he reached into his money pouch and handed the coins over. Bourbon stuffed them into his pocket and continued to ride.

They had barely rounded a corner when a slender, bespectacled man rode out of the bushes just ahead.

The man halted his horse. "You must be Lieutenant McDonald."

"Yes. Dr. Hay?"

"Pleasure to meet you. Sorry I had to leave before you arrived. Patients in Gouyave waiting for me. Mr. Benjamin Webster will witness the documents in my place."

"Thank you. My humble apologies for the delay."

"You are very welcome." He gazed at Malcolm's head. "If I may say so, that is a dangerous knot you have there, Lieutenant."

"Just a little accident." At that moment, he remembered the jar of honey Charlotte had given him for Dr. Hay. Malcolm reached into his saddlebag and handed the jar to the doctor. "From Mrs. Turnbull. She said 'tis for your tea, not medicine for your patients."

"Thank you." He laughed but returned the conversation to the swelling on Malcolm's head. "And you have been riding all day with an accident like that? How is your vision?"

"A little dizzy, slight headache but not a bother."

"Not good. I suggest you stay the night at Monsieur Fédon." Dr. Hay turned to Bourbon. "Please convey to Monsieur Fédon that I insist the lieutenant be given quarters for the night. He should not be riding."

"*Oui*, Dr. Hay. Shall we go now?" Bourbon's speech slurred with impatience.

Dr. Hay turned to Malcolm. "I hope Bourbon is giving you a pleasant tour for all the money I paid him."

Malcolm looked over at Bourbon. The man glanced away.

"As a matter of fact," Malcolm said. "He enjoyed doing this so much, he said he will give you back the money."

"Not necessary," Dr. Hay said.

"In that case," Malcolm said. "Bourbon would like to give you the money to donate to Father Pascal's church."

Bourbon stiffened his upper lip and reached into his pocket. He handed Malcolm's money to the puzzled-looking Dr. Hay and rode off.

Dr. Hay looked back at the Frenchman. "Unusual fellow, but the only one I could find willing to do this on short notice. Most British riders are fearful of coming up here alone."

Malcolm explained how Bourbon demanded money from him, saying he had not received payment.

"You handled it well," Dr. Hay said. "Catch up to him. You are only a half-mile away. See you at the post tomorrow. I will have my servant prepare you a good taste of Gouyave's cooking." He rode off down the hill.

Malcolm increased his pace to catch up with Bourbon. The Frenchman rode in silence, visibly dejected by his failed attempt to swindle Malcolm.

A few minutes later, Bourbon pointed up at the hill ahead, and an excitement ran through Malcolm.

Belvidere House began to take shape through the trees.

Bourbon muttered a few words, which a cool breeze quickly swept away into the rustling trees.

Malcolm squinted at him. "Pardon me?"

Bourbon stopped and glared at him with bloodshot eyes. "I said a deal between an Englishman...and a *gens de couleur libres*...is a deal blessed by the devil."

Chapter Nine

Kojo guided his horse on a cautious walk along the treacherous ledge of the precipice, even though he had ridden it a hundred times before. He worried as much for the information he carried, as for his own life. Winds bellowed behind him, and around the sheer cliff that rose to Mount Qua Qua, one of the highest peaks on the island. Far below him, jagged white rocks waited in the shadows, in case he slipped, to send him to an early reunion with his African ancestors. He had travelled this way as recent as that morning, to find the young slave with the swollen belly.

Venus Darling, he used to fondly call her. But no more.

This route got him from the coastal Beauséjour Estate to the central mountains and back faster than any other way he knew. But he did not return the same way with the girl. Too risky. If she jumped with her rope tied to his saddle or made his horse nervous with her screeching pleas, she would take all three of them—and the unborn baby to certain death.

Kojo's father, killed in battle as a young brave warrior from the Kingdom of Dahomey, would be disappointed if his son suffered such an ordinary end like a careless fall off a cliff. Kojo's mother used to remind him how much of his father's physical gifts he had inherited—broad shoulders, commanding height, strong face. But even after the horrific separation from his motherland on an agonizing ocean ride and twenty-seasons of enslavement, Kojo had yet to use his warrior abilities in his own battles. Only then could he join his father and grandfather with honor. He even owed his name to his grandfather, a Ghanaian trader.

This day, however, gave him more hope than any day since his capture in Africa. The information he carried reassured him that he was another step closer to victory and honor.

He was just fourteen when he and his eleven-year-old sister fell victim to the brutal kidnapping that ripped them from their homeland and family. The memories of that day and the following years still flowed in his veins like the thickened heat of volcanic lava. His fiery teenaged hatred used to lead to insubordination, followed by severe plantation whippings. But he eventually molded his rage into a calm purpose, calculated for victory, honor, freedom—and sweet revenge.

Revenge sweeter than the juiciest sapodillas he could find anywhere on the island.

That purpose drove him to cultivate a personal aura of trust, willing to follow every command of his master without flinching—even if it meant drawing blood from his African brothers and sisters.

It pained him that their respect for him came from fear, not admiration. Maybe one day they would understand.

For now, his mission outranked the need for

admiration.

He excelled in pretense. So well, in fact, Massa Turnbull happily proclaimed to his English visitors that *his* Kojo was the embodiment of the perfect slave, conditioned for obedience and work. Evidence, Massa Turnbull would proclaim in Kojo's submissive presence, that God granted African labor in the service of King George and Christian civilization.

Little did he realize that slave had conditioned Massa.

Massa Turnbull trusted Kojo to leave and return to the estate alone, and on a horse, not in chains. And with a rifle, not just a cutlass. Kojo learned to keep his head bowed in public, and to address all white men with the docile "Yes, Massa" at their every wish. Kojo became a reliable messenger on horseback, an unflinching exactor of punishment for Massa's pleasure, an untiring worker—a perfect slave.

The perfect *deception*.

He thanked the gods for never letting his face betray what lay in his heart.

Occasionally, small communities of runaway slaves, maroons, would inform him of a bad seed in their midst who might give up an entire community to their slave masters. These communities lay concealed deep in the central mountain range, constantly on alert for search parties.

Capture meant severe floggings, loss of a leg, human dung stuffed into their mouths, or excruciating death.

Massa Turnbull gave Kojo strict warnings about maroons. He told Kojo the name maroon came from the Spaniards as *cimarrón*, which meant wild and untamed. Massa explained that since the taste of freedom in the wild excited their passions to be primitive again, only the severest of punishments could restore the obedience God meant for them to have.

So Massa believed.

But Kojo preferred what a slave from Belvidere Estate

once told him. The slave had overheard Monsieur Fédon's Mestive mother, the one the girl called Grandmère, say that maroon came from an Amerindian word, *si'maran*, which meant flight of an arrow.

Over the years, slaves transferred from Jamaica brought rumors of a maroon woman who ran a colony of freed slaves fifty years earlier in the Blue Mountains of Jamaica. So successful she was in fighting off the British with her gifts of Obeah powers, they signed a peace treaty with her. An Asante from Ghana, her followers called her Queen Nanny, and named a maroon town after her, Nanny Town. Even after she died, the maroons signed another treaty with the British, agreeing to return runaway slaves in return for bounties.

Kojo never asked for a bounty, but he became a reliable one-man runaway hunter, with the help of his maroon friends.

He returned troublesome runaway slaves to their masters.

With a single stroke, he protected the maroon communities and earned yet more trust from Massa Turnbull and his white circle.

He used the little freedom that Massa granted, to collect and pass along information amongst slaves and maroons. From Sauteurs in the north to St. George's in the south. From Grenville, which faced the rising sun, to Gouyave, which faced the setting sun.

In recent years, he sensed a rising tide of bitterness for the British masters, from slaves, maroons, and *gens de couleur libres* landowners like Monsieur Fédon.

But also, from white Frenchmen.

Kojo had waited twenty seasons for these signs. He would exercise caution. He would exercise cunning. He would exercise patience. But at every opportunity, he would fan the flames burning in the veins of his oppressed brothers as it did in his.

He finally rounded the corner into the afternoon

sunlight. The slippery path gave way to rolling terrain covered in perfumed shrubs, bent in submission to steady easterly winds which howled through the tree line. A *tatou*, which Massa Turnbull called an armadillo, scampered away to safety. If Kojo had his rifle ready, he could have taken it with one squeeze of the trigger. But a shot this high in the mountainside would echo across the entire valley and send his maroon brothers into panic.

The message he had for them this day would lift their spirits, not send their already troubled souls into a frenzy.

He dismounted and pushed his way against the wind and through shrubs to an embankment ahead. He tied his horse to a tree and climbed the mound. In the distance, foggy mountains wrapped around Grand Étang Lake, its round glassy surface like a mirror to the blue sky. The still lake and its dense surroundings pulsed with the spiritual presence of Oshun, the much-loved Yoruba deity of fresh waters.

The view exhaled an aura of deeply-held secrets he could feel, but not see. Secrets that slipped into the invisible world, like water slowly vanishing from the surface of a hot rock. Older slaves even told of a secret underground flow from Grand Étang Lake to Black Bay, on the coast that faced the setting sun. In all his rides between the lake and Black Bay, he had never seen any openings in the ground that might link the two.

But the lake did give up some secrets to him and the maroons. Like the caves in the hillsides. Cloaked by thick jungle, the caves provided disguised shelters for small groups of runaway slaves. They also escaped detection with techniques like smothering cooking smoke with layers of banana leaves.

For their bravery and daily risks, Oshun blessed the maroons with abundance, but not relief from the fear of capture. Hunger was rare. The fertile soil bore huge yams and potatoes, clear rivers overflowed with mullets, and the valley floor attracted plenty of wild game for meat. Oshun gifted them steady breezes that stirred the greenery with pleasant jungle fragrancies. And he kept the air alive with the music of birds, insects, and occasional monkey chatter.

White masters had brought the Mona monkey to the island as pets from the West African jungles Kojo loved as a boy. For the Mona monkeys, as well as the maroons, the risks of freedom meant more than the wretchedness of slavery. Many of the monkeys did what the maroons did: they ran away to Oshun's paradise.

As a boy in the Kingdom of Dahomey, Kojo had learned to imitate the chatter of the Mona monkey. Now he used it to announce his visit to maroon country.

He cupped his hands around his mouth, sucked his lungs filled with air, and chattered three choruses.

The chatter echoed down the valley and bounced off the facing hillsides.

He waited. No answer.

He hollered another three choruses.

No answer.

Three more choruses.

Three new choruses chattered out of the thick canopy below.

He responded with two choruses. Two more floated back up to him.

Now all he had to do was wait.

He sat with his back against a tree listening to the winds howl around him. A relief from the oppressive Beauséjour. He shut his teary eyes so Oshun would not see his suffering. The guilt that shredded his insides.

The breeze calmed him, and he dozed off.

He was not sure how long he slept.

But he awakened abruptly when a hand grabbed his hair from behind and another thrust the sharpened edge of a cutlass against his throat.

Chapter Ten

Lieutenant McDonald did not make a favorable first impression on Rosette when he and that Frenchman rode up to Belvidere House. It distressed her to see the exhausted Englishman, his dusty face marred with lines of sweat and a painfully ugly knot on his head, riding an equally drained horse. Next to him, that rotten-toothed French drunk on his skeletal mare. Both men looked like they amply deserved each other's revolting company as they struggled up the hill in the afternoon heat. Even the workers, busy rolling mats and setting up drums in the front yard for the night's *Saraka*, made fleeting glances in the men's direction. And, to make matters even more disgusting, these white men had kept her father waiting for more than three hours.

The words she could use to describe them would shock even Papa.

And what with the Englishman casting unwelcomed boyish glances at her with his icy blue eyes? Perhaps because she stood barefoot on the verandah. Or maybe her white dress, bright red bandana, and dark skin presented him with more contrasting colors than he ever saw in his dreary life. It was possible he had never seen a colored girl standing in a Great House she called home. Whatever the reason, his and the Frenchman's demeanors provoked much revulsion in her.

If Papa had not asked her to sit next to him during the signing, she would have promptly excused herself and returned to Grandmère's room to read more *Robinson Crusoe*. Oddly though, Papa seemed more formal and respectful than he otherwise would have been when rudely inconvenienced. He marched down the steps to greet the men when they dismounted.

"Welcome to Belvidere Estate," Papa bellowed, shaking their hands. He yelled over his shoulder. "Rosette, please ensure the servants have tall glasses of cool passion juice for our visitors. 'Tis been a long day, especially for Lieutenant McDonald. Have one for Mr. Webster as well. I can see his carriage on the way up the hill now."

Rosette hurried into the kitchen to place Papa's request. The wooden floor creaked, as if expressing empathy for her having to participate in his strained hospitality for these two hooligans. But she calmed her resentment, remembering the reason for their visit. She would simply endure their company while they drank passion juice, signed a few papers, and exchanged a few shillings. Then, she would watch them ride away into the sunset, never to be seen again.

She returned to the verandah just as Mr. Webster rode up in his horse-pulled carriage. He exited with an air of dignity, his nose held high as he adjusted his black jacket and hat.

Papa continued the charade, shaking Mr. Webster's hand. "Mr. Webster, what a privilege and honor it is to have you attend on short notice."

"My pleasure to partake in such a noteworthy

occasion," Mr. Webster proclaimed in the manner of an emperor expecting his every word to be written for posterity.

While the lieutenant removed his saddle bag and handed the horse reins over to a waiting worker, the Frenchman shuffled up to Papa and Mr. Webster.

Mr. Webster took an immediate step back in his shiny black boots, his arms wrapped firmly across his robust chest, and his face disfigured with disgust, as if a pig had accosted him with exhaled sewage.

"I must leave now," the drunkard said in French to Papa.

Papa looked puzzled. "The signing will only take a few minutes. Wait to accompany Lieutenant McDonald back to Gouyave."

"Dr. Hay requested that he remain in Belvidere overnight, on accord of his head wound."

Rosette could not have envisioned a more preposterous outcome from the conversation. It puzzled her how eager Papa seemed to accommodate the Englishman overnight.

"But of course," Papa said loudly. "I am honored to provide quarters for Lieutenant McDonald."

Lieutenant McDonald marched up, a pained smile beneath his bulging forehead. "'Tis no bother. Just an accident."

"I never protest Dr. Hay's advice," Papa said.

Lieutenant McDonald seemed resigned to Dr. Hay's recommendation and Papa's insistence that he stay the night.

The lieutenant thanked the Frenchman, who then mounted his miserable horse and disappeared down the hill.

Papa introduced Mr. Webster to Lieutenant McDonald and invited them into the house with a wave of his hand.

At the door, Lieutenant McDonald looked around with some hesitancy. "May I have a bucket of water to at least have a presentable face before we sit?"

"By all means." Papa laughed and turned to Rosette. "My daughter will show you to the washroom."

Papa seemed determined to ruin what for her should have been a highly spirited day, but she complied without looking at the lieutenant. "This way, please."

With an air of elegance, Mr. Webster held his hat and followed Papa across the living room to the study at the back of the house. Lieutenant McDonald followed Rosette in the other direction, past the kitchen, and down a dim hallway to the washroom.

She pointed to the door. "There is water and soap with a towel in there."

"Thank you most kindly." Despite his sweaty whiff, his voice and crispy British accent held a surprisingly youthful and polite quality. He paused, reached into his saddlebag, and handed her a small bag. "From Father Pascal."

"Oh, thank you," She restrained her smile and turned a firm stare on the washroom door to avoid looking at him. "I will wait here to take you to the study."

She nibbled on a few of Father Pascal's treats while she waited and licked the sugary residue off her fingertips.

A few minutes later, the lieutenant timidly stepped out of the washroom with the saddle bag hung over his shoulder, and carefully shut the door behind him. The dusty British ruffian that had evoked such revulsion in Rosette became a young man with flushed skin, brown hair in a tidy ponytail, and a discolored head wound. He looked lost in a world he had never stepped in before.

The steady disdain she had so persistently nurtured for the Englishman before meeting him, now stood on wobbly legs. Standing this close before her, he exuded a disarming humility.

His blue eyes must have seen the approval on her face.

He smiled. "Do you think Monsieur Fédon would feel better about discussing business with me now?"

His warm, steady gaze touched her, but she kept her

composure without answering his question. "This way—"

"Pardon my poor manners." He bowed slightly, his right hand at the ready as if expecting a handshake. "My name is Malcolm."

She recalled maybe once or twice when she allowed an Englishman to shake her hand, and always in Papa's attendance and with his introduction.

"So sorry." She wiped her sticky fingers on her dress.

"Those treats were marvelous, were they not?" A knowing smile spread across his face. "I did not let a single bit of coconut escape my fingers either."

His light-hearted tease soothed her embarrassment. She shook his hand and quickly withdrew hers. "Rosette."

"Very pleased to meet you, Rosette."

Most whites, especially the British, neither engaged in casual pleasantries with the Fédons, nor acknowledged their presence.

Her handshake with Malcolm, even for a second, felt different from her other handshakes. Holding his hand while they stood alone in the darkened hallway felt strangely forbidden, yet—delightfully so.

She turned and headed to the study. Malcolm's boot steps followed in cadence with her brisk walk. She resisted the temptation to look back to see if he was making fun of her walk but decided that this might be a marching habit drilled into British soldiers. He seemed a soldier first, and boy next.

She wished the opposite was true.

Rosette sat next to Papa at the table in his crowded study. Mr. Webster sat across from him, and Malcolm sat across from her. A stack of papers, a porcelain inkwell, and two quill dip pens waited in the middle of the table. At the end of the table, Maman sat with Grandmère at her side.

A servant waited in the corner by the door, almost unseen, but alert to refill empty glasses with passion juice.

Malcolm sat erect, with an aura of formality, but flinched when he brushed strands of his hair hanging over his swollen forehead. She speculated that he had been drinking with the Frenchman and must have fallen off his horse on the way to Belvidere. She dared not ask him, fearing he might consider her impolite.

It surprised her that she cared what he thought of her.

Another servant placed a tray of freshly baked coconut cakes and tarts Maman had prepared just for the occasion. Despite holding the bag of treats from Father Pascal in her lap, Rosette reached across the table for one of the tarts. Malcolm did too—at the same time. Their hands brushed, and they both quickly pulled back.

"I am so sorry," she said.

He insisted. "Please, after you."

They each took a tart and nibbled in silence.

Papa leaned across the table with a burning match to Mr. Webster's cigar until it flashed flame and smoke. Papa lit his, and soon both cigars sent clouds of smoke around the room. A steady mountain breeze blowing through the open rear windows twirled the smoke into the high ceiling and escaped with the remnants through the side windows.

Papa tapped his thick knuckles on the polished table. "We have many pages. Let us begin so we do not intrude on Mr. Webster's valuable time."

Mr. Webster puffed his cigar. "I am in no hurry, Mr. Fédon."

If only Mr. Webster knew how much it aggravated Papa to be called *Mister*.

"My name is *Monsieur* Fédon," she had heard him scold a man one day. "I am a Frenchman, not an English pig."

Malcolm lifted the first page, read it aloud, and passed it to Mr. Webster, who read it to himself before passing it to Papa. Papa glanced at the page with a studious frown and handed it to Rosette. She read it to herself.

"...for conveying unto and to the use of the said Julien

Fédon his Heirs and Assigns forever a certain Coffee and Cocoa Plantation Tract or parcel of Land in the parish of Saint John called Belvidere..."

She finished reading the page and set it in the middle of the table. Malcolm read another page and passed it the same way.

Rosette read it.

"by Admeasurement Four hundred and fifty Acres of Land...the buildings thereon and one hundred Slaves, Sixteen head of horned Cattle and five horses..."

It annoyed her that the deed listed the slaves between the buildings and the cattle. She considered some of these slaves her friends, having known them since she was just a toddler in Grand Pauvre. "Why do we have the slaves in this sentence?"

Mr. Webster squinted. "What do you mean, young lady?"

"They are people," she said. "We have them listed with buildings and animals."

"They are property, with value," he insisted. "This is a standard British contract. There is no harm done to them. Just business."

"'Tis distasteful. In any case, this page has a mistake," she said. "It should be eighty slaves, not one-hundred. Papa already had twenty slaves when we moved here to lease the land a year ago."

Mr. Webster turned to Papa. "Mr. Fédon, is that correct?"

"Yes," Papa said. "Colonel McDonald and I agreed on eighty slaves. The total for everything should be fifteen thousand."

Rosette read aloud the price statement on the page. *"Fifteen thousand pounds Current Money of the said Island of Grenada."*

Mr. Webster turned to Malcolm. "Lieutenant McDonald, do you agree with me amending the number of slaves to eighty and assigning my name to it, since it does not change the price?"

"Yes, sir."

Rosette handed the page to Mr. Webster, who the scribbled the correction. During the pause, she glanced over at Maman and Grandmère. Both smiled. Grandmère winked at her.

Both women looked alike, even though they were only related by marriage. Cocoa-brown skin, high cheeks, and long thick hair now rolled up and covered in matching red headscarves for the *Saraka*. Both Mestive, descendants of negro and Amerindian, in a world ruled by white customs. But they exuded with pride for Papa's big moment.

This estate was more than ten times the size of the coffee plantation he had recently sold in Grand Pauvre to afford the move to Belvidere. But he had negotiated a purchase price only five times what he received for his Grand Pauvre plantation. Maybe because so much of Belvidere remained virgin land, uncultivated and wild.

One day, soon after moving to Belvidere, Rosette and one of the servants had ventured up the uncultivated hills across the river. They jumped from rock to rock over the racing waters to the other side and climbed the hill until they were out of breath. Rosette loved the damp earth beneath her bare feet, the never-ending views of misty-green mountains and valleys, birds singing in the trees, and juicy yellow mangoes tantalizing her taste buds. The winds blew with appetizing flavors too numerous to identify.

But when the girls returned to the house an hour later, sweaty and joyous from the adventure, Papa scolded them.

He had yelled. "You do not know who might be lurking up there. Do not do it again."

Regardless, all of Belvidere would soon be his, slaves, land, rivers, and forbidden hills—as forbidden as holding hands with Malcolm in the darkened hallway.

Today, Papa would sign his own name. Of Grandmère's eight children, Papa was probably the only one with the desire to learn. Rosette wondered how much more distant she would be from her father had she not appointed herself his writing tutor.

The reward of sitting next to him now far surpassed those discouraging moments when he would slam down the pen in frustration and stomp off. But he would return, and she would be waiting with pen, paper, and patience.

Mr. Webster handed the corrected page to Papa, who glanced at it and handed it to Rosette. A proud grin stretched across Papa's face. She read the correction and waited for the next page. Two following pages listed the names of the slaves.

When the fire in Mr. Webster's cigar died, Papa struck another match and reached over the table to the English gentleman. Papa held the match to the cigar, but his eyes glazed in a hardened stare at Mr. Webster.

She wondered what emotions flowed in her father's vein. The chances of a free French mulatto sitting across the table from two Englishmen in such a transaction seemed so remote. Yet, here they sat. Exchanging money for land and lives.

The remaining pages went smoothly, with no remaining errors. By then, Rosette had begun to grow tired of the repeated words that Malcolm read aloud from each page. The *'for conveying unto,'* *'land in the parish of Saint John called Belvidere'*, and the *'assigns forever'* seemed to go on forever.

She tried in vain to block out Malcolm's words—but not the pleasant tone of his voice. She liked how his lips and tongue worked together in clear pronunciations of the legal terms. *'That in compliance with the said last in part recited Articles and for the considerations therein...'*

Instead of trying to comprehend what *'considerations therein'* meant, the only consideration she held was how his lips would feel on hers. A surprising warmth ran through her. Embarrassed, she looked out the window.

The ill feelings she had held for Malcolm since awakening that morning seemed to have dampened with the cool sound of the flowing river. Was his physical proximity more disarming than all the resentment she had cultivated for the British over the past few years?

Grandmère might understand. After all, did she not fall in love with, and married, a white man? A Frenchman who once enslaved even her own mother.

Malcolm waved the last page. "Finally, we get to sign."

Papa and Maman signed, followed by Mr. Webster and Malcolm as witnesses. Papa counted ten shillings and pushed them across the table to Malcolm.

When Rosette read the signed page, she chuckled at his middle name, Neill.

The servants poured brandy for the adults, including Malcolm. They toasted, shook hands, and accompanied Mr. Webster outside to his waiting carriage.

Rosette wondered if the celebratory occasion and friendly atmosphere had further warmed Papa's enthusiasm towards the two Englishmen. The same way her contempt for Malcolm had subsided.

But her heart sank when she looked at Papa as he watched Mr. Webster's carriage rattle down the hill.

Papa puffed his cigar, his jaw muscles rigid. His eyes held a cold dead stare that surprised Rosette—and worried her.

Chapter Eleven

Kojo grabbed the hand holding the cutlass to his throat and jerked the attacker down. With a thrust of his shoulder into the man, he heaved him overhead and onto his back. Kojo swooped up the loose cutlass and stood with his foot planted on his attacker's chest.

"Friend or foe?" Kojo asked.

The bareback man laughed and leaped to his feet, dusting his hands against ragged trousers. "Just your friend, Simon, keeping you alert."

They embraced in a back-slapping moment.

Simon stepped away and gave Kojo a side glance. "Two visits in one day? Did your *Venus* escape again?"

"No, my brother. And she is not my *Venus*."

"Any punishment for her?"

Kojo wondered how much he should tell Simon. A hundred slaves had witnessed the whipping of the girl and Massa Turnbull's vicious temper against a white boy.

Eventually, Simon would hear about it from the *shoo-shoo* whispers that spread news from plantation to plantation, from slave to slave, and from slave to maroon.

Secrets poisoned trust. The friendship and trust Kojo shared with Simon held more value than any secrets. Their lives depended on it. If Massa Turnbull ever suspected Kojo's double life, Kojo would die a slow agonizing death. Simon held Kojo's life in his hands, and Kojo held Simon's life in his hands.

The screams still tormented Kojo. But he knew worse would have befallen Venus if the white boy had not grabbed Kojo's arm, or if Massa Turnbull had taken the whip to do the job himself. Maybe having a baby in her belly saved her life. On another day, she would have lost a leg. Or left to die hanging from a hook through her rib cage. He had warned her about running away. Repeatedly. But her stubbornness took over her mind, and she vanished one night, like she had done twice before.

Massa Turnbull had been lenient when Kojo returned her on those occasions, because of her tender age. Massa locked her up in the musty dungeon for a week, because he knew she feared the rats and centipedes. For that week, he fed her nothing but bread and water. But this last escape lifted Massa Turnbull to frightening heights of rage. When weeks dragged by, and she did not crawl back begging for his forgiveness, he called a meeting of his English friends. The housemaids told Kojo that Massa Turnbull swore, if Venus did not return soon, he would get the governor to amass a militia to sweep the entire island for runaways.

Kojo was forced to act to save the maroon communities from extermination. He begged Massa Turnbull to let him find her. Even with her swollen belly, it took him a week, with Simon's help.

Kojo searched his mind for ways Venus could have escaped punishment, but he kept returning to one answer— her own death.

"She got off easy," Kojo told Simon about the young

McDonald grabbing his arm during the whipping, and Massa Turnbull knocking him to sleep with a pistol blow to the head.

Simon listened intensely to the account and gazed up at the mountains when Kojo finished.

"Times changing," Simon said. "But not fast enough. We be long dead and gone before every white man wake up like that boy."

"Bad blood between Massa Turnbull and the white boy not over. Never see Massa Turnbull so hot."

Simon squinted at him. "What else bring you back here?"

"Good news. Monsieur Fédon own Belvidere Estate today."

"White man actually let him buy it?"

"Massa Turnbull say so."

"I do not trust." Simon sucked his teeth with a hissing sound. "Salt look like white sugar."

Kojo liked to talk to Simon. The maroon had a refreshing view of situations. A way of seeing things Kojo rarely noticed in the enslaved. Freedom, however scant, provided nourishment to the maroon's spirit and mind. Even Simon's skin glowed with a clean vitality not seen among Massa's dusty field slaves. Many returned to their shacks at night too exhausted and disheartened to wash away days-old sweaty grime with a bucket of river water. Simon frequently told Kojo about their leisurely baths in the rivers and sulfur springs, which explained the vigor he exuded. Beneath a headful of crazed curly hair, Simon's eyes blazed like a torch in the night, and his thoughts slashed through circumstances with the sharpness of his cutlass.

Simon had changed from the day Kojo first met him on the coast of Benin. The African catchers had taken Kojo and his sister on a rowboat down the river to the sea, a three-day journey. In a gut-wrenching moment of screams and sorrow, they separated him from his sister. Then they blindfolded him and dragged him to a dungeon. It suffocated with other unfortunate souls and their pungent waste.

Later that day, they led him to an auction block where he stood next to a bareback boy about his age, both raining big teardrops and shaking at their knees. Two white men with long hair and shaggy beards spoke strange words and marched up to the boys. They forced open Kojo's mouth with smelly gloved hands, pinched his arms, and poked at his ribs with a stick. Then did the same to the boy next to Kojo. The white men handed money to the black catchers, shackled Kojo to the boy, and pulled them to the port where they packed them into a ship with hundreds of moaning people.

Kojo never forgot how the stench overwhelmed his senses deep in the bowels of the ship. The groans of other captors in the darkness muffled the boy's sobs next to him. From the deck overhead, the clanks of heavy chains mingled with screams that followed harsh claps of whips.

Kojo and Simon exchanged names in guarded whispers, mainly because the smells of puke and diarrhea seemed to thicken through their open mouths. They shared the horrors of their kidnappings. Black men had snatched them from their compounds while the boys' parents were away gathering food from the jungle. They tried to talk about their families, friends, and hunting victories but kept returning to the cruelties and bodily inspections they had witnessed and endured.

Both boys admitted that they harbored the same fear: when they arrived in the white men's land, they would be eaten.

That belief worsened a few days later when men with whips led Kojo and Simon with a group of captors up to the deck, a procession of Africans shuffling to the clanks of heavy chains around their ankles. The white men made them sit around a big pole in the blinding sunshine, made more intense by the days in darkness. Huge white sheets roped overhead dragged the ship across the water.

The men tied an older man to the pole. An African translator explained that the man had tried to jump overboard to join his ancestors in death. They whipped the man until he collapsed to his knees with raw red skin hanging off his back.

They rubbed salt in his wounds and let him bake in the sun awhile. Then they whipped him again. By then, his screams and howls had faded to silence—except for the whip clapping the man's bloodied back and white sheets applauding in the wind overhead. When his body stopped jerking, they untied him and heaved him into the sea, the reason he was punished to begin with.

Kojo understood the message clearly.

The white man owned, not only the lives but the deaths of the human cargo.

Three weeks later, the ship docked in Grenada. Despite the shackles that scraped his ankle skin almost down to the bone, despite the hunger and despondency, the moment Kojo stepped on deck remained within him through the many rainy and dry seasons on the island. The memory, cast in fresh air and intense sunlight, sealed an unwavering decision. Regardless of how long it took, he would one day be free to return to Africa. And those who enslaved him yesterday would bleed tomorrow.

He saw Simon again at the St. George's auction the next day. An Englishman bought them, and they slaved on his plantation in St. David's for eight years. During the chaos of the French invasion fourteen years ago, Simon confided in Kojo his plans to run away to the central mountains, at the risk of his leg or his life. When the British reclaimed the island, and Massa Turnbull purchased the two young men, Simon made his move.

They decided then to remain a team. Kojo on the inside. Simon on the outside.

Both men arranged meeting places and times to meet in secret. They remained trusted friends. Sometimes their conversations revived memories of Benin. Sometimes they planned. Sometimes they just sat and smoked cigars.

Simon reached into his pocket and removed two cigars. They lit each other's cigars and sat puffing.

Kojo chewed on his and savored the bitter tobacco juice before breaking the silence. "Another ship come this morning. They pack them tighter these days, like saltfish in a crate. More than two hundred souls."

"Two hundred more fighters for us," Simon said.

"The delivery drivers say they used to smell the ships from Hospital Hill, looking down on the port. Now they start smelling them at the river, a mile away."

"Maybe they pack more because they worry their white king might stop soon the ships."

Kojo puffed his cigar. "Our kings in Africa also have to stop the captures."

"Greed is a bigger king than white king and black king together." Simon pushed back his bushy hair with his hands and stared at Kojo with a questioning squint. "You no come back here to talk about kings."

"Monsieur Fédon say tell you about new rules starting today."

Simon puffed on his cigar. "Yes?"

"He said you can cultivate the lands on the Belvidere side of Mount Qua Qua. Nobody go up there."

"What he want from us?"

"No more trying to get his slaves to run away. No trespassing on the work lands. No more stealing."

"We do not steal. The gods give the land to us. When we take from the land, it is a gift from the gods."

Kojo spat tobacco juice at his feet. "The French and British do not believe in our gods. Monsieur Fédon and the landowners say it is stealing."

"It is they who steal!" Simon leaped to his feet and slapped his chest. "They steal work and sweat from Africans and pay them nothing."

"My brother, we know that. With patience, we will

change all that soon."

Simon dragged a puff on his cigar. When no smoke came out, he looked at the cigar with disappointment that wrinkled his brow and protruded his thick lips. "My people have no more patience."

"Remind them that we have only one chance to do this right or we all hang from trees with our guts open like slaughtered pigs."

"I know you believe in Monsieur Fédon. But my people see no difference between brown men and white men."

"He is more like us than them."

Simon shook his head. "Why you say that? He own land and slave like white men."

"Monsieur Fédon hate the white Englishman as much as we do."

"He hate the white Englishmen, but not the white Frenchman. Remember the French brought Africans here first."

"It no matter," Kojo said. "He still in a cage. He just own a cage inside a cage."

Simon laughed. "Yes, brown man with a cage inside a cage."

"For now, we must take what the brown man give us until we strong enough to destroy them both. Our brothers in Saint Dominique doing same thing. I wait long time. I could wait a little more." Kojo inspected his cigar, no longer lit, dusted off the ash end and stuck it in his pocket. "I must go. Madame Turnbull go be troubled."

Simon looked at the burnt-out tip of his cigar. "Tell Monsieur Fédon cure his tobacco for two more sunsets. I no like steal tobacco that cannot keep fire. He need patience too."

Chapter Twelve

Confusion muddied Malcolm's thoughts as he glanced over the vast expanse of rolling Belvidere hills, still lush green in the fading sunlight. A steady tobacco-scented wind blew from behind him, carrying the distant sound of the river's turbulent wash. Along the front yard of the dignified Belvidere House, workers hammered the final touches on shelters and flag poles for the night's festivities. The two-storied brick house, gray bricks with white window frames, held an unobstructed view across the valley to the Chadeau plantation, owned by Monsieur Fédon's younger brother, Jean-Pierre. Rosette had told Malcolm after the signing, that on a clear day, her father and his brother would wave and shout obscenities at each other in laughing fits.

Why did Father sell such luxuriant acreage and home at such a bargain price just a year after purchasing it? And to a man he called a mixed breed French mongrel with no loyalty to white or black?

Beneath his iron deportment, Father harbored an overflowing reservoir of bitterness for the outcome of the American War. When Lord General Honorable Earl Cornwallis surrendered His Britannic Majesty's forces at Yorktown in October 1781, Father sank into misery as a prisoner of war.

Father grudgingly recalled the mile-long columns of dejected British troops, marching between equally long columns of victorious American and French soldiers, to lay down their arms in surrender. Two years of prison squalor away from his family and the long, harsh Pennsylvania winters froze his heart with disdain. He reserved his fiercest anger for the French and the negroes who fought against the British. In addition to the thousands of French troops on the American side, out of every four American soldiers who besieged Yorktown, one was an African.

Father's distaste for Monsieur Fédon might certainly have come from his horrid experiences in America, the reason he had Malcolm conduct the sale rather than waiting to do so himself on his return from England.

But why sell the estate to a man he hated?

Color and French heritage notwithstanding, Monsieur Fédon possessed none of the qualities that should trigger such loathing and fury. He appeared to be a diligent businessman, proud father, loyal family man, and respectful of his workers, doing the best with all the blessings of His Majesty's colony of Grenada.

Father probably reaped a handsome profit from the sale. Grenada provided Father his best opportunity yet to redeem himself after the American loss. In the years before Malcolm began his military career in the service of King George, Father had frequently sat the family around the dinner table in Liverpool to tell them of his plans to own a prosperous slave plantation in Grenada. His goal, he said, was to build an extravagant country home in England. Like the Paxton House owned by Grenada Speaker of the House of Assembly, Ninian Home.

The mansion sat just west of Berwick-upon-Tweed on the north bank of the River Tweed, near the Scottish-English border. Father had visited the governor there once when both were on holiday from the islands. Father returned home with an enthusiastic description of the sprawling house, complete with library, picture gallery, colorful gardens, croquet lawn, and a walking path alongside the River Tweed.

Governor Home's sugar plantation in Paraclete, to the north of the island, provided him a reliable source of wealth. It allowed him to pay fifteen thousand pounds for Paxton House, the same price Monsieur Fédon agreed to pay Father for Belvidere. But the Belvidere agreement only required Monsieur Fédon to make a deposit of ten shillings, with annual payments over ten years. Hardly a practical plan for Father to purchase the country home that he wanted for his retirement.

Even the drunkard, Bourbon, said the Belvidere deal was an agreement blessed by the devil, and Mr. Turnbull greatly detested the idea of Monsieur Fédon owning it.

Why?

Something felt rather odd about the Belvidere affair.

A voice as soft as the footsteps on the grass behind him interrupted his thoughts. "The river is in the other direction."

He turned to face Rosette, and his heart raced. Her deep bronze complexion glowed in the red sunset and her smile quickly washed away his concerns about the Belvidere sale.

His composure fluttered. "Riv... River?"

Her dark eyes held an amused twinkle in the fading light. "Father said you were going to take a river bath. 'Tis the other direction."

"Yes...yes, of course. Just enjoying the view."

"You should be getting ready for tonight. Papa might not be so forgiving if you are late twice today."

"Agreed. Please show me the way."

They walked in silence across the front yard and down a trail that disappeared into the tree line.

She pointed into the trees. "Just follow that shortcut to the river. The water is cool. But be careful. The rocks are slippery."

He chuckled and touched the swollen side of his forehead. "I do not want to get a second horn."

Rosette laughed for the first time since he met her that afternoon, and he wondered why she did not laugh more frequently.

"Yes," she replied, "if the workers see you return from the river with two horns, they might think you are a white devil."

He instantly saw her embarrassment.

Her smile faded, and her lips trembled. "I am so very sorry," she whispered.

Just then, her mother's voice sailed from the house. "Rosette, come back here, child."

Rosette turned and ran back to the house.

Malcolm wished she had not left so soon. He wanted to tell her that he liked her humor. And her laugh.

Rosette found Papa sitting alone in his study, staring out the window at the twilight sky. He leaned back in his chair, his legs on the table, his boots crossed at the ankles. Tobacco smoke thickened the air, and the only discernible light in the room came from the glow on his cigar. The first drumbeats, singing, and food aromas from the Saraka festivities drifted freely through the open windows.

She tapped on the open door before walking in. "Papa?"

"Come in, my child."

"Did not mean to interrupt."

Papa must have sensed she was there for more than idle conversation. "Something on your mind, my dear?"

She hesitated to tell Papa how she had just insulted

Lieutenant McDonald. "Is Uncle Jean-Pierre attending tonight?"

"Yes, of course." His voice filled the room. "You will hear him before you see him. With all his workers. They are bringing more food and drums. This is as much my brother's celebration as it is ours."

"It pleases me to hear that, Papa." Rosette loved her uncle Jean-Pierre, his African wife, Aunty Margueritte, and their two teenaged daughters. The cousins attended the same tutoring classes that Grandmère paid for. She would have much to tell them tonight, especially about Malcolm.

The cigar glowed with another puff. "You did a magnificent job today at the signing. You impressed those Englishmen, especially Lieutenant McDonald."

At the sound of Malcolm's name, the door opened for her to address the true reason for visiting Papa. "I am afraid I squandered any goodwill he had for me today."

"Yes?" Papa dropped his feet to the floor.

She explained her slip of the tongue, about Malcolm looking like a white devil if he received another bump on his head.

Papa's uncontrollable laughter started a coughing frenzy that brought one of the servants rushing into the office with a glass of water.

When his composure returned, he wiped laughter tears from his eyes. "My dear daughter, Englishmen have worse names for us."

"Should I apologize to him?"

"Why?"

"Because I did not say it to hurt him."

"Did it hurt him?"

She had not thought of that. "I know not."

"Then ask him. If he says yes, ask him to tell his people to stop using their names on us too." Papa puffed his cigar. "Wait, do not ask him. He already had enough hurt today."

"Did he fall off his horse?" she asked.

"No." Papa explained how Malcolm sustained his head wound from Mr. Turnbull. "Kojo told me what happened. Lieutenant McDonald is either a brave young man or does not understand this whole affair very well."

"'Tis astonishing that he stood up to Mr. Turnbull, Papa. That makes me feel even more miserable."

"Okay. Apologize. For you."

"Thanks, Papa."

He puffed a while, and his tone lowered almost to a growl. "Make him the only Englishman you ever apologize to. None deserve to keep their heads."

Rosette walked out of the office and raced upstairs to her room to get ready. She peeked out her window. Across the front yard, flaming torches burned into the darkness, casting yellow light over hordes of workers in white and red. Heavy drumming filled her soul, and from down the hill, a chorus of singing from Uncle Jean-Pierre's arriving workers lifted over Belvidere House.

Only then did the chills from Papa's last words begin to subside.

Chapter Thirteen

Spellbound, Malcolm stood alone on the verandah watching the Belvidere night descend around him with an embrace of sensations he knew neither how to accept nor reject. His English upbringing left him little room to grasp the outpouring of raw exertions that flowed from the crowd of Africans before him. Bathed in the yellow light of flaming lanterns, their black skin glistened with sweat from joyous dancing. Vigorous drum beats throbbed his insides. The echoes rolled like thunder over the moon-glazed hillsides to greet a chorus of singing from a group shuffling up the hill. The smoky aroma of peppered meats and vegetables soaked the air and enticed his neglected appetite.

King George and his Christian mission to spread civilization seemed woefully distant and diminished here.

A surge of sadness and anger overwhelmed Malcolm. How can these people of such rich exuberance tolerate a life chained to plantations by fear and brutality? How much longer before they erupt against their masters?

Maybe they would not rebel against Monsieur Fédon. Even as a slave master, he shared at least some of the skin color and resentments of his slaves. Enough so to allow them the freedom to partake in some of their native African customs.

Monsieur Fédon marched up with a bottle in one hand and two cigars in the other, his boots hammering the wooden floor. "You look perplexed, Lieutenant."

"Just enjoying the energy."

"Me boy, you are feeling the spirit of the warrior, Shango. It comes with drumming and dancing. He gives courage, so there is much for them to celebrate." Monsieur Fédon held a cigar to him. "Let us have a smoke for the Belvidere sale."

"Thank you, but I do not smoke. My coughing might be louder than the drums."

"Then you must have a drink of rum." He uncorked the bottle, said a few words with his eyes closed, sprinkled a few drops on the floor between them, and took a swig.

Malcolm accepted the bottle from Monsieur Fédon and lifted it to his lips. The rum burned its way down his throat and made his eyes water. He struggled to hold his composure, lest Monsieur Fédon thought him unfit for such a manly ritual.

They stood side by side, passing the bottle between them, and watching the display of drumming, dancing, and singing.

Monsieur Fédon pointed at the singing group of about fifty dancing their way up the hill. "My brother, Jean-Pierre, leading his workers."

Jean-Pierre wore all white, but no shoes, like the group behind him. When they reached the yard, his group dispersed into the crowd, and Jean-Pierre mounted the steps to the verandah.

Monsieur Fédon greeted him in a crushing embrace.

"Your dancing is improving, brother," Monsieur

Fédon said. "But your singing needs improvement. You will embarrass your mother."

"Your wife tells me your singing gives her nightmares!" Jean-Pierre stepped back and pointed at Malcolm. "When you sent a message that you have an Englishman visiting, I did not expect one so young."

"And bold too," Monsieur Fédon said. "He stood up to Mr. Turnbull this morning and paid a price on his head for that."

Jean-Pierre held Malcolm's hand in a firm handshake. "Pleased to meet you."

"My pleasure," Malcolm said.

Monsieur Fédon swung his arm over Jean-Pierre's shoulder and grinned. "Tell us the truth, Lieutenant. Who is more handsome?"

Jean-Pierre looked five years younger than Monsieur Fédon, maybe forty, same dark brown complexion, but not as tall. His smaller frame, when coupled with his warm smile and voice, made him a less intimidating figure.

Malcolm considered his options to Monsieur Fédon's question. "I can tell right away that you are brothers, and you are both equally handsome men."

The Fédon brothers laughed, but Monsieur Fédon's next words betrayed a bitter edge. "Jean-Pierre is more valuable to me than fifty Englishmen. When other family chose to live in Trinidad under the Spaniards, rather than in Grenada under you British, Jean-Pierre chose to remain here with me. We are not afraid."

Malcolm wondered if the rum had begun to raise the man's temper. He tried to return some civility to the conversation. "We should not be afraid of each other."

"Tell that to your father's friends like Mr. Turnbull and his tyrant friend, Ninian Home."

Under starry skies and lost in a sea of dancers dressed in red and white, Rosette surrendered to the rhythmic beats from an army of goatskin drums. She closed her eyes and became one with pained voices around her singing of loss, punishment, struggle—and retribution. The drumming rolled on, summoning Shango, the God of thunder, song, and dance.

Rosette's hands twirled upward. Her body gyrated without her command. The drums pounded powerful sensations through her body.

Harder and harder.

A spiritual path opened before her, a path to the other world. The drumming rolled with increased urgency, beckoning her to enter paradise. The world of the ancestors, where an abundance of pleasure, wisdom, and strength awaited all who dared to take the journey.

The drums hammered faster and faster.

She could see it now. She could feel it now, with mounting desire. The power of Shango possessed her humanity, her womanhood. Deeper and deeper the drum beats drove into her. Lifting her higher and higher with the yearning to enter the other side. Finally—an explosion of sweet release. A heavenly river rippled down her body. It swept her off her feet. In blissful surrender, she floated away to the other side, her soul in flight, soaring to boundless heights with a smile of victory.

She entered the land of Shango.

And the drums kept pounding.

She danced, for how long she did not know. But when she finally returned to her body and opened her eyes to the earthly world, a big moon watched the festivities from where it hung between the trees. Her insides felt anew, refreshed, pure. Purpose and courage warmed her heart. There was no better time, no better place to plan for the unknown than here and now. All she ever wished for will come true. All her fears will be vanquished. All her enemies will be destroyed by the wisdom of Shango.

The Fédon family will overcome British oppression. Papa's purchase of Belvidere Estate was the first step. Up here in the mountains, away from demeaning eyes and scornful whispers, he could be his own master.

True, Papa was a slave owner, but a different slave owner. She had heard the countless heartbreaking stories from slaves Papa purchased from other estates. Papa was stern with his slaves too. She would cover her ears with her pillow to smother the screams when he exacted punishment.

But he had more in common with his workers than he did with English people.

The slaves labored for him, but more from respect than fear.

The British scorned nights like this, but Papa understood why the slaves should keep their African ways. Many came from Yoruba cultures of Dahomey, but others were Igbo from the Bight of Biafra, and Bantu from Central Africa, all represented here this night in a common display of faith.

Papa believed Shango gave the slaves a connection to their homeland, a source of strength to cope with their hardships, and a way to reduce their desperation. Desperation that frequently led to violent outbursts against slave owners—and merciless reprisals.

After all, despite being a slave owner, he too understood oppression.

Shango promised deliverance, but deliverance had to be fought for. With the spirit of Shango, Rosette intended to stand at her father's side in every battle he fought.

Malcolm's heart raced when Rosette came running out from the crowd, looking happy and delightful in her full white dress and red headscarf, like a flower in full blossom. Her mother, Maman, followed arm in arm with a slender dark woman.

Rosette raced up the steps and into Jean-Pierre's embrace. "Uncle, so glad you came."

"But of course, Princess."

The woman with Maman strolled on to the verandah in timid but graceful steps and stood at Jean-Pierre's side.

Monsieur Fédon gazed into Maman's eyes and kissed her on the cheek. "You look lovely, my dear,"

Jean-Pierre introduced the other woman to Malcolm. "Lieutenant, this is my wife, Margueritte."

Malcolm held her outstretched hand in a brief handshake. "Pleased to meet you, Madame Fédon."

"Nice meeting you, Mr. McDonald." She avoided eye contact, bowing her head with a shy smile.

After a few minutes of conversation, the two women drifted down the steps to rejoin the festivities, and their husbands retreated inside leaving Rosette alone with Malcolm on the verandah.

"My Aunty Margueritte was a slave for an Englishman," Rosette explained. "I see the scars on her back when she bathes in the river. She bought her freedom earning money working on her free Sundays as a seamstress in Gouyave."

"She is very introverted."

"Slavery can do that to people. Only around white..."

"White people?"

She glanced away. "Yes. Sorry if I offended you."

"No need for apologies. I understand more tonight than when I left Fort George this morning."

"I apologize for making that white devil joke."

He laughed. "I thought it quite humorous."

"You did, honestly?"

"Honestly, I swear," he said.

She seemed relieved, her smile aglow in the abundance of lantern flames lighting the night. "What did you really think when I said that?"

"You really want to know what I was thinking?"

"Yes, please."

"I was thinking how much I enjoyed your company."

She tugged at her braids and looked away. "Papa told

me what happened to you in Beauséjour today. Kojo told him."

"It was unfortunate."

"The people are starting to talk about you," Rosette said. "I do not know if 'tis a good or bad thing. They might expect you to choose sides one day."

The drumming and singing filled the silence between them. The moon rose in full glory over the hillside and stars flickered in the sky, so low they looked within hand's reach. He wondered if Rosette would ever let him hold her hand again.

What would his family think if they knew he stood next to a black girl, feeling earnest sentiments for her, and wishing they were both alone so he could kiss her inviting lips? Mother would be appalled and would probably demand that Father ship him back to Liverpool promptly to be reacquainted with the fair maidens in her Anglican church.

Father's anger would probably lead him to challenge Malcolm to a deadly duel. And Malcolm's brothers? They would eagerly rush him with questions. Does she kiss like white girls? Is her black skin as smooth? Does she dance?

"Were you dancing out there too?" he asked Rosette.

"Were you watching me?"

"There were so many dancers, I could not tell. But I wish I had seen you."

Her smile faded. "What you see out there is more than meets the eye. Shango drumming and dancing give these Africans the courage and the way to face their unknown future. For some, dancing is the fighting ritual of warriors. Shango is the energy of justice and revenge. That is the future they celebrate tonight."

Malcolm lost track of how long they talked, so enchanting her presence, so alluring her deep dark eyes, so intriguing her words that seduced his thoughts down unfamiliar paths. Paths submerged deep below the mass of enslaved humanity, where grief, anger, and pain simmered.

He thought of the little girl he saw that morning watching down from the ridge overlooking the Beauséjour fields and wondered what pain she might have already endured in her delicate years to have such a mangled leg.

So much of what he perceived on the surface now held no stock.

The songs the workers sang in the fields were not songs of gratitude, as he thought. Singing strengthened their resolve to live another day, another day closer to salvation and liberation—and revenge.

Slave desperation and French mulatto resistance now threatened to merge against British rule. The powder keg sat at the ready, its short fuse awaiting the perfect spark at the perfect time.

Malcolm felt a need to raise this observation with Dr. Hay.

Rosette fetched them two plates of food from the food tent, returning up the steps with grace and a heartwarming smile.

He pulled up a chair across from her and consumed with great pleasure the plate of delicious stewed beef, fried plantains, and spicy greens. His appetite fully satisfied, he felt ready for bed. His head hurt, and fatigue from the full day had begun to set in.

Reluctantly, he stood from his chair. "I must say goodnight."

She stood. "I hope you sleep well."

"Maybe I will see you tomorrow before I leave?"

"For my good, I hope so." She offered her hand.

He held it in a brief shake, although a little tighter and longer than they did by the washroom that afternoon.

"For my good too," he said.

He headed down the steps and around the corner towards the small guest cabin behind Belvidere house. The Shango drumming and dancing faded behind as he passed Monsieur Fédon's darkened study.

They might expect you to choose sides one day. He

wondered what Rosette meant. *Shango is the energy of justice and revenge. That is the future they celebrate tonight.*

Her words sounded ominous, but nothing he saw or heard revealed any hint of a slave rebellion.

Rosette had said her father rarely invited white men to their festivities. "They would not understand."

"This knot on my head was my invitation to stay here tonight."

She had chuckled. "I am glad you stayed."

Alone with his thoughts, he walked the lawn past the corner windows of the study. Cigar smoke drifted out. Two men sat in the darkness. Two cigars glowed. Probably Monsieur Fédon and his brother, Jean-Pierre, their conversation muffled by the drumming.

Malcolm walked past the last window and glanced back into the study.

A third man sat at the table facing the two smokers.

It puzzled Malcolm that no one had entered the house through the front door while he and Rosette spoke on the verandah.

Why would a visitor enter the house through the back door?

Under candlelight in the guest hut, Malcolm changed into a nightshirt and collapsed on the bed. He stretched past his carbine and reached into his saddlebag on the floor to retrieve the book his brother had sent him. He read a few pages and stopped at a paragraph.

He read it again, a quote from a letter Edmund Burke had written in 1777. *People crushed by laws have no hope but to evade power. If the laws are their enemies, they will be enemies to the law; and those who have most to hope and nothing to lose will always be dangerous.*

How could the words of a British intellectual so well describe Malcolm's own growing anxiety about slavery in

Grenada?

Just today, the things he heard and witnessed shook his confidence. Slavery no longer seemed buttressed on laws of God and King. *Shango* defied those laws. The spirit ruled the fields, hidden amongst slaves, whispering songs of liberation and revenge.

Mr. Turnbull did not have to look for strange ideas about freedom coming from faraway places like Paris.

Those ideas were always among his flock. Embedded under their skin. Since their birth, as it did with white men. And brown men.

The King's laws of slavery—which listed men for sale as if they were buildings and cattle—were enemies to the essence of man.

All men.

Doubt slipped through the door into Malcolm's mind, left ajar and unguarded during the Shango dancing and during his conversations with Rosette. He tried to push the thoughts out and shut the door, but Edmund Burke's words pushed back with the strength of its troubling truth.

Those who have most to hope and nothing to lose will always be dangerous.

Sleep sat heavily on his eyelids. On the end table, he placed the book face down opened to the pages he just read. He blew out the candle and drifted off to sleep with his headache throbbing to the drum beats outside.

How much later, he knew not, but the sound of a horse thundering past his window awakened him.

It faded down the hillside.

Roosters crowed, a sure sign that sunrise was on its way. Gray predawn light peaked past the thin curtains blowing in the cool morning breeze. The plantation bell announced the wakeup time for the slaves. A gang driver somewhere on the hillside shouted orders, and a whip clapped. Cooking fires soiled the morning air with smoke, while a braying donkey added to the growing morning chaos. He filled his lungs with the fresh air, savoring the rich aroma of wildflowers and coffee. His headache had faded overnight, and now he felt revitalized.

A few minutes later, urgent hoof beats of arriving horses drew closer on the far side of the great house. They stopped.

Shouts and heavy footsteps. The unmistaken metallic sound of soldiers running with weapons.

From the front of Belvidere House, steady banging on doors.

A man yelled.

A woman screamed.

Malcolm yanked up his trousers and pulled on his boots.

More screams.

He grabbed his carbine and scrambled out the door.

A man shouted in anger.

Mr. Turnbull.

Chapter Fourteen

Dr. Hay never thought he could detest a man more than he did Mr. Turnbull. Rage burned through the doctor's veins. Nothing seemed to sooth him. Neither the gentle sounds of the morning waves washing the Gouyave shoreline behind his house, nor the steaming cup of coffee his servant just served him.

The turmoil began with the rapid banging on his door a half-hour earlier. One of his soldiers had upsetting news: Mr. Turnbull had cajoled a few soldiers from the Gouyave militia post to serve a legal document on the Fédon family in Belvidere.

It was within Mr. Turnbull's prerogative, as a ranking member of the Grenada council, to procure British soldiers to enforce the law—in the absence of any available military authority. Dr. Hay, commanding officer of the St. John's Regiment, residing less than half-a-mile from the militia post, possessed that military authority granted to him by

His Honor, Governor General Matthew.

The regiment consisted of thirty-two of His Majesty's natural-born subjects, thirteen commissioned officers, forty-six French adopted subjects, and eighty-six free people of color. In addition to his medical obligations, Dr. Hay dedicated many hours to ensure the regiment exhibited the highest levels of loyalty and preparedness. In one of his surprise inspections several weeks ago, only one of their muskets misfired. Dr. Hay's report to the governor must have bubbled over with pride and satisfaction, for the governor paid the soldiers a much-valued visit soon thereafter.

So why did Mr. Turnbull not exercise the slightest pretense of common respect for Dr. Hay's authority? The audacity of the man to impose his will on Dr. Hay's soldiers before discussing the legal issue at Belvidere—whatever that was. Dr. Hay still had no clue what compulsion drove Mr. Turnbull on his way to Belvidere Estate while the ink on the sale contract was still wet.

Did the man suspect what Dr. Hay already knew?

Mr. Turnbull had engaged in casual conversations with Colonel McDonald about purchasing the estate some months ago, before the colonel's departure for England. But nothing came of it, and Dr. Hay assumed the proposal dead. Obviously, Colonel McDonald would not have wanted to sell his friend the estate under the dubious financial arrangements Dr. Hay recently discovered.

Was it possible that Turnbull had been driven to anger over Kojo's visit to Monsieur Fédon yesterday? But why should he? Kojo acted on Charlotte Turnbull's orders to deliver the news that Lieutenant McDonald would be late for the signing.

Dr. Hay never questioned Kojo's loyalty to the Turnbulls, but he sometimes wondered what fires burned behind the slave's dark eyes.

He recalled having to amputate a runaway slave's leg at Beauséjour after Mr. Turnbull, in a maddening state, crushed it with blows from an ax handle. Dr. Hay had requested Kojo's help in holding the crazed man to the bed as he performed the ghastly operation in a shack pungent with human odor. The man screamed through jaws clenched around a piece of wood as Dr. Hay sawed through skin, muscle, and bone to remove the mangled limb. He stitched excess skin over the exposed bone and muscle, thankful for the antiseptic blend of rum, honey, and clove oil that fought off the smell of stale sweat and blood.

Kojo remained silent and unflinching throughout the ordeal—until he fetched Dr. Hay's horse for the return ride to Gouyave.

"Thank you, Kojo," Dr. Hay said when the slave handed him the reins. "And sorry for what you had to endure in there."

Kojo held a steady gaze at him. "I know what the doctor think I think." He glanced up at Mr. Turnbull's great house. "Every tree have crooked branch. You not one."

Dr. Hay expected a dark day of reckoning between Kojo and his master, but not today. He doubted Kojo was the reason for Mr. Turnbull's ride to Belvidere.

On Dr. Hay's return from Belvidere late yesterday, he learned from a neighbor that the intoxicated Mr. Turnbull had been spewing unholy profanities in one of the seaside taverns. He yelled that no French mongrel, especially a man of dubious loyalty to His Majesty's colony like Monsieur Fédon, should ever own a square-inch of Grenada's soil. And he, Mr. Turnbull, would do all in his power to halt such purchases.

True, the Belvidere sale troubled Dr. Hay, but his anxiety had far less to do with Mr. Turnbull than with information he recently received from London.

Colonel McDonald had not disclosed the whole truth about the estate to Monsieur Fédon.

Dr. Hay doubted Mr. Turnbull knew this.

But whatever the man's ill-timed motivation in taking soldiers to confront Monsieur Fédon, it could only spark an already explosive situation.

Upon hearing the worrisome news from his soldier, Dr. Hay immediately ordered him to ride with haste to catch up with Mr. Turnbull and to deliver him a hurriedly scribbled note. Dr. Hay demanded that Mr. Turnbull halt his ride to Belvidere and return immediately to Gouyave, so they could discuss the issue.

About ten minutes later, heavy banging on his door almost made him drop his coffee. He had not expected Mr. Turnbull to return this soon. He rushed to the door even before the servant could answer it.

The last person Dr. Hay expected was the bearded Mr. Webster.

"Mr. Webster, what a surprising honor," he said. "To what do I owe such an early visit?"

Had he known his friend would visit, Dr. Hay would have had his servant remove the old medical kit off the gallery table, wipe clean the sea salt off the furniture and place a new cloth over the table. At least, he would have ordered her to pick up the loose papers scattered across the floor when she opened the windows to let in the sea breeze at dawn. His house already choked from dusty books and papers which clung to overladen bookshelves and fluttered with every puff of wind.

"Sorry for the intrusion." Mr. Webster glanced back at the other houses overlooking the courtyard. "May I come in?"

Dr. Hay stepped aside and waved Mr. Webster in. "Forgive my lapse in respect. Please come in and have a seat. Tea, coffee?"

"Thank you, but I have just a few minutes." Mr. Webster removed his black hat and stepped into the living room.

Dr. Hay led him to the gallery overlooking the sea and showed him to a chair that the servant hastily wiped. She stood by the window waiting for more instructions, but Dr. Hay pointed her back to the kitchen.

Mr. Webster pulled on his beard. "I am on my way to St. George's. But I have a serious matter you should know about."

"The sale?" He wondered now if Mr. Webster had also gotten wind of Colonel McDonald's game with Belvidere Estate.

"Not at all. It went well yesterday, and Monsieur Fédon seemed in high spirits."

"Mr. Turnbull?" Dr. Hay asked.

"Yes. On my way down here, I saw him with two of your soldiers riding with much urgency to Belvidere. The conversation was brief."

"I have deep reservations about that man," Dr. Hay said.

"I also saw your rider racing to catch up with him, but I doubt anyone would change Mr. Turnbull's mind at this point."

"Did he tell you what legal issue he intended to raise with Monsieur Fédon and the estate sale?"

"'Tis neither."

"Neither?" Dr. Hay's concern and curiosity heightened.

"Mr. Turnbull is on the way to arrest the man's wife, Madame Fédon."

Chapter Fifteen

"My mother has done nothing!" Rosette rushed out the front door to the verandah and thumped the chest of the soldier pulling Maman by her arm. If Papa had not taken the early ride to Grenville, someone would be dead by now. "Leave her alone."

The other soldier stepped forward and pushed Rosette back against the wall.

Mr. Turnbull stood to the side and yelled. "We are enforcing the law. Step aside and let it be, or else you will also be arrested."

Maman screamed, losing one of her shoes as they dragged her down the steps. "I have not broken any of your crazy laws."

Rosette recovered and sprinted down the steps after them, panic lifting her screams over the hillsides.

"Halt, soldiers." Malcom ran around the corner, his half-buttoned shirt blowing in the wind, and a rifle in his hand.

Everyone froze.

"Not you again." Mr. Turnbull humped down the steps towards Malcolm. "I am here to enforce the law, and you had better not interfere."

"What law has Madame Fédon violated?"

"The Act to require all free Mestives, Cabres Negroes, and other colored free persons residing in or who may hereafter arrive in these islands to register their names for the purpose of proving that they are free. Mrs. Fédon has no such documentation. She will be imprisoned until she can prove she is a free woman of color."

Rosette yelled. "'Tis a bloody lie you tell, Mr. Turnbull." She recalled the 1780 marriage certificate she had discovered before their move to Belvidere. *Mariage de julien foedon et de marie Rose cavelan mûlatres libres.* "Do you know what *libre* means? It means free. She was documented as a free woman thirteen years ago."

Mr. Turnbull bloated with indignation. "Young woman, know your place or else you too will be off to prison. We do not have to respect anything you French mongrels did under French rule in 1780. She will have six weeks in prison. Ample time for you to prove me a liar, or else she will be sold as a slave. 'Tis the law."

Malcolm marched forward. "Mr. Turnbull, have you received Dr. Hay's permission to use his soldiers for this arrest?"

"I am a member of the Grenada Council. I do not need his permission."

"You most certainly do, sir." Malcolm turned to the soldiers, including a corporal who looked like one of the soldiers he dressed down at the market square the previous day. "My name is Lieutenant McDonald of the Sixty-Seventh Regiment, under the command of Colonel Hector McDonald. Mr. Turnbull ordered you here under false pretenses. Release her at once."

The soldiers looked at each other, loosened their hold

on Madame Fédon, and stepped away from her. Rosette ran up to her mother, and they embraced, tears dripping on each other's shoulders.

Mr. Turnbull pointed at Malcolm. "You...you will regret this! I should have finished you yesterday."

"You should thank me." Malcolm nodded towards a crowd of workers, silently inching from the fields towards them, machetes in their hands. "If you tried to leave with Madame Fédon, they would have skinned you alive. Up here in these mountains, no one would find your overfed torso. And of course, I would not remember a thing. After all, I have a severe head wound. Remember? Even Dr. Hay can testify to that."

Mr. Turnbull spat at his feet. "I am not done with you." He struggled on to his horse and rode down the hill in a thunderclap of galloping hooves.

Chapter Sixteen

Kojo knew not why Madame Turnbull fetched him from his horseback patrol around the fields, but it worried him. He stood at the open doorway on the rear verandah of the Beauséjour great house holding his battered straw hat to his chest. The rattle of dishes and mouthwatering cooking aroma filled the silence as he stared down at Madame Turnbull's bare white feet. He expected that she might have a reason to deliver a storm of bitter words she usually stocked away to fill the void in Massa Turnbull's absence.

Had she discovered Kojo's rendezvous with Simon in the mountains yesterday? He reported to her as soon as he returned to the estate, before sunset. She seemed relieved when he told her that Monsieur Fédon was grateful to be informed of Lieutenant McDonald's delayed arrival to sign the Belvidere documents.

Something else must have happened for her to order his presence this early.

She stood on the inside floor, a step up from the verandah, which placed her at eye level with him.

"You send for me, Madame Turnbull?"

She lifted his chin with her finger, but he kept his sights on her feet.

"Kojo, look at me when I speak to you." She spoke in a surprisingly low voice. "I do not bite."

True, she never bit, but in the years since Massa Turnbull returned from the American colonies with his cheerful young bride, she had gradually mastered the sharp verbal edge that white people used to slash the pride of their slaves. The toxic estate life slowly robbed her tender ways.

On just her word, Massa Turnbull could have him flogged worse than he, Kojo, had flogged Venus the day before. But for now, his respect for Madame Turnbull stood higher than his fear of her.

She still preserved some of her female ways—especially the fleshly passions that awakened in Massa Turnbull's absence. Kojo had seen her leading other men up the creaky stairs to her chamber and heard pleasure moans coming from her windows. He always looked the other way and commanded the house servants to say nothing.

She never asked him to keep her secrets. She did not have to. Every slave learned early that silence and absolute loyalty wove a protective shroud, from behind which they could fake ignorance and hide their true feelings.

So far, secrets and silence bonded well on Beauséjour Estate. His own skin and life depended on that bond—especially since Madame Turnbull continued to cast temptations in his direction, like a fisherman casting a baited hook. In the rare moments he unwillingly found himself alone with her, she stared him down with hungry eyes, but her gentle squeezes to his hard shoulders aroused only alarm in his loins.

He knew better than to let her generous curves, moist

lips, and white skin force him to surrender his will. Kojo's loyalty to his father's warrior legacy stood diligent watch over his burning desires. He would stand rigid, poking holes in his straw hat until she would sigh and walk away.

To a white man, a white woman's desire to lay with a black man was as unthinkable as clouds raining blood. And when caught in the act, the woman had only to claim rape to defend her purity and to sentence her lover to an excruciating end.

During his first year in Grenada, on another plantation, Kojo was forced to stand with other slaves to watch the punishment of a slave found naked with the master's wayward wife. The master used butcher knives to slash open the throbbing red and white insides of the slave. His gut spewed a raw nauseating odor. His screams gurgled, and his eyes rolled so just the white gazed up at the heavens, as if in a plea for forgiveness and a merciful death from the gods.

Death arrived late with its mercies—after they slashed off his manhood and hanged him from a tree like a slaughtered pig, his bowels swaying like rope from his open stomach.

Kojo learned later that the unfortunate slave had no choice. The woman had warned him that if he refused to please her in bed, she would claim rape. Either way, his agonizing destiny was sealed.

Kojo would never have to beg for a merciful death or forgiveness, because he would never be ensnared. He held his guard and waited for Madame Turnbull to speak again.

She handed him a jar. "'Tis honey. Use it sparingly on Venus's back. Dr. Hay says it soothes the pain and speeds the healing."

"Pardon me, Madame—"

"You must do it." Her voice grew stern. "Saying sorry would be insufficient."

"But—"

He knew. And he knew that Madame Turnbull knew.

He dared not speak to her like this in the presence of Massa Turnbull. Resisting the orders of a Massa's wife was disrespectful and intolerable. It would draw more blood than insubordination to a master himself.

Kojo meant no disrespect. He just never expected that facing Venus now would stir such painful disturbance in his soul. He learned years ago to lock himself outside the pain he inflicted on his African brothers and sisters, in his reluctant obedience to Massa.

But this all changed with Venus—

"Listen to me, Kojo." Madame Turnbull stood her ground. "I am a woman like she is. I know what she wants from you. She knows why you had to do what you did."

He struggled to restrain the turmoil boiling in his chest, forcing his words to escape in barely a whisper. "Please understand, Madame. Kojo cannot. Kojo do not know how."

"Then I will come with you. Wait for me while I fetch my shoes."

"Please, no need go there to—"

She snapped. "Stop it right now. We will go together, and that is final."

"Sorry, Madame. I get your horse."

"No. You and I together will walk there."

Kojo tightened his jaw in frustration. Massa Turnbull would never allow his wife to venture to the slaves' ugly lodgings, especially on foot. If he heard that she did, and with Kojo as escort, someone's skin would burn. And it would not be Madame Turnbull's.

She disappeared into the house, leaving him standing with his hat and the honey jar in his hands—and a bitter mood clouding his thoughts.

She returned with a plate overflowing with eggs, sausages, and biscuits, and placed it in a woven palm basket along with the honey and several fruits. "Venus is with child. She needs to eat more too. 'Tis your baby, right?"

A tear rolled down his cheek. "*Oui*, Madame."

Hesitantly, Kojo led Madame Turnbull down the back steps to the stone path that cut across the great house lawns and towards the tree line in the distance. The path snaked along the ridgeline overlooking the fields. The boiler house, its roof blackened from thick plumes of smoke belching skyward from the chimney. When an occasional shift in the wind's direction sent smoke up the hillside towards them, Madame Turnbull lifted her apron over her nose.

Kojo held the basket and kept glancing back, cautious not to walk too hastily as to leave her behind. Or too slowly that she might keep pace at his side, a thought he dreaded. She wore the same craggy low-heeled riding boots she brought from the American colonies eight harvests ago. But where the path turned rocky or uneven, especially with smoke in the way, he slowed to ensure she stepped on flatter ground where he landed the leathery soles of his bare feet.

In her company, he felt like he was juggling eggs while standing on burning coals.

It frightened him to think what it would look like to the watchful eyes down below if she slipped and he felt a duty to help her to her feet with a hold of hands—a white soft hand in a rough black hand. He trusted the slaves, but not the white overseers who supervised the sugar processing. One overseer recently reminded Kojo that even as Massa Turnbull's favorite whipping boy, he would always be a field nigger.

Kojo imagined ripping the man's throat apart with his bare hands. But in practiced submission, he kept his head bowed until the man exhausted his venom. Recalling the incident reminded Kojo that any kindness to Massa's wife might, through hateful eyes, look suspicious.

And it mattered not that she was fully clothed.

Under the full-length stripped apron with wide lower

pockets, Madame Turnbull wore a white bodice and blue petticoat for the brief walk to the ramshackle slave commune. Two ribbons of blue silk secured a flat straw hat to the crown of her head and met in a neat bow under her chin. Long pins kept her hair in a tight bun at the back of her head, but a few strings of red hair escaped and blew wildly around her freckled cheeks.

She would look and feel out of place in the dismal hamlet sulking behind the tree line, unseen from the great house. He tried to discourage her from visiting Venus, but this was her decision, beyond his station in life to influence. She had been there before, maybe as many times as the fingers on one hand. But the last time must have been more than two sugarcane seasons ago when she rode her horse there to assist one of the servants in labor.

Madame Turnbull broke the silence. "I want Venus to get well so she could have a healthy baby and come work for me in the kitchen again."

"That good news for her, Madame."

But his mind swirled gloomy thoughts of Venus delivering a slave baby to a white world, where his color ensured a lifetime of brutal labor and his village lodgings attracted contempt.

It enraged him when other white people came to the hamlet. They looked down their noses upon the residents as deprived, unhealthy, living like animals, and too uncaring to improve their own surroundings. Deserving of nothing but slavery.

How many of these people ever realized that the conditions they saw were the bitter fruits of slavery—not of the people? He recalled the daily pride and diligence with which, as a boy, he swept the family's front yard in Dahomey.

He had no doubt that the spirit of white people would be just as bent if fate changed their roles with the Africans.

But he reminded himself, the bent spirit of slaves ensured their survival, like trees bending in hurricane winds. Bent, but not broken. That spirit of endurance carried the slaves from one moment of anguish to the next. It allowed them to live one more day. Then another and another until the promised day of reckoning.

That spirit was a gift from the warrior god, Shango.

A few whites, like Dr. Hay and Madame Turnbull, appeared to recognize just a little of what lived beneath the slaves' skin. Kojo had seen the way those two looked into the eyes of slaves during conversations with them, past their downcast shadows, and into the life light granted by the gods to all earth's children—of all colors.

This connection, he believed, allowed Madame Turnbull to venture into the slave commune, however rare, and despite the stench that turned others away at the tree line.

The first assault came from the smelly brown dunes of distillery waste—Massa called it bagasse—that wallowed in their own fly-buzzing stench in open roofed sheds. They clustered where the ridge path meandered down to meet the tree line, an intersection of worn paths the slaves shuffled across each day from their shacks to the fields and back.

Kojo glanced awkwardly at Madame Turnbull. She clasped the apron over her nose.

Accustomed as he was to the odor, Kojo noticed it more after visiting the great house. There, the spicy flavors from the kitchen stimulated his taste buds, and the intoxicating aroma of gardenia perfumed his nostrils. If he ever closed his eyes to dream of Africa, the scent of discarded sugarcane waste always whipped him back to the harsh reality.

Bondage had a smell.

To Kojo, Massa treated slaves no differently from the way he treated sugarcane. He burned the fields to season them for harvest, just as he shackled and beat the slaves to season them for hard labor and obedience.

He chopped and squeezed the cane for the juice with the same unfeeling manner that he chopped and whipped the slaves for punishment.

He boiled the juice for sugar just as he baked the slaves under the sun for their labor, from fore day morning to sunset, in fields choking with dust, smoke, and ash.

And, when no more juice could be drained from the cane, Massa dumped the foul-smelling carcass in rickety sheds to keep out rain and allow ventilation. Similarly, each day, when no more work could be drained from the slaves, Massa dumped them into the slave village, a nauseating collection of rickety shacks, towards which Kojo now led Madame Turnbull.

They passed the bagasse sheds, pungent with the waste used to flame the boilers or mixed with cattle dung for fertilizer.

Kojo's hardened bare feet crunched on the worn trail as they rounded the corner behind the tree line. A steady breeze whispered in the treetops and washed the air for a moment.

Madame Turnbull removed the apron from her face. "Venus might have the baby in a few weeks. Do you have a boy name and girl name yet?"

"Madame, in my country we wait nine days after born."

"I would like to make a baby basket for her, with the baby's name on it."

"That be nice, Madame."

"How about the other girl, Lovely?"

Kojo's guard went up at the mention of the brown-skinned girl who spent all her time amongst the shacks, her leg twisted by polio. Even her name she received in a cruel fate nine harvests ago, before Madame Turnbull's arrival at Beauséjour. When Massa visited the latest addition to his slave stock, he looked disappointed. He took a fleeting glance at the squirmy baby, yellowish in complexion from mixed blood, and said in a tone lacking in pleasure and filled with sarcasm, "Lovely."

More versed in French than in English, the slaves

assumed 'Lovely' was the name Massa intended for the baby. From that day forth, the name latched on to the girl as strongly as Madame Turnbull's longing to know who fathered Lovely.

"She help out lots, Madame," he said. "Especially with cooking and with the sick."

"Still not speaking?"

"Maybe she go talk when the gods ask her."

Madame Turnbull sighed. "Me thinks she looks like my husband."

Kojo recognized the bait. He paused to ensure his answer remained the same one he had given her since she first set her sights on the baby. "Some workers say she face favor one of the overseers. Massa fire him long time. He done gone England."

"That is all you ever say."

"'Tis all I know, Madame. Kojo sorry."

How could he ever tell her the truth without destroying the trust Massa had in him, and maybe placing his own life in danger?

Now out of sight from the rest of the estate, she drew abreast of him and nudged his elbow with hers. "I hope you protect my secrets as well as you protect my husband's."

Fear rippled down his spine. He swallowed hard. "*Oui*, Madame."

"Was Lovely's mother beautiful?"

Madame never asked him that question before.

He felt unprepared, exposed. He smothered his anxiety. "Madame, this no safe place for beauty."

They drew alongside the first house, a ramshackle hut of sticks, dried plantain leaves, and palm. Through an open window and narrow doorway, it exhaled a pungent odor of stale sweat and decaying vegetation. A pair of muddy feet dangled out the doorway, probably of a nightshift slave sleeping after a long night, and in preparation for the next. A family of skinny chickens, enjoying more freedom and less pain than slaves, scratched and plucked happily alongside an open trench filled with human sewage.

On the other side of the path, in front of another hut, a dog with half its fur lost from mange and its rib cage covered by a thin sheet of skin, barked lazily at Kojo and Madame Turnbull. On a muddy flat between the following two huts, an old woman with one arm looked up from a boiling pot she stirred on a wood fire. She gazed at them with open jaws like she had just seen her ancestors.

Kojo pointed ahead to another shack, about the fourth on the left. "'Tis where Venus stay."

"Which one is yours?" Madame asked.

"Same one."

Just then, Lovely limped out of the hut, a scruffy dress clinging off her boney shoulders, the walking-stick in one hand and a tin cup in the other. She scooped a cupful of water from a wooden barrel next to the doorway and turned to reenter. She looked in Kojo's direction and scurried back into the house, spilling water and almost tripping over her stick.

Kojo squeezed his way into the hut and waited for Madame Turnbull to enter. She walked in slowly, removed her hat, and stared at Venus lying on the floor.

Venus rested motionless on her side with just a skirt on, her back to the door and her face towards the rear wall. A blanket separated her from the hard dirt floor. Her arms cradled her full stomach, and her breath came in shallow rhythms.

Lovely backed into the corner, her shivering hand tapping the cup against her walking stick.

It must have taken a few moments for Madame's sight to adjust to the darkness and to see the deep red gashes across Venus's back.

Madame gasped, and her hands went up to her mouth. She dropped to her knees next to Venus. "Oh my God, no!"

Venus's words came in a whisper without turning her head. "Madame, so sorry you see me this way."

Madame Turnbull shook her head. "You say sorry to

me? Why? I let this happen to you."

"No fault yours."

They talked a bit, about baby's names, about Venus returning to the kitchen, and about her learning to read and write.

"Keep talking, my dear. It will keep your mind off the pain." Madame turned to Kojo. "Let me have the honey."

He handed her the jar.

She looked up at him and patted the blanket. "Kneel next to me."

He complied. She poured a bit of honey on his fingertips and held his hand. A rough black hand in a soft white hand. She guided his fingers in a light dab against Venus's back.

Venus flinched and groaned.

"'Tis well, my dear," Madame Turnbull said. "Kojo will take good care of you."

She repeated it. Her white hand, his black hand, and honey on Venus's back. Until neither he nor Madame could hold back the tears.

Madame Turnbull rushed out the door bawling like a baby, her apron to her face.

Chapter Seventeen

Malcolm led the way on a steady gallop towards Gouyave, prepared to shoot Mr. Turnbull if the man attempted again to arrest Madame Fédon. Indeed, had Monsieur Fédon not left Belvidere for Grenville early that morning, he might have been forced to defend his honor in front of his wife. Now, she followed Malcolm on horseback, along with Rosette, the soldiers, and Zab, one of the Fédon's field slaves. Could Father's sale of Belvidere Estate to Monsieur Fédon have triggered Mr. Turnbull's rash behavior?

Malcolm also worried that his promise to visit Charlotte at sunset could lead to another confrontation with Mr. Turnbull—if discovered. Their two previous encounters ended in catastrophe. On the first, Malcolm suffered a head wound. On the second, he received a death threat.

It mattered not that his father, Colonel McDonald, considered the man a friend. Malcolm's relationship with

Mr. Turnbull had soured quickly in the twenty-four hours since they met. He doubted spending a night with the man's wife could make it any more dangerous.

Rather than await Monsieur Fédon's return from Grenville, Malcolm had convinced Madame Fédon to seek Dr. Hay's counsel immediately. As a British Justice of the Peace, he could offer sound advice and acquire appropriate witnesses for her certificate. It would behoove her, Malcolm explained, to obtain as soon as possible a sworn verification of her station as a free person. Lest Mr. Turnbull resorted to more extreme measures to apprehend her again. Rosette agreed with the merits of the idea and successfully convinced her mother of the same.

They sent a rider to Grenville to inform Monsieur Fédon of all that had transpired, and of the plans to rectify it before his return.

Notwithstanding Malcolm's growing kinship with the Fédons, especially his infatuation with Rosette, he felt obliged to extend to them all the security he could as an officer in His Majesty's Army. He held his carbine at the ready, loaded, but not cocked, for fear that the jostling on Father's horse could lead to an accidental discharge.

The two soldiers Mr. Turnbull had ordered to arrest Madame Fédon now rode compliantly behind her and Rosette. Zab, Monsieur Fédon's trusted field-hand, covered the rear. The muscular chap with a penchant for fierce loyalty to the Fédons, carried multiple cutlasses.

Mr. Turnbull could neither be trusted nor underestimated.

They arrived in Gouyave around midmorning, in heat thick with the aroma of slaughtered cattle, fresh fish, and crops from the market. Malcolm scanned the crowds for Mr. Turnbull. No sign of either him or his horse. They turned right onto the coastal road. To the left, several cargo vessels groaned against a jetty that stretched out into the blue sea.

Seagulls shrieked overhead.

Malcolm wiped the sweat off his brow as the soldiers guided them through a stone archway that opened into a sandy courtyard. Several two-story houses encircled the yard, and a few people glared from behind thin window-curtains. The group dismounted in the shadows of a coconut-tree cluster in the center of the enclosure, leaving Zab in custody of the horses. The two soldiers escorted Malcolm and the Fédons towards one of the houses, their boots pounding the stone path lined with red hibiscus. High above the roof, a Union Jack flapped in the sea breeze. They stopped at the entrance, and the lead soldier knocked on the heavy wooden door.

When Dr. Hay answered the door, the aroma of freshly baked bread greeted them. He wore a rumpled suit, his hair disheveled and his spectacles barely clung to the tip of his narrow nose. His enthusiasm rose when he recognized his visitors.

"My word," he exclaimed to Madame Fédon. "You are exactly who I need to see. Come on in, please. Mr. Webster told me of your predicament. Just wait till you see who is here."

Malcolm waited at the open door to let Rosette enter ahead of him.

"Thank you, Lieutenant." Her grateful smile and soft words rewarded his heart.

The soldiers remained outside while Malcolm followed Dr. Hay and the Fédon women into the house. They entered a drawing room congested with overflowing bookcases. A salt-scented breeze washed through the house, fluttering loose papers on a large table. They crossed a thick rug and entered a rear gallery, its louvered windows overlooking the sea and the jetty. Bareback men shouldered burlap bags of crops down the length of the jetty and up daunting ramps to the ships. A slave driver cracked his whip, sending menacing claps louder than the waves bashing the seawall.

Three men sat at Dr. Hay's table, two colored and one white. They stood as the women approached. Madame Fédon and Rosette exchanged polite handshakes and broad smiles with them, especially with the colored men. They obviously knew each other, given the warm greetings befitting old acquaintances.

When Dr. Hay introduced the men to him, Malcolm's confidence in the doctor soared like seagulls over the sea. The colored men were French esquires, Joseph Verdet and Francois Philip, and the white man was a British Justice of the Peace, Esquire Walter Carew. Rosette whispered to Malcolm that Monsieur Verdet attended her parents' 1780 wedding as Monsieur Fédon's best man, and Monsieur Philip purchased the Fédons' estate in Grand Pauvre before their move to Belvidere.

Dr. Hay had obviously recognized the sensitivity of the conflict between Mr. Turnbull and Madame Fédon and had already started the wheels rolling to acquire the appropriate representations for her document.

"At my request," Dr. Hay said, "these gentlemen responded immediately to rectify this injustice."

The round of handshakes completed, they all sat around the table, Malcolm next to Rosette.

Their knees touch, but neither withdrew.

While the servant poured tea and served buttered bread, Dr. Hay penned the oath on a crisp sheet of paper.

> *"Certificate of Freedom for Marie*
> *Rose Cavelan Fédon*
> *By John Hay and Walter Carew,*
> *Esquires*
> *two of His Majesty's Justices of the*
> *Peace for the said island of Grenada*

> *Be it remembered that on the 16th day of*
> *July in the Year of our Lord 1793, Joseph*
> *Verdet and Francois Philip Esquires, of the*
> *island aforesaid, being two credible*

> *Freeholders within this Island, personally came and appeared before us and declared solemnly upon Oath, that the said Joseph Verdet and Francois Philip, and each of them, have known a certain Mestive Woman named Marie Rose Cavelan, of the age of Thirty eight Years, or thereabouts, the Wife of Julien Fédon, a Mulatto and a Planter, residing in the Parishes of Saint Mark and Saint John, for the space of five years and upwards; and that during such space of five Years, the said Marie Rose Cavelan was regarded and reputed to be, to all intents and purposes whatsoever free from Slavery and always behaved and demeaned herself decently, and as becoming a free Person of her complexion."*

When Dr. Hay pulled out a King James version of the Bible upon which Monsieurs Verdet and Philip were to lay their hands to take the oath, the two Frenchmen glanced at each other.

Malcolm recalled his captain's caution before he left Fort George the previous day. *Be careful in Gouyave. We have a few British subjects there, but most of the people still think they are French.*

These men would certainly be amongst the thirty-four French and mulatto estate owners who signed the Declaration of Loyalty to Great Britain. But even Mr. Turnbull uttered grave warnings about their intent.

They are all wolves in sheep's clothing.

Nonetheless, the men took the oath, their Catholic French hands probably scorching on the sacred Bible of the Church of England.

Overcome at the happy conclusion of what had to be a taxing morning for Madame Fédon, she pulled an embroidered handkerchief from her purse and wiped her tears. Rosette comforted her with a hug while the men engaged in hearty handshakes.

Dr. Hay addressed Madame Fédon and Rosette. "Keep the certificate safe in Belvidere. I have it registered in my log, but I advise you to record it at the Registry in St. George's at your earliest convenience."

Madame Fédon shook his hand. "I cannot thank you enough, Dr. Hay."

The certificate might have given joyful solace to Madame Fédon, but it struck Malcolm that missing were the two men this event affected the most, Monsieur Fédon and Mr. Turnbull.

The certificate could be the commencement of a war between them.

In the searing noon heat on the street outside Dr. Hay's courtyard, Malcolm prepared to say farewell to Madame Fédon and Rosette.

Madame Fédon shook his hand. "Lieutenant, I will tell my husband all that you did for us today. He will be most grateful."

"It was my duty, and my pleasure, Madame."

Rosette too shook his hand. "Maybe you will visit Belvidere again someday?"

"I hope so."

She paused, seemingly for him to say more. But with Madame Fédon present, he withheld telling Rosette of the fondness he possessed for her, and of his equally deep desire to be in her company again. They stared at each other in a silent moment, her plump lips slightly parted, full of sensual promise. Her dark, curious eyes swept caressing gazes on his face, from his forehead to his lips and back again. A free and pleasing visual exchange, unburdened from the punishing dictates that trapped slaves in submissive eye-avoidance.

Monsieur Fédon's stubborn defense of his dignity had come to fruition in his daughter, a young tropical flower who brazenly blossomed in Malcolm's heart.

Abruptly, Rosette turned and hurried towards her horse, her boots stomping the stone walkway, her blue petticoat rustling, and the tails of her red polka-dot head-wrap riding the wind behind her. He followed to assist her on to the horse, as he would for maidens in Liverpool. But before he could utter the words and offer his palm, she mounted on her own will.

His mood collapsed. He bit his lip in disappointment. His gawking speechless fascination with Rosette might have robbed him of an opportunity to present her a worthier gesture of the genuine affections he harbored.

Gladly for him, though, Madame Fédon probably did not witness the awkward moment, preoccupied as she was with Dr. Hay's chivalry in assisting her onto her horse.

When all were mounted and ready to depart, Dr. Hay chatted briefly with the militia escort. In a remarkable deed to pacify Monsieur Fédon, Dr. Hay assigned four armed soldiers to escort Madame Fédon and Rosette back to Belvidere. He gave strict orders to the soldiers—two French adopted subjects and two of His Majesty's natural-born subjects—to protect the Fédon women and their slave, Zab, at all cost.

However, Malcolm silently debated whether the certificate and Dr. Hay's generosity would be sufficient to restore Monsieur Fédon's wounded pride.

At least, Madame Fédon would sleep in her husband's arms tonight on Belvidere Estate—not in a smelly British stockade crammed with runaway slaves, drunks, and thieves.

Malcolm watched Rosette and the group disappear into the dense greenery on the slow rise towards Belvidere, without as much as a glance from her. If his lapse in good manners offended her, the culprit was his weak-kneed impotence in the face of her native beauty.

Perhaps the disappointing farewell was for the best. They may never see each other again. His fascination with her would surely dissipate with the passage of time. Best to keep his true feelings locked away from her and others. Sentiments that would dismay and embarrass his own father and family. Most certainly, they would discourage such mismatch of color, religion, and heritage. Best to wait and reveal this only to his brothers in some distant future. Maybe in a Liverpool pub where inebriation unlocked old secrets of the heart.

Dr. Hay led Malcolm on the horseback climb up to the Gouyave militia post. Malcolm pointed down the hill to the churchyard, where Bourbon rested in the shadows of a tree with a horse tethered nearby. "Interesting fellow."

"More like a vagrant," Dr. Hay said. "Roams the entire island. Staying in one place just long enough to earn a drink or two. He knows the island well. I hire him on occasion as a guide. But trust him not with your silver."

"So I learned."

They rode up to the front walls of the militia post, and the soldier manning the gate pushed it open. They handed their horse reins to an attendant. Malcolm grabbed his saddle bag and followed Dr. Hay across the compound to the officers' mess, where he introduced Malcolm to two British officers in crisp uniform. They had a hearty meal of fish broth, figs, and a local dish of greens before retreating to the adjutant office next door.

The four men huddled around a table. Malcolm pulled out a stack of dispatches the Fort George captain had given him for delivery to the Gouyave militia. It included mail, military orders, transfers, training plans, and a memorandum from the commanding officer-in-charge during Father's absence.

The memorandum cautioned the militia to be alert for efforts to undermine British rule. It ordered the militia to monitor the 'mood, manner, and words' of French adopted subjects. Especially the free people of color, the *gens de couleur libres*, amongst whom Monsieur Fédon figured prominently on the commander's list.

At the mention of Monsieur Fédon, Dr. Hay and Malcolm relayed the events that occupied them that morning.

Dr. Hay adjusted his glasses on his nose. "Monsieur Fédon may be an honorable man at times, but he can spread his vexations far and wide, to the French, Catholics, coloreds, and slaves. Mr. Turnbull's recklessness can light his fuse. We must monitor Belvidere."

One of the officers leaned forward. "We also have to be watchful of our own militia. More than half are free French coloreds."

The other soldier joined in. "I remember how few of them joined the fight against the French invasion just fourteen years ago."

"'Tis a night we have no desire to repeat." Dr. Hay turned to Malcolm. "I beseech you to plead our case to Colonel McDonald when he returns. The threat looms more urgent here in the countryside than in St. George's. We have whites against blacks. Browns against whites. Slaves against masters. Catholics against Anglicans. French against British. It is a recipe for calamity. We are dangerously outnumbered. We need more British regulars and cannons."

"I agree fully," Malcolm said. "The danger could escalate if the slaves unite with their mulatto masters. I will report as such to my chain of command at Fort George, and to Colonel McDonald. I expect his return from England within sixty days."

Distant thunder interrupted the discussion and reminded Malcolm that he should soon head south—to visit Charlotte. The two officers handed Malcom additional documents for distribution at Fort George, and he inserted them into his empty saddle bag.

Empty?

At that moment, Malcolm realized he had forgotten his

book in the Belvidere cabin, on the table next to the bed.

On horseback at the main Gouyave intersection, Malcolm adjusted his hooded poncho in the drizzle and prepared to say farewell to Dr. Hay.

"Lieutenant, it was a pleasure meeting you," Dr. Hay said. "I will be sure to report my favorable impressions of you to Colonel McDonald when he returns."

"Thank you. I will also tell him of the tremendous responsibilities you shoulder here in Gouyave. And the dangers."

"I hope it improves."

"With you in command, I am optimistic."

"Dr. Hay!" A messenger on foot rushed up to Dr. Hay and handed him a folded note. "Mr. Turnbull gave it to me two hours ago. I have been trying to find you."

"My servant knew I was at the militia post."

"She did not answer your door."

"Always disappearing." Dr. Hay sighed. He read the note and turned to Malcolm. "'Tis Mr. Turnbull, on his way north to Paraclete Estate to visit his friend, the Speaker of the Assembly, Ninian Home. He wants to meet with me to demand Madame Fédon's arrest when he returns in two days."

Despite the worrisome news, Malcolm perked up. "Should I ride to Belvidere to warn the Fédons?"

It surprised him how quickly he jumped at the opportunity to see Rosette again—instead of Charlotte. He had only known them a day, yet they both intrigued him, more so than the women in St. George's. The city women seemed more disposed to either exude pretentious social status at fancy British events or to attempt to separate him from his money in smoky taverns.

Rosette appealed to his mind, Charlotte to his body.

Dr. Hay grinned. "Your ulterior motive with Rosette is quite transparent, Lieutenant. Smitten though you may be, it is not of necessity that you ride up there again. From my observations, your one night at Belvidere was medically sufficient for your head wound. Indiscretions between a British officer and the daughter of an influential French mulatto could trigger bigger conflicts than we could manage with cannons."

"I respect your advice and admire your perceptions."

"Only because I am twice your age, young man."

They laughed, but Dr. Hay persisted. "You already went beyond the call of duty today. You must get going to Fort George before this weather catches up to you. I will take care of Mr. Turnbull."

They shook hands and saluted.

Comforted with the news that Mr. Turnbull headed north for two days, Malcolm said goodbye to Dr. Hay, and bade a mental farewell to Gouyave, Belvidere, and Rosette.

He turned his horse and galloped south for a rainy night with Mr. Turnbull's wife.

Chapter Eighteen

The rumbling thunder and roaring winds were no match for Papa's fiery mood when Rosette rode up to the great house with Maman and their militia escort. Under menacing dark clouds rolling over Belvidere, Papa stomped back and forth across the verandah and pounded his fists on the banister.

He shouted at the soldiers and dismissed them into the first raindrops without a word of gratitude. "Be gone with you, and never return."

They rode off down the hill before either Maman or Rosette could thank them.

Papa yelled at Maman. "Who gave you permission to leave these premises with my daughter, and in the company of filthy British soldiers?"

Maman glared at him. "Lieutenant McDonald escorted us."

Rosette attempted to join in. "Papa—"

"Do not intrude." He barked.

She handed the reins to a waiting servant and stepped out of the drizzle. Papa's booming voice followed her into the drawing room where she stood watching her parents.

"The audacity of that scalawag Turnbull to treat us as slaves," he yelled above a clap of thunder. "If he had attempted this in my presence, his head would be gone."

Maman's voice barely passed the door. "But dear, you would then be a murderer at their mercy."

"This would not be murder. This would be defending my honor as a citizen of this island and a property owner of upstanding record. An assault on my wife is an assault on me."

"Dr. Hay arranged the certificate to put this at rest." She handed it to him.

"This is an outrageous insult. If my friends were not on here, I would rip it to shreds. I do not want this in my sight ever again."

Rosette slipped upstairs and down the hall where she tapped on Grandmère's door. She opened it when she heard her grandmother's soft voice. "Come in, *Pitit cheri mwen*."

Rosette entered the gardenia-scented room and shut the door, leaving Papa's shouts behind to compete with the storm. At times, she could not tell thunder and Papa apart.

The exertions of the day had finally taken its toll on Rosette, from Mr. Turnbull's shocking incivility to the long back and forth rides between Belvidere and Gouyave. Malcolm's aloofness in Gouyave, unlike his openness the previous night, also wore on her with questions. What did she do to deserve that? Had she misunderstood his British ways?

She sat on the soft bed next to Grandmère and read a few chapters of *Robinson Crusoe* to her. The comforting patter of raindrops on the roof and Grandmère's relaxing companionship called her to sleep.

The book slipped from her hands. She dozed into a

dream of naked Indians and slaves, slave ships and islands, mutiny and savagery, black skin, white skin, and brown skin.

Rosette knew not how long she slept. When she finally opened her eyes, Grandmère was seated at the shut window, the glass fogged against the drenched outdoors.

Grandmère smiled. "Papa called for you earlier. I snuck out and told him you sleeping."

"I did not hear him. Must have thought it was thunder."

Grandmère laughed. "Your Uncle Jean-Pierre is visiting. Go see them in the library."

Rosette kissed Grandmère and raced downstairs.

She tapped the open library door and walked in. "*Bonjour.*"

The library was choked with cigar smoke that rose to the ceiling. Papa and Uncle Jean-Pierre sat facing each other across the table, leaning on their elbows in low conversation.

Uncle Jean-Pierre stood and embraced her warmly with a kiss on her forehead. "How is my dear Rosette doing?"

"Better now that I had a good sleep."

Papa waved her to a chair. "Have a seat. But no cigars."

They laughed.

Papa turned to Rosette and puffed his cigar. "You were right about young McDonald. He is different."

"How so?" Rosette resisted saying anything that might reveal her feelings for Malcolm.

"Your mother eventually told me what happened this morning. Colonel McDonald will be displeased with his son's behavior."

"It was he who insisted he take us to Dr. Hay."

"And he stood down Turnbull and the two soldiers," Papa said. "Maybe the boy has more French than British blood."

"Lieutenant McDonald may not receive that as a compliment, Papa."

"You can tell him—if he ever returns to these parts."

The thought of never seeing Malcolm again disheartened her, but she tried to convince herself that it mattered not, especially since she knew him for less than a full day. She wondered what else Papa wanted to talk about since his conversation with Uncle Jean-Pierre seemed more intense than the chat about Malcolm.

"Anything else, Papa?"

Papa glanced at Uncle Jean-Pierre, then looked at her with a solemnity that curled his brows. "Have you heard about Vincent Ogé?"

"Yes, Papa." Rosette's tutor had told her about the man who led a recent rebellion in Saint Dominique.

Vincent Ogé, a *gens de couleur libres*, slave owner, and land-owner, came from a large family with a French father and colored mother.

Just like Papa.

French whites controlled the government and political power in Saint Dominique.

Just like the British in Grenada.

Monsieur Ogé started a rebellion of free-coloreds, but the Spanish captured him and turned him over to the French whites. The French brutally executed Ogé, breaking him on the wheel two years ago.

The thought of Papa dying in excruciating pain on a wheel, with every bone in his body broken, sent apprehension pulsing at her temples. She had promised Shango and the ancestors to stand with Papa in any life-and-death struggle he embraced. But Papa would need more than Grenada's *gens de couleur libres* to fight the British.

He would need the slaves. And he would need the French.

If rebellion in Grenada became inevitable, the British as the enemy made sense. Mr. Turnbull as an enemy made sense.

But Malcolm?

Papa must have sensed her forebodings. "Do not be troubled, my dear. I just wanted you to know that what happened in Saint Dominique would not happen in Grenada."

She breathed a sigh of relief.

But Papa's next words promptly revived her qualms. "Fools like Ogé learn from their own mistakes. Wise men learn from the mistakes of others. Your Papa is no fool."

Despite Maman's warnings that Rosette could catch a cold if she walked barefoot in the wet, she slipped out the kitchen door and headed around the house. The soaked grass under her naked feet helped her feel connected to Belvidere, to the cycles of rain and sun, the mountains, and the people.

While thin mists whispered by, more ominous clouds gathered over the peaks for another onslaught. Papa had released the slaves to their quarters with orders to the drivers that if the rain stopped for as long as it took to eat a meal, they were to ring the bell and return the workers to the fields. But even the birds and the chickens retreated into the dense trees. The chirps, cackle, and song that enriched the air around the house on sunny days rendered to an eerie silence. Not a rooster strutted with machismo across the green yard, daring not to challenge thunder rolling down from the mountains.

A break opened in the clouds. A sliver of sunlight peaked through, just enough to lift Rosette's mood after the unsettling conversation with Papa.

Papa taught her to value friends and family. But he also taught her about enemies. His lessons were profoundly simple: enemies brought pain and despair. In Grenada, the British were the enemy. To be free and happy, enemies must be destroyed.

Simple.

But when the line between friend and enemy became blurred, life no longer seemed that forthright.

Simplicity provided comfort and security, like an eggshell around an innocent yolk. But once the shell broke, the security vanished forever. In just a day, three men, Papa, Malcolm, and Mr. Turnbull, intersected at once in her life, and the impact cracked her simple protective shell.

Papa, family. Mr. Turnbull, enemy. Simple.

Malcolm? Complicated.

Like an exposed yolk, she felt vulnerable. She now needed Grandmère's counsel more than ever. Or maybe Father Pascal's. Maman was already too preoccupied with the demanding task of keeping Papa on a level path. She recalled Maman seated next to Papa during one of Father Pascal's visits. Maman patted Papa's calloused hand during the priest's message of longsuffering as if to ensure he fully absorbed the meaning.

"When you live your life in the furtherance of God's work, He will provide you with the strength and patience to persevere," Father Pascal said. "He will provide you with the forte to protect the weak and the enslaved. He will provide you with the compassion to embrace the downtrodden. But if you turn your back on His Word, neither friend nor foe will recognize you. God will abandon you, and your heart will turn stone-cold."

Rosette did not worry about her heart turning stone-cold. Malcolm's brief visit in her life most assuredly confirmed that her heart was alive with longing. Even after his departure, having failed to communicate any similar sentiments, desire still burned in her.

In a light drizzle, she wandered towards the cabin Malcolm had occupied the previous night. At her touch, the door creaked open easily. She stepped in. She shut her eyes and inhaled the masculine presence that he had left behind, scented with body powder and strong leather. A gust sprayed cool raindrops on the back of her exposed legs. The heavens opened with a deafening downpour. Thunder shook the cabin. She latched the door against the wind. Rain pinged the windows. She pulled the curtains shut.

Feeling alone with him now, she moved towards the bed that he slept in just hours ago. The firm mattress welcomed her, and she welcomed his pillow. She cuddled it along the front of her body and inhaled his fragrance.

She shut her eyes, letting his voice massage her insides with tender tones, inviting his strong hands to roam her body. In ecstasy, Rosette became one with Malcolm.

Thunder shook Belvidere and returned her to the cabin. Despite the turbulence outside, she felt at peace on the bed. She knew not how, but for sure, all would be fine.

She gazed around the small room.

A book, opened face down on the end table, beckoned her curiosity.

Malcolm must have forgotten it.

She glanced through the open pages. A paragraph leaped out at her.

People crushed by laws have no hope but to evade power. If the laws are their enemies, they will be enemies to the law; and those who have most to hope and nothing to lose will always be dangerous.

She thought about Malcolm's coolness with her in Gouyave. Maybe she had frightened him last night with conversation about Shango and African warriors seeking revenge. Yet, if Malcolm understood these words from Edmund Burke, then he understood her more than he revealed.

She held the book to her chest.

She had to see him again.

Soon.

Chapter Nineteen

Neither pelting rain, roaring wind, nor rumbling thunder deterred Malcolm and the horse on the steady trot to Beauséjour Estate. He had to get there before dark, to see if a red sweater hung on Charlotte's bedroom balcony, the warning signal she would use if Mr. Turnbull returned unexpectedly to the estate.

Malcolm's hooded poncho kept the rain off his face, except when an occasional gust attacked head-on. At first, he feared the thunder and lightning would panic Father's horse, but it kept its ears loosely forward in a vote of trust in Malcolm's handling. Father had no doubt trained the horse to ride in foul weather and to handle sudden noises.

A perfect horse for battle.

He was mindful though, of the risk of the animal breaking a leg on uneven ground or in a hole covered by water. He pulled back on the reins occasionally to allow the horse time to slosh carefully past deceptive ground on the muddy path south.

The messenger's note to Dr. Hay in Gouyave reassured Malcolm: Mr. Turnbull was heading north to Ninian Home's Paraclete Estate. Nevertheless, what if the bad weather had goaded Mr. Turnbull to a change of heart during the two hours the messenger searched for Dr. Hay? If he had instead returned to secure his property, then what should Malcolm do?

In daylight, it would be easy to see Charlotte's red sweater from the main road, a disappointment though it would be.

In the dark, he might be tempted to ride up to the estate house for a closer look—and a deadly confrontation with Mr. Turnbull.

Malcolm had to get there quickly, before nightfall.

With another half-hour's ride ahead, darkness began an early descent. Tempestuous clouds rolled over the sea, blocking the dying sun. The troubled sea pounded white waves against the rocky coastline.

Premonition gnawed at him.

Did Dr. Hay suspect Malcolm's destination? The doctor seemed more concerned with the Fédon's wellbeing. Regardless, given Mr. Turnbull's violent disposition, Dr. Hay might hardly entertain such suspicions of infidelity, especially of Malcolm. Surely, any man voracious enough to risk his neck for a naked embrace with Mr. Turnbull's wife, under his own roof, would have to be a pleasure-driven maniac.

Even as Malcolm rejected such a label for himself, he would readily confess to his inability to resist Charlotte's charm. But if Father discovered this, would he understand?

The thought of Father renewed Malcolm's misgivings. His most troubling fear would be to disappoint his father with a scandalous affair.

Malcolm considered a torrent of reasons why he should have no repentance. Charlotte invited Malcolm; he had not pursued her. He empathized with her sense of neglect, given the despicable man she married. It was deserving of Mr. Turnbull, for his attack and threats on Malcolm. A wife in need she was, Malcolm doubted he would be the first, or only one, she received in her bed.

He had one final reason. Try as he must, he could not disavow his strongest motivation for riding as diligently as he did to get to Charlotte.

He wanted her as much as she wanted him.

Regrettably, although Charlotte might be alone for two nights, Malcolm could enjoy her company for just one. Any delay in returning to Fort George might raise alarm amongst his military superiors, ever watchful over Colonel McDonald's son.

Finally, he rounded the corner to Beauséjour Estate. The abandoned fields sulked in the final gasp of ashen light. Not a man. Not a woman. Not an animal in sight. The windmill stood motionless, locked in place. The boiler house chimney pointed skyward, smokeless, like an unlit cigar.

The decrepit slave village, pushed haphazardly into dense shrubbery to the left, looked downcast and exhausted, its inhabitants probably in their only escape— sleep. Large drenched trees wept raindrops down on the thatched roofs and elephant-ear leaves below, with splatters that echoed in the rinsed air.

High on the hill, the great house stood white and waiting against the gray sky.

No red sweater.

A woman stepped on the balcony. She spread her arms and beckoned with urgency.

A shaft of sunlight thrust through the forbidden sky, lighting her hair like fire and exploding its reflection off her window.

Malcolm's concerns evaporated. Nothing could go wrong now. Euphoric anticipation rushed up his spine.

He spurred his horse to a full gallop up the hill.

Malcolm listened to the tapping of gentle rain on the balcony floor outside Charlotte's bedroom. Clean sea breezes blew through the open door, lifting the curtains in joyful waves, dancing yellow candlelight around the room, and rendering the room a most agreeable temperature.

Charlotte's deep breaths blew against his chest.

He wished he had words to describe the pleasure that awaited him when he parted the mosquito net to her high-post bed and joined her under the white sheets an hour beforehand. He would bottle such words and guard them with his life.

He inhaled the fresh linen scent of her skin. The same fragrance that lit his desire when Mr. Turnbull introduced her the day before. Her ravenous kisses, flavored with red wine, still excited him. And her pleasure moans, encouraged by drumbeats of thunder through her open balcony door, still played in his ears with arousing effect. Like it did again and again before their spent bodies collapsed on her sprawling bed in a hangover of pure delight.

The room held every bit of Charlotte's color and vitality, painted in a blazing sunset orange, adorned with thick rugs and sumptuous drapes. A wooden lift-top chest sat against the wall adjacent to her balcony door. It held a bouquet of scented fresh flowers that deodorized the air and brightened the room even in candlelight. A gigantic painting filled the far wall with red and blue birds in flight. A twinkling crystal chandelier hung from the ceiling beam. Above it, a wide mural. Mythical babies with tiny outstretched wings, floating amidst puffs of white clouds.

Charlotte's breathing stalled, and her eyelashes brushed his skin. "You like it?"

He kissed her. "Yes, much cozier than my Fort George barracks."

"I mean the mural."

"All those happy babies? If the world had half this happiness, it would be a far better place."

She sighed. "I always wanted a baby."

"You are still young. And beautiful."

"Well, thank you, my handsome young lover."

They laughed.

"I envy Venus," she said. "Slave she is, sleeping on hard ground, slashes on her back, and I envy her for her baby. Strange, is it not?"

"How is she?"

"Visited her this morning. Only God knows why 'tis so difficult for babies to live more than a fortnight on these plantations. A rather strong girl Venus is, her baby might be just as strong."

"Do you know the father?"

"Kojo."

Bewildered, Malcolm asked, "Kojo? The same Kojo who whipped her?"

"Yes. Quite strange what this life does to people."

"He had tears in his eyes when I grabbed his hand yesterday."

"And he helped me clean her wounds this morning," she said. "She will bounce back. She wants me to teach her to write, so she can one day write her baby's name."

"Will Mr. Turnbull permit that?"

"Once the baby is born in a few weeks, I will solicit him to return her to the kitchen as a servant. When he is away or out in the fields, I will sit her at the table with pen and paper."

"Suppose he disagrees?"

She touched his lips with her fingertips. "I have my ways."

Jealousy pulsed through him. How could she stomach the company of such a pig?

She sat up and pulled the sheet over her shoulders. "You know, there's a brown child in the village. Kojo says her father is an overseer Mr. Turnbull fired years ago."

"Yes?"

"This happened before I arrived. The girl is now about

twelve, deformed by polio. They call her Lovely, but the poor child is anything but. No one can tell me what became of her mother. I often wonder if she is Mr. Turnbull's baby. If another woman can give him a baby, why not me?"

He searched his mind for another conversation. He let his thoughts drift to the swish of curtains blowing in the sea breeze. "I saw no one when I arrived."

"I sent them back to the village when the bad weather started this afternoon. I had Kojo shut down the boilers and lock down the mill. If the winds are too strong, Mr. Turnbull must fish the windmills sails out of the sea. Glad I sent everyone away. 'Tis a perfect night for us."

"What about the overseers?"

"One of the two white ones left for St. George's yesterday. When Mr. Turnbull is away, they take turns at the taverns along the port. The free colored women are all too happy to lay with them for the jingle of a few shillings. The other overseer probably has one of the servants in his cabin right now."

"And Mr. Turnbull approves all this?"

"Not in the least. Overseers and slaves alike remain tight-lipped about everything around here. And I am quite happy with that. I do not need them watching me instead of the machines. In this weather, we can afford to delay the sugar processing for a day or two."

"I gave the honey to Dr. Hay," he said, suddenly remembering her preference for honey over sugar.

"Thank you. He also knows why I use honey in my tea."

"Tell me."

"Maybe 'tis better I show you." She gazed out the balcony door into the night, now pale blue from the rising moon. "The rain has stopped."

Just then, he thought he heard a noise outside.

He placed his finger to his lips. "Listen."

Up the hill towards the house came the muddy clomps of a horse.

Chapter Twenty

Kojo was not there when it happened. But he knew the one-armed old woman felt lucky to be alive. Lena, they called her. He sat in the doorway of the shack and watched Lena trap Madam Turnbull's honey jar between her ribcage and her left arm, which ended at her mangled elbow. She could no longer work the mill or the fields. Instead, she cooked around the village and, when needed, tended to babies and the sick with voiceless Lovely at her side. Tonight, they cared for Venus.

He stared over his shoulder into musty gloom he still shared with Venus—even after the whipping that sliced her skin and crushed her heart. He wished she told him why she ran away again but now was not the time. She rested on the hard mud floor with a baby pushing her insides and cuts burning her back.

Lovely held a lit candle in one hand and leaned on her walking stick with the other. Lena scooped out some of the honey into a wooden bowl and sprinkled a mixture of herbs and lime juice. An offensive odor filled the air. In yellow candlelight, the same color Lovely's brown dress used to be years ago, Lena showed the young girl how to stir the mixture into a green paste and to apply it with care to Venus's open wounds.

At Venus's first painful wince, Kojo stood and walked away, soppy mud squishing between his toes. From the dark, decrepit huts on either side of the rain-soaked path, deep snores, coughs, and sobs mixed with low voices burdened with despair.

Massa Turnbull had asked him why the slaves never bothered to build stronger houses with stones from the river behind the village. The white devil never understood that slaves went to sleep each night dreaming it would be their last night in slavery.

Slavery deserved shacks with hardened mud floors. Freedom deserved stone.

He knew the risks from the day he possessed Venus on the hard mud floor. In a short-lived moment of escape, their sweaty bodies gyrated as one in a frantic desire to lift each other above their plantation misery.

Their daily choices, from fore day morning to late night, always remained caught between pain and more pain.

Whether he boiled his sugarcane juice or labored his slaves, Massa Turnbull did not believe in waste. Everyone gave all they had to keep Mr. Turnbull's hilltop great house happy with fine wine, filled plates, and white linen.

Some gave their dignity. Some gave their arms. Others gave their lives.

To the living, pain never left, whether to the flesh or to the soul.

It was still too early to forget, just one day after he captured and whipped Venus to please Massa. Rats, prowling to feast on her open cuts, kept him awake last night. He stayed next to her, silent, not touching. Just comforting her injured presence with his. He listened to her breathing as it nurtured his first and only hope for a son.

A gift in her swollen for his long line of proud forefathers.

Unable to keep his eyes shut, he gazed out the window at the moon just rising over the hill and peeping through the trees. He hoped for salvation, any uplifting sign from his ancestors, as he did on that big-moon night twenty seasons ago before he sailed in chains from Benin. Now, as then, no encouragement came. Instead, his own words now delivered punishment, ripping his soul into shreds the way his whip slashed Venus's once perfect skin.

Let me do it, Massa. Please, let me do it, Massa.

And Massa had let him do it. Now she lay on the floor in pain because of Kojo.

But she would have been in *more* pain if that young Englishman did not stop him. And, if Massa had done it himself, she would have been in *even more* pain. Perhaps with a leg bashed and chopped off.

Daily choices. Pain or more pain.

He fumbled in his pocket and withdrew the cigar Simon had given him in the mountains yesterday. He had carried it around in his sweaty rags, taking instructions from Madame Turnbull. She had him shut the windmill, rope the animals, and smother the fires in the boiler house. Now the damp cigar unfurled to a clumpy mess in his hands.

In growing disgust, Kojo rumpled the useless tobacco leaves in his hand and tossed them into the bushes.

When he returned to the shack, old Lena had already left with her candle, but Lovely remained seated on the ground next to Venus. A spray of moonlight glazed Lovely's dress, as dirty brown as her skin. Even in the pale light, her big eyes shone like her mother's.

A wave of melancholy swept over him, but his emotional dam held. He grabbed one of the thin blankets Madame Turnbull had sent him after her awkward visit that morning.

"You sleep with us tonight?" he asked Lovely.

He knew better than wait for a verbal response. Her words were fewer since her mother departed eight seasons ago. Her silent stare gave him the answer he needed.

He unfolded the blanket at the corner. "Sleep here. Use your stick if you see rats." Despite Lena's assurance that her herb potion not only healed wounds, but also repelled prowling rats, he took no chances. "I go use me cutlass."

Lovely curled up in the corner with the blanket.

Kojo stretched out next to Venus, the cutlass in his hand. Sleep came a little easier. For how long, he knew not.

He awoke suddenly.

A horse galloped up the hill. Unusual this time of night. The second one since Madame Turnbull ordered all the slaves to their huts.

Another visitor heading up to the great house? Or Massa Turnbull returning already?

He adjusted his position to go back to sleep. The cutlass scratched the dirt.

It awakened Venus.

A soft cry came from her. "Water. Water please."

He jumped up in pale light. Lovely and her blanket remained undisturbed in the corner. Unlike last night, not a rat darted around the hut. As Lena had promised, the pungent smell of her medicine must have repulsed the rats.

He filled a cup in the water basin outside and returned to hold it to Venus's lips.

When she finished the cup, she held his hand in the darkness and kissed it. "Thank you."

"I so sorry I hurt my Venus. It hurt me too."

"I know your heart," she whispered. "After what I do, you carry me on you horse all down from the mountains yesterday."

True. Until they arrived at Beauséjour—to convince Massa that she had walked the whole way full with baby.

Maybe, Kojo had hoped, Massa would show mercy on

her.

He did not.

Kojo glanced away to avoid her seeing his wet eyes. Moonlight swept the room to Lovely's empty blanket. She was gone.

Kojo knew where.

He squeezed Venus's hand. "Coming back just now."

He grabbed his cutlass and hurried out the door into the night.

With a big moon out, Lovely was again looking for her mother.

But if Massa found her first, he might order Kojo to flog her. This time, Kojo had other plans for Massa.

Chapter Twenty-One

The horse trotted in the night, ever closer to the great house. Malcolm worried now that Mr. Turnbull's message that he would be gone for two days was a ploy to trap him in the act with his wife. Malcolm had challenged the man's order to whip Venus, defied his attempt to block the Belvidere sale, and embarrassed him in front of the Fédon women and two British soldiers. What better revenge for Mr. Turnbull than to exact violent retribution on Malcolm, caught in his wife's bed.

Charlotte rolled off the bed and slipped on a dress coat. "Stay right there!" Her whisper quivered as she rushed to the balcony.

She quickly stepped back into the room and grabbed the candle. "I cannot tell who the rider is. I am going downstairs. If anyone comes into the house, stay on the bed. The floor creaks."

"If 'tis your husband, I just cannot lay here and let him find me."

"He never comes to my room. I go to his."

She turned to the door, leaving Malcolm dumfounded by her last words.

Her footsteps creaked out the room and down the stairs.

The horse stopped outside and snorted. Boots landed on soft ground and shuffled up to the front verandah. The door knocker pounded.

The door latch clanked open. Low voices. The door slammed shut.

Footsteps stomped away. Trotting hooves faded down the hill and into the night.

Charlotte walked into the room with the candle. "That was Bourbon, delivering a note from Mr. Turnbull. He is returning here around ten o'clock tomorrow morning."

Strange.

Malcolm did not want her tempting him to stay longer than one night, so he did not tell her of the message Dr. Hay received saying Mr. Turnbull would be in Paraclete for two days. Why would Mr. Turnbull then send Charlotte a message hours later saying he would be back in one day? Bourbon and his horse were still sheltered under the tree in the churchyard when Dr. Hay received his message. It would mean that Mr. Turnbull changed his mind halfway to Paraclete, returned to Gouyave after Malcolm had already departed, and hired Bourbon to deliver his new plans to Charlotte during the downpour.

If Mr. Turnbull truly wanted to keep her abreast of his plans, why did he not send her an earlier message as he did to Dr. Hay?

Something felt odd.

"Let us go for a walk," she said. "I want to show you a secret about sugar."

He reached for his clothes on a chair and glanced over his shoulder at her.

Charlotte stood with her back to him, holding a piece of paper in the candle flame.

They headed out the back door under skies that beamed in full-moon radiance. A sea breeze chilled the night in a manner that made Malcolm think Grenada had stolen a summer night from Liverpool. The flora, inspired by the earlier showers, released a delightful blend of fragrances. Clicking chirping insects emerged from their hiding places to celebrate the end of the storm with a high-pitched chorus that blanketed the hillside.

It marveled Malcolm that just hours earlier, he and Father's horse battled deafening rainfall from Gouyave to Beauséjour.

The island's weather intrigued him with its ability to switch temperament with little warning. In one moment, thunderclouds with lightning. In the next, starry, full-moon skies. Frequent 'passing clouds' would block out scorching noon sunshine to deliver unexpected showers. The island also had a peculiar reminder of the surprises lurking behind every hour of every day—it routinely rained at the same time the sun blazed.

On those days, Malcolm had heard slaves express their premonitions. "The devil and he wife fighting again."

In England, cloudy skies meant just that. Gray skies for ceaseless days and days like it would never end. Not like Grenada.

He wondered what effects the constantly changing weather had on the shifting roles of the island's residents. Here was gorgeous Charlotte, wife of a prominent sugar producer and legislator, in the secret company of a British officer almost ten years her junior. Monsieur Fédon, himself a descendant of a slave, owned a hundred slaves. Just recently, Kojo captured his run-away pregnant lover and flogged her to please his master. And Dr. Hay, physician and esquire, commanded the militia defending one of the most important towns in Grenada.

Nothing appeared as it seemed.

Nothing Father ever taught Malcolm about Grenada

prepared him for this perspective. Father's lessons always focused on the higher calling of loyalty and service to God, King, and Country. A well-oiled mercantile system undergirded these great purposes. Slave labor produced products in the colonies. These products generated profits and taxes in England. Taxes supported the government and military. Profits supported the mercantile class on their climb up the aristocratic ladder—worthy of the exertions of every God-fearing Englishman like Father.

From afar in England, the arrangement looked flawless, inspired from the heavens, ruled by the king.

Up close?

It steamed with abnormality, an odious danger on the verge of calamity.

Malcolm wondered if those social contradictions would one day implode the fragile harmony—or disharmony—of His Majesty's colony.

What else could Charlotte want to show him this night that could possibly tantalize his imagination any more than it already was?

With heightened curiosity, he held her warm hand on the walk across the ridge overlooking the moonlit sugarcane fields. They stopped where a narrow track broke off from the ridge and led downhill. She cozied up to him, her loose hair blowing in the breeze.

She pointed at the fields below. "Fieldwork begins down there before sunrise."

She explained that the overseers or the drivers, usually Kojo, would whip latecomers. Around nine o'clock each morning, the slaves would be fed a breakfast of boiled yams and seasoned vegetables. They then toiled in the sun till noon, when they received another break for the same meal, this time with a little meat or saltfish added. So named, she added, because it was more salt than fish.

Malcolm chuckled. "My soldiers at Fort George complain about their one pound each of beef and bread, plus butter, peas, and rice. They can also purchase extra food at the market or grow their own vegetables."

"Mr. Turnbull tells the slaves they can grow their own too, but they have very little time to care for their crops. By two o'clock, the bell and whips chase them back to the fields until sunset. During the sugarcane processing months, they work the fields like this for sixteen hours a day, with maybe a half day off on Sundays. I do not comprehend how these poor souls do it with such little sleep."

"A troublesome enterprise indeed." Malcolm's admission surprised him.

"I should be offended—but I am not." She pointed at the windmill; its sails held rigidly like upheld swords against the glowing sky. "'Tis where the cane stalks are taken immediately after being cut, before they ferment and spoil. The wind-sails turn three rollers inside the mill to squeeze out the juice from the cane. The juice then flows downhill in a pipe to be boiled and processed into sugar in the boiler house, over there."

Except for the chimney at one end, the oblong-shaped boiler house, on lower ground from the windmill, looked like a giant coffin bathed in moonlight.

"Does the processing stop when the slaves return to the village at night?"

"No. Except for stormy days like today, it is around the clock during the six months of processing. I dread those days and nights. Some who work the fields all day might also work the mill a few hours at night. The rollers used to be wood. Now they are heavy iron and more dangerous to those who feed the cane to the rollers. Accidents occur when they work long hours with little sleep. 'Tis why I want to show you the—"

"Look." Malcolm pointed at the windmill. "I thought I saw someone enter."

"Cannot be. Should be no one out here tonight."

Just then a flame lit up on the inside.

"That is worrisome. Come with me." Charlotte picked

up her pace, pulling Malcolm by the hand.

They hurried down the narrow trail to the flat and turned right on the wagon road, their boots crunching the pebbled surface. Discarded stalk trimmings littered the worn compound, and a sweetness in the air grew thicker as they approached the windmill. A pipe, as large around as a man's leg, connected the foundation of the windmill to the boiler house down the hill.

The daunting stone mill held a commanding pose on elevated ground, broad at its base and tapering towards a summit that stretched higher than nearby trees. At its crown, a wooden box clutched a shaft that supported four canvas-covered wind sails. The canvas flapped in loud protest against the breeze and their wooden frames complained in tired groans. The mill displayed walls as thick and impregnable as the fortress walls on Fort George, with an open arched entrance—twice the height of the tall man standing on the inside.

The man, in a pair of ragged pants, had his back to them. He held a flaming torch in one upheld hand and a cutlass at his side in the other hand. Raised scars traversed his muscular back like young snakes. He faced the iron rollers—three vertical torso-sized drums locked within metal brackets on a stone table.

Charlotte and Malcolm's footsteps grew closer. The man turned around.

Kojo.

"Kojo." Charlotte mounted the ramp to the entrance, her voice echoing within the mill. "I expected you to be asleep like all the others."

He lowered his head. "I was, Madame."

"Venus needs you at her side."

"Yes, Madame. She sleeping. But Lovely done gone again. I come here to make light. For if she lose she self."

"'Tis full moon. She will find her way back like the other nights." Charlotte stepped into the mill and stood next to the stone table housing the rollers, beckoning Malcolm to join her. "Kojo, remember Lieutenant McDonald from yesterday?"

Kojo held his sights on the dusty floor. "Yes, Madame."

"I want you to show Lieutenant McDonald what happens when someone gets their arm caught in the rollers."

Kojo glanced up at Malcolm and then down to the floor again. "You sure, Madame?"

"Of course, I am," she said. "Now, please do as I ask."

Malcolm pondered the ease with which Charlotte bent the will of such a robust man. The same man who extracted flesh-ripping punishment on other slaves—and on the pregnant mother of his unborn child.

The breeze whistled through the archway. Kojo's torch blazed, adding smoke to the thick sugary aroma within the walls. He set his cutlass in front of the rollers, their surfaces plastered with cane splinters. A contraption of wheels-with-teeth connected the rollers to a thick metal pole that stretched high into the dark ribcage of the mill. Below the rollers, a gutter filled a round opening in the middle of the table.

Charlotte explained that the wind sails outside spun at about four to six revolutions per minute, rotating a shaft in the darkness above. The shaft engaged a wheel bolted to the pole, which in turn sent the drums rolling against each other at an unstoppable pace. When the rollers squeezed the cane stalks, the resulting juice flowed into the gutter. The gutter led down through the bowels of the mill to the pipe outside, through which it streamed to the boiler house for sugar processing.

Charlotte turned to Malcolm. "Mr. Turnbull often says the rollers are so tight, they can squeeze ink from a written page."

"How much cane can they squeeze each day?"

"About two acres," she said. "Unless bad weather forces a shutdown."

She explained that on stormy days like today, a team of able-bodied men would push a lengthy restraining log outside to align the wind sails into a neutral position with the wind. This slowed the sails enough to be locked in place.

Kojo set the torch in a holder on the inner wall, next to a heavy machete, wider and thicker than the cutlass. In the light, the exquisitely sharpened cutting edge looked silver next to the rest of the dark metal.

With his sweaty skin glistening in the torchlight, Kojo retrieved a few sugarcane stalks and tied them together in a bundle the size of his muscular arms. He sat the cane on the stone table, which helped secure the rollers in an unyielding entrapment of metal bars and wrist-sized bolts.

"These rollers spin fast," Charlotte said. "When the workers feed them with cane, if they are too sleepy or careless, their fingers can get caught. There is no way to stop them. The wind keeps blowing, the sails keep spinning, and the rollers keep pulling and squeezing. First the fingers, then the hand, then—"

"Then you grab the shoulder." Kojo thundered. He slammed the machete on the bundle of sugarcane with such might, juice sprayed into the air and splintered pieces flew all over the floor. He lifted the remnants of the bundle. "You lose arm. You save life, like old Lena."

Charlotte looked up at Malcolm with a pitiful gaze. "There is always someone on watch to chop off the arm."

"No!" A child screamed outside. "No just arm. Everything gone."

"Lovely?" Kojo called out. "Come here, girl."

A small figure with a walking stick hobbled into the light at the bottom of the ramp. The dark brown-skinned girl Malcolm had seen on the ridge when Kojo was flogging Venus. In a tattered dingy dress, and hair in unruly coils, she leaned sideways on bare muddy feet, one twisted and shorter than the other.

Malcolm's heart bled sadness as the girl's big eyes

teared up and her thick lips blubbered almost incoherently. "She...all...gone."

Charlotte turned to Kojo. "She speaks now? Who is she talking about?"

"Her mother."

Charlotte glared at him. "'Tis high time you tell everything, Kojo. What happened to her mother?"

"She work here one night—"

"Two nights," Lovely yelled, her voice shivering. "All day field work. All night millwork. Two nights. No sleep."

"Why?" Charlotte asked Kojo, her voice raised to a high pitch. "Everyone knows accidents happen to tired workers."

"I know, Madame." Kojo glanced at Malcolm and stared at the floor.

"Speak up, Kojo," Charlotte shouted.

Malcolm, sensing his presence might inhibit the man's will to speak, walked up to Kojo and held his shoulder. "Mr. Turnbull is not here. Tell us what happened."

The muscles along Kojo's angular jaws pulsed. "Massa make she work all day and night as punishment."

He explained that Lovely's mother used to take special care of her daughter. Even carried her tied to her back as a baby when she worked the fields. It surprised no one that four-year-old Lovely would also show up when her mother faced punishment at the mill.

Kojo pointed at Lovely, his voice faltering. "Lovely stand right way she is now. She see when she mother finger get catch."

"Not finger." Lovely bawled. "Not hand. All Mammy gone. Machine take Mammy and not bring she back."

"Who was supposed to watch her with the machete?" Charlotte, in tears, pushed for more. "For God's sake, Kojo, speak up."

"No machete," Kojo said quietly.

"Mammy gone," Lovely screamed. "Massa Turnbull mill take Mammy." She turned and hobbled down the roadway, vanishing into the fields' moon-drenched embrace.

Malcolm turned to go after her, but Charlotte stopped him with her hand on his chest. "Let her go. She might not need to hear the rest of this." She turned to Kojo, her voice firm, demanding. "Why in God's name was there no machete that night, Kojo?"

Kojo's lips trembled when he looked at Malcolm.

Malcolm nodded approval.

Perhaps also with Lovely gone, Kojo spoke more readily. "Massa say no sleep and no machete for she because she have another man. He say he go sell the man to a wicked Englishman in Grenville."

Kojo's willingness to whip Venus now made more sense to Malcolm. Given the choice between the whip and the crushing rollers, Kojo had gladly chosen the whip as the more merciful punishment.

"What business was that of Mr. Turnbull if she had a lover?" Charlotte asked.

"Madame...before you and he make husband and wife...Massa take her to he upstairs room every night."

"I knew it all along." She slumped against Malcolm. "Did he sell her boyfriend?"

"When she boyfriend hear about selling, he and she runaway. They stay with maroons in the mountains. He name Simon. But she soon come back alone."

"Why?"

"Simon try to stop her. But she come back for Lovely one night. Massa catch she. He put she in the mill, no sleep, and no machete."

"Was Lovely's father Simon?"

"Madame, I fraid to say."

"I swear on my mother's grave. I will never tell Mr. Turnbull a word you say."

"Madame. I sorry. Lovely is Massa baby."

Charlotte's tears kept Malcolm's chest damp that night. He slept barely a wink before the chaotic sounds of bells, whips, and roosters awakened him. Aware of Mr. Turnbull's plan to return to the estate around ten o'clock that morning, Malcolm thought it wise to leave early for St. George's. He had little appetite, just enough for a cup of black coffee and a piece of bread. Having ordered the servants not to show up until she sent for them, Charlotte prepared him a sandwich lunch and filled his canteen with lime juice sweetened with honey.

Worn out from the long night, she bade him a teary-eyed farewell. They embraced and kissed before he slipped out the back door to retrieve his horse from her small stable hidden between the trees. He saddled up and followed the trail she asked him to use to stay out of sight.

The trail took him to the far uncultivated side of the estate, and to a wooded lookout that sloped down to the main road. He paused at the top, hoping that the view of the blue sea would wash away his sugar-mill nightmares. The sea breeze rustled the leaves around him. In the distance to the right, the windmill spun, and the first belch of smoke rose from the boiler house chimney. A somber procession of slaves and donkey carts flowed to and fro between the fields and the mill.

An intense distaste for what it all stood for bubbled up in him.

He recalled with sadness, Kojo's parting words the previous night. Charlotte had asked what happened to the woman's body after the accident at the mill.

"She everywhere," he said. "That why Lovely looking everywhere for she."

He said the workers collected whatever recognizable body parts they could salvage and buried her in a shallow hole in the wooded graveyard behind the village. Any body parts not found suffered the same fate as the sugarcane. Blended with bagasse to fire the boilers or mixed with bagasse and animal dung to fertilize the fields.

"Massa no believe in waste," Kojo had said before his slouching return to the slave village in the moonlit night. "Now she everywhere. Even boil with cane juice. Massa put more lime and ash to hide it. Lovely mother even go England, mixed with sugar for them people tea."

She everywhere. Mixed with sugar for them people tea.

Even hours later, the thought stirred nausea in Malcolm's stomach. He leapt from his horse and vomited at his feet. Black coffee and white bread.

He walked his horse away from the pile and sat against a tree, unable to summon the motivation to ride away just yet.

Lack of sleep weighed on his eyes. He dozed under the tree and lost track of time—until a hawk screeched overhead.

The sun felt hotter, reflecting on the sea in glittering intervals, like polished silverware dispersed across a blue glass table-top. Waves crashed in sheets of white along the shore. The wagon road scarred the coastline, meandering as far north towards Gouyave as he could see. The road he traveled the previous night, and the one Mr. Turnbull would ride to return to Beauséjour.

Malcolm's chain watch said a quarter to ten.

He decided to wait for another look at Mr. Turnbull, who surely made the devil proud.

A rider rounded the corner past the slave village and turned up the roadway to the great house.

Charlotte stepped onto the balcony and waved.

Even at the distance, Malcolm recognized the man—not whom he expected.

The slender frame, long nose, and glasses reflecting sunlight *did not* belong to Mr. Turnbull.

And, it became clear now, the note Bourbon delivered to Charlotte the previous night, the one she burned, *did not* come from Mr. Turnbull.

Charlotte's bed, still warm from Malcolm's restless night, prepared to welcome another man—Dr. Hay.

Dr. Hay leaned into his horse and sped up the hill towards the great house.

Malcolm rode just as fast as he could on the road to St. George's.

The further away he got, the more he missed Rosette Fédon.

Chapter Twenty-Two

"But Papa, we could all get in trouble if caught." Rosette did not understand why Papa would ask her to do something that risky. In the week since Mr. Turnbull's gross intrusion into their lives, Papa cloaked a dark, secretive mood around himself. He met frequently in his library, behind closed doors, with Uncle Jean-Pierre and other visitors, some of whom she had never seen before. Some white. Some black. Some brown.

At first, she thought the men were meeting to discuss plantation business. But when Papa sat her in the smoky library and closed the door, with the same sour mood clouding him, she balked at the idea he proposed.

He dragged on his cigar. "We live in risky times, my dear."

"I doubt Lieutenant McDonald would cooperate," she protested. "He is just an acquaintance. We only met a week past."

But Papa had made up his mind. "My dear, I would not ask of you a task beyond your aptitude. Think about it and give me your answer before we leave for St. George's tomorrow."

When, a few days earlier, Papa announced plans to register Maman's Certificate of Freedom at the Court House in St. George's, Rosette asked to ride along with them. She intended to use the occasion to return Malcolm's book—if she found him.

There were things of the heart and mind about which she hoped they would talk.

Papa's idea could jeopardize her family's freedom and any chances of a lasting friendship with the English lieutenant.

Yet, Papa's request—not a command—allowed her the freedom to decline, without leaving a smudge of disobedience. He had elevated her to a position of equals, and, in so doing, lifted her own confidence to new heights.

However, disagreeing with Papa could be a blow he may not soon forget—or forgive.

Next morning, they mounted their horses and waited for Maman to join them. Rosette pulled up next to Papa. "If this is important to you, it is also to me. I will do my best."

He flashed his first smile she had seen in days. "That is all I ask. Just do not tell your mother. You know how she worries."

Indeed, Maman worried, and many times with reasons Rosette understood. At Maman's prodding, Papa chose to take the east coast route to St. George's to avoid riding past Beauséjour Estate. Any escalation in the rancor between Papa and Mr. Turnbull could lead to severe legal vexations for Papa. Mr. Turnbull possessed two powerful advantages. He held a distinguished position in the Grenada Legislative Council, which wrote Grenada's laws, and retained the sympathetic ear of Mr. Ninian Home, the Speaker of the Grenada House of Assembly.

When Dr. Hay visited Papa a few days ago, he said as

much. Bursting with renewed rambunctiousness and oozing stale grog after his two-day visit with Ninian Home, Mr. Turnbull boasted to Dr. Hay of the Speaker's support in any future legalities with the Fédons.

Further, Mr. Turnbull cautioned, Dr. Hay had made a grave mistake in approving Maman's Certificate of Freedom without prior consultation with either the Speaker or himself. The certificate would stand, but at a most humiliating reduction in Dr. Hay's credibility. His actions signaled a suspicious loyalty to the French mulattoes. Mr. Turnbull intended to spread that perception amongst the Assembly members.

In Mr. Turnbull's mind, the doctor's loyalty should be reserved only for His Majesty's white English subjects.

Dr. Hay further advised Papa that, given Mr. Turnbull's propensity for mischief, the certificate be immediately registered in St. George's.

The four of them—Rosette, her parents, and Zab—took the Windsor Road over the mountains to Grenville and turned south along the east coast towards St. George's. Despite the silk bow tied beneath her chin to secure her light blue bonnet, Rosette held the brim in the wake of the easterly winds roaring ashore from the Atlantic. The gusts agitated high waves to her left and rushed the green mountains to her right with a persistence that made even the largest trees howl in bent obedience.

The horses plodded along in the rising heat, not in the least disturbed by loose leaves and twigs blown their way. Zab's horse carried two baskets, one with a change of clothes, and the other with gifts of fruit, baked coconut treats, and cigars. Rosette had helped Maman pack the gifts for Papa's sister, Aunty Marie-Louise and her husband, Uncle Charles Nogues, a tailor in the bustling town.

Rosette always enjoyed the overnight visits to St. George's, the last perhaps six months ago. The town buzzed with a vibrancy of agricultural commerce, British fashions, and fancy four-wheeled carriages that rarely made it as far north as Gouyave or Grenville.

But as they drew closer, an old memory and her promise to Papa tightened anxiety around her stomach.

Papa, in the lead, pointed to a turnoff in the road that left the coast and rose along the southern end of the central mountains. "This will take us to Uncle Charles, but I have a stop to make on the way."

In an area called St. Paul's, they rode on to a small estate scented with spice and fruit. The brown-skinned owner, a tall, athletic man, named Louis La Grenade, invited them inside. While Madame La Grenade sat them in the drawing room and served cool drinks of passion fruit, Zab remained outside with the horses. Papa and Monsieur La Grenade disappeared into a back room.

About a half-an-hour later, the men emerged with Papa in front. "Thank you for your kind hospitality. We must get on our way."

He hurriedly led them to their horses and bade a frosty farewell to the La Grenades. Papa gritted his teeth and remained silent on the ride. Whatever the purpose of his conversation with Monsieur La Grenade, it did not bear the kinds of sweet fruit that grew on his estate. In hot sunshine and drizzle, they started the winding road down towards St. George's.

High in the hills to the left, the insurmountable walls of Fort Frederick, which the French started after their 1779 invasion, watched over the town. Ahead, Fort George held the high ground at the harbor entrance, overlooking the traffic of ships exiting and entering the horseshoe-shaped port.

When they arrived at Uncle Charles's house, uphill from the port, Papa pointed at a ship skulking low into the entrance of the harbor, evidently laded with heavy cargo. It displayed worn flags and dingy sails.

"Fresh from Africa," Papa said. "Looks like *The Recovery*. And flying the bloody Union Jack."

Zab looked at the slave ship. His lips trembled, and his

head slumped. Maman and Papa followed Auntie Marie into the house, but Zab remained on his horse.

Rosette was unsure if the nauseating smell came from the ship pulling into the port, or that horrid memory that clutched her mind and refused to leave. Perhaps five or six at the time, she accompanied Papa on one of his business trips to the port. In a racket of sliding grates and cracking whips, a black procession of human misery shambled out of the hulls with chains heavier than the starving legs that dragged them. Crazed seagulls shrieked and dove at the human excretions the slave crew shoveled overboard. So offensive and potent the stench that fouled her senses, Papa had to catch her just before she fainted at his legs.

Determined not to let it happen again, she hurriedly unpacked and retreated into the small house, where comforting hugs and kisses from her aunt and uncle awaited.

Once the greetings subsided, Papa immediately pulled Uncle Charles aside and launched into a vigorous tirade about Monsieur La Grenade.

"The man has become more a *Mister* La Grenade that a *Monsieur* La Grenade," Papa growled.

"Fear not, my friend," Uncle Charles said. "Remember he signed the Public Declaration of Loyalty."

"So did thirty-four of us. But that does not mean we wrap our grievances in their flag and look the other way."

Rosette had little desire to hear more. The thought of that sickening day on the port with Papa sapped her mood. She fled to the backroom Aunty Marie had prepared for her.

The memory followed her.

She collapsed on the bed, struggling with fatigue and the urge to puke at the same time.

Papa shouted so loudly at Maman in the drawing room, Rosette worried that neighbors or even soldiers might show up at Uncle Charles's house. "She can go to the fort by herself to return a book."

"She is just a child." Maman protested.

Aunty Marie stood over a wood fire in the backyard stirring a pot. Uncle Charles was away from the house, at his tailor shop a brief walk away.

"She is no longer a child," Papa yelled.

Rosette intervened. "I can take Zab with me."

Maman and Papa glared at each other. Then agreed.

Rosette rode ahead at a slow pace in the midafternoon heat, with Zab just behind her. She felt a little out of place, her first time on the city streets without her parents. But at the thought of seeing Malcolm again, her racing heart overwhelmed her apprehension. The clops of horseshoes on the stone surface bounced off the houses lining both sides of the street—houses of brick walls and red clay-tile roofs. Papa once told her that after fires razed the town in 1771 and 1775, the British passed a law requiring that houses no longer be wooden structures. The roof tile, he said, came from cooking oil containers that many of the ships visiting the port used as ballast. Wooden louvered shutters paired the sides of open windows, where thin curtains floated in and out on the breeze.

Dogs asleep on doorsteps paid them no mind. But some residents seated at the windows displayed unwelcoming stares and finger-pointing at Zab. The sharpened cutlass strapped to his horse, when added to his imposing height, muscle, and rock-hard face, made him stand apart from the better-dressed residents they passed along the way. His muddy bare feet, ragged pants, and ripped shirt barely clinging to one shoulder, must have compounded the offense they felt. Evidently, these folks thought St. George's an extension of His Majesty's England and intended to keep it that way—without the likes of Zab.

Smoke drifted from backyard cooking houses with aromas of spicy fish, stewed chicken, and boiled beef. But it did little to subdue the stench rising from the port, hours after the slave ship discharged its human cargo.

The downhill road flattened on a left turn, past a handsome church with a steeple, and then took a steep incline towards Fort George. Two armed soldiers in red and white uniforms guarded a wooden gate built into massive brick walls.

One of the two guards at the gate viewed them with a suspicious scowl. "Halt."

Rosette gathered up her courage. "I am here to deliver papers...to Lieutenant McDonald."

"Give them to me, and I will give him."

"Sorry, I must give him directly."

He danced his head mockingly, his pimpled face reddening with sarcasm. "Well sorry, young lady. You will just have to take your papers and leave."

"I am sure Colonel McDonald would be displeased to learn that papers important to his son were not delivered in time because of some low-ranking soldier."

The other soldier laughed. "Come with me. The duty officer will find him for you."

"Your horse and your gorilla remain here," the first soldier said.

Zab seethed.

Rosette responded in French. "I could slap you on accord of your stupidity. But I will not soil my hand on such a diseased face. Plus, I doubt it will improve your lack of intelligence."

The second soldier, apparently capable in French, laughed loudly, holding his rifle in one hand and his stomach with the other.

"What did she say?" asked the pimple-face soldier.

"I will tell you when I get back."

The second soldier, still chuckling, led Rosette on foot through the gate and up a brick passage that stared down a column of black shiny cannons pointing out to sea. She counted eighteen. She followed him up three flights of steps, and into an office overlooking the inside of the fort, and with stunning views of green mountains, white beaches, and blue water.

The soldier explained their presence to the duty officer behind a desk. "She has papers for Lieutenant McDonald."

"Not just any papers," Rosette added, gazing out the windows. "Colonel McDonald is aware of them."

The officer glanced up. "Show me."

"I cannot."

"The lieutenant is not here today." Just as quickly the duty officer returned his attention to a log book in front of him. "You might find him in one of the taverns around the port. That is if one of those whores do not already have him."

Rosette had been preoccupied scanning the walls and cannons. "Pardon me?"

The officer glared at her. "I will not repeat myself." He turned to the soldier. "Get her out of here now."

In fading afternoon sunshine, Rosette and Zab rode down the hill towards the smelly port. She had promised Papa to do her best to meet with Malcolm. It looked like her best required her going into taverns to find him.

But would Papa understand?

Chapter Twenty-Three

Nothing seemed to work for Malcolm. Neither the grog he had been guzzling for the past hour nor the earsplitting ruckus from his fellow soldiers seated around the wooden table. The crowded tavern, filled with smoke, and darkened within dingy stone walls and shut windows, diminished his sense of time and place. But even the chaos did little to separate him from the throbbing reminders.

For all he cared, this could have been in Liverpool, with its flags and dim lanterns. One reminder that he sat on a slave island was the colored woman at the back of the tavern. She smiled under a bright turban and licked her lips in conversation with a well-dressed white man. She wore a low jacket that barely contained her ample half-exposed breasts, which glowed in the lantern light. Especially when she cupped them in her hands and adjusted them with regularity. The man handed her a coin, and they disappeared down a dark hallway.

Malcolm felt nothing.

How could he, after all he had seen a week beforehand?

When he left Fort George to formalize the Belvidere sale, he was clueless about the exposures that would ambush and shatter his confidence in all things British. When he returned to the fort, a tightness in his chest signaled a troubling disharmony between what he experienced in Belvidere and Beauséjour and his upbringing. The boundaries with which he had grown up proved incapable of containing his uneasy sentiments. They escaped at will to whisper distressing doubts in his ears, especially when he tried to sleep at night.

Something felt wrong.

Very wrong.

The pain in his chest told him that. The sickening odor of the slave ships told him that. His memories of Beauséjour, Gouyave, and Belvidere told him that. The vicious whipping, Mr. Turnbull's depressed slave village, and the broken sorrowful child they called Lovely.

Oh, what grief, for her to have seen her mother chewed alive and discarded like garbage.

Where were God, King, and Country in this unnatural arrangement that punished the desire for freedom with brutality, and rewarded brutality with wealth?

He now understood why slave anger on the island simmered thicker and hotter than boiling molasses.

But slaves were not the only ones harboring resentment against the British.

French mulattoes like Monsieur Fédon, who owned slaves themselves, cultivated deep bitterness against their British rulers. Despite signing the Public Declaration of Loyalty to King George, they would never be accepted as an equal in the halls of the Legislative Assembly. Too many obstacles stood in their way. French heritage, skin color, and Catholic religion. And men like Mr. Turnbull, eager to crush their well-being in His Majesty's colony.

Malcolm had seen the signs of damning things to come.

The surprising Shango energies in the dancing slaves revealed a power, cleverly disguised in their subservient plantation roles, but too potent to deny, too deep to repress.

How much longer would proud men like Monsieur Fédon and angry slaves like Kojo tolerate the onslaught on their dignity?

One of the soldiers at Malcolm's table punched him in the shoulder. "Are you here with us?"

"Yes...yes." Malcolm guzzled his drink.

"You know," another of the soldiers started, "since your journey to the countryside, you have not been the same. Did a French beauty steal your heart in Gouyave?"

They laughed.

Malcolm did not.

He recalled what Charlotte had told him at Venus's whipping.

Tis not only what will happen to her. Tis also what will happen to you.

Something did happen to him.

If his change in demeanor was that obvious, certainly Father would notice it when he returned to Grenada. What a bitter disappointment if Father saw but a few of the thoughts that swarmed his son's mind. Malcolm hoped it would not become common knowledge that he had offended Father's friend, Mr. Turnbull. Or even more unforgiving, that he had engaged in sinful fornication with the man's wife.

Malcolm might face the unimaginable wrath of an infuriated father—armed with the punitive power of an Army colonel.

Charlotte's entanglement with Dr. Hay also shattered Malcolm's faith in her. But why should it? Malcolm had welcomed her lures and deceptions to get him in her chamber. What made him think she would not do the same for other men? He pitied that such a lovely woman with a pleasant heart and ecstatic feminine passions had to crave depravity to fill what had to be an agonizing void in her life.

Brief interludes with men provided her only relief on an oppressive plantation, rigged with daily pain, fear, suspicions—and repressed anger.

Perhaps Charlotte would be a happier woman if she remained within the tranquil confines of the great house. He imagined her wrapping the comforts of a pretentious life around her, surrounded by exciting murals and polished mirrors. Idyllic days would be spent sipping expensive red wine and honey-sweetened tea, maybe even caring for little white babies of her own. Busy days would occupy her with lavish dinner plans for Mr. Turnbull's wealthy associates. They would all sit like royalty around the long shiny table, under chandeliers that swung from Beauséjour's high ceiling beams.

But alas, Charlotte's soul had wings. Her flights had taken her from the luxuries of the great house to the throes of the slave village. She traveled across the fields, saw the sweat, heard the cries, and walked down the slaves' horrid memory paths. She absorbed their tragic stories of fractured spirits and mangled bodies.

Their pain brought her guilt.

Their blood brought her tears.

No great house big enough, luxurious enough, or far away enough, could save her from the punishing life she inherited as Mr. Turnbull's wife.

In all the gloomy discord that tugged at Malcolm, the only light came from Rosette—his memory of how her smile, her intelligence, her laughter, intrigued previously untouched parts of his inner self.

Until he could see her again and hold her hand, his only medicine came from daily visits to his favorite tavern. Here, he would numb his mind with grog, a potent concoction of rum, lemon juice, and cinnamon. Together with thick clouds of cigar smoke that overwhelmed the odor of slave ships, and the jubilant singing of drunken Englishmen, the tavern atmosphere built a protective wall between his feelings and the unhappy world outside the doors.

Delilah, the big brown woman who owned the tavern, stood at the door in hand-waving conversation with a girl wearing a blue bonnet. The wavering lantern light accented her chocolate complexion in a shade that reminded him of Rosette.

It seemed this past week, every colored girl reminded him of her.

Delilah pointed in his direction. The girl stared at him and nodded.

Rosette!

Malcolm wriggled out of his seat and shouldered his way through a sea of rowdy drinkers to get to her.

His heart thumped. "Rosette. What are you doing here...in a place like this?" Embarrassment curdled in his throat like spoilt milk.

"Looking for you," she said matter-of-factly.

Delilah plopped her fists into her bulging waist. "Lieutenant, me ain't want you bring no girls to work—"

Rosette groaned. "I tried to tell her I was just looking for you to return your book."

Malcolm placed his hand on Delilah's shoulder. "Rosette is my friend. Only a friend."

Just then, a pimpled face soldier stepped through the doorway, his sights glued on Rosette.

"You again?" He spat. "Come sit on my lap so we could make up."

He stretched past Malcolm and slapped Rosette on her behind.

Malcolm's fist landed squarely on the soldier's temple.

The soldier crumbled at Delilah's feet and lay still.

Delilah called out to one of her black help. "Drag he ass across the street. Always causing trouble 'round here."

"We must go." Malcolm held Rosette's hand. "You do

not belong in a place like this."

Malcolm sat next to Rosette on a log facing the sunset. He poured out everything he regretted not telling her in Gouyave. Her departing words of kind regard had presented him with an opportunity to express similar sentiments. Instead, inhibited by her mother's presence, he had held an awkward silence that must have offended Rosette.

"I wanted to tell you how fond I was of you," he said. "My apologies for any injury I might have caused to your feelings."

"No apologies necessary." She giggled.

Despite his light-headedness from the grog at Delilah's tavern, Malcolm had preserved a sensible presence of mind to choose this spot for the conversation with Rosette. They sat on a tree-covered incline facing the shore. It afforded them a view beyond the harbor entrance to a golden sunset over the sea.

The easterly winds kept the odor from a slave ship pushed up against the far ridge of the inner harbor. Earlier, at Delilah's tavern, a drunken sailor who had arrived on the ship from Africa, had described the scent thus. "The vapors are strong enough to poison the devil."

Regularly, the smell crawled up the ridge to the Anglican Church and Fort George, where the oblivious Union Jack soared from flagpole heights—safe above the nauseating vapors. Ignorant of the suffering.

Mercifully, the winds blowing from behind Malcolm and Rosette had visited hillside cooking fires before proceeding down to the shore. Light charcoal smoke scented with freshly-baked bread and spiced meat freshened the area.

About a dozen ships crowded the horseshoe-shaped bay. They swayed without care on the calm water, their loose sails and ropes slapping lazily against the tall wooden masts. Along the far port road, in the sunset shadows of

Fort George, obstinate rows of brick warehouses with red-tiled roofs discharged precious cargoes onto ships destined for England. Long columns of workers, with swollen bags on their backs, traversed the busy docks and climbed boat ramps like orderly ants in the fading light.

Early glows from lamp posts signaled the coming night, and too soon, time for Rosette to return to her Uncle Charles's house.

"I am glad you came." He reached for her hands.

She kept them clasped in her lap. "I do not want to encourage any misguided presumptions on your part, Lieutenant McDonald." A mischievous sparkle lit her dark eyes. Her lips glowed in the twilight. "I only came to return your book. You can ask Zab over there."

Zab sat under a tree ahead of them, facing the sea and puffing on a cigar. The horses fed on pasture grass nearby.

Malcolm gazed into her face. "Zab would not see if I kiss you."

"Do not be too confident." She glanced away. "My father has eyes everywhere. Plus, your impulse may be insincere, and comes only from your drinking."

Indeed, he had been drinking Delilah's grog. "But the thought to kiss you first crossed my mind when you pointed me to the river in Belvidere," he recalled, smiling. "I was not drinking then."

"My first thought to kiss you came earlier," she whispered. "That afternoon when I sat across the table from you, during the signing of the Belvidere documents."

Afraid he might miss yet another chance with her, he leaned closer. She closed her eyes. He closed his too.

They kissed briefly.

When he paused and sat back, her dark eyes shined with delight and stared into his with a purity that caressed his desire.

Her plump lips parted. "Why did you stop?"

His arousal poured forth, the likes of which not even Charlotte's passion could inspire. He wrapped his arms around her slender body, and their lips met again in a moist union that warmed his body in the sunset breeze.

Finally, she sighed and pushed her hand on his chest. "I wish not for this to end, but I must leave soon. Maman will be worried."

"Not Monsieur Fédon?"

"He knows Zab will take care of me."

A bugle sounded the attention call from Fort George. The waving colors of the Union Jack descended behind the angular walls crowning the fort.

"I should be standing at attention," Malcolm said. "But holding you in my arms is infinitely more gratifying."

He wondered if he would have broken the flag-lowering tradition a week ago, before his journey to the countryside. Regardless, he wore civilian attire and sat far enough away to justify his lackadaisical attitude.

She pointed at Fort George. "An officer up there told me you might be in one of the taverns. So many of them, I almost gave up. I was taken aback to learn of the frequency with which you visit those...places."

Embarrassment slowed his reply. "Only since a week past. I have found it most difficult to reconcile with all I experienced during my visit to the countryside. I must admit, Delilah's grog does provide some relief, though temporary."

"I hope meeting me did not add to your discomfort."

He kissed her hand. "My dear, meeting you has been the most welcoming of my time on the island. I do hope you feel the same."

She kissed his bruised knuckles, sore from the contact with the soldier's head. "My only fear is how quickly my heart has opened to you."

"Please leave it open."

She giggled. "You now have the keys."

The final red of the sun dipped into the sea. This moment with Rosette, her hand in his, felt complete, at peace. A fleeting taste of bliss. He embraced the feeling, wanting it to last forever. But knowing that nothing did.

She broke the silence. "Do you get to fire those big cannons up there?"

"I was trained to fire them in England."

"'Tis a well-defended fort. I counted eighteen cannons."

"Actually, we have a total of twenty-three to defend the harbor."

"So how did the French overtake it in 1779?"

Impressed with her interest in military matters, he explained that Fort George defended the harbor, but not the higher hills surrounding the city. "The French landed on the coast and marched overland to Hospital Hill up there." He pointed to the hills to the right, overlooking Fort George. "They overran some small fortifications and turned a few abandoned cannons down on Fort George below. The battle was done almost before it started. It was a most humiliating surrender for our British soldiers."

"Is that why the French started building Fort Frederick?"

"Yes, and three other forts." He pointed way up the hills to the north and to the east behind them. "Forts Frederick and Adolphus were named after King George's sons. Fort Matthew, after Grenada's Lieutenant-Governor at the time, and Fort Lucas, after the owner of the property on which it was built. All quite unique."

"Unique?"

"Those new forts are called 'back-to-front' forts." He said the French had started them in 1779. And, when the Treaty of Versailles returned the island under the Union Jack in 1783, the British immediately gave top priority to the forts, which they just completed that year, 1793. He explained how their gun ports faced inland rather than the sea, from where most islands expected invasions. "The French learned their lesson well. Now St. George's is completely defended, from naval attacks by Fort George and from land attacks by the four 'backward facing' forts.

St. George's is perhaps the best-defended port in the British Empire."

"You trust my secrecy."

"I wish all our enemies knew this," he said. "It would prevent future attacks. I have had arguments with Father about this. The best way to prevent attacks is to let the enemy know or believe you are invincible." He went on to tell her about the sheer walls, big cannons that weighed more than a ton, and cannon balls that weighed twelve, sixteen, and twenty-four pounds. "The cannons for the twenty-four pounders could fire a hundred times per day, even in Grenada's tropical heat. Attacking St. George's in 1779 was brilliant. Attacking it today would be suicide."

She looked into his eyes, hers aglow in the twilight. "I am afraid, for Grenada. For you and me."

"We have nothing to fear." He kissed her again and led her towards Zab and the horses. "By the way, you can share everything I told you with Monsieur Fédon. But tell him you heard it from a few drunks at the tavern. If Father finds out, he will ship me back to England in disgrace."

"I do not want you ever to leave," she said. "You can trust me,"

Chapter Twenty-Four

When Rosette and Zab rode up to Uncle Charles's house, he and Papa were sitting on the road-side steps, both puffing on cigars under the first stars of the early night. Zab took the horses around to the backyard while Rosette headed up the steps with her saddle bag.

Papa stood, chewing his cigar, his fists clenched at his sides. "Young lady—"

"Please Papa, not now." She pushed past him. "I need pen and paper before I forget everything."

When Rosette finally stopped writing under the table lamp, she handed several pages to Papa where he sat next to Uncle Charles.

"Jesus," he muttered, handing the papers to Uncle Charles. "'Tis more than I expected."

"I told you I would do my best." She beamed in his admiration. "But all it shows is that France will never again capture Grenada like it did in 1779."

"Who have you been talking to?" Papa squinted at her. "I deserve to know all that transpired after you left here this afternoon."

"I had to go to seven taverns to get you what you asked for. Zab is sworn to tell you just that. I beg of you, please do not put him in the situation to either lie to you or betray his word to me." She hugged him. "Trust me, Papa."

He dragged on his cigar a few times, sending puffs of smoke towards the ceiling. "You honored my request beyond my reasonable expectations." He grinned at Uncle Charles. "My dear daughter is grown up."

Uncle Charles nodded. "You are a most fortunate father. She will always be at your side."

"Did you return Lieutenant McDonald his book?" Papa asked.

The book.

The book still sat in her saddlebag. She had forgotten to give it to Malcolm. And he had forgotten to ask for it. Papa might now believe that she had not seen Malcolm, and therefore he could not be the source of all the valuable details of the forts.

Good.

She smiled inside for the good fortune her flawed memory brought her. "No, Papa. I have to go look for him again tomorrow to return his book."

Maybe this time, Papa would trust to let her go alone.

Too delighted to eat, she gave Zab her plate of stewed chicken and vegetables.

Rosette turned in early. No sooner had she climbed into bed, she faded into a deep sleep with Malcolm's kisses on her mind and her pillow in a tight embrace.

"You sure 'bout that?" Kojo asked, stunned. He had expected the baby to come around the time of the next full moon. "Awready?"

"Yes, she go have baby, tonight," Lena whispered to Kojo in the dark, outside a shack hidden at the back of the village.

He glanced past her, over the shrubs and through the open doorway of the windowless shack. In candlelight, Venus sat moaning on a low stool, a thin white sheet up to her waist. Her exposed breasts full and ready to feed his son—if the gods so will.

Lovely held a bowl out towards Venus. She took the bowl but placed it on the mud floor without looking at it. She held on to Lovely's hand.

"Go now," Lena ordered him. "And stay way. Come back after nine sunsets."

She shuffled back to the shack, with a length of rope she and Lovely tied across the top of the doorway. They removed the white sheet from Venus and hung it over the doorway.

No longer able to see Venus, Kojo walked back to his shack. The mating croaks of bullfrogs and the happy chirps of unseen crickets surrounded him. He too felt the happiness. He would soon stand with the pride of a father. Perhaps of a son who would one day join him in victorious battle and return with him to freedom in Motherland Africa.

The smell of cooking smoke lingered within the village, trapped in dense bush that clung to the shacks. Boiling vegetable peels diluted the harsh aroma of wild meat like armadillos and cane rats, which the slaves wrapped in leaves and roasted on burning wood embers.

Kojo felt little need to eat. Hope now satisfied his hunger. For that, he owed so much to Venus. Her strength, forgiveness, her grace in pain, all lifted his spirit.

His baby would receive the same noble traits.

Sleep came easy and peaceful on the mud floor of his shack.

He knew not for how long he slept before a baby's cry sliced the morning air over the slumbering village. It awakened Kojo even before the first cock crowed.

A teardrop slipped down the side of his face.

He was now a father.

A proud one.

The more Dr. Hay read the papers before him, the more unpleasant his feelings about the sale of Belvidere Estate from Colonel McDonald to Julien Fédon. He sipped his early-morning coffee for relief, but his temples still throbbed, like the waves pounding the shore outside his window. As a doctor, he would have prescribed himself an hour of Charlotte's bedroom passions, but he pushed the thought—and the memory—away. No purpose in dwelling on an opportunity that might not occur again for months.

The Belvidere documents on his table could spell catastrophe, certainly more so than if Mr. Turnbull discovered Dr. Hay's occasional rendezvous with Charlotte. Such a discovery might simply mean removing one plantation from his busy medical rounds.

Partly due to Dr. Hay's role as Esquire and head of the Gouyave Militia, it behooved him to stay abreast of property transactions on the island, especially in the parish of St. John's, which encompassed Gouyave and Belvidere.

Sales of land, animals, and slaves revealed much about their buyers and sellers. Early knowledge of developing conflicts allowed him to resolve them peacefully or squelch them with his troops before they got out of hand. Concerns Dr. Hay took seriously as head of the militia.

These transactions also exposed secrets and deficiencies in loyalty to King George.

This would hardly be the first Fédon document in Dr. Hay's possession. One of the first came some years earlier from his good friend, Webster Benjamin, Registrar of the Grenada Supreme Court. A copy of a deed signed and registered at the Grenada Supreme Court on February 18, 1784. In this Deed of Manumission, Monsieur Fédon gave freedom to a "Cabre Slave commonly called or known by the name of Isaac Marseille of the Age of One Year and Nine Months." Most slave owners celebrated the birth of healthy slave babies, as it increased their stock without the financial outlay to purchase them. When Monsieur Fédon granted twenty-one-month-old Isaac his freedom, without mention of the mother, Dr. Hay knew why immediately. Monsieur Fédon was the baby's father.

Also, when Monsieur Fédon, made a 'mark' to sign the deed, it indicated to Dr. Hay that the man was illiterate back in 1784.

However, these papers Dr. Hay now held came not from the Supreme Court in St. George's, but from afar, a law office in England. Throughout the years, Dr. Hay had developed a strong confidential friendship with a distant cousin employed at the British firm Lushington and Law. The man sent him a generous flow of newspapers and documents on events in England, especially if they affected the island colonies. Of course, he could have retrieved some of the island documents himself by riding to the Court in St. George's and requesting them. But such frequency and interest in transactions with which Dr. Hay had no part to play, would have raised eyebrows, even from his friend Mr. Webster.

Dr. Hay read the document that most heightened his concern about the Belvidere sale. It held the title "Abstract of sundry Securities and Transactions to and by William Lushington and James Law Esqrs., and Lists of the Deeds in their possession." It showed that when Colonel McDonald arrived in England, Lushington and Law made him a "Loan of £3000 Sterling upon Mortgage of a Plantation called Belvidere in Grenada."

> *Reciting that Colonel Hector McDonald was seized in fee of an Estate called Belvidere situate in the said Island of Grenada and that Messrs. Lushington and Law had agreed to lend Colonel Hector McDonald £3000 upon the Security of s'd. Estate.*

> *The Plantation called Belvidere in the parish of St. John in Grenada containing*

400 acres more or less and all the Negroes and Stock then upon the Estate and all other Negroes & Stock which should be upon or belong thereto whilst any money should remain due upon the Security thereby made.

The loan agreement called for regular payments to Lushington and Law, until 1803. The document spelled out an unequivocal fact: The loan agreement obligated Belvidere to Lushington and Law.

Colonel McDonald had signed over Belvidere as collateral for a loan and sold it at the same time.

Monsieur Fédon held no legal rights to Belvidere Estate.

The colonel had enticed him into a dangerous swindle.

Indeed, unbeknownst to Monsieur Fédon, he now managed an estate he believed he owned, in order that Colonel McDonald repay a loan upon which the estate stood as collateral.

Unless Colonel McDonald had miraculously paid out the £3000 loan in one year rather than ten, Belvidere Estate rightfully belonged to Lushington and Law.

Monsieur Fédon was working to help Colonel McDonald repay his loan.

Monsieur Fédon just did not know that.

If he discovered this, the repercussions could be worse than if Mr. Turnbull discovered a caring doctor tending to his young wife's insatiable needs.

The next morning, Rosette and her parents departed Uncle Charles's house for the city. Under sunny blue skies, they walked down the stone road that she and Zab had travelled the day before. Papa's heavy work boots pounded the road and probably drew more curiosity from passersby than Maman would have liked. Back in Belvidere, he had dismissed her gentle prodding that he packed his dress shoes for the courthouse visit.

"I might own Belvidere Estate," he had said. "But I do not want my St. George's friends to mistake me for a British aristocrat. I am not an imposter."

He had been born a working man, and a working man he would die.

Papa preferred to walk, instead of ride, to the city because it allowed him to stop and chat with friends. Some he greeted with back-slapping embraces and thunderous laughter. Others in ominous tones, too low for Rosette to hear the words over the sounds of rattling carriages and yelling food vendors. Women squatted in front of sizzling roadside coal-pots, rolling blood sausages and parched corn with wooden sticks. The smoky aromas overwhelmed any residual scents from the port. Papa bought one of the finger-burning sausages, which they shared on the way.

Not surprisingly, the walk down the busy road, past open windows and sleeping dogs, seemed to take considerably longer than Rosette's horse ride with Zab the previous day.

Perhaps it felt longer because of her bubbling anxiety to see Malcolm again.

Where the main road into the city intersected the street with the church, she turned left towards Fort George while her parents headed right to the courthouse. She had offered to accompany them, but Papa insisted that registering Maman's Certificate of Freedom would be a boring formality. With Mr. Webster in attendance, it would receive expedited attention.

Maman had expressed concerns about Rosette visiting the fort alone, but Uncle Charles quickly put those to rest. Each morning, British soldiers routinely marched along the walls of the fort in a display of military colors and shiny rifles, attracting spectators of all ages. Rosette's presence would hardly raise an eyebrow.

She agreed to meet her parents at the market square in

an hour. With a lift in her step, she happily strode past the church toward Fort George, in her white bonnet, lime-green petticoat, and flat shoes. Closer to the wardrobe city girls her age wore, she hoped to make a virtuous impression on Malcolm, especially after her inappropriate entrance at his tavern the previous night.

Bystanders waited in sunlight for the parade, ladies with umbrellas, gentlemen smoking pipes, and girls in petticoats. Relieved that the soldiers at the gate to Fort George were not the same ones from the day before, she strolled up to them.

One of the soldiers held up his hand. "Stand over there with the others."

"Lieutenant McDonald is expecting me."

Without delay, he sent another soldier to seek Malcolm.

Her heart fluttered when the gate opened a few minutes later, and he stepped out.

"You look absolutely gorgeous," he said.

The blush warmed her face. "Thank you, Lieutenant. And you look quite dashing yourself."

"You are generous. I was expecting you."

She wondered if that was the reason his brown hair looked washed and neatly brushed back into a tail. He wore a white cotton shirt that blew loosely in the breeze. His tan slacks held sharp creases down to his black shoes, polished to a brilliant shine in the mid-morning sunlight.

She handed him the book and giggled. "My apologies."

"Apologies not accepted," he said with a sly grin. "I am glad we both forgot. 'Tis the happy reason I get to see you again."

"Seeing you also brings me much cheer, I must confess."

"Perhaps we can forget the book once more, and plan another meeting?"

His smile reassured her that his passions the previous evening had been fueled by more than Delilah's grog and fleeting sunset moods.

"I find this game most enjoyable, but Papa will soon become suspicious."

Just then, the guards pushed open the large gates. The sounds of light drums and flute led a platoon of armed soldiers out of the fort in a march of crisp red, white, and black uniforms adorned with shiny silver buttons. The soldiers paraded along the road, demonstrating a series of precision movements with bayonet-fitted rifles.

The spectators applauded.

Rosette wondered if these soldiers, and Malcolm, ever would face a French attack on Grenada again. Her parents frequently recounted the jubilation that filled the Fédon's Grand Pauvre house, when seventeen years of British occupation ended with the return to their beloved French ways and Catholic practices.

But the celebration was short-lived.

Four years later, the treaty that ended the American Revolutionary War also handed Grenada back to the British. Retribution followed, dressed in oppressive laws that stole French lands, cancelled British debts to French creditors, and imposed slavery on free blacks and mulattoes who could not prove their free status.

Rosette was just old enough to remember the sadness that overcame the family, including Grandmère. The grief in the Grand Pauvre house felt like a family member had died most shockingly. The mood followed them, like a storm cloud over their heads, all the way up the mountains to a new start on Belvidere Estate.

But Mr. Turnbull's attempt to enslave Maman proved that Belvidere was not far enough for the Fédon family to escape. British oppression persisted across the island, despite the overwhelming number of free coloreds and blacks compared to whites. Even here among the spectators at Fort George, whites were greatly outnumbered.

Several British gentlemen stood erect against a background of blacks and coloreds, like chalk lines on a blackboard. In light jackets, string ties and wide hats, they locked arms with ladies in extravagant petticoats, some fanning themselves in the rising heat. One white woman tugged at her male companion and chinned smug glances at Rosette and Malcolm.

The group of blacks and coloreds mingled behind in plain fashions and reduced formality, some in unrestrained liveliness.

The soldiers marched back into the fort to applause, and the crowd slowly dispersed.

"I must go meet my parents at the market square," Rosette said.

"'Tis going to be a boisterous day with the slave auction. May I escort you?"

She looked around. "Would it bring you much discomfort to be seen with a girl like me?"

"Do you mean the most beautiful and intelligent girl in Grenada?"

"Oh my." She exclaimed with giggling sarcasm. "You dare not compare me with your beautiful girlfriends in England?"

He reached for her hand. She let him hold it.

His tone grew serious. "There is no one I could compare you to, in Grenada or England."

She could not bear the wait to talk to Grandmère again. To ask her what she felt when she, a Creole girl, fell in love with a white Frenchman so many years ago.

Arm in arm, Rosette and Malcolm strolled towards the market square in the center of St. George's.

Kojo followed Massa Turnbull in oppressive heat towards the auction block, a small wooden platform on the far side of the crowded St. George's market square. The square sat trapped between the base of the hill and the open sea. Shoppers and vendors haggled in voices raised almost to anger, across tables stacked with sunbaked vegetables, red meat, and fresh fish. Kojo inhaled air thickened with a blended aroma of human sweat and raw food, while his leathery feet kicked dust over patches of struggling grass. A breeze sprinkled the humidity with a stingy flavor of cooking smoke—too stingy to brighten the sea of stunned black faces that stood ahead.

The new barefooted arrivals stood in a tug-of-war with heavy chains that hung from their arms and legs. Their skin, washed with a putrid composition of gunpowder, lemon-juice, and palm-oil, glistened in the sunlight. A woman bawled for an untold loss, but a loss Kojo recognized. A loss only a mother suffered—when ripped from her child. She howled with the force of hurricane winds, from so deep within her, Kojo knew it blew from her sacred womb.

The crack of a whip drew blood on her arm. She muffled her howl. Eyes bulged in silent pleas. A little girl, standing alone, cried and shivered in the blazing sunlight.

Kojo's stomach tightened, like the aching memories around his heart. Like the shackles that had tightened around his ankles. His anger boiled. But equal to the power in his muscles, he also possessed the strength to restrain himself.

He followed Massa Turnbull without betraying a hint of the fire that raged inside.

Massa Turnbull approached a finely dressed man who held a stack of papers, his bearded face in the shadows of a wide hat. They flipped pages and walked among the captured, pointing, poking ribs, and pinching muscles. They examined eyes, ears, and teeth, much like Massa Turnbull did when he purchased his last horse in Gouyave.

Massa Turnbull stopped at a young mother, not much older than Venus, her chained arms embracing a little boy, also in chains.

Massa rubbed her face and purred.

She trembled.

He turned to Kojo. "Just look at this fine specimen. Her strong shape, and these fingers, perfect for kitchen work.

She would be good help in the house for Mrs. Turnbull, do not you think?"

"Massa know best, Sah."

"We will take her, but not the boy. We have enough pickaninnies and most are useless in the fields."

"Massa right." Kojo looked away from the girl's questioning stare and chose his next words carefully. "No matter how Kojo flog the little wretches for laziness, they work better with their mothers. And mothers work better with their pickaninnies close by."

He waited for his suggestion to sneak into Massa Turnbull's thick skull.

Massa Turnbull chewed on his cigar, eyeing both mother and boy. "I think—"

Suddenly, he yanked his cigar from his mouth and threw it to the ground. Brown teeth showed in his open mouth. He glared across the square.

Monsieur Fédon's daughter and the young British soldier, Malcolm, strolled arm in arm, talking to, and looking at each other like they were the only ones in the square.

Massa Turnbull huffed up to them, Kojo at his heels.

Massa Turnbull poked his stubby finger at Malcolm. "You are a disgusting embarrassment to your father."

Malcolm stiffened, and squeezed his hold on Monsieur Fédon's daughter's arm. "Pray tell, sir. To what do you refer?"

"Such public display with a mongrel." He spat on the ground. "You have squandered the last of your goodwill here in His Majesty's colony. I am sure your father will find space on the next ship to Liverpool."

Malcolm released the girl and made a fist. "Sir, you have offended my last nerve."

Just then, a voice boomed over the crowd. "Let me through."

Monsieur Fédon charged towards them. Madame Fédon hurried behind him, her brows furrowed in alarm.

Chapter Twenty-Five

Rosette grabbed Malcolm's clenched fist. When she and Malcolm floated into the steamy market square, arm in arm, she had not expected an embarrassing fight between Malcolm and Mr. Turnbull. Maybe a raised eyebrow from Papa and a knowing smile from Maman. But Papa now roared towards them, fire in his eyes. Maman struggled to keep up with him, her desperate pleas to calm him as fleeting as raindrops on a hot stone.

Papa halted in front of Mr. Turnbull and barked, "Well, well, Monsieur Turnbull. I understand you made an uninvited visit to my Belvidere Estate. Might there be any additional matters I can help you resolve?"

Mr. Turnbull spat. "Not yet, *Mister* Fédon. Not yet."

"Then I will deem future unannounced visits as hostile." Papa turned to Rosette and Malcolm. "Any more of this conversation I should partake in?"

"No, Monsieur Fédon." Malcolm held Rosette's arm,

gazed into her eyes, and turned to Papa. "I was just telling Mr. Turnbull here how fond I am of Rosette. And of my intention to beg your permission to visit her again at your Belvidere Estate."

In afternoon sunlight, Kojo settled on the driver's bench of the open wagon and shook the reins. The horses dragged the rattling wagon behind Massa Turnbull's black carriage on the rugged road to Beauséjour. The market square chaos faded behind, making room for a shadow to drift over Kojo's thoughts. His mood darkened, such that by the time they arrived at Beauséjour, even the gold sunset lost its luster.

From behind him, the young mother's anguished sobs tortured his conscience like the toothache that throbbed his head. She sat in the wagon, chained with two men among bags of supplies and food provisions. After his encounter with Monsieur Fédon in the market square, Massa Turnbull's temper boiled. He quashed Kojo's hint that mother and son be purchased together.

Massa ordered him to rip the young mother apart from her pleading son. Kojo had clenched his jaws so forcefully to keep from chopping off Massa's head, that he broke a tooth.

The screams, jangling chains, and Massa's shouts haunted Kojo.

He dwelled on the dismal future that awaited his innocent baby boy, now probably nursing peacefully at Venus's breasts. Kojo expected to see him for the first time in a few days. Would Kojo's son someday endure what the young boy did just hours ago in the St. George's market square, only to face a life of bleeding skin, hunger, and sweltering rage? Kojo's ancestors would consider him an unworthy outcast if he handed down this existence to another generation.

At Beauséjour, Kojo guided the horse up the hill behind

the black carriage until they reached the great house. Massa's carriage turned left and pulled up at the base of the wide steps. Kojo continued past the house, heading down a narrow track to the slave pen used for new arrivals, within view of the great house. The slave pen, a darkened cave of mossy stone walls and iron gate, sat embedded in a thick canopy of hanging branches and crawling vines.

He dismounted and lit a lantern at the entrance. He trudged to the back of the wagon with a whip at the ready. The men looked surrendered to their destiny, but the young woman's eyes glistened with tears and her lips puckered in anger.

She yelled at Kojo in a dialect he did not recognize, but he guessed the words were vicious arrows meant for him. He grabbed the chained men off the wagon, one at a time, and shoved them into the dank, musty hole. He locked their chains onto iron bars anchored into the walls.

When he returned to the wagon for the young woman, she spat in his face, she screamed at him, she scratched at him. He felt nothing but pity for her. He lifted her fragile frame into the pen and locked her next to the men. Her howling began anew, and it surged a red-hot mixture of anger and guilt through Kojo's veins.

He knew why. Like the toothache that throbbed in his head, his ancestors drummed urgent messages in his mind.

Massa Turnbull huffed up in fading light, his boots crunching leaves and dried dirt. "Shut up that savage."

"Yes, Massa."

Kojo rushed into the shadowy pen. He stood over the weeping woman and jerked back the whip. She recoiled in the shifting lantern light, lifting her chained hands to her face, the white in her teary eyes glaring between her fingers. He cracked the whip. It slashed into the wall just above her head. Powdered masonry showered her hair.

She gave him a puzzled look and stopped crying.

He returned to Massa's side.

"No food for them tonight." Massa Turnbull pulled a

big key from his belt and locked the gate. "Tomorrow, we start breaking them in. I want the girl washed and in the kitchen at sunrise. Meet me here with water. I will open the gate."

"Yes, Massa."

After all those years, Massa still never trusted him with the key to the new slaves.

Massa hung the key on his belt and marched back to the great house, his bulky head leaving little evidence that he had a neck.

The ancestors drummed more rage into Kojo. The message became clearer. The time drew closer.

When Rosette returned to Belvidere with her parents at sunset, tired from the ride but elated nonetheless, she sprinted up the steps and raced down the hall to her grandmother's room. Grandmère would be waiting for her to read the closing chapter of *Robinson Crusoe*. But first, Rosette wanted to divulge all that had occurred on the overnight trip to St. George's, especially Malcolm's endearing gestures to win her.

She knocked on the door, and, not hearing a response, pushed it open.

Grandmère looked comfortable on the bed, propped up on two pillows, an opened book in her lap. But she held a pained look on her face, her eyes in a fixed gaze at the ceiling, and her lips slightly apart.

Rosette jumped on the bed. Grandmère rolled over stiffly into Rosette's embrace, her wrinkled skin cold to the touch.

Rosette screamed. "Grandmère!"

Next morning, Kojo approached the slave pen with a cutlass in one hand and a bucket of water in the other. Just then, a scream cut sharply into the predawn calm. It sounded like a child in the great house. Lovely? But what would she be doing in the house at this hour, instead of attending to Venus and the baby in the village?

He placed the bucket at the gate and hurried back to the house.

Another scream. This time, Madame Turnbull.

Kojo ran around the back of the house and up the steps to the open kitchen door.

Lovely stood with her back to him, her hands to her face. Across the dining room, Massa Turnbull watched from the staircase in his work clothes. Madame Turnbull struggled on to a chair at the dining table. She wrapped her arms around Venus.

Venus hung by a rope that stretched from her neck to the ceiling rafters, her hands flopping lifelessly at her side.

Protruding from a covered basket on the dining table, tiny white feet. Unmoving.

A paper stuck to the basket, with scribbly letters.

Massa Baby.

Chapter Twenty-Six

Malcolm gulped a mouthful of Delilah's rum punch and stared at the door in disbelief. Charlotte strutted in and scanned the tavern, her long red hair loose on her back. It had been a few months since he last saw her, the morning he rode away from Beauséjour as Dr. Hay rode up the hill. What would the wife of an upstanding member of Grenada society want in such establishment of ill repute?

Malcolm stood from his chair and rushed to her, elbowing soldiers in his way.

She brushed past him and headed to his table. "No need to leave your drink. I need one too."

He pulled up a chair for her. They sat facing each other.

He broke the awkward silence. "Mrs. Turnbull, I—"

"Have you forgotten my name already?"

"Sorry. Still confused and shocked."

"If your drink helps, then I need one too."

He waved at Delilah. She huffed up to the table and eyed Charlotte with a sideward frown.

Malcolm pointed at his drink. "The lady would like one of these."

Delilah plopped her fists onto her plump waist and glared at him. "Another friend, eh?"

Charlotte squinted at him questioningly. Delilah stomped off.

Malcolm gulped his drink. "Dr. Hay brought me the news."

"Lovely got there first." She sniffled. "When Venus disappeared from the shack with the baby, Lovely went looking for her. 'Tis why Venus asked me to teach her to write a few words. She just needed two, *Massa Baby*. That was her plan all along. It was most horrid."

"Did Mr. Turnbull say anything?"

"He seemed oblivious." She glanced up at the ceiling. "Kojo once told me something strange. Now I know what he meant. He said, 'Madame Turnbull, young girls on plantations have it hard, hard, hard. They have to keep their Massa off their back in the day, and off their belly at night."

Delilah returned with a mug of rum punch and handed it to Charlotte. "Nice hair, darling."

"Thank you." Charlotte took a gulp and licked her lips. "Just what I needed."

Delilah lumbered off.

"Any news yet about Kojo?" Malcolm asked.

"I thought he would remove Mr. Turnbull's head with his cutlass, right there and then. He calmly followed Mr. Turnbull's orders without emotion. He wrapped them in a sheet, took a gun and a shovel, and disappeared into the woods on the horse. Never returned."

"Maybe he joined the maroons."

"We thought so too, but some strange things happened thereafter. We heard a single gunshot echo from way up in the mountains. That night, the horse returned with blood on its face, but no cut. I believe Kojo buried Venus and the baby, then shot himself close to the horse to scare it back to the estate."

"How tragic."

"That was not all. Next morning, Mr. Turnbull discovered the new slaves, two men and a girl, gone. Vanished. But the gate was still locked, and his keys were hanging on his belt in his workroom. I overheard the servants saying Kojo's spirit freed the slaves. Mr. Turnbull is getting nervous."

"He might need you now more than ever."

"Too late." She held Malcolm's hand. "I came to say farewell. I am sailing for Boston tomorrow."

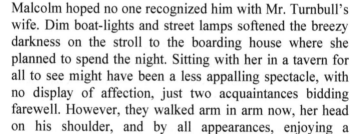

Malcolm hoped no one recognized him with Mr. Turnbull's wife. Dim boat-lights and street lamps softened the breezy darkness on the stroll to the boarding house where she planned to spend the night. Sitting with her in a tavern for all to see might have been a less appalling spectacle, with no display of affection, just two acquaintances bidding farewell. However, they walked arm in arm now, her head on his shoulder, and by all appearances, enjoying a romantic evening. If exposed, it would surely bring dishonor to his prestige as a British officer and incite Father's wrath, an especially more punitive outcome.

Malcolm still worried that Father might discover his warm acquaintance with the Fédons and growing attraction to Rosette. Malcolm might be able to explain that he spent the night on their estate, on Dr. Hay's insistence, after the head injury from Mr. Turnbull. But if Father also discovered that Malcolm had engaged in a scandalous affair with his friend's wife, it would be the equivalent of putting a flaming torch to a loaded cannon. The explosion would wreck Malcolm's relationship with his father.

Now, he just wished for an uneventful walk with Charlotte.

Passersby, a few stumbling out of boisterous taverns, expressed no curiosity in Malcolm and Charlotte.

"I came...to say farewell." Her words slurred on breath flavored with rum punch. "But you have not even tried to kiss me."

"My fondness for you has—"

"Stop it." She faced him and held his hands, her hair blowing in the wind, her white bodice struggling to restrain her heaving breasts. "I do not want you to be fond of me. I want you to desire me, one last time—like you did before."

"I will always remember you."

"'Tis that girl, is it not? Mr. Turnbull told me about you and Monsieur Fédon's daughter. He was most disturbed by your blatant public display of infatuation for her."

"I attended her grandmother's funeral in Belvidere but have not seen her since. The family is in deep grief."

"I cannot compete with such a young beauty." She sighed. "You rode past my house but did not visit."

"Your husband will not take kindly to my presence."

"You could have asked one of the slaves. I was alone. He was on business in Grenville for a few days."

He wanted to ask her why she did not have Bourbon deliver an invitation to Dr. Hay, but thought better of it. He empathized with the loneliness that coated her voice, the pain that simmered in her eyes, visible even in the night.

Charlotte seemed lost between two worlds, and again fleeing one for the other. She tried to transform her Beauséjour existence to her liking, to escape Boston. But slavery persisted around her. Cruelty persisted. Death persisted. And not enough pleasure in her bed could shelter her from the ugliness that surrounded her on Mr. Turnbull's hill. As long as she remained under his roof, she remained a benefactor of a plantation system that crushed human souls—hers too.

She had to leave.

Malcolm would miss her, but it felt like she wanted to

use him to cross the bridge from her dreary past to her uncertain future. It lacked the reckless lust that drove them to ecstasy under her sheets. Malcolm wanted to hold her and reassure her, but the memory of Rosette's voice, laughter, and grieving tears, gave him pause.

Just standing alone with Charlotte felt contrary to his wishes, now that Rosette had moved into his heart.

Charlotte touched his lips. "You could at least accompany a lonesome lady to Antigua. I might be there alone for days before finding a boat to Boston."

"I have military duties here."

Charlotte wrapped her arms around his neck and kissed his unresponsive lips. She dropped her arms and stepped back, her face downcast. They turned and walked in silence until they reached the lamp-lit entrance to the boarding house.

Her tears welled up. "You are too young to deserve the wrath of a woman scorned. Farewell, my friend." She turned and ran into the boarding house.

Chapter Twenty-Seven

Colonel McDonald marched off the ship ramp with his bags and stepped on the pier of the St. John's harbor in Antigua, the gateway to the Caribbean. Glad to feel solid ground beneath his boots again after the three-week journey across the stormy Atlantic, Colonel McDonald's spirit heightened at the thought of seeing his son again. It had been months since he bade farewell to Malcolm in St. George's harbor. But now, with just a few days away from Grenada, and under blue skies and flocks of squawking seagulls, he marched with purpose in his red and white wool uniform.

Despite the extended front and rear brims of his black hat, the late morning sun pelted scorching heat on his head, the likes of which he never suffered in England. Even as the sea breeze struggled to blow some relief, beads of sweat trickled from his forehead. But the thought of reuniting with Malcolm erased his discomfort. He lifted his steps with renewed vitality and pride.

He inhaled the burnt sweetness of molasses, the unmistakable scent of sugar wealth. Slave drivers cracked whips and barked orders at parades of slaves carrying bags of sugar and rolling barrels of rum to ship ramps. Moored ships groaned impatiently against the pier. Other ships sailed the harbor, their high masts and white sails sharing the skyline of green hills and sugarcane fields. In the distance, columns of smoke rose above sugar processing boiler houses. Vibrant signs of the ever-expanding British Empire, despite the painful loss of the American colonies.

A young soldier marched up and saluted. "Colonel McDonald, I have been assigned to assist with your luggage and ensure your accommodations."

"Thank you, soldier."

"I secured a room for you." The soldier took the two bags from the colonel. "The hostel is quite busy, given the lodging of in-transit passengers from Grenada."

"Grenada?" Colonel McDonald's interest heightened at the opportunity to catch up on Grenada news. "Please get me their names."

"Most certainly, sir," the soldier said cheerfully. "Some left yesterday for England, but at least one remains in search of a ship sailing to Boston."

It appalled Colonel McDonald that American ships, licensed as British colonial ships before the revolution, continued to sail into British West Indies ports with the same legal privileges granted to British vessels. He raised those concerns with a Member of Parliament back in Liverpool. But the Honorable Member simply repeated the prevailing sentiment among the decision makers—trade superseded old bitterness.

Bitterness?

Colonel McDonald vehemently disagreed. He exercised his God-given duty to regard the American backstabbers with the same fiery revulsion with which he regarded traitors and snakes. Their rightful destiny should be the immediate separation of their heads from their bodies.

The same for the likes of Monsieur Fédon. But the colonel had a more exquisite plan for the French mongrel, who by now, would be comfortable with the notion that Belvidere Estate belonged to him.

How vain, to think a British commanding officer would relinquish such a grand estate to someone like him. The colonel had revealed his plan to his friend and legislative Speaker, Ninian Home. But not to Mr. Turnbull, who had expressed interest in buying the estate. Turnbull's big mouth would have had the colonel's plans spreading like wildfire all over the island.

One day the estate would be back in the McDonald name. Fédon would be destitute, hopefully on a ship to Trinidad. What a fitting reward for the stinging humiliation the colonel suffered at the hands of the American and French degenerates in Yorktown. The memories still pulsed: dead horses, dying soldiers, and diseased men in muddy red-soaked trenches.

The colonel looked forward to finally explaining his plan to his son. It was best Malcolm did not have full knowledge of the Belvidere plan when he rode there to have the sale documents signed.

The young soldier led the colonel off the pier and down a bustling waterfront street. Horse-drawn carriages rattled past, and fancy women strolled by under even fancier umbrellas, their floral perfumes reminding the colonel of feminine pleasures that awaited him in Grenada.

The smoky aroma of roast beef awakened his appetite. He desperately needed a meal besides the daily salted cod and rancid bread he had on the ship.

The young soldier must have seen the way he inhaled the flavors. "A generous meal awaits you, sir."

The colonel laughed. "You remind me of my son. I can always trust him to say and do the right thing at the right time."

"I am sure he holds you in equally high regard, sir."

The soldier led him into a stone building with doors and windows wide open to the sunny afternoon. A big man seated behind a desk looked up when they entered the doorway and jumped to his feet.

The young soldier walked up to the desk. "Colonel McDonald has a room until the next ship leaves for Grenada. He will need a meal immediately, and a list of your occupants from Grenada."

The man pointed down the hall. "The dining room is open. Our chef prepared a hearty meal of beef and vegetables, with a tasty turtle soup." He flipped the pages of a log book. "We have one remaining Grenada passenger, awaiting a ship to Boston. Her name is Mrs. Charlotte Turnbull."

Colonel McDonald's heart raced. "Are you sure? Alone?"

"Yes, sir. She has not left her room since her arrival yesterday. Seemed rather sad, like she lost—"

"Please ask her to join me in the dining room in an hour. I will need fresh bath water and soap immediately."

Colonel McDonald pushed his empty plate across the table where he sat alone in the small dining room. Two hours earlier, he had checked into his room upstairs, secured a proper bath, and changed into clean clothes in anticipation of seeing Charlotte. The meal was substantial in size and taste, but he would have enjoyed it more with her company. He spent most of the time at the table expecting to see her walk through the door in all her splendor, her laughter, enticing smell, and unrepressed femininity.

To no avail.

Despite the clerk's repeated assurance that the colonel's invitation had been delivered, there was no sign of her.

How unlike her to ignore his request. Especially since they had not seen each other for such long months. Maybe the journey from Grenada had been unkind to her stomach, and reduced her happiness, as the clerk had observed.

But he and the clerk were wrong.

For just then, Charlotte walked in, her freckled face aglow in a wholesome smile that he hoped came from her seeing him. A looped braid held her red hair up at the back, and loose curls hung at the nape of her slender lily-white neck. She wore a pink low-buttoned bodice and flowered quilted petticoat that glorified her full curves.

The colonel's mood rose at the splendid opportunity to renew his affection for her. He stood, and she floated into his arms.

"I missed you," she whispered in his ear.

He tamed his longing to carry her upstairs. Had he been Malcolm's age, he might have already had her under the bed sheets.

"The feeling is quite mutual, my dear." He kissed her politely on the cheek. "Please sit."

They sat and chatted a while, he about England, she about events in Grenada.

She glanced out the window. "The Governor and legislature are quite intent on driving the French from Grenada. Some landowners have already abandoned their estates and moved to Trinidad with their slaves."

"I am surprised it has taken them this long."

"But not the likes of Monsieur Fédon, having just purchased your Belvidere estate."

He kept his silence. The Belvidere estate was a business affair unfit for the tender opinions of women. It gave him immeasurable satisfaction that he could rely on Malcolm's competence and loyalty to conduct such matters in his absence.

She studied his face. "Your son is ever as handsome and wise as you are."

"And how, may I ask, did you get to know so much about him?"

"I met him once, when he visited Mr. Turnbull...on his

way to Belvidere."

"I am proud of him," he said. "His loyalty and service to King George incites great admiration and respect among his Liverpool family and friends. He wrote me that all went well with the Belvidere papers."

"Mr. Turnbull also said so."

"Good." He leaned towards her. "How long will you be in Boston?"

She sighed, tucked loose hair behind her ear, and looked out the window at the coloring horizon. "Looks like we might have a lovely sunset. Shall we go up to the balcony?"

He retrieved a bottle of red wine and two glasses from the chef and led Charlotte up the stairs to a sheltered balcony overlooking the congested waterfront. Glad to see the balcony unoccupied, he pulled up wicker chairs for them beside a small table. He filled their glasses, and they toasted.

Seated next to him, she gulped her wine and returned the glass to the table. "It feels perfect being here with you where no one knows us."

"You never answered me. When are you returning to Grenada?"

Her second gulp of wine almost emptied the glass and her eyes moistened with sadness. "I may never see you again." She held his hand. "I am not returning to Mr. Turnbull."

His heart sank. "Why did you not tell me this before?" He pulled away his hand from hers. "You could have written. I will have living arrangements for you. I cannot let you do this."

"You have a wife and a happy family. My family is in Boston. I live a lonely life." She recounted some of the events that occurred during his departure: Venus's hanging, *Massa Baby*, Kojo's strange disappearance, and Mr. Turnbull's increasingly barbaric treatment of the slaves. "Things are getting worse. I could not stomach another week."

"Come back with me. I will provide you a room in St. George's. I shall make Mr. Turnbull understand your desire to be independent of him."

Colonel McDonald had a greater taste for Charlotte than Mr. Turnbull had for his own wife. He did not share Mr. Turnbull's desire for dark women. The man tarnished his own line, even producing a mixed-race offspring with all the deformities befitting such unnatural mixing of blood. And to call her Lovely. The man had no redeemable gumption, except for his legislative ability to pass laws the colonel intended to use against Monsieur Fédon.

"Not just Mr. Turnbull. Grenada is on edge. I feel it when I look into the eyes of the slaves."

"You are too close to these Africans. They do not value life the way we do. 'Tis why they do what they do. And why we do what we do. God's way."

She glared at him and refilled her glass. "I beg to differ."

"I am a soldier, not a saint." He sipped his wine. "I have not the patience to indulge in shallow reckless sentiments."

He admitted to himself, Charlotte's sentimentality flowed deeper than most of the other women he befriended along the way. Everything about her breathed more life into him, even when she expressed opposing views.

The silence between them surrendered to the vibrancy of the busy harbor below, sounds of a thriving British colonial center. Horses clopped resolutely on the stone roads, built by the taxes on plantation goods. Filled wagons clattered in haste towards the pier, perfuming the air with burlap bags of tobacco and sugar. Seagulls yelled over bobbing vessels readying to deliver goods to English homes across the Atlantic. All powerful evidence that Britain's global mercantile machinery rolled uninterruptedly, keeping the Union Jack flying high on every continent across God's planet.

Soon, he too would reap the status and wealth accorded those with unwavering faith. The colonel's friendship with influential men like Ninian Home would assure a smooth transition from military officer to master of his own estate in the King's colony of Grenada—and a luxurious mansion in England to welcome his silver years.

Maybe Charlotte's dim view came from her female nature, hardly equipped to comprehend the global and personal implications of commerce. The gentle nature granted to women matched well with the duties of bearing and nurturing babies—and for pleasing men.

Charlotte leaned towards him. "If opposites attract, that explains why you and I are here today."

Her voice teased with the naughty tone that had first led him to cast aside Mr. Turnbull's friendship in favor of ravenous moments with his wife.

He held her hand and kissed it. She embraced him with a yearning and an open-mouthed wine-flavored kiss that aroused him.

They left the empty bottle and glasses behind.

Her door opened easily into a simple room ablaze in sunset red. They helped each other undress, even as their hungry lips sought each other's. The salty film of sweat on her neck lifted his excitement. They rolled across her bed, too eager to squeeze under the sheets. She closed her eyes and spread her knees. He braced himself on top of her, her legs in a tight embrace around his waist. He thrust his manhood into her with a delight that ran up his spine.

She moaned and clawed at his back. They tightened their hold on each other in gyrating rhythms that grew harder, louder, and sweeter than he remembered in her Beauséjour bed.

They exploded together in pulsating pleasure he felt would never end—until she whispered in his ear.

"Oh, Malcolm."

Chapter Twenty-Eight

Maman thought Papa's first ominous signs started after his mother's sudden passing because he had not taken time to properly grieve. Rosette disagreed. It came earlier, like the first winds of a storm. A little cooler, a little stronger than usual. But it kept building. She felt the first reverberations in Papa's voice when he confronted Mr. Turnbull in the St. George's market square before she discovered Grandmère had passed away in bed.

In the following days, his mood kept getting sulkier. More abrasive.

And Rosette became more worried.

Papa slammed the banister with his fist when Bourbon rode up with news from Turnbull's estate. Three new slaves vanish. A baby and two adults dead, Kojo among them. And when Father Pascal visited to prepare Grandmère's burial services, he delivered another blow. The legislative assembly just authorized the seizure of more Roman

Catholic property, including his church in Gouyave.

The funeral services would be held in the Belvidere great house, not in the church.

The torrent of bad news left Papa little solace to grieve. Rosette restrained her own grief, doing all she could to calm Papa and to remind him to not turn his reading of the eulogy into a call to arms against the British.

The one shining moment came when Malcolm unexpectedly rode up to the estate before the services. Through teary eyes, she watched him console Papa, Maman, and Uncle Jean-Pierre. Malcolm held Rosette's hands in his and expressed kind words of condolences that warmed her heart. He spent a full day and a night on the estate, again at Papa's insistence, but she had precious little time to thank him adequately—and privately—before his return to St. George's.

She wondered if Papa's generosity to Malcolm, for protecting Maman against Mr. Turnbull, would ever be exhausted.

Now a week later, Papa's jaw muscles remained tightened, he chewed his cigar ends to smidgeons, and spent more time staring up into the hills with intense contemplation.

Something about the Belvidere hills captured his daily attention.

From her window now, Rosette watched Papa and Uncle Jean-Pierre lead a long row of ragged workers, some she had not seen before, up the sunny hillside. They carried bags over their shoulders, cutlasses, and shovels in their hands. The workers gathered around Papa. His hands punctured the air with forceful gestures, and his voice bellowed, though she could not comprehend the words from the distance.

The workers scattered into the thick greenery, chopping vines and shrub as they went. Within hours, they cleared a wide expanse of land in the shadows of large trees and began emptying the contents of their bags into the earth, like they were planting new crops.

Rosette returned to her chores and was sitting on the verandah shelling a basket of peas when Uncle Jean-Pierre returned from the hillside by himself, sweaty and muddy. She fetched him a jug of water with a glass and returned to her chair.

He gulped down his first glass. "Thank you, my princess."

"What is Papa planting up there?"

"Yams, potatoes, dasheen—basic ground provisions."

"Not coffee and cocoa?"

She dared not question Papa's plantation decisions, but Uncle Jean-Pierre allowed her greater latitude.

He grew serious. "Your father is a wise man. Have faith."

It seemed an odd response to her question.

Papa allowed his slaves time on Saturdays and Sundays to cultivate their own gardens of ground provisions at the bottom of the hill, just past the slave village. He supplemented those with occasional boxes of saltfish.

Papa's revenue came from export crops, cocoa, and coffee. Not slave food like yams, potatoes, and dasheen.

Confused by Uncle Jean-Pierre's response, she prepared to ask him more questions, but the sound of a horse galloping up the hill distracted her.

Bourbon rode up to the steps and dismounted. He handed Rosette a letter and pulled Uncle Jean-Pierre aside in whispers.

Surprised, Rosette opened the letter. Her heart raced.

Dearest Rosette,

It saddens me at the loss of your grandmother and my inability to console you in person. But I hope to lift your spirits with the likelihood of good news. I have suggested to Dr. Hay, and he has enthusiastically agreed, that assigning me to his Gouyave militia as a training officer shall be a most feasible arrangement. Of course, in confidence with you, I wish this in order that I see you more frequently, with Monsieur Fédon's permission. My transfer request has only to receive the blessings of my father, Colonel McDonald, on his impending return to the island. I now spend most of my liberty at the port, praying for his prompt arrival and approval.

Please convey my best regards to Monsieur and Madame Fédon.

With sincere affection,

Malcolm

Rosette held the letter to her chest.

Suddenly, Papa's strange obsession with the hills and his increasingly sulky moods no longer felt as worrisome.

Malcolm's pride swelled at the sight of Father descending the ship ramp. Colonel Hector McDonald stood tall, adjusting his red waistcoat and black hat. White leather belts crossed his chest with buckles that glittered in the afternoon sunlight. Gold epaulettes hung at the shoulders. His black top boots pounded the pier as he stepped off into the boisterous river of sweating workers and rolling carts.

Malcolm hurried up to him. "Father, welcome back."

Father looked past him with cold blue eyes. "Soldier, get my luggage at the top of the ramp and follow me. Make haste." His words pierced the air with the sharpness of a battlefield command.

Unsure how to interpret Father's uncanny demeanor after his long absence, Malcolm assumed a matter of extreme urgency had seized his attention on the ship.

Malcolm hurried up the ramp to the waiting bags and dashed down with them. He led Father to a waiting horse carriage, which took them along the busy waterfront and crawled up the hill to Fort George. Father held his stone-faced silence, despite Malcolm's attempts to solicit news about the family in England.

When they pulled into the fort, Malcolm grabbed the bags and followed Father into the commanding officer's quarters. Other soldiers approached respectfully to extend welcome-back greetings to Father. Their words also fell on deaf ears.

When they arrived at the door to his room, Father turned sharply to Malcolm. "Lieutenant McDonald, you are hereby ordered to return to your quarters and remain there until further orders from me. You are to communicate with no one. Whether spoken or written. Is that understood?"

"Yes, but—"

"Is that clear, soldier?"

"Yes, sir."

Father unlocked his door, pulled the bags in, and slammed the door shut in Malcolm's face.

Aghast at Father's shockingly icy display hours earlier, Malcolm gazed out his window at the hillsides, painted red in fading daylight. What could have happened? Malcolm feared eventually Father, on returning to Grenada, might discover his son's reckless liberties with Charlotte, his confrontations with Mr. Turnbull, or maybe his fondness for Monsieur Fédon's daughter. But something lit Father's aggravation even before his arrival in St. George's.

Marching boots echoed down the hall towards Malcolm's room. Heavy banging on the door. It swung open. Father marched into the darkening room and pushed the door shut behind him.

He adjusted his uniform and pointed to the chair. "Have a seat, son."

Malcolm sat with his gut tightening.

Father paced the room, his hands laced at his back. Shadows hardened his facial features, and his boots pounded the floor.

"My utter disappointment in you is worse than I ever thought possible. As my son, and as a promising officer in King George's Army."

"Father, pray tell to what I must apologize—"

He stomped his boot and glared at Malcolm. "Do not dare pretend."

Malcolm held his silence and stared at the floor.

"Your name slipped in Antigua...most untimely. Charlotte...Mrs. Turnbull wanted to protect you, but I got the truth out of her."

"It was just once—"

"It matters not." Father marched up to the window and gazed out, his back to Malcolm. "I had the occasion to talk at length with Mr. Turnbull at the legislative meeting this afternoon. He disclosed everything else. Your hostility towards him and your coziness with the Fédons raise serious doubts about your loyalty. I never thought I would hear those words about my own flesh and blood. You disobeyed my instructions when I left. I warned you about that snake, Monsieur Fédon."

"I can explain it all, if I be given but just a few minutes."

He spun around. "Too late. Your request to join Dr. Hay's Gouyave militia is denied. Pack your bags. You leave for Liverpool on the first ship tomorrow."

The ship cut deep into the sea, shedding a white wash along her sides as she plowed northwards past Gouyave. Malcolm held on to a pulley rope on the starboard side of the ship and watched the mountains slip by against the blue sky. He imagined somewhere up there in the Belvidere mountains Rosette's heart throbbed for him as much as his for her.

How cruel a fate, that their innocent passions suffered under the harsh rigidity of customs and surrendered to the selfish loyalty demanded by country and family.

Rosette would surely be crushed—just days after he lifted her hopes with his plan to join the Gouyave militia to be closer to her.

Soon, his absence and silence would confuse her. But the truth would be more devastating than confusion. It might come to her as a rumor from Bourbon, or as confirmation from Dr. Hay. Eventually, she would learn. Lieutenant McDonald had suddenly and unexpectedly departed for England. Without a farewell visit. Without an apologetic note. With callous dismissal of all they said to each other, and all they felt for each other.

Never to see each other again.

He attempted to calm his rising fury with the thought that his situation could be far more distressing. His abrupt expulsion from Grenada did not compare to the agony that slaves endured. Ripped from their African homeland, packed like sardines in foul holes below deck, naked and shackled, and forced into a lifetime of labor and suffering in alien lands.

Never to see their families again.

What strength they possessed.

How dare Malcolm lament his situation. At least no chains locked his limbs. He stood in fresh air above deck, and in three weeks he would be home in Liverpool with his mother and brothers.

Free.

Yet, his pain persisted. The further the ship sailed from Gouyave, the harsher it clawed his insides.

The pain sought an outlet, a release, an escape.

Then, he found it.

Anger.

The path to his redemption boiled with anger. At everything he held dear and swore to defend. He despised England and her pretentious civilization. He loathed the odious system of slavery, armed with brutality and clothed in hypocrisy. It ripped people from their families and homes, chained them, labored them, suffered them in the name of a King they knew not.

He hated those who climbed rungs of human agony to reach heights of pretentious aristocracy, leaving behind hanging mothers and smothered babies, crushed limbs and shattered souls.

He hated Mr. Turnbull.

Malcolm hated his father.

Chapter Twenty-Nine

The days stretched into weeks, and Rosette's concern stretched into suspicion. Not a word from Malcolm. She read his letter again and again. The message stated clearly his sincere intent to seek her affections. His desire to be closer to her, his optimism for a hasty transfer to Gouyave leaped out of the page. So, where was he? She spent many a day on the verandah peeling peas as a pretext but staring down the hill at every sign of a horse between the wind-blown trees.

Rainy days. Cloudy days. Sunny days.

Whenever a rider galloped up the road to the house, she would stand in heart-racing anticipation. Inevitably, she would collapse into the chair in gloomy disappointment, even when her Uncle Jean-Pierre rode up to assist Papa in the hills.

The distant hills helped to distract her from her rising doubts about Malcolm's honesty. She would sometimes gaze up at the steep terrain, where Papa and Uncle Jean-Pierre poured all their attention in recent weeks. They directed the workers to chop down huge trees with heavy axes, clear bushy grounds, and dig holes.

One day, two white Frenchmen she had not seen before rode up the road with Bourbon. They joined Papa and Uncle Jean-Pierre in the hills for about an hour, gesticulating in all directions over Belvidere. Papa then led them back down to the house where they retreated into his library for a few more hours of food, drinks, cigars, and low conversations behind closed doors. Just before sunset, the Frenchmen mounted their horses and followed Bourbon in the Grenville direction.

Papa neither introduced Rosette to his visitors nor even acknowledged her presence on the veranda. She chewed a handful of bitter raw peas to fill her growing despondency.

Papa's cool distance from her and his secrecy only heightened her curiosity.

The next day, Sunday, with Papa in Gouyave and an off day for the workers, she climbed the hills alone to inspect the secret enterprise. Rows and rows and rows of baby elephant ears, the young green leaves of the taro root the slaves called dasheen.

The slaves cultivated their own dasheen from smaller gardens behind the slave village at the bottom of the hill. They also grew plantains, a starchy yellow banana, which, along with the light purple dasheen, they boiled, fried, and roasted on open fires. The sweet, earthy aroma floated up to the great house each day. Rosette especially loved the fried plantain, as sweet as the baked treats Father Pascal had sent with Malcolm on his first visit to Belvidere.

She followed the dasheen rows to where the cascading muddy fields flattened and rounded the hill. Ahead, out of sight from the great house, even more, lengthy rows of plantain suckers rising from the rich soil as far as she could see into the woods.

More slave food than Papa's slaves ate in a year.

Why?

She returned to the veranda and speculated that the French visitors might be buyers, who in turn would sell the produce to plantations in Grenada or elsewhere. But she could not name a single estate owner who chose to buy this much food for their slaves. Instead, they allowed them scanty time to plant their own food on marginal lands.

And why had Papa not included her in his business discussions with the Frenchmen, like he did when Malcolm came to complete the Belvidere purchase?

The thought of Malcolm reawakened her aching heart. At sunset, she swallowed a few raw peas, dropped off the basket of unpeeled ones in the kitchen, and went to sleep without supper.

The next morning, the rumble of logs awakened her.

Then a piercing scream.

She pulled her window curtain and stared at the commotion at the top of the hill. Soon, Papa and other slaves struggled down the hill, carrying a slave on a makeshift stretcher of tree limbs and clothing.

Rosette changed and hurried downstairs to the veranda, where Papa, Uncle Jean-Pierre, and a couple of other men circled the man on the floor. He lay writhing in obvious pain, his leg swollen and bent at a most unnatural angle.

Papa shouted at Zab. "Fetch Dr. Hay in Gouyave. Here is a note if anyone stops you. Make haste."

Zab galloped his horse down the road.

Papa popped open a bottle of rum and held it to the man's lips.

By the time Zab raced back up the hill with Dr. Hay two hours later, the man with the broken leg had swallowed half the bottle of rum. He mumbled in half-consciousness. While others held the man, Dr. Hay aligned the broken leg and applied a splint of chopped tree limbs and straps.

Dr. Hay adjusted his glasses and turned to face Papa. "He should not stand on it for at least a week. You would not get much work from him."

"Nothing wrong with his hands. He could peel peas." Papa nodded at Rosette. "'Tis more than I get from her, just sitting there with a full basket waiting for that English officer to show up."

Dr. Hay removed his glasses and squinted. "You mean Lieutenant McDonald? You have not heard?"

Rosette perked up. "Heard what?"

"He is probably already in England. Left rather abruptly some weeks ago. Transferred to an artillery unit in Liverpool."

Rosette covered her mouth in shock.

Papa slammed his fist on the banister. "That bastard."

She turned and rushed through the door towards the washroom, vomit rising to her throat, bitter with the taste of raw peas.

Papa's words trailed after her. "The next Englishman to step foot here will have his head crushed...not you, Dr. Hay."

Chapter Thirty

One year later

High on the artillery battery wall overlooking Liverpool port, Malcolm tugged at his collar to brave the cold westerly winds dragging thick gray clouds across the sky. Days like today reminded him how the passing seasons had dampened his initial happiness to be home again. He reached out for sunny memories of Grenada to warm his spirit. But those recollections bounced around in his aching hollowness, stretched between irreconcilable worlds.

Liverpool held his body. Grenada held his mind. Rosette held his heart.

If Father intended to reinsert him into the bosom of Mother England, to rekindle the civic loyalty and family morals that fired Malcolm's boyhood years, he could not have picked a more strategic location and time. England reeled under constant military threats from a turbulent and aggressive Revolutionary France, embroiled in a vulgar assault on its royal heritage. They arrested, humiliated, and guillotined their own king and queen in a manner Malcolm thought befitting the savagery of a butcher shop.

He glanced around for reassurance that Liverpool would never succumb to such incivility. In every direction, Liverpool proudly displayed the symbols of her commitment to God, king, and enterprise. Church spires, St. Nicholas being the most prominent among them, towered skyward with bells that gonged their pious presence over the town and surged Malcolm with boyhood memories. The massive Workhouse for the poor on Brownlow Hill. Windmills at his every glance, for grounding corn into flour. Chimneys exhaled smoke above earthen and glass works. Custom houses and warehouses lined the harbor front, where a forest of masts, white sails, and proud Union Jacks floated in and out of the elongated harbor like a never-ending parade.

The harbor traffic hardly surprised Malcolm. Liverpool had earned the distinction as the home port for eight of every ten slave ships flying the Union Jack. The burgeoning commercial wealth from the colonies widened the outskirts of the city with new roads and buildings absent before Malcolm first left for Grenada.

Father had reassigned Malcolm to the Liverpool artillery barracks, on the south side of the entrance, the gut to the port, in anger over Malcolm's imprudence in Grenada. But the England that once nourished his every noble endeavor with pride and allegiance now seemed heartless to the suffering that fed her prosperity. His family and friends might as well have walked around with their noses to their navels, as unwilling and unable they were to lend their unwavering views to his colonial experience.

Even his plump, loving mother and his brothers had reacted with raised eyebrows soon after his surprise return to Liverpool when he said he preferred honey to sugar in his tea.

"My, my," Mother said at their supper table. "Your taste has really changed. Why so?"

His changed taste in sugar notwithstanding, if only Mother knew about his new taste in female companionship, she might need smelling salts to revive her from the shock. He decided not to recount the night he spent on Beauséjour Estate, when Kojo demonstrated how sugar cane rollers crushed slaves' fingers, limbs, and bodies. Surely, details of plantation gore in the West Indies would not find eager ears around a supper table abundant with food he relished since he last enjoyed them a year past. Boiled leg of mutton flavored the air over spreads of cheese, breads, potatoes, and English puddings.

"Maybe I just had too much in Grenada," he said to pacify Mother's interest in his distaste for sugar.

He also doubted that his younger brothers, enthralled with maidens, church activities, and cricket matches, would find it appealing to engage in far-flung conversations about slave anger and suffering. Such an exchange would be terribly out-of-place in their elegant Duke Street home, endowed with shiny floors, richly upholstered furniture, and paintings depicting happy families in luxuriant gardens. Under Father's strict guidance, the family avoided the port's ugly scars and obscene stench.

Footsteps behind Malcolm interrupted his thoughts.

A young soldier hurried up and saluted. "Sir, the major requests your presence right away."

Malcolm led the way down to the steps and to the stone walkway that stretched past cannons to the two-storied barracks.

The soldier cleared his throat. "Sir, a mailbag was just delivered from Grenada."

"I doubt anything for me. 'Tis been a year, and no word from anyone."

Before leaving Grenada, Father had warned Malcolm that letters between a British soldier and adopted French subjects might be deemed traitorous in such times of war.

Father addressed all his letters to Mother, who then passed along any news of interest—but nothing on the Fédon family. And no letters from Rosette.

Why should Malcolm expect mail from her? He departed the island without as much as a farewell note. Under father's strict orders, he had no way of letting her know of the unfortunate turn of events that sent him to Liverpool instead of Gouyave.

The bald major sat at his desk chewing an unlit cigar when Malcolm pushed open the heavy door and took a seat at his superior officer's direction. "I have a matter of importance to discuss with you." He handed Malcolm an unopened letter. "But read this first."

Malcolm immediately recognized Father's handwriting on the outside. He removed the seal and read the terse letter.

Father announced that Ninian Home had been appointed Governor, but soon thereafter his wife passed away from the contagious Bulam fever, brought to Grenada on a slave ship. The governor planned to return to his Paxton House Estate, just west of Berwick-upon-Tweed on the north bank of River Tweed, for a period of mourning and rest. But first, he had business matters to attend to in Liverpool. Father had requested, through the major's chain of command, to release Malcolm from his barracks duty to make accommodations for the governor and accompany him as needed—even to Paxton House if the governor requested.

The letter gave the name of the ship and an approximate arrival date one month hence. Malcolm, Father instructed, should spare no expense to ensure the governor's satisfaction and comfort during his time of bereavement.

The letter gave no hint that a father had just written to a son after a year of silence between them.

The major removed his cigar. "I have been providing Colonel McDonald periodic reports on your progress here.

Even with a comfortable home just a short ride away, you spend many long hours here training the troops and maintaining excellent discipline and readiness among them. I recommended to him, and he has approved through my chain of command, that you be promoted to Captain."

Captain Malcolm McDonald galloped his horse from the windy hilltop battery towards the harbour, and into the chaotic stench of horse dung, dead cats, and open sewage, made more unbearable by the recent rains. Meagre sunlight slipped through clouds like a full moon on a foggy night. Loaded wagons rattled over rough stone-paved roads. Sailors, some black, hollered instructions to fellow workers from high atop masts. Closely moored ships with mundane names like *Othello* and *Mermaid* seemed to mock him with self-indulgence, rubbing and groaning against each other. Their scented cargoes of West Indies sugar, coffee, and tobacco barely disguised the odour of human cargo discharged in the islands.

He dismounted at the base of the steps to the imposing brick custom-house and tied off his horse. Seagulls screeched against the gray sky overhead. He shut his eyes and imagined the clouds parting to let the Grenada sun beat on him. Memories rushed in with Rosette's smile, her lips seeking his. But then the bitter sadness came roaring back.

He headed up the steps to the front door.

He approached the custom-house officer manning the counter, the same one he had spoken to several times over the past few days. He expected the man to repeat the same answer to his question regarding the arrival of the ship from Grenada with Governor Ninian Home. True to Malcolm's expectation, the man glanced over a few pages, shook his head and shrugged his shoulders. No sign of the ship yet—but any day now.

Malcolm gave the man written directions to his barracks and some money. "Please have a messenger find me promptly, as soon as the ship enters the harbour."

"Count on it, Captain."

Since the major had already released him of his regular duties to await the governor, Malcolm decided to take a slow ride along the busy waterfront. Within minutes, he had had enough of tall masts, yelling sailors, and smelly ships. He thought of dropping in on Mother, who, with the boys away at military college, might be home alone with the servant. But by the time he reached Duke Street, away from the waterfront vexations, he dug his heels into the horse and sped north instead.

He wanted to get away from it all. Liverpool, its people, his family, the ships, the odours, the churches—all felt like a heavy, ill-fitting coat suffocating him.

He no longer belonged here.

Malcolm had become a man without a home.

He finally slowed on Hunter Street. To the left, a small gathering of Quakers—suited men with black wide-brimmed hats—stood in vigorous conversation at the front door to a new building. A poster on the front wall caught his attention. It showed a well-dressed black man. And in bold letters, *The Interesting Narrative of the Life of Olaudah Equiano or Gustavus Vassa, the African.*

One of the Quakers, an older man with white hair, in as much contrast to his black hat as it was to his boyish face, strolled up and waved at Malcolm.

"Good morning, Captain." He pointed at the poster. "If you are intrigued, you can join us for a cup of tea, and I will introduce you to Mr. Vassa."

Malcolm needed no persuasion. He dismounted and tied his horse.

The man shook Malcolm's hand. "My name is William Rathbone."

"Malcolm McDonald."

William introduced him to the other men. "We are members of the Liverpool Committee for the Abolition of the Slave Trade. Mr. Vassa travelled all the way from

London to promote his book and to speak to our group tonight."

Malcolm followed William through the doorway and into a plain room with wooden benches and a podium. To one side of the room, several men hunkered around a table in low conversation, sipping tea and nibbling crumpets. A narrow hallway led to a kitchen, from which floated the clinks of dishes and a delightful aroma of freshly baked treats. It revived with fondness the memory of the day his and Rosette's hands touched when they both stretched for baked coconut treats on the Belvidere table.

On the other side of the room, a black man sat at a table facing a line of several people. He scribbled on the inside cover of a book and handed it to the first man in line. They shook hands.

The black man bore a remarkable likeness to the man named Vassa on the poster, with a prominent nose and melancholy eyes. He glanced over his shoulder at Malcolm and smiled.

Here Malcolm stood, a British military officer, sworn to defend King and country, at war with France, in the company of men planning to undo a key fountain of British prosperity and military power—the slave trade.

Yet, these men, this place, felt so welcoming.

He wondered what Father might say if he knew where Malcolm stood today. It suddenly struck him that his fear was not of the ferocity of Father, but of Colonel McDonald, the military commander. The winds of time and distrust had finally swept away the last residue of respect that once bonded Malcolm to his father. Fear and disdain took its place.

Mr. Vassa must have sensed Malcolm's apprehension. "Thanks for coming, Captain. I have many years of obedient service with officers like you." He spoke with a surprisingly clear British accent.

William turned to Malcolm. "'Tis not often we have officers brave enough to show up in uniform at our gatherings. Please stay a while."

They chatted for a few minutes, and, when the last person in line strolled away with a signed book, William walked Malcolm over to Mr. Vassa's table.

Mr. Vassa stood and extended his hand in a strong but warm handshake. "Very pleased to have you here today, Captain."

"Please call me Malcolm."

"I have travelled the world with military men like you. You have my utmost respect."

"My respect to you as well, Mr. Vassa. For writing what appears to be a popular and important book. I would very much like to purchase one."

Malcolm handed him the money.

Mr. Vassa signed one of the books stacked on the table. "My real name is Olaudah Equiano, but when I was a mere boy, a British lieutenant in Virginia purchased me and renamed me Gustavus Vassa. After a Swedish nobleman. He must have assumed no one would know the difference."

They laughed.

Mr. Vassa gave him the book. "I hope you can return for our evening event."

Malcolm studied the book. "I never judge a book by the cover. By your courage alone, I judge it with high regard. I will read as much of it today. Then I will return to hear your talk this evening."

Foggy darkness cloaked Malcolm's ride to the Quaker meeting house. Except for an occasional horse rider or rackety carriage, the streets were empty of the commercial traffic that congested the daytime harbour routes. His horse's shoes clopped on the stone road, and solitary oil lamps burned pale yellow in the misty night, silent witnesses to Malcolm's troubled thoughts.

After reading Mr. Vassa's gripping book to the last page, Malcolm's head throbbed. Young Vassa, at age eleven, was kidnapped with his sister from the Kingdom of Benin. Malcolm recalled that slave catchers kidnapped Kojo around the same age, but from the Kingdom of Dahomey.

Still, the book had cast a new light on Kojo's torturous life. Did Kojo choose to join Venus and her baby in death rather than remain imprisoned in slavery? Vassa wrote that he too considered taking his own life. However, Africans feared suicide would forever break the bonds with their ancestors.

Taking one's life led to a second but more dreadful end. Eternal death. Hell.

Most slaves preferred to crawl through their horrid existence one day at a time, waiting for a day to fight and live in freedom—or die with honor.

Malcolm found it difficult to believe Kojo would dishonour his ancestors with suicide.

And Venus? Certainly, she died a desperate death at her own hands, taking her baby with her. According to African beliefs, the baby would be received in the warm bosoms of her ancestors. But would they see Venus's death as dishonourable?

So much Malcolm did not understand. The reason he read Vassa's book.

Vassa survived the horrendous middle passage, and slaved in Barbados, Monserrat, Virginia, on ships at war, and finally in London. There, he purchased his freedom, learned English, and became a Christian.

Now Malcolm spurred his horse on to hear more from this man of raw courage.

Quaker men filled the room on Hunter Street. Malcolm squeezed in and sat in the back row.

William Rathbone stepped up to the podium, welcomed first-time visitors, and made a few opening remarks. "As some of you might have recently heard, our Honorable Member of Parliament, Wilberforce has again submitted the bill in Parliament to abolish the slave trade.

And yet again, has failed to get the needed votes."

Moans and the shaking of heads among the audience.

"But the fight continues," Mr. Rathbone said. "Tonight, I am pleased to introduce two speakers with first-hand experience from both sides of the trade. One from here in Liverpool, will share his experience as a sailor on a slave ship. The other, a former slave, travelled all the way from London to share with us the inhumanity suffered by those African souls."

Mr. Rathbone introduced the first speaker as Edward Rushton, founder of the School for the Blind on the east side of Commutation-row. Heavyset with thick black hair, Mr. Rushton wore a patch over one eye. The other eye remained shut.

Mr. Rathbone held his hand and led him to the podium.

Edward cleared his throat. "I became an apprentice on a slave ship at age sixteen. I am here tonight because of God's will and the sacrifice of a self-less slave who drowned while saving me from a sinking ship. I still carry him in my heart every day. His name was Quamina."

What bitter irony.

The silence so filled the room, Malcolm feared even the sound of his head turning against his upturned collar might draw attention.

Edward continued his story, explaining how he lost his sight when he contracted the contagious ophthalmia while caring for affected slaves on his ship. He recounted gory details that mirrored those in Vassa's book. The stench. The sick. The dying. "The poor wretches were packed into less space than a dead Englishman's coffin."

When Edward finished, William introduced the next speaker, Mr. Vassa.

Mr. Vassa shuffled up to the podium as if the world had abandoned him to bear the full weight of his excruciating memories alone.

He gazed upon the audience. "Am I not a man and a

brother? When I boarded the ship in chains at age eleven, I believed the white men were going to eat us. If you are cannibals, I doubt these skinny limbs could feed you all tonight."

Nervous laughter.

"I no longer believe that white men are cannibals. And white men should no longer believe Africans are beasts of burden. If our Christian Parliament changes their beliefs, the country will follow. When they begin to think of us as men, only then will the slave trade be abolished. Otherwise, they can no longer believe themselves Christians."

The audience applauded.

He continued. "We have only to look at slave rebellions to see that Africans fight for the same freedoms that white men yearn for. Look how they fight in Jamaica, Saint Dominique, St. John. There will be more. The French Revolutionaries know this and will use it as a weapon against the British Empire. If Parliament continues to hold these cursed beliefs that subjugate Africans to such terrible conditions, slave rebellions will continue to echo with their cries of *Vive la Republique*!"

Chapter Thirty-One

High above Belvidere, the cool winds of Mount Qua Qua whistled past Rosette's ears, as if delivering a secret message: change had landed on Grenada's shores, and the footprints led all the way to Belvidere Estate. Over the past year, she had seen the hidden crops and disguised fortifications grow. She observed the increased number of visitors for Papa. New faces, urgent expressions, meetings in the library. Intense conversations, always in French whenever she walked past the shut library door. Close enough to hear the language. But never close enough to understand what they planned—until today.

This day, Papa took her on the muddy climb to Mount Qua Qua. To reveal the truth, he had said. With cutlass and stick in hand, they hiked up the steep trails to the peak. He led her past two camps, so cleverly tucked into the woods, she had no view of them from their house. Low blockhouses of stone and logs in compounds protected by walls of felled trees, their sharpened branches pointing out menacingly.

Sweaty but exhilarated after the two-hour climb to the summit, she gazed around from a vantage point next to a huge rock. The island opened before her with greenery on greenery, hills on hills, in every direction. To the south, under sunny skies, a thin mist drifted over the extinct volcanic lake, Grand Étang, making it look like a giant bowl of steaming bland soup.

Papa's jaws tightened. His eyes focused into the distance. He spoke about the smoking embers blowing from the French Revolution with promises of *liberté, egalité, fraternité*.

"Our French Revolutionary leaders asked me to bring Grenada into the fight for freedom, equality, and fraternity," he said. "I accepted. The British must go."

"What does that mean for us, Papa?"

"We must prepare. Many workers and warriors will come to Belvidere for shelter. Our plantains and dasheens are almost ready to feed them. But enemies will also come, that is why we build camps in the hills."

Howling winds filled the silence without calming her misgivings. Rosette had hoped Malcolm's father would miss him as much as she did, and return him to Grenada. But if the French and their slaves rose up in victorious rebellion, the British would be gone. Malcolm would never return. And she would never know why he discarded her sentiments so uncaringly.

Try as she did, she could never get Malcolm to leave her thoughts the way he left Grenada. How could she forget? What they shared felt so pure, so real. Yet, his departure so shockingly cold, the betrayal so deep, it hardened her heart. Father Pascal had warned Papa about his heart turning to stone. He should have also warned Rosette.

Maybe it was best she never learned why Malcolm abandoned her. Best he never returned. If the slaves rebelled, as happened in Saint Dominique, no Englishman would be safe in Grenada.

Malcolm had departed her life. Now she wished he would depart her mind forever. She had more pressing concerns before her.

She turned to Papa. "I want to help."

"My dear, your help is being my daughter," he said. "I met with Madame Josephina."

Rosette knew too well the power Madame Josephina held over her Yoruba followers. A freed slave and Papa's friend, she kept alive Shango rituals that gave hope to slaves. Madame Josephina had also planned the Shango ceremony the day Rosette met Malcolm.

"She gave all the signs," Papa said. "Right now, we stand on the very middle of the island. Think of it as the middle of a cross. Madame Josephina assured us victory to the west and the east, Gouyave and Grenville. She said the north will deliver us a mighty prize, but we do not know what that means yet. If all fails, in a straight line south from here is Mt. Sinai, then Westerhall Bay, the bottom of the cross. 'Tis where I will go for deliverance."

On the way back down the slippery trails to Belvidere, Rosette pondered Papa's message.

'Tis where I will go for deliverance.

Why would Papa have an escape plan? The British would surely capitulate against an island-wide rebellion. A rebellion the French would supply and support, maybe even with their own troops. Did he have doubts about the viability of his plan?

Papa suddenly halted and pulled back his shoulders.

Two men stepped out of the tree line ahead of him. Both barefoot and in rags, they carried cutlasses. One quite taller and bigger than the other.

Papa turned to her. "Wait here."

He left Rosette on the trail and slashed his way across the brushy path towards the men. He embraced them. They talked, their words lost to her on the windswept mountain.

A few minutes later, Papa embraced them again and headed back towards Rosette. He turned and raised his fist. "*Vive la Republique!*"

The men raised their fists and yelled back. "*Liberté!*"

Papa led her down the hill. "My dear, do not reveal anything you saw or heard today."

"*Oui*, Papa."

Rosette shivered, but she knew it came from more than just the wind. Change had begun to blow across Grenada, and the uncertainty chilled her.

"Papa," she said. "That tall man back there looked like Mr. Turnbull's slave. Everyone thinks that he shot himself more than a year ago. Was that Kojo?"

Chapter Thirty-Two

The change in Governor Ninian Home's deportment surprised Malcolm. He had seen the governor a few times in Grenada, while he was still Speaker of the legislature. But the change in the man, most likely from the grief of losing his wife, took Malcolm by surprise. Governor Home's once upright posture and confident footsteps gave way to a haggard shuffle down the Liverpool ship ramp. He wore a black oversized coat that looked like it would drag behind him, were it not for his high-top boots. He seemed hidden inside his bushy sideburns, his collar upturned against the cool winds, and a thick wool scarf that pillowed his drooping head. He walked older than his mid-sixties might suggest, and held his bag in such labored effort, Malcolm felt compelled to shoulder his way through the waiting crowd to rescue him before he stumbled.

"Welcome to Liverpool, Your Excellency." Malcolm reached for the bag.

Instead of surrendering the bag, Governor Home dropped it at his feet and took Malcolm's extended hand in a feeble handshake.

"I am so pleased you could meet me." The governor's trembling smile lifted neither the sadness in his voice nor the sagging skin under his weary blue eyes.

"It is my deepest honor and privilege, Your Excellency." Malcolm bowed his head respectfully, hoping the formality might improve the governor's state. "My deepest condolences on the sudden passing of Lady Home. She will be greatly missed."

Malcolm escorted him to a waiting carriage which took them to the best hotel Malcolm could find on Scotland Road.

The governor's grieving spirit remained deflated in the following week as Malcolm ushered him to and from meetings with shipping companies and government officials. After they walked out of the last meeting on the harbor front, the governor turned to Malcolm.

"I have an urgent request of you," Governor Home said. "I must return to my country house for a brief visit before returning to Grenada. I would very much desire your company and assistance on that trip to Paxton Estate."

The request raised Malcolm's hope that in the comfort of his country home, the tight-lipped governor might eventually reveal news of Grenada, especially of the Fédon family and Rosette. Or equally important, open the subject of Malcolm's return to the island.

"I am totally at your disposal, Your Excellency," Malcolm said. "I am thrilled that you ask."

A week later, he accompanied the governor on a northbound ship that sailed up the scenic River Clyde. The distant hills, though barren and rocky, still reminded Malcolm of Grenada's more lush terrain. At Glasgow, the governor commissioned a rider to notify his estate staff of his pending arrival with a guest. He also hired a four-wheeled hackney coach, drawn by two horses, for the rugged journey that took them east past Edinburgh. They spent the night in a cozy guesthouse at the seaport of Dunbar, and early next morning headed south.

Despite the rattling wheels and shaky coach, Governor Home dozed for most of the journey in his seat across from Malcolm. His head rolled from side to side like a ball. His face, ashen with grief, troubled Malcolm. How could a man, so distraught by the loss of his wife, profit in a human trade that crushed the lives of millions? Maybe God had taken the governor's wife as punishment.

But surely, Malcolm wondered, if white slaveowners deserved the wrath of God, should not black slave-traders, and brown slaveowners like Monsieur Fédon also face the same consequences? And why would God create men, regardless of color, with such reduced capacity to comprehend the suffering they inflict on others?

Around noon, the coach wheeled onto the streets of Berwick-upon-Tweed and turned inland on the Scottish north bank of the majestic River Tweed. The blue sky and puffs of white clouds mirrored off the sun-glazed river with a serenity that seemed to stop time, gently inviting Malcolm's thoughts to leave his tribulations behind.

Now drawing closer to his estate, the governor sat up rejuvenated, and his eyes sparkled anew with the glare from the river. He pointed out the window. "There she is. Paxton House."

Malcolm peered ahead in the green distance. The brick mansion stood proud with tall windows and commanding pillars, gifted with a grand yet charming presence on a crest overlooking the river and rolling plains beyond. The carriage meandered up the slight hill, past immaculate treed grounds alive with alert deer, chirping birds, and sunny daffodils.

"It is spectacular," Malcolm said.

"Eighty acres to spend my retirement. Miles of the best salmon fishing. I bought the house unfinished in 1773 from my cousin, thanks to the earnings from my Grenada plantations."

Malcolm reflected to himself that God probably created such distant tranquility for men like Governor Home to wash their bloodstained souls from the plantation brutality and human degradation that created their wealth. Maybe only men devoid of guilt could remain unscathed in their tropical Great Houses, surrounded and aroused by the horrors of their own making.

Men like Mr. Turnbull.

That night, Malcolm and Governor Home ate dinner together at the end of a long table covered with white cloth and adorned with sculptured centerpieces. Malcolm counted thirty-eight empty chairs, which faced meticulous table settings of chinaware, silverware, and crystal glasses. The spacious dining room, with luxuriantly large paintings and Persian rugs, glowed under hanging candle-chandeliers.

At the direction of a portly butler, eager kitchen staff moved hastily around the lavish table's end, carving meats and filling plates. Roasted turkey, sausage meat, potatoes, pickles, and stewed celery enriched the air with potent aromas that unleashed Malcolm's appetite. He devoured his first plate and gladly accepted another, bringing a grateful smile from the butler.

Meanwhile, the governor nibbled in a silence disturbed occasionally by hissing and cracking from the blazing fireplace. The only evidence that he was alive came from the clinks of his silverware on his plate and slow movement of his jaws under his powdered silver-gray wig. The man's wealth traveled thousands of miles to buy him the luxuries that embraced him tonight. Yet, they could not penetrate mere inches beneath his skin to lift his spirit. A gloom dampened his presence under his navy-blue jacket and black pantaloons.

Malcolm had enjoyed a warm bath in a room

extravagant with thick towels, back brushes, and fragranced soap. He changed into formal jacket and slacks for the supper that now left him thoroughly satisfied.

Later, the butler ordered them a variety of cheeses, tarts, and puddings, and ensured a steady flow of whiskey for the governor and port wine for Malcolm.

Malcolm would have much preferred Charlotte Turnbull's Spanish wine, and of course, her Spanish honey for his tea. Not desiring to offend the grieving governor by refusing the product which built his wealth, Malcolm sweetened his tea with sugar—but left the cup discretely unattended.

The whiskey must have recharged the governor's mood. After a few glasses, he leaned back in his chair and eyed Malcolm with a scrutinizing glare.

"I wish I had a family, a wife, even a son to whom I can pass all this," the governor said in a raspy voice. "Colonel McDonald will someday have a home like this for you. He is a most fortunate man to have you, a proud officer and fine Englishman."

"Thank you, Your Excellency. I hope he thinks so as well."

The governor sipped his whiskey and scratched at his bushy sideburns. "Mr. Turnbull seems to think otherwise of you."

Malcolm felt no surprise that Mr. Turnbull's rum-soaked dribble had eventually reached the governor's ear. The two men shared business and legislative interests on the island, and Mr. Turnbull regularly chose the governor's Paraclete Estate in Grenada's north for his binge-drinking escapades, including the night Malcolm spent with Charlotte. Malcolm now wondered how much of the man's rum-laced poison had influenced the governor—and Father.

Malcolm chose his response with care. "Mr. Turnbull's impression of me might be prejudiced by unfortunate circumstances. I do believe a renewed acquaintance with him might change his mind."

The lie hung in silence. Honesty be damned. He just wanted the governor to get him back to Grenada.

The governor cleared his throat. "I promised Colonel McDonald I would give him a proper assessment of your fitness to return to duty in Grenada. I must say, despite Mr. Turnbull's skepticism, my last week with you has given me encouragement."

"Thank you, Your Excellency."

The governor wiped his mouth with a cloth napkin, pushed away his mostly untouched plate, and stood. "Come with me."

Malcolm followed the governor down a carpeted hallway wide enough to fit two coaches side by side and decorative ceilings high enough for three men to stand on each other's shoulders. They climbed an elegant spiral staircase to more expansive hallways with candle-lit walls, huge gold-framed mirrors, and paintings.

The governor pointed at some of the paintings as they walked past. "I am sure you recognize *Frederick the Great* by Rosalba Carriera. *The Holy Family* by Antonio del Massaro da Viterbo. *The Madonna and Child with St Jerome* by Galbiani."

A servant pushed heavy double-doors that opened into a library furnished with fine Chippendale chairs, desks, and wall shelves filled with neat rows of books. Sculptured busts and heads shared the walls with more paintings. Malcolm wondered how much more enraged slaves would become if they saw the extravagance squeezed from their sweat and blood.

The governor led him to a wall covered with smaller paintings of an immaculate sugar plantation, its sprawling great house surrounded by palm trees and rolling fields of green.

"That is Paraclete Estate in the north of Grenada," the governor said. "I am proud of what we accomplished there. My slave merchants tell me many of my workers would have been slaughtered by their own kind in Africa. They are better off with me than awaiting massacres back in their jungle villages."

Malcolm held his silence.

The governor shuffled across the library to a large desk. He pulled open a drawer and withdrew a letter, which he handed to Malcolm. "'Tis a copy of a letter I wrote to my Paraclete Estate manager a few years ago."

Malcolm read the letter.

"Sir,

I have learnt with very severe concern that your conduct lately has been in many ways improper... Before I left Grenada, I gave you the best advice I was capable of... Kindness and humanity to the slaves was one of the things I endeavored to impress most strongly in your mind.

"The poor things are so dependent upon the white people over there and so much in their power, that wantonly to use that power is the height of cruelty. A manager of a plantation should consider himself as the father of the slaves, and treat them with tenderness. They are human beings as well as ourselves. I will not keep any overseer that ill treats the negroes in any way."

Malcolm wondered if such compassionate awakenings might be too little too late for Grenada. He handed the letter back to the governor. "Quite profound, sir."

The governor's blue eyes teared up in the candlelight and his lips trembled. "The irony is that while I give humanity to the slaves, a slave ship delivered the Bulam fever in Grenada to take my wife away."

"I am so sorry, sir."

"There is much to learn about this enterprise, my son." He placed his hand on Malcolm's shoulder. "As odious as it seems, our generation did not start it. We received it, with its ills and merits. It is foolish that a dog born with a tail would ask why. Its duty is to learn how to wag it with effect. Our plantation system sustains the British Empire. The Quakers condemn it, but nowhere in the Scripture is it condemned. Now, the French Revolutionaries poison the slaves' minds with visions of freedom. Ideas the slaves never experienced and never would understand. Just look at the calamity these French imbeciles started in Saint Dominique. **They just use the slaves. Promise them freedom. As soon as they claim victory, they will restore slavery. Mark my words.**"

"Do you think they will attempt to do the same in Grenada?"

"We see increasing numbers of suspicious French wanderers on the island. With your father's troops and Dr. Hay's militia in Gouyave, we ship them off to Trinidad just as soon as we find them. We do not need any more of them. The likes of Monsieur Fédon is enough. I cannot wait for him to pack up and join the rest of his siblings in Trinidad."

"But he just purchased Belvidere Estate."

The governor squinted at him. "Eventually, it will revert right back into your father's hands, together with all past payments. You do not think he really wanted to hand over such a magnificent estate to that traitor, do you?"

Chapter Thirty-Three

Dr. Hay pushed the stack of papers into his desk drawer and locked it quickly before his servant answered the heavy banging at the front door. The plump black woman thundered across the living room and pulled open the door, unseen from where he sat in the breezy seafront gallery.

"Dr. Hay." Her voice rose to a high pitch over the sound of waves pounding the shoreline, a sign the visitor was one of considerable importance. "Dr. Hay."

"I will be right there." He slipped the key into his vest pocket, adjusted his glasses on his nose, and hurried to the front entrance. A bit of embarrassment reminded him how much he needed to tidy up his paper-strewn bookshelves and living room, especially for when he received unexpected visitors.

Colonel McDonald stood just outside the door, erect in his uniform—a double-tailed scarlet coatee with close-fitting white pantaloons tucked into his tall riding boots. Under cloudy skies, several other soldiers stood back in the courtyard under the coconut trees, their Brown Bess muskets and fixed bayonets clinking against their swords and water canteens.

"Colonel, what a pleasant surprise." Glad he had secured the papers in his locked desk, Dr. Hay wondered if the colonel might mistake his relief for delight, at yet another of the colonel's unwelcomed intrusions—the third in as many months. If only the colonel knew the desk hid papers that revealed questionable transactions around the Belvidere sale, with his name prominently displayed throughout. "Please, come in."

They shook hands.

Without blinking his cold blue eyes, the colonel removed his black hat in the steady glare that always troubled Dr. Hay, but even more so today.

The colonel cleared his throat as if about to deliver an urgent declaration. "My apologies for the unannounced visit. I made an impromptu call on the militia post. Your sentries told me I might find you at home."

Dr. Hay led the colonel across the untidy drawing room to the gallery at the rear of the house. If he dared ordered his servant to clean up the mess, he might spend the rest of his life trying to find an important medical book or legal document. He had not anticipated his roles as doctor, Justice of the Peace, and Militia head would have him submerged in so much paper. Recent changes in the migration laws only swelled the flow of official papers, as new French residents and visitors had to be rounded up and deported. Suspicion thickened the air over Gouyave as fast as Dr. Hay's stack of deportation orders thickened on his desk.

They sat at the window table, and the servant hurriedly served tea with crumpets. But the colonel's cup and plate remained untouched in front of his stoic composure, rigidly locked in his thick military uniform. Dr. Hay always considered the uniforms too hot and unhealthy for soldiers in the tropics. Despite the sea breeze flowing through the windows, beads of perspiration gathered at the colonel's forehead. His musty odor filled the gallery, though not as putrid as the chamber pot the servant emptied into the sea each morning. Only the ribbon at the tail of his tightly plaited silver hair fluttered in the breeze.

The Colonel struck a match and eyed the departing servant. He lifted a pipe to his open mouth, exposing a dark, chipped tooth, and sucked on the pipe as he fed the flaming match to it. He glowered past the rising smoke. "I wish for our conversation to be private."

Dr. Hay now worried that Colonel McDonald had learned of the confidential letters between him and his cousin in London. Realizing that hesitancy to respond to the colonel's request might betray guilt, Dr. Hay immediately gave the servant some money and sent her off to shop at the market.

When the door shut behind her, the colonel leaned across the table toward Dr. Hay. "I am afraid we are not doing enough to suppress the French revolutionaries here in Gouyave."

"With all due respect, Colonel, pray tell me what more we can do under the law. We already detain and ship out any new French people of suspicious intent."

"Right under your noses here in Gouyave, you have two culprits who wander around, spreading ideas that undermine King and Country."

"If you mean Father Pascal and Bourbon, they are long-term residents. Father Pascal has an unblemished record of service and fellowship to our residents. Despite losing his church and presbytery to the Anglicans. Bourbon is just a vagrant, delivering messages to pay for his drinking. He spends half his life recovering under that tree by the church."

"I have a confidant in Grenville who saw Bourbon board a ship for Guadalupe and returned two weeks later in the accompaniment of French-speaking newcomers."

"I understand your concern, Colonel. But should not the Grenville port be under the jurisdiction of their militia?"

The colonel slammed the table. "What happens in Grenville affects us all."

Dr. Hay leaned back in his chair and adjusted his vest. "Colonel, you have my word that we are doing our utmost to forestall any suspicious activities."

"Good. Governor Home is back on the island. He expects nothing less. He will be travelling by in a few days to visit his Paraclete Estate, along with Mr. Turnbull."

"I will ensure proper security and an escort."

The colonel puffed his pipe and watched the smoke twirl into the drawing room with the breeze blowing through the window. "The governor—"

A loose stone outside clapped its way down to the sea. The colonel glanced quickly out the window. A seagull screeched past. A wave roared ashore, its crash drowning out echoes from yelling sailors and flapping sails on ships that bobbed along the pier. Stones clattered with the retreating wave. Horses clopped on the stone road past the open window at the far end of the gallery. All the sounds that had become so ordinary to Dr. Hay, they no longer begged for the urgent attention the colonel displayed.

Apparently deciding his suspicions of prowling ears lacked merit, the colonel continued. "The governor also indulged me to assign a new training officer for your Gouyave militia. I expect equal diligence from him as I do of you."

Dr. Hay leaned forward over the table. "I am confident that you and Governor Home would approve a fine officer."

"Of course. And I expect the new officer to be also weary of the French, especially that mongrel in Belvidere. I can hardly wait for them to be long gone from the island."

Dr. Hay suspected the colonel had a personal reason for the visit. But he had to be sure. "Is it premature for me to know who this officer might be?"

The colonel sucked on his pipe, letting the smoke escape with the breeze across the drawing room. "He should be arriving from Liverpool in a fortnight or so. Captain Malcolm McDonald."

Rosette knew the day of reckoning loomed close. The number of cutlasses, spikes and other weapons outnumbered the likes of anything she had ever seen. Some arrived in burlap bags strapped to horseback, but most came in open carts driven by Uncle Jean-Pierre's men. Papa's workers carried them up the hill to the camp in chattering clanks of metal. She also knew their purposes but sought comfort in Papa's words that they may not be needed.

The British had muskets and cannons.

The people had cutlasses. But the slaves outnumbered the Englishmen twenty to one.

Papa assured her that the slaves and *gens de couleur* would overwhelm the British in days. They would surrender—without the need for catastrophic bloodshed. French Republicans stood ready to reinforce the rebels with regular French soldiers and weapons. Furthermore, with the Bulam fever spreading among the congested population in St. George's and undermining their will to fight, Governor Home would have no choice. He would quickly give up, sparing his fellow countrymen the massacres that befell Saint Dominique.

"We have no need to attack St. George's," he said. "Thanks to the information you retrieved, about the number of cannons on the forts, we decided a frontal attack on the city would be catastrophic. If we control the rest of the island, the city will strangle."

Papa had said it would serve the interests of both the British and the French if the British surrendered before they lost control of the slaves.

That was a fire no one wanted.

He had shown her the letters from the French Commissar in Guadalupe, Victor Hugues. Hugues had kicked the British out of Guadalupe with the same strategy of using the slaves as a weapon. Now, the French revolutionaries prepared to do in Grenada what worked for them before. From all the way in Paris, they approved Papa as the Commandant-General for the Grenada revolution.

Up in the camp, Papa had shown her on their return from the Mt. Qua Qua climb, were the plans, the men, the weapons that would change Grenada for the better. They would reverse the offensive laws and restore dignity and humanity to the *gens de couleur* and slaves.

Liberté, egalité, fraternité.

Her anticipation grew with each passing day. In a strange way, it comforted the ache that throbbed in her heart whenever she thought of Malcolm. The more she indulged her attention on the new dawn Papa prepared for Grenada, the more her memories of Malcolm seemed to fade into a foggy distant past—and the more her present burned with exhilaration. This day, she could no longer resist the temptation to return to Papa's camp.

When she saw one of the house servants carrying two pails of water up the hill, she raced after her to help.

The woman looked nervous. "Massa Fédon be vex if I take you up there."

"Do not worry." Rosette reached for a pail. "Here, let me take one of those."

When they struggled into the encampment thirty minutes later, sweating and heaving, Papa plodded towards her in his muddy boots and sweaty shirt. His jaws bulged as he chewed mercilessly on his unlit cigar.

"Young lady," he yelled. "You are very stubborn. You do not belong here."

"Sorry, Papa." Rosette stepped between him and the terrified servant. "She told me to go back home, but I had to see."

Uncle Jean-Pierre must have heard their raised voices from where he stood in the doorway to the shack. He hurried over, saving her from what could have been a humiliating scolding.

"My princess." He hugged her warmly. "Your Papa has great respect for you. You are as strong as you are smart."

Papa chuckled, and his agitation seemed to dissipate. He looked around the camp.

Relieved, she followed his gaze. Men sharpened cutlasses, burned and shaped tree limbs into spikes, and cleaned muskets. Between the trees for as far as she could see, women dug holes and plucked dasheen roots from the ground. Others stirred huge steaming pots balanced on rocks over crackling fires. Boiling plantains sweetened the cool mountain air.

"By the way," Papa said. "That young English officer you foolishly befriended is returning, to take up a post in Gouyave. For his own good, I hope he arrives too late and never steps foot on Belvidere."

Her heart sped, even though she knew it was all for naught. Malcolm had betrayed her deepest trust and Papa would never forget that. While she longed to unleash her anger at Malcolm, his return—in the face of Papa's temper, or during a French takeover—might have dangerous consequences for him as a British officer. She did not hate him sufficiently to reap gratification from his pain. She just wished Grandmère was still alive to explain why love and hate made such close neighbors. Her own mother, Maman, seemed entirely too preoccupied with Papa's sleeplessness and low appetite to be concerned with Rosette's disastrous infatuation with a white man.

Rosette's bitterness towards Malcolm had not risen to such a boiling point that she would want him dead if she came face-to-face with him.

Papa might, but not her—not yet.

"Papa, I no longer care to know his whereabouts," she lied.

Papa placed his hand on her shoulder. "Good girl. He is as much a white devil as his father."

A glimmer of curiosity lingered. "But how did you learn of his imminent return?"

Papa chewed his cigar. "We have eyes and ears everywhere. Even in Dr. Hay's house."

The sound of clinking metal awakened Dr. Hay in his upstairs bedroom. He glanced at his clock, bathed in moonlight on the window table facing the sea. Two o'clock. The noise subsided. A breeze rustled the coconut trees along the shore and charmed his thin window curtains into a silent dance.

He listened.

Nothing.

He shut his eyes and prayed for sleep to return.

Maybe paranoia had gotten the best of him. Earlier that afternoon, a few English residents alerted him of their suspicions. Rumors abounded of a secret meeting at Julien Fédon's Belvidere home. Dr. Hay noticed that the street outside the gallery window seemed unusually quiet, and some of his French neighbors had their courtyard doors and windows shut most of the day. One Englishman even told him of a canoe pulling up to the pier with two men heretofore not seen in Gouyave.

Dr. Hay considered calling up the St. John's militia, but since the parish stretched ten miles from north to south, he doubted the troops would arrive at the post before dawn anyway. Of the one hundred and eighty troops under his command, he trusted maybe forty-five, those being His Majesty's natural born subjects. The remainder consisted of French adopted subjects and free people of color, all with doubtful loyalties to the British flag.

He wished he had a capable officer such as Captain McDonald, with whom he could plan preemptive measures tonight. For that, he would have to wait another week before the ship arrived from Liverpool.

He retired to bed around eleven o'clock but tossed and

turned in bed, for how long, he knew not. But eventually, he had fallen into a troubled sleep, with a sense of approaching dread—until those strange metallic sounds awakened him at two o'clock.

He believed now all he needed to do was calm his imagination. He adjusted his pillow and prepared to return to sleep with the help of the gentle breeze and soft moonlight.

Just then, through his window overlooking the courtyard, came footsteps and muffled voices.

He rolled out of bed and peeked past the curtains.

In the courtyard below, an untold number of men. Cutlasses and muskets glistened in the silver light. The group moved in unison, like an enlarged beast, slowly crowding towards his front door.

Oh, Merciful God Almighty, no. His worst suspicions had come true.

Fierce banging at his door shook the house.

Visions of human slaughter swarmed his mind. He had read about the bloody slave uprisings in Saint Dominique. Whites dragged from their beds and chopped mercilessly in streets that ran red with blood. The fear climbed to his throat. He swallowed.

He had to act. Quickly.

A strong voice drummed the night. "Open up before we burn you out."

With no time to change out of his nightshirt, he hurriedly grabbed two pistols and his keys hanging on the bedroom wall. Barefoot, he tiptoed down the wooden stair, slowing when it creaked.

More hammering on the door. "We hear you in there."

He crept past the front door and across the gallery to the window that opened over the quiet street. He climbed out and landed awkwardly on the stone sidewalk. He ran across the street but froze before he reached the other side.

A mob of men—some colored, some black, some he recognized—immediately emerged from the shadows and into the moonlight, muskets and cutlasses at the ready.

"Grab him," one shouted.

"Kill *L'Anglais*," another yelled.

Realizing the folly of attempting to outgun so many, Dr. Hay lowered his pistols and submitted to his fate.

A young mulatto man Dr. Hay knew casually as Lavallée, broke from the crowd, a bayonet affixed to his musket. Dressed in pale yellowish nankeen cotton and gold epaulettes, he lunged at Dr. Hay. The sharp tip of the bayonet pierced Dr. Hay's arm. He screamed and dropped his pistols to the street. Blood oozed down his arm and dripped in warm splats on his bare foot.

He recalled that July night in 1779 when he had cheated death during the French attack on St. George's.

He resigned himself to the awful truth.

He may not cheat death a second time.

"Kill *L'Anglais*," the men screeched. "*Vive La Republique*!"

House windows opened along the street. The attending French free colored women pointed at his undressed state and laughed with much satisfaction.

His deteriorating prospects received a frantically needed boost when his servant huffed through the attackers with reassuring boldness. She appeared annoyed, surely at the commotion that would have awakened her in her little outside room attached to the far end of his house. But more certainly at the ruffians who suffered indignations upon Dr. Hay, the man who successfully applied for her freedom to be in his employment. He waited precious seconds for her divine intervention to rescue him.

Instead, she pointed a stubby finger at him and shouted. "Look the pockets for keys. He have guns and powder lockup in the cellar."

His jaw lowered in disbelief. "This, after I purchased your freedom?"

Fury spat out with her words. "I born free. You people thief it. Tonight, I take it back."

He stared into her eyes, hoping some glimmer of memory might return her to the day he applied medicine on the whip slashes she suffered from her previous owner. Or the nights he doctored her fever, or the tears of joy they both shed that day he showed her the Certificate of Freedom he penned and signed to authorize her new status as a free black woman. But the anger in her eyes did not belong to the same woman who shared his roof and sanctuary these past five years. How did such potent wrath go undetected under her cotton-soft demeanor and submissive devotion?

Obviously, slavery had assaulted her inner core. Deeper than he could see or feel.

His hopes shattered in a nauseating mix of disgust and fear.

Another man walked up with a pistol in one hand and a blazing torch in the other, his sweaty dark face and raging eyes aglow in the light. He wore the same circular red, blue, and white French cockade in his hat as the other men. They parted and let him through.

"Our French brothers have landed in Grenville," he yelled. "We have no more use for *L'Anglais* pigs." He pulled the keys out of Dr. Hay's pocket and handed them to the servant. "Open every door and drawer for the men."

With the keys jingling at her side, she led several men towards the front door.

The man held his torch high and turned to the crowd. "Who among you deserves to dispatch this Englishman?"

Lavallée squeezed past the man, pulling a pistol from his waist. He cocked it and placed it at Dr. Hay's head.

Dr. Hay closed his eyes, whispering a prayer for speedy deliverance.

"No." A familiar voice rose with authority over the street. "Leave that one for General Fédon."

Dr. Hay squinted past the torchlight at the big man marching out of the night.

"Kojo?"

Chapter Thirty-Four

On the street outside Dr. Hay's house, the fiery Lavallée waved his pistol in the doctor's face. "Liar you are. Turnbull rode past in his carriage yesterday. Was tyrant Governor Home with him?"

Kojo grabbed Lavallée's pistol arm with one hand and, with the other, held his cutlass to the man's neck. "Stop before I chop off your head."

No one, not even Lavallée, wanted Massa Turnbull more than Kojo did. The anger rolled like thunder on the back of his memories. He recalled how easy he could have removed Massa's head the day Venus went to meet her ancestors, and took the baby with her. He was standing just feet behind Massa with his hands locked on the handle of his sharpened cutlass. But Madame Turnbull stepped up to Kojo, touched his hand and stared into his face with her teary eyes. Just long enough for Kojo's head to calm his heart.

A dead Massa and a runaway Kojo might bring British dogs, muskets, and cannons into the jungle interior. Simon and his runaway maroons would have been butchered. And General Fédon would have been fighting in Grenville at that very moment without them.

Kojo glared at Dr. Hay. "Where Massa Turnbull?"

Kojo had waited for this day for many moons, but especially since the day he begged Massa to let him flog Venus. *Let me do it, Massa. Please, let me do it, Massa.* To save her from an even more brutal attack at Massa Turnbull's wicked hands, and the wicked choices he gave his slaves.

Pain or more pain.

She would have been in more pain, if not for that young Englishman, who stopped him and earned a pistol-pounding to the head from Massa Turnbull.

Kojo recalled Venus sobbing on the mud floor, her back shredded by his own hands, and her belly swollen with a baby he thought came from his own seed. Under pale candlelight, she allowed him to apply honey to her ripped skin. He even stayed awake to keep prowling rats away from her raw flesh.

Tonight, in the street outside Dr. Hay's house, with the sounds of rebellion in the air, Kojo recalled Venus's labored breathing, the putrid medicinal paste, Lovely in her filthy yellow dress. Madame Turnbull holding his hands to apply honey to the wounds. Then came that shocking day—the screams from the great house, the rope stretching from the ceiling, and motionless little white feet protruding from the baby basket on the polished table.

That was how Kojo learned Massa Turnbull had planted his ugly seed in Venus.

Venus did not take her life. She sacrificed it, like a warrior in battle. Her weapon? The truth. Although she did not die removing Massa's heart, she removed the next best thing from him—his wife.

She honored her ancestors.

Tonight, Kojo aimed to help her complete the task. He needed Dr. Hay to help him find Massa Turnbull.

"I know nothing of Mr. Turnbull's whereabouts." Dr. Hay stared at the blood dripping from his arm and spreading around his feet. "Do you wish I die this way? I will need a piece of rope, yarn, or cloth to stop the bleeding."

Kojo yanked a piece of Dr. Hay's shirt and tied it around his arm. "Massa Turnbull ride here yesterday?"

Dr. Hay looked into Kojo's eyes. "Mr. Turnbull and I are hardly friends. I heard he rode past on his way north. But I did not see him, and do not know his destination."

"Ha-ha," Lavallée shouted. "I bet with that tyrant governor."

"No," Dr. Hay said. "I heard it was just Turnbull in the carriage, with his little girl, Lovely."

A few minutes later, Kojo led Dr. Hay towards the house for a change of clothes. They shouldered through the growing crowd, past blazing torches and loud threats.

"Stay with me, "Kojo said. "Monsieur Fédon want you safe in Belvidere."

They entered the chaotic house. Men rummaged through Dr. Hay's kitchen wares, books, and desk drawers. Others tramped out the door with Dr. Hay's muskets, powder, wine, and his militia flag. Books and papers lay scattered across the floor. When his servant leaned over to unlock the top drawer of his desk, Dr. Hay lunged towards her, his eyes wide with panic.

"No," he shouted. "Those are my papers...my letters."

Lavallée charged towards him with a fixed bayonet. Kojo quickly stepped between them and pushed the revolutionary away. Kojo never understood why white people valued papers so much. Massa Turnbull used paper to buy and sell African brothers and sisters. He used paper to sell sugar. He even used paper to remember the words of their god, in a book they called the Bible. Kojo had nothing but disdain for the god and paper ways of the white man that only brought pain to the black man.

He grabbed Dr. Hay by his shoulder. "Forget papers. Get clothes."

Kojo followed the doctor upstairs to his chamber and watched as he untied the cloth from around his arm. He handed Kojo a length of yarn rope to replace it. Kojo tied it off and held the shirt sleeve up for the doctor to medicate his own bayonet wound.

Dressed now in a loose shirt, gray pantaloons, and black boots, Dr. Hay reached into a trunk and pulled out a handful of paper money and coins. He attempted to hand the money to Kojo.

"For safekeeping," Dr. Hay said. "When this is over, I will give you some."

He shoved them into Dr. Hay's vest pocket where his watch sat. "I no want no money."

They headed downstairs. A few revolutionaries remained, scavenging through the kitchen. The desk laid tipped over on its side, open and empty. Dr. Hay's servant gone. Dismay seemed to burden his shoulders.

Kojo watched Dr. Hay shuffle through the drawing room scooping up papers and books off the floor. The doctor stuffed them into a small box with pens, ink, and a few personal belongings. He pushed the box aside but held on to a few clothing items and blank pages of paper which he inserted into his medical satchel.

He faced Kojo like a hungry dog begging for food. "Can I take this?"

Kojo nodded.

Dr. Hay sheepishly headed out the door, adjusting his hat in the night breeze. Kojo led him across the courtyard and into the boisterous street. The crowd had grown, with more freedom fighters threatening more white prisoners.

A few minutes later, a mulatto on horseback gave the order to begin the march to Belvidere. He led the group out of Gouyave, waving a French Revolutionary Army flag high against the moonlit sky. In big bold letters across the flag, the words *Liberté, Égalité, Fraternité, ou la Mort.*

Kojo turned to Dr. Hay and pointed at the flag. "What that mean?"

"Liberty, equality, or death."

"I die for one. Liberty."

Despite Kojo's high spirits now that freedom loomed ahead, he felt a tinge of sorrow for Dr. Hay. The doctor hobbled in his boots with some difficulty, having hurt his foot when he jumped from the window. He had always treated Kojo as a man, not a slave. When they reached the first river, Kojo hoisted him on his back and carried him across the rushing water, the slippery stones being no threat to Kojo's broad leathery feet.

"Thank you, Kojo," Dr. Hay said when Kojo landed him on the other bank.

"Sah," Kojo said. "Me do it because me want to. Not because me fraid not to."

The sound of river turbulence, shuffling feet, and clinking weapons filled the silence between the two men.

Kojo's act of generosity felt liberating, without being ordered, without fear, of his own making, his own choice. Freedom. The reason he ran away from Masa Turnbull. The same day he tearfully buried Venus and the baby. The reason he faked his own death with the blood of a wild animal, so Massa would believe him dead in the jungle.

Kojo had returned to the great house that night. Crept through an open kitchen window. Slowly opened the closet where Massa kept his work clothes and keys. Kojo freed the three new slaves, the young mother and the two men. He convinced them to wait for him while he relocked the gates and returned the keys. Then he led them up the mountains to join Simon and the maroons.

To wait and prepare for this night of liberation.

Tonight, after two seasons of agonizing patience, Kojo's dream had come true. Shango, the god of revenge, had for years nurtured Kojo's temperance for this day.

Kojo was now the hunter, and Massa, the prey.

The scream sliced the misty sunrise and jolted Kojo, just as the lengthening trail of rebels and prisoners reached the Belvidere Estate great house.

They had walked all night, with Dr. Hay at Kojo's side, stopping only to pick up more slaves who abandoned their estates and captured their masters. Most of the prisoners still wore sleep shirts that stopped at their knees and exposed pale legs. The news of the rebellion spread like the fires licking into the sky from hilltop great houses and surrounding fields. All night, at the constant urgings of French mulattos, the triumphant yells of *"Vive La Republique!"* rang in Kojo's ears.

He wondered if the rebellion was for the slaves—or for France.

Kojo turned towards the scream. A horse galloped towards them, a girl barely hanging on. Desperation masked her brown face. She wore a red dress around her pudgy frame, and one of her legs seemed too short to reach the leather stirrups. He recognized the horse immediately, Madame Turnbull's mare that Kojo had groomed and saddled so many times in Beauséjour. The horse must have recognized him too. It pulled up alongside him, and the girl rolled off, right into Kojo's waiting hands.

She felt hot and sweaty, even in the cool air.

"Lovely?" he asked.

She opened her eyes ever so slightly. "If I see you, it be I dead too?"

"No, I live. You live too."

"Even Massa thought you dead."

"Not all thought is so." He carried her to the verandah steps and sat with her cradled in his arms.

Dr. Hay checked her pulse and cupped her cheek in his palm.

"Severe fever," he said. "Could be Bulam. We must get her out of this mist immediately."

The front door flew open, and Monsieur Fédon's daughter ran out. "What happened to her?"

"Massa in Paraclete Estate." Lovely's voice barely made it higher than a whisper. "I run away. I want talk Monsieur Fédon."

"He is not here. You can talk to me."

Kojo worried General Fédon had not yet returned from Grenville, the scene of the other attack on the British. Had the British defeated the mighty general?

Lovely's eyes closed. Her breaths came in short wheezes. She spat a dark fluid.

Dr. Hay turned to Monsieur Fédon's daughter. "We must get her inside. I need boiling water and rosemary bush."

Kojo stood with Lovely in his arms and followed Monsieur Fédon's daughter up the steps. He paused at the front door.

Monsieur Fédon's daughter turned to him. "It is quite all right, Kojo. You can come in."

He wondered how she knew his name. He did not know hers. "Thank you, Miss..."

"Rosette."

"Thank you, Miss Rosette."

He and Dr. Hay gently placed Lovely on a couch, while Rosette puffed a pillow for her.

Madame Fédon offered them coffee, which only Dr. Hay accepted. When a kitchen boy showed up with the steaming cup that scented the room with a rich aroma, Dr. Hay handed him a coin from his pocket. No sooner had the boy disappeared into the kitchen, he returned.

He handed Dr. Hay a piece of bread and the money. "Madame Fédon say no money."

Kojo turned his attention to Lovely. He had last seen her that morning in Massa Turnbull's dining room. Now, she seemed more grown in the ways of a woman. Round breasts pushed out against her red dress where once a dingy yellow dress covered a flat chest. And where she once had a skeletal frame, she now had a full belly.

She must have noticed his puzzled curiosity. She took his hand and held it to her protruding stomach.

A tear ran down her cheek, and her chin trembled. "Massa make baby."

Kojo tightened his jaw in anger. Massa was wicked. Now Massa crazy. He done plant baby seed in his own offspring.

Chapter Thirty-Five

Rosette left Lovely asleep on the couch and rushed out the door when yells of '*Vive la Republique!*' and '*Vive Le General*' rose up the hill. Her heart leaped with joy at the sight of Papa, having worried about him all night since he and Uncle Jean-Pierre rode off with dozens of armed men into the full moon shadows. Papa rode proud and high on his white horse. Behind him several other riders, *gens de couleur libres* and white men in uniform, waving national flags of the French Republic. Among them, Bourbon trotted a new horse and looked more like an alert soldier in his black cocked hat than the drunkard she thought she knew.

A huge crowd followed, choking the roadway as far as she could see between the trees. Their singing took wings over the trees and echoed off the hillside in an uplifting chorus that gave her the chills.

She now knew for sure—the Grenada Revolution had begun.

She recalled sitting on this very spot on the verandah, talking to Malcolm. They had talked about the Shango drumming and dancing, and she explained how the ceremony gave the Africans courage to face their uncertain future. Shango energy of justice and revenge had come alive today, with Papa as the leader.

Papa dismounted at the base of the steps. Maman joined Rosette on the verandah, and they ran down to greet him. His eyes glistened with intensity, but he held a stiff posture, chewed his cigar with vigor, and kept a cold distance from Rosette and Maman. Despite his typical coarse demeanor, he appeared even more so this morning, like a man changed by what he had seen—or done.

He directed his men, some wearing scanty blood-splattered rags, to take their prisoners up to the camp where the Gouyave prisoners were already locked up in boucans. Uncle Jean-Pierre pointed the people to thatched-roof shelters around the estate where boiling pots scented the hillsides with the sweetness of plantains. Papa and Uncle Jean-Pierre climbed the steps with Bourbon and a few of the French soldiers. They chatted briefly with Kojo, bareback with a red bandana around his head, and other mulattos in uniform.

Then Papa turned and watched the crowd flow past, men, women, and children in a victory parade. They waved at Papa, their black faces aglow with joy. Some sang. Some played the fiddle. Some led cows and goats. Others carried bundles of clothes, food, blankets. But together, they carried a spirit of liberation long denied them.

If only Malcolm could share this moment with her. Not as an Englishman. Not as a soldier. But he as a man. She as a woman. She wanted to be one with him, to experience this height of exhilaration together.

But Malcolm was now the enemy.

The disappointment tugged her heart. For relief, she lost her attention on the singing crowd.

So enthralling the scene, Rosette almost forgot she had

an important message to deliver. She squeezed past Bourbon and reached for Papa's hand.

"Papa, I must talk to you."

He pulled away his hand. "Not now, my dear."

"'Tis about the governor and Mr. Turnbull."

He whipped around. "Why did you not say so?"

Papa, Uncle Jean-Pierre, and Kojo followed her into the living room, where Lovely slept on the couch.

Dr. Hay sat nearby under the scornful eyes of Lavallée. They stood as Papa entered.

He nodded at them without handshakes and faced Dr. Hay. "I hope Madame Fédon has extended her best hospitality to you."

"She has. And Rosette as well, under the circumstances."

"I dare say, Doctor, you must understand our circumstances more deeply than all the other Englishmen on the island."

"What I wish for is harmony between our people."

Papa chewed his cigar. "On this, we have full agreement. Unfortunately, to cook and enjoy an egg, the shell must be broken."

Rosette nudged her father slightly on his elbow. "Papa, excuse—"

He pointed at Lovely. "Who is she?"

"Her name is Lovely, Mr. Turnbull's daughter. She travelled to Paraclete with him yesterday. She said the governor was already there with friends, Assemblyman Alexander Campbell, and others. She said they received an alarm last night that French soldiers had landed in Grenville."

Papa glanced over at Jean-Pierre and grinned. "It worked. 'Tis what we hoped they would believe."

"Papa," Rosette said, "the governor sent a fast rider to St. George's with an order for Colonel McDonald to organize reinforcements. They sent boats to other islands like Martinique to request emergency help. The governor and his group left Paraclete to get on a sloop named *New Diamond*. They are sailing to Gouyave because they do not yet know that it is in the hands of revolutionaries."

Papa squinted at Rosette. "Why would Turnbull's daughter give away such valuable information?"

Kojo cleared his throat. "Monsieur...General Fédon, Sah. I know her since a baby. Massa Turnbull kill she mother in the sugar mill. The girl have baby in she belly for she own father. She want him dead too. She ride horse all night with fever, over mountain and river, to tell us."

Papa removed his cigar. "We must not waste any more time. Madame Josephina was right. We have a prize to collect from the north."

It now appeared the Shango woman's prediction for the first three points of the cross might come true in the first day. Papa already had victories in Gouyave and Grenville. If he captured the governor and his officials, Papa would never have to escape south to the fourth point for deliverance.

Victory for Papa meant defeat for the British, which meant she would never see Malcolm again.

Kojo worried that the plan to capture the tyrant Governor Home and Mr. Turnbull seemed too simple. In the midmorning heat, he hoisted the British flag over the abandoned Gouyave militia post, which overlooked the sea and Father Pascal's empty church. He rode down the deserted stone road to Dr. Hay's house and pulled another Union Jack up the rooftop pole. As Jean-Pierre instructed him earlier, he hastened south to meet him at the next bay, among a row of canoes concealed between the trees. There, Jean-Pierre hid with a force of eager revolutionaries.

From the sea, and despite the two flags, Gouyave might have appeared suspiciously quiet for a Tuesday. No shoppers. No horseback riders. No women or children. Even the dogs stayed off the streets. If the *New Diamond*'s captain ignored those signs and pulled up to the jetty, another armed group waited out of sight in Dr. Hay's house and courtyard.

However, if the Englishmen suspected a trap and continued south, Jean-Pierre's group would launch their canoes to cut them off and board their sloop. But even a single-mast sloop would out-run any canoe.

Kojo kept his doubts to himself and waited.

He did not have to wait for long.

Wearing a blue French coat and black cocked hat, Jean-Pierre adjusted his long glass and hollered. "Here they come."

In the distance, a single-sailed vessel rounded the point and hugged the shoreline. It slowed outside of the town, but remained offshore, gliding a steady route past the jetty.

"Prepare to launch," Jean-Pierre shouted at the men crouching in the sand behind their canoes.

The sloop sailed passed the town and made a slight turn towards the shore.

Jean-Pierre held up his hand. "Wait. They suspect something."

The sloop dropped sail, and an anchor splashed overboard. The crew lowered a small boat, and several men climbed in, a few with muskets. Oars stretched out, and the men began to row towards the shore.

"Now." Jean-Pierre ordered.

His men roared down to the water carrying their canoes. Kojo jumped into one and pulled his cutlass. The convoy of canoes sliced across the blue water towards the sloop and the small boat. The leading canoe fired off a volley of gunshots.

The remaining men aboard the sloop began to scamper about. They pulled up the anchor and the sail. The sloop drifted seaward. The wind filled the sail, and the sloop picked up speed, away from the canoes and away from the small boat.

The men on the small boat turned it around and began to row vigorously towards the fleeing sloop, now headed out to sea with increasing haste.

More gunshots from the canoes.

The men in the small boat stopped rowing and placed their hands in the air. The canoes circled the boat.

It did not take long for Kojo to recognize Massa Turnbull amid other dignified white men. Just as Monsieur Fédon said, the north delivered a big prize.

Massa looked at Kojo like he had seen a ghost.

Kojo tightened his grip on his cutlass.

Chapter Thirty-Six

Malcolm's officer friends liked to use Martinique as the most compelling reason for King George to seize and keep as many of the sugar-rich islands as possible—regardless of the cost in blood. Now three weeks after departing Liverpool, Malcolm would see for himself as his ship sailed into Martinique's Fort Royal, his final port call before Grenada. He recalled Rosette telling him that her late grandmother, Monsieur Fédon's mother, had come from this green mountainous island, equally treasured by France and Britain. An island that had seen its share of hurricanes, earthquakes, naval battles, land invasions, and slave revolts.

On the peninsula guarding the entrance to Fort Royal, massive stone fortifications watched over the harbor. They reminded Malcolm of a recent conversation with friends at a smoky Liverpool pub. Over drinks, they laughed about how Britain invaded and captured Martinique in 1762, only to trade it and the neighboring Guadalupe back to France.

In exchange for those two islands, France gave Britain all of Canada. And, just a couple of years ago, the Martinique Assembly, made up of wealthy estate owners, invited the British to reoccupy the island rather than have their slaves freed by the reckless French revolutionaries.

One of the soldiers in the Liverpool pub laughed. "Captain McDonald, when you make your port call in Martinique, please tell any French Revolutionaries you find there, they can only give us Canada once. If they want Martinique returned to them, do they have a continent to offer this time?"

The thunderous laughter faded in Malcolm's memory, his attention more absorbed on Grenada, and what it would be like to see Rosette again. He worried though, would she ever want to set eyes on him after so many months without a written word from him? If she allowed him but a few minutes to explain his sudden departure from Grenada, might she forgive him for any anguish it caused?

But larger obstacles might await him. Certainly, Mr. Turnbull would reignite his animosity, especially if Malcolm's infatuation with Rosette blossomed into a deeper relationship. For sure, Governor Home and Father would be less than accepting of a McDonald in love with a Fédon.

It surprised him that he allowed his thoughts to be so frank about love.

Maybe because his arrival in the warm islands, so much closer to Rosette, strengthened his equally warm sentiments for her. How else could he explain why his fondness for her persevered during his bleak, lonely months in Liverpool, through foggy winter days, and windy summer storms?

In late afternoon sunlight, he stood next to a lifeboat on the port side and held on to a hanging rope as his ship breezed into the congested harbor. It closed in on a pier teeming with soldiers hurrying towards a waiting ship. Several squads pushed and pulled wheeled cannons up ramps. Donkeys pulled wagons loaded with bagged supplies.

All in frantic haste.

His ship nestled up against the pier. One of the sailors yelled to a dock worker securing the ropes. "Ahoy, there. What is the hustle and bustle yonder?"

"They are headed to Grenada to put down a slave rebellion. The bloody island is on fire."

The words so shocked Malcolm, he almost fell overboard. He leaned over the side of the ship and called out to the dock worker. "Any idea who started it?"

"A mad man named Fédon. Even owns slaves and an estate called Belvidere. They pulled English people from their beds in Grenville and killed them in the streets. Governor Home and forty others are prisoners. Fédon swears to remove their heads if the British do not surrender."

The high plumes of smoke rising from Grenada distressed Malcolm. Even from where he stood on the *Beaulieu* sailing south along the island on the way to St. George's, visible flames hungrily devoured mansions and boiler houses. Where rolling green acreage of cultivated fields once flourished, black wasteland smoldered like a sea of burnt meat. The sinking sun behind him swept a misty red against the hillsides, so red, it looked like the entire island was aflame.

After hearing the news of Monsieur Fédon's rebellion, Malcolm had decided to seek immediate passage on the *Beaulieu*, one of the navy ships hurriedly preparing to depart for Grenada. Otherwise, he would have had to remain in Fort Royal another three or more days while the ship that carried him from Liverpool offloaded merchandise from England and restocked supplies for the Grenada leg.

The Army major in charge of boarding the soldiers for Grenada regarded Malcolm with skepticism. "Captain, I have had a mammoth task rounding up troops from the Ninth and Sixteenth Regiments for this mission. You are the first and only one to request, with such enthusiasm, to go to an island burning with fevers, fires, and death."

"My new assignment is with the Gouyave militia," Malcolm said. "I am sure I will be needed there."

He left out the fact that his father, Colonel McDonald, commanded the regular troops on the island. Malcolm felt no compulsion to discuss with the major whether his wish to reunite with his own father might be behind his urgency to transfer to the navy ship. Indeed, it surprised him how strongly his need to see Rosette displaced any motivation he might have otherwise felt to be at Father's side again.

The major penned Malcolm's name in his log. "I am sure General Lindsay would be overjoyed to have you in his ranks."

"General Colin Lindsay, from the Gibraltar siege?"

"Yes, Grenada is vital to the Crown. They are sending the best to crush those savages. Welcome aboard."

The ship rushed him past the burning island now, but not fast enough to outrun the scent of the smoky breeze. It intensified his concern for Rosette's safety. She would no doubt firmly support her father's rebellion. The major called them all savages. Would Malcolm have thought the same had he not met the Fédon family?

The Monsieur Fédon he knew was hardly a savage. Did Fédon hate the British and the Anglican church? Yes, with reasonable justification. Did he hate slavery? He and his family thrived off slavery all his life, although without the savagery practiced by those like Mr. Turnbull.

Savagery.

How ironic, Malcolm thought. The British did not see in themselves, the very thing they despised most about the other side.

If the British, under seasoned warriors like Colonel McDonald and General Lindsay responded with overwhelming force against the rebellion, Rosette and her family would be in grave danger.

He had no idea how, but he needed to rescue her from the chaos—before it got worse.

That night, Malcolm marched through the doorway of the Fort George planning office in St. George's. He snapped to attention, his heart pounding with anxiety. "Captain McDonald reporting for duty, sir."

Father kept his focus on the maps spread across the table before him. General Lindsay and several other officers stood around him in the yellow lamplight, all in glittering military regalia. The general, tall with slender features, wore bushy sideburns like an unwelcomed addition to his face. Earlier that evening, Malcolm had watched the general disembark from the *Beaulieu* onto the St. George's waterfront, where residents hurried around in panic. The panic, from the bloody rebellion that now controlled the entire island except St. George's, seemed to have wafted up the hill from the smelly port and seeped through the fort walls into the room.

The tension felt thick enough to slice with a sword.

Among the solemn circle of officers, the general was the first to acknowledge Malcolm's presence. He glanced at Father and then at Malcolm. "I must say, given your name and handsome features, you two share some family connection."

Despite not seeing each other for more than a year, Father looked up grudgingly and glared at Malcolm for what seemed like enough time to ride a horse to Belvidere.

"Gentlemen," Father said. "This is Captain McDonald, fresh from Liverpool. He has personal knowledge of Gouyave, Belvidere, and, if I dare admit—the traitor, Commandant-General Fédon. Captain McDonald would be most resourceful in crushing those negroes."

Father did not mention that Malcolm was his son. And Malcolm thought it not in his place to reveal this as he shook hands with the general and other officers.

Father handed him a hand-written page. "You might want to read this from the governor, dictated by Fédon, of course."

> *Gentlemen,*
>
> *General Julien Fédon, Commander of the French Republican troops (which are now of considerable number), and the prisoners held at Belvidere, who are forty-three in number, have requested that I acquaint you with the said General Fédon's positive declaration made to me and the rest of the prisoners, which is briefly as follows: "That the instant an attack is made on the post where the prisoners are now confined, that instant every one of the prisoners shall be put to death." We therefore hope you will take this our representation into your most serious consideration, and not suffer, if possible, the lives of so many innocent persons to be sacrificed.*

Forty-three signatures followed, including those belonging to Governor Ninian Home, Dr. Hay, Assemblyman Alexander Campbell, and Mr. Turnbull. Then, a final paragraph:

> *P.S. General Fédon is of the opinion, that I have not sufficiently expressed his sentiments in that full manner he wishes should have been done, and requests me to add, "That he expects all the fortifications to be delivered up to him on an honorable capitulation."*

Father turned to Malcolm. "His Majesty's Council in St. George's has assumed full executive powers. They have requested a contingent of Spanish soldiers from Trinidad to help us protect the town. We have received forty so far. The Council also ordered the immediate recapture of Gouyave and a full-scale attack on Belvidere to rescue the prisoners. Your arrival with General Lindsay today is timely to achieve those objectives."

"Yes, sir," Malcolm responded.

"Captain." Father's sharp tone matched in hostility with his cold eyes. "Report to the officer's armory at once. Get full combat gear. Acquaint yourself with the men and get some sleep. You will accompany General Lindsay and his troops at four o'clock in the morning to retake Gouyave. Since you are our only commissioned officer with firsthand knowledge of Belvidere and the traitor General Fédon, you will lead the attack on Belvidere."

He hoped no one heard his hard swallow or saw his Adam's apple descend. "Yes, sir." Malcolm saluted and made an about-face towards the door.

"One more thing," Father said.

Despite the damning nature of the Grenada crisis, Father's words seemed even more threatening. Malcolm made a snappy about-face and braced himself for another of Father's verbal ice storms.

Father crossed the room and stretched out his hand to Malcolm. "I am glad you are here." They shook hands—briefly. "Do not let me down again."

Father abruptly returned to the table and fixed his attention to the maps.

Malcolm marched out of the office into the clammy night. Tiny lights dotted the hillsides around St. George's like a city of fireflies, drenched in fear and in the deadly grip of the Bulam fever. His arrival in Grenada felt like the preparation for a funeral, the island he had so loved and missed, now dying. Soon to suffer the same fate as the bond with his father—a bond he once cherished like life itself.

Obviously, Father held for Malcolm a reservoir of

disdain. Malcolm's cozy association with the Fédons, his disrespect for Mr. Turnbull, and his bedroom rendezvous with Charlotte Turnbull, all fed the bitterness that soaked Father and poisoned his demeanor.

Malcolm no longer had a father. He had a commanding officer.

Now, more than ever, Rosette seemed the only remedy for the ache that gnawed his insides. He wanted desperately to see her. But she now slept in the heart of a bloody rebellion.

A rebellion that Malcolm's duty to King George and solemn oath as a British officer demanded he annihilate.

How could Malcolm possibly do that, without destroying his only reason left for living?

If he had to, would he dare betray his father to save Rosette?

His eyes welled up.

Chapter Thirty-Seven

Papa's roar from downstairs shook the Belvidere great house and awakened Rosette before sunrise. She did not make out his words, but someone must have delivered more bad news even before the sun greeted the cool morning. The cries of babies in the Belvidere hillsides slipped through her windows, along with smoke from early cooking fires.

Each day, it pained her to watch Papa's mounting pressures simmer into growing rage. He expected a British surrender by now, seven days after the rebellion started. Seven days after Kojo and Uncle Jean-Pierre delivered the prize from the north, Governor Ninian Home, along with Mr. Turnbull, Alexander Campbell, and others.

Uncle Jean-Pierre told her of Kojo's attempts to behead Mr. Turnbull when they landed the frightened Englishmen from the boat in Gouyave. It had taken several men to restrain Kojo, with Uncle Jean-Pierre reminding him that the prisoners were worth more to them alive than dead.

When the prisoners arrived in Belvidere, Papa complained loudly that even under threats of death, the governor refused to order a surrender of the forts in St. George's.

"I am a prisoner," Rosette heard the frail governor declare to Papa in the library. "I have lost all my official power and authority. But I can write the council to convey your wishes."

"These are not wishes," Papa yelled. "They are bloody demands."

Rosette had read the last letter the governor wrote to the Grenada Council, in which he repeated Papa's threat—any attack on Belvidere, and continued refusal to surrender would lead to the executions of all British prisoners. The British prisoners held in the camp on the hill now included Dr. Hay. But Papa still allowed him to roam the hillsides, attending to wounded rebels and the sick, with watchful guards at his side.

Overnight, Papa's Belvidere Estate became a hilly sanctuary for a steady flow of slaves, now in the thousands. Just a couple nights ago, Kojo spoke to Papa about riding to Beauséjour to get Mr. Turnbull's slaves. The growing mass of people scattered in the Belvidere fields and in the hills, under trees and under thatched roofs. Many lazed around cooking fires. To feed them, Papa organized the slaughter of up to ten cows each day.

The smell of boiled beef, plantains, and dasheens thickened the air in an offensive blend with the scent of raw cattle entrails and human waste.

To avoid depleting the fields he had cultivated over the past eighteen months, Papa ordered daily food forages across the island, especially to abandoned British-owned estates. In the first few days, Rosette's spirit soared as Papa celebrated the return of hunting parties with much foodstuff and animals.

On the second day of the rebellion, she stood next to Papa watching a foraging group climb up the hill with bulging bags of vegetables and supplies. Behind them, cows and donkeys dragged two wheeled-cannons seized from the Gouyave militia post.

Papa plucked his cigar from his mouth and yelled. "Six-pounders. Bravo. With this protection and food, the British will starve long before we do."

Despite Papa's threats, the British held firm. And Papa's moods grew sourer, especially as the groups returned with less food in the last few days. Sometimes, they returned empty-handed. Increasingly, the groups clashed with British patrols and suffered wounded and dead. They even told of horrid battles with other slaves who remained loyal to their British masters.

Rosette overheard one returning group, some bloodied, speaking of killing fifty other slaves who refused to join the rebellion. Another fifty chose to join the mass of desperation spreading across Belvidere.

The wounded and diseased kept coming.

The stories and rumors of death, by violence and disease kept coming.

But Rosette needed no reminder. Just down the hall, in Grandmère's old bedroom, the Bulam fever slowly robbed Lovely's meager strength. Since Dr. Hay had less time to attend to her, Rosette took over his efforts to keep her hydrated with rosemary tea and soup. He insisted Rosette limit her time with Lovely, since she too might contract the infectious disease.

He said the Spanish called it *Vomito Negro.*

Black Vomit.

As fast as Rosette spoon-fed her, Lovely expelled her bodily fluids from both ends in gushes of black liquid. Her bony frame caved in around her bulging stomach, but her smile beamed gratitude each time Rosette entered the room to feed her or empty her pan.

Papa's early-morning outbursts drummed downstairs

as Rosette rolled out of bed and changed clothes. His shouts followed her down the hallway and into Grandmère's old bedroom.

Lovely lay in bed covered with a white sheet up to her chest. Her smile welcomed Rosette into the room. "I glad you come. Time I go." She rubbed her belly. "Baby go too. This no place for baby."

Rosette held her hand. "No. You have become my friend. You cannot leave now."

"You my only friend." Lovely blinked feebly, her breathing in shallow spurts. "But I want see my mother."

"She would be very proud of you."

Lovely squeezed Rosette's hand and closed her eyes. Lovely released one long final breath.

Rosette wanted to cry, but her grief seemed lost as to where, or to whom, to express itself. Not to Maman, who busied herself around the estate ensuring that meals reached the hungry first. Not to Uncle Jean-Pierre, who spent most of his time in the hills supervising the fortifications. And not to Grandmère, who joined her ancestors almost two years ago. Not even Father Pascal, who could be lost anywhere around the expansive Belvidere Estate, among the crowds, delivering the last rights to another departing soul.

Rosette pulled the bedroom door shut behind her and headed downstairs to find Papa.

He stood in the middle of a group of anxious French soldiers and *gens de couleur libres* rebels, yelling orders. His shouts thundered in her head, and lack of sleep ached her body. She wished, just for today, Papa would leave his temper up the hill in his camps.

Maybe if she got his attention just long enough to let him know that Lovely lay dead upstairs, he would hold her and let her bawl her pain into his big shoulder.

Instead, he turned to her with blazing eyes. "Did you not hear me call you?"

"No Papa. I was with Lovely. She is d—"

"British soldiers are on the way from St. George's. Captain McDonald has been ordered to attack Belvidere."

Malcolm? The news felt like a hot dagger in her chest. *He be damned.*

At that moment, a bitter truth burned through her like a fever. Surrounded by family and thousands of supporters, loneliness had become her only true companion.

What cruel fate could have allowed Malcolm into her heart, only to turn him into an enemy about to unleash more pain and death on Belvidere?

A wave of unsettling emotions rushed her insides. Even though she had not eaten or drank anything since awakening, she felt like throwing up. She ran out the door to the verandah, her stomach in nauseating spasms.

She leaned over the banister. And vomit gushed out of her mouth—in a stream of black.

Malcolm marched alongside General Lindsay in the early morning light, ahead of four hundred troops on the way north to Gouyave. Swords clinked, and horse-drawn cannons on wheels rattled behind them. The sea breeze blew only pint-size relief from the suffocating uniform of a black wool hat, thick coat, britches, and boots. Somewhere offshore, about a hundred lucky soldiers sailed to Gouyave aboard the *Beaulieu.* An additional two hundred soldiers, many falling sick or recovering from fever, had been left in St. George's and Fort Frederick to protect the city, under Colonel McDonald's command.

Along the way, charred fields and destroyed great houses disfigured the landscape, much to Malcolm's dismay. Even so, when they reached Beauséjour Estate, the devastation shocked him. Where once Mr. Turnbull's handsome, great house sat, its smoldering skeleton now clutched the hill. Blackened windows, like gaping eye sockets, gazed down at burnt fields as far and as wide as Malcolm could see. Where once donkey carts hurried to and from the mill and a hundred slaves labored in green fields, neither a soul nor an animal beckoned. Only a hawk floated overhead. A cool breeze whipped up a swirl of ash with an aroma of burnt sugar.

Malcolm recalled the rainy evening he rode from Gouyave to meet Charlotte in her luxuriant chamber. Such downpour would have hardly dampened the anger that brewed in the slaves, but it might have spared the estate from the worst of the fires.

The stone-mill walls survived with burnt splotches, but only tattered cloth flapped where the sails once spun diligently against blue skies. He remembered all too well the night Charlotte and Kojo introduced him to the mill's brutal efficiency, its unforgiving power—to remove limbs and crush human bodies. And how could Malcolm forget the broken little girl, Lovely, still waiting in the moonlight for the mill to return her mother, long-devoured by the rollers. The woman's mauled remnants had been ploughed as fertilizer, mixed with bagasse to fuel the boiler house fires, even processed and disguised as sugar for English tea cups.

Malcolm's mood began to slip, but General Lindsay intervened. "Captain, this looks like a good place for the men to get some rest."

"I will pass the order, sir."

The general unbuttoned his coatee and dabbed his sweaty eyebrow with a handkerchief. "We will need all the rest we can take now. God knows what is awaiting us in Gouyave."

Malcolm called over a few platoon leaders and gave the order for the men, regular and militia, to rest. He also directed them to prepare a squad to conduct a reconnaissance of the scorched hillsides around Beauséjour Estate for any possibilities of ambush.

He took a swig of water from his canteen and glanced across the road to where the slave village hid. Thin smoke rose above the green canopy, mercifully spared from the fires that ravaged the fields.

"Have the squad report to me before leaving for the hills," he ordered. When the soldiers showed up a few minutes later with fixed bayonets, Malcolm pointed to the tree line bordering the village. "Let us start there."

He checked his carbine and led the men to the mud path that snaked into the shanty village. Smoking ash heaps lined both sides of the path, marking where huts once stood. A profound sadness overcame him.

One of the soldiers stopped next to Malcolm. "What madness, for these slaves to burn their own dwellings."

Malcolm rested the butt of his carbine on his boot. "What would you do if you traded places with them?"

A gust broke the silence, rustling through the trees overhead and carrying what sounded like a cough.

Was it the wind, or the river rushing down the ravine?

He listened.

Yes, a cough. It came from the only hut left standing ahead.

He readied his carbine and crouched toward the doorway. The men followed.

Another cough.

He stopped just yards away from the hut. "You in there. Present yourself with your hands up."

Slow movements, then a croaky female's voice struggled from inside. "Sah, the old lady sick. I no want you sick too."

"I am not here to hurt you. Anyone else with you?"

"Me alone."

"By what name are you called?"

"Lena." A one-armed woman shuffled out from the interior darkness to the doorway. She had thick white braids, bloodshot eyes, and cheeks sunken around her toothless mouth. Her scanty dress, as tired as she looked, clung to her thin body like it would not last another day. "Kojo spirit take everybody and leave fire everywhere." She looked down at his boots and paused, as if to catch her breath. "Two sunset ago."

Malcolm turned to the soldiers. "Continue the patrol from here, past the tree line and up the hill behind the great house." He waited until the men disappeared past the last smoking ash heap, then he turned to Lena. "You know Kojo?"

"Long time, before he dead." She shivered. "He spirit come to free us from Massa Turnbull. He say Massa is prisoner in Belvidere."

"You saw Kojo?"

"He spirit, with me own eyes."

"I thought he died too. Why did you not go with him?"

"I too old, too sick to climb mountain." She squinted briefly at him, then returned her gaze to his boots. "How Massa soldier like you know Kojo?"

"I was here two years ago when he whipped Venus to save her from Mr. Turnbull."

"You." She looked into his eyes for the first time and lifted her trembling hand to her chest. "You, I remember. If I not sick, I hug you."

"Did Kojo say anything about Belvidere and Monsieur Fédon?"

"Free people all over the estate. They worship General Fédon."

"Any French soldiers?"

She shook her head. "I know nothing about that kinda thing."

Malcolm could barely wait to ask the next question. "Did he talk about General Fédon's daughter, Rosette?"

The old woman's eyes lit up. "Yes. She and Dr. Hay, everywhere helping the sick and hurt." She lifted her amputated arm, cut above the elbow and crisscrossed with scars. "Dr. Hay fix me when sugarcane rollers take me hand."

"Any more about Rosette?"

"He say she now sick. Poor thing. Like me...she have the Bulam."

He leaned on his carbine to hold a steady footing. "Rosette? Are you certain of this?"

"Me head bad with old age. But I know he say that. It take little Lovely in Belvidere too."

His insides howled. If the Bulam took Lovely, it could also take Rosette. The Bulam fever came ashore on the slave ship, *Hankey*, eighteen months prior, soon after Malcolm had departed for Liverpool. The sickness swept St. George's, taking one in three lives infected with it, including Governor Home's wife. Now it worked its way around the island. If thousands of slaves congregated on Belvidere, it could be catastrophic. The thought of losing Rosette now, having gotten so close to see her, would bring him unspeakable pain.

"Would you see Kojo again?" he asked.

She shook her head in the negative. "I tell him I stay here and dead here."

Malcolm knew, even if Kojo, spirit or not, planned to return for her, she would never reveal that to a British officer.

"Do you have food, water?" he asked.

"Kojo leave me boil provisions from Belvidere. I have to go down to the river for more water."

She pointed her reduced arm at an old barrel by her door. Ash and burnt splinters floated on a meagre level of grimy water.

He could not imagine the old woman hiking to the ravine and back in such a feeble state. "Stay here."

He hurried towards the sound of the river along a worn path behind her hut. He scampered down to the water's edge and refilled his canteen.

When he returned, Lena clung to the doorway frame with her one hand, her nails thick and muddy. Tears streaked down her dusty face.

"No need to cry," he said. "I will make sure someone comes by tomorrow."

"I cry because I have black man and white man kind to

me. But they enemies."

"Kojo is not my enemy." He placed his canteen at her feet. "I must go now."

"I hope nobody hurt you," she said. "And you no hurt nobody. They just want freedom."

Her words struck him like Mr. Turnbull's pistol grip to his head. "I know. Please get well."

She cleared her throat and smacked her lips against bare gums. "If Kojo spirit come in me dreams, I tell he, 'white soldier feel strong about General Fédon girl.'"

Maybe Lena read his shocked reaction upon hearing of Rosette's illness. If Lena saw Kojo again, she just might tell him of this. Malcolm did not dare take the chance that Rosette might receive a message from Kojo that inadequately measured Malcolm's sentiments for her. In the days ahead, she could die from the disease, or he in battle. Now, more than ever, he wanted her to know, even if they never saw each other again. But in a time of open warfare between Fédon and the British, communications from Malcolm to Rosette, however pure in intent, might carry the stain of betrayal. He searched his mind for the perfect way to say what he felt, but the words seemed to have a mind of their own. They flowed out of his mouth as though Rosette stood before him.

"Malcolm loves Rosette," he said. "Please tell Kojo's spirit he must tell her for me."

Lena's weak smile lifted her sagging cheeks. "You and Dr. Hay, best white men." She pointed her elbow stub at the main group of soldiers gathered on the road and grew serious. "That you big Massa soldier over there?"

He glanced over his shoulder to where General Lindsay conferred with other soldiers. "Why do you ask?"

She shivered and spat dark liquid. "He go have big trouble in Belvidere."

Kojo hid with his horse in the bushy hilltop overlooking

Beauséjour, and, through his long glass, watched the last British soldier disappear around the twisting coastline towards Gouyave. He dug his bare heels into the horse's ribs and took it on a cautious trot down the hill. He slowed at the tree line, on the shadowy path into the village, looking around for any sign of a hostile surprise.

Nothing—except a cough from Lena's hut.

He pulled up the horse next to her open doorway and dismounted.

Lena lay shivering on the hardened mud floor, next to his bowl of cooked provisions, untouched except for nibbles on the ground. Her pungent medicines and stale puke must have failed to keep away the rats. A canteen he had not seen before sat next to the bowl.

He kneeled over her. "Come with me. Dr. Hay go care you."

"If you is spirit, take me home to me ancestors."

"No. I live." He told her about the day he left the estate to bury Venus and the baby. "I shoot agouti and send back the horse with blood to make Massa think I shoot meself. I free the new slaves and lock back the slave pen gate to confuse him."

"You smarter than Massa." She chuckled as if a bubble had stuck in her throat. "White soldier boy come back."

"I see him from the hills through the long glass."

"He say, 'tell General Fédon's daughter his heart have love for her.'"

"That might be good medicine she need. Bulam have her sick bad."

"Poor thing." She pointed at the canteen. "He give me. But I no can eat or drink nothing no more."

Kojo puckered his lips. "He come back to put us under Massa again."

"He say you not he enemy." She held a weakening gaze on his face. "You know, we used to 'fraid you and think you enemy too, as Massa big man. Now we know you hard on us to make Massa happy. And if Massa happy...you hope Massa kind to us. Thing is, Massa never happy. Nobody never happy here."

He bowed his head to hide his wet eyes. Two sunsets ago, Kojo led a hundred freed slaves over the mountain to Belvidere. When they reached the estate safely, he felt their gratitude in their hugs and handshakes, but they must have choked back any words they had to express their constant fear of his whip.

Even the young mother he had freed from the slave pen rushed up to him leading a young boy by his hand. He too fled his plantation and found his mother in Belvidere, two seasons after Kojo unwillingly tore him from his mother's arms in the St. George's market square. Their thankful embraces touched him.

Lena's words cut a straight path to the silent guilt he had harbored for so many years. A deep sigh of relief escaped him.

"They know," she said. "You give them gift from the gods. Freedom. I still 'member. I was a little girl, seven or eight seasons, when they catch me..."

Her breathing rose and fell, like the slave ship that took Kojo across the deep ocean from Africa. Maybe those were the same rhythms that returned Africans to their homeland, preparing now to return Lena.

She continued. "But I still 'member them free days. I climb up hills to see ocean, ocean, and more ocean. Water for so. Wind blowing in me face, whistling in the trees. Dancing in the rain. Birds singing. Life was music..."

Her smile brightened her face, even as she shivered. She closed her eyes. Her shoulders lifted with her breath, each more labored than the previous.

Truth stared at him. She would never make it to Belvidere. Yet, he could not abandon her here. Nor could he stay. British soldiers might return at any time.

He knew what he had to do.

He lifted her delicate body, hot to the touch, and

walked out of the hut. He propped her on the horse and climbed up behind her. He held her around her stomach with one hand and held the reins in the other.

"Belvidere?" she asked. "Too far. I no can make it."

"No, not Belvidere."

"Where you take me?" Her words came in a whisper.

"Home." He struggled to keep his voice from cracking. "To feel free music again."

He heeled the horse into a comfortable trot up the hill, away from the sugar mill that took Lena's arm and Lovely's mother. Past the tree where his whips tore the skin of so many of his African brothers and sisters. Past the charred great house where Madame Turnbull used to touch his hand, and where Venus and her baby met their ancestors. He guided the horse on to the wooded trail he took the last day he lived under Massa Turnbull's boot.

The trail led high away from Beauséjour. Higher and higher they went.

She looked up at the bright blue sky, with puffs of white clouds floating past. "I can touch clouds. Where we now?"

"Out of plantation. We free."

She squeezed his arm. "I like free."

He rode until the trees thinned and the terrain smoothened on a windy top. He slowed and pointed at the wide expanse of sea. The blue water reflected glittering slivers and attracted flocks of white seagulls. High above, a solitary black frigate drifted with stretched wings and forked tail.

"Feel like home." Her words now came as soft as a gentle breeze.

He picked up speed.

The wind blew in his face. Her white head bobbed against his chest. Birds whistled in the trees.

She laughed aloud, waving her one arm and elbow stub in the air until he slowed.

"Again," she squealed—in the voice of a little girl.

He turned the horse around and sped back to the far edge, hoping she would not feel his tears dripping on her head and fevered cheeks.

"It raining," she yelled.

He slowed and turned the horse around.

"Again. Please."

She must have said it, and he must have sped the horse for as many times as the fingers on two hands.

"I am home," she shouted with a renewed burst of energy.

She grew quiet, and her body relaxed against him.

When he lifted her off the horse, Lena's smile held a youthful glow he had never seen on her before.

He buried her on the hill overlooking the sea. Next to Venus and her baby.

Then he returned to the slave village, retrieved the canteen, and set Lena's hut on fire.

Freedom deserved more than a thatched roof and a hardened mud floor on a slave plantation.

Chapter Thirty-Eight

Dr. Hay's stomach growled from hunger and fear in the cramped hut. He expected he and the others—now fifty-one of them—would be killed anytime now. Their lives clung precariously on General Fédon's mood, a flimsy string of hope which threatened to break without notice. He had heard about the night the general led the revolutionaries into Grenville, the same night Lavallée and others took Dr. Hay prisoner in Gouyave. They led British residents out of their bedrooms at gunpoint, and into the streets where they shot and chopped them to death in the moonlight, in the general's presence.

When Dr. Hay's moment arrived, he planned to request that he be shot.

He had spent the morning on the estate below with an escort of guards. First, to extract a musket ball from the arm of a rebel, wounded when General Fédon led them in an ambush of a British patrol.

Thereafter, Dr. Hay visited Rosette at the general's calling. She rolled and tossed in bed, her bedpan splattered with black fluid and her brains roasting in the throes of fever. Her hallucinations came very much in the erratic ways of a woman. In one instant, she expressed love and longing for Captain McDonald, much to the chagrin of General and Madame Fédon standing at her bedside. In the next instant, Rosette swore in gutter language unbefitting a young lady of class, that if she saw the captain again, she would remove his head with her father's cutlass.

Dr. Hay left the house having provided little assurance to the Fédon's that Rosette would recover from her rapidly deteriorating condition. He dreaded that if he gave any false hope, and she died, the general's grief might change to anger. Anger that might lead to Dr. Hay's execution or even a massacre of the prisoners.

Now squeezed back into the suffocating prison hut, Dr. Hay's stomach grumbled in anticipation of their daily three small plantains and two ounces of half-boiled beef. Given the lengthy climb from where the cooks prepared their food in the camps below, the women showed up once daily, around three o'clock in the afternoon. Already an hour past, Dr. Hay sat squeezed into a muddy corner by the door, gazing through a space in the side wall and wondering why the women ran late.

The hut, twenty-two feet long by thirteen feet wide, held a raised platform in the middle with intimidating stocks on each of the four sides. This left a mud path about two feet wide between the platform and the outer walls. Two of the men enjoyed good fortune with hammocks for sleeping, having the foresight to carry them on the forced march up the hill. The platform thus allowed maybe twenty-eight of the others to rest at night. The remaining captives were obliged to stand or lay on the mud floor, damp from daily rainfall that dripped through the thatched roof or seeped in from outdoors. Most of the men shivered in wet clothes.

Dr. Hay had written notes to General Fédon decrying the deplorable conditions that led to severe colds among the men. Coughing and sneezing persisted around the clock. The prisoners began to lose weight, especially Mr. Turnbull, whose once thick rolls around his neck gave way to flaccid skin. Governor Home, himself frail and weakening, insisted on giving up his platform space to others, especially to Matthew Atkinson, a boy no more than twelve years old.

"Sleep well...Matthew." The governor's coughs interrupted his words. "I might need your strength to carry me back down this hill. Dead or alive."

Relief came sparingly. General Fédon permitted the men to build a fire outside to dry off, six at a time. And, with prudence and secrecy, a free negro woman who worked for Dr. Hay some years back, regularly slipped them a jug of warm toddy. When the occasion blessed them, she also delivered rum, oatmeal, and salted fish, but steadfastly refused his offer of money. Meanwhile, Dr. Hay's note to General Fédon, requesting more rum to keep the men warm and their spirits high, went unanswered.

Dr. Hay squinted through a narrow gap between the wooden planks, expecting at any time to see the pots balanced on the heads of the negro women who served them.

Instead, General Fédon slogged up to the hut in the accompaniment of several armed men, including Kojo. The general stood in muddy boots, a giant against the smoky mist that rose from the camps below. Grinding a cigar in his mouth, he called for the guards around the hut. Among them, Lavallée, who had stabbed Dr. Hay in the arm with a bayonet in Gouyave. A wound struggling to heal in the absence of adequate medical supplies.

"The British are marching towards Gouyave," General Fédon yelled, with obvious vigor for his prisoners to hear. "If they attack Belvidere, I want all the prisoners put to death immediately."

Several of the prisoners shrieked.

Lavallée stomped his boots on the threshold of the prison door, his pistol and dagger held high. "I shall require no other weapons in my hands to execute your orders."

The guards crowded the door with cocked firelocks and drawn cutlasses.

Some of the prisoners reacted with dismay, their cries for mercy drowning out the sobs from young Matthew where he sat on the platform close to Dr. Hay.

"Be steady," the governor said, his own legs in the stocks. "Act like men."

General Fédon faced the hut. "Your council offered a reward for my head. My head is not worth a penny compared to the lot of you in there." He laughed and turned to one of his men. "Time to go see Josephina. She has plans for Gouyave."

The general about-faced and stomped down the hill with a couple of his men.

Kojo remained in conversation with a negro man Dr. Hay had never seen before.

Mr. Turnbull elbowed the doctor and lowered his voice. "That man with Kojo is a runaway. Simon. Used to be mine too. Kojo sure fooled us. These blacks are as treacherous as snakes."

Dr. Hay looked up at Mr. Turnbull. "I suggest you keep such declarations to yourself. They regard us with equal scorn."

Mr. Turnbull glared through a gap in the planks and called out. "Kojo, all is forgiven. Plead our call for mercy to the general. When this is over, you and Simon can return to Beauséjour without consequence. 'Tis not too late to save your skins."

Kojo snapped around to face Mr. Turnbull's direction, fury burning in his eyes, his face hardened with such ferocity that Dr. Hay had never seen in the man before. "Too late for Venus. Too late for Lovely and her mother. Too late for you."

"I will always be your Massa," Mr. Turnbull yelled. "You know how well I treat—"

Lavallée tugged at the shaky door. "I will have his head right now."

Kojo rushed up to him and grabbed him by the shoulder. "No. Only General Fédon say so."

"You will never touch me again." Lavallée thrusted his dagger at Kojo, who stumbled back and fell in the slippery mud.

Lavallée raised his dagger arm to strike Kojo.

Simon, standing just behind Lavallée, swung his cutlass against Lavallée's neck. Blood sprayed.

Lavallée stood transfixed, his eyes opened wide, his face distorted in grave confusion. Simon swung again, almost dislodging Lavallée's head from his body. He collapsed in the mud.

Another guard raised his cutlass and rushed Simon from behind. Kojo, now on his feet, cut the man down with his cutlass in a sickening moment of cries, blood, and gurgles.

Simon finished the guard off like slaughtered cattle.

The other guards dragged the dead men into the woods and returned to their posts.

Kojo and Simon headed back down the hill, their hands and clothes bloodied.

The cooking women never came to the hut that day. But it mattered not to Dr. Hay. After the killings, his hunger fled. Seated with his back against the wall, he dozed.

He knew not how long he slept, but when the shouts at the door awakened him, nightfall approached.

"Dr. Hay." Zab, one of General Fédon's guards, pushed open the door. "Me do not know what you do. General Fédon vex like a lion. He waiting for you in the house with cutlass. You seeing you maker tonight."

"Dr. Hay, tonight I will have your head." General Fédon whacked his cutlass against the great-house banister with such rage, the blade twanged, and wooden splinters rained through the yellow torchlight to the verandah floor.

The impact resounded like a gunshot. Dogs howled, and questioning shouts rose from the encampments crowding the estate. Shadowy figures raised heads around cooking fires, as if in dreaded anticipation of Dr. Hay's imminent execution.

He stood between Zab and another guard at the bottom of the steps and struggled to control his demeanor. "Pray tell...General. For what do I owe you my profound apology?"

"Apology?" He prodded his cutlass in the air above his unruly head of hair. "Traitors do not apologize. They die."

Dr. Hay adjusted his spectacles and held his silence, lest he said something that would only aggravate the general further. Yet, he wondered what boiled the man's temper.

Madame Fédon rushed on to the verandah from inside the house. "Julien. Please, Rosette is finally asleep upstairs."

The general whipped around. "Go away, woman."

"I just might," she screamed. "This mess is getting out of control."

"Then good riddance." General Fédon pulled a piece of paper from his soiled vest and turned back towards Dr. Hay. "This came from your house. You knew of Colonel McDonald's swindle, and you covered it up. For this, you will die now."

The general lifted his cutlass and stomped down the steps towards Dr. Hay.

Dr. Hay's knees trembled. He expected to die. But not at the hands of this man. Dr. Hay had shown so much deference to the family, at the painful loss of face in the British community.

God, where is your just and merciful hand?

Madame Fédon ran down the steps past the general to Dr. Hay. "Please, you must have an explanation for my husband. We cannot lose you. My daughter needs you. We all need you."

Dr. Hay cleared his throat. "Colonel McDonald knows not that I have this knowledge of his financial affairs. My cousin in England wrote me privately, most of it after you had already purchased the estate. I do not comprehend fully how these transactions affect you, but I am equally appalled by the appearance of deception. Kill me if you must. But 'tis the absolute truth. I swear it."

General Fédon pointed the tip of his cutlass at Dr. Hay's nose. "What about his son?" he roared. "The one who delivered those fraudulent documents. The one who abused my hospitality and deceived my daughter. What about him?"

Dr. Hay sighed, relieved now some of the general's anger dispersed in the Belvidere breeze. "General, I doubt his willful participation in any falsehoods. I stand by his reputation as an honorable young man. I think his father kept him as unaware as he kept the rest of us."

"It matters not what you think. He too will suffer the same fate as his father." He turned to the guards. "Take him back to the hut. If Colonel McDonald's son fires a single shot at this estate tomorrow, Dr. Hay will die with the others."

Two hours after marching into Gouyave, Malcolm realized why General Fédon abandoned the town. But it was too late. He galloped his horse up the hill in red sunset to the militia post and rapped on the door of the office that General Lindsay occupied.

"Come in," the general hollered.

Malcolm pushed open the door and stepped into the office, looted of everything not nailed. The general sat on the floor reading a dispatch, his skin flushed. A bottle of rum stood against the wall next to him.

"Any enemy activity to report, Captain?"

"No, sir," Malcolm said." All troops are positioned. Those from the *Beaulieu* have also landed and are at their assigned posts. The *Quebec* is expected overnight with another one hundred troops. All very quiet, sir. Too quiet."

"When the king's army come marching in, all cowards flee."

"Agreed, sir. But I believe 'tis the reason they left a generous supply of rum in every store. The men did not even have to break the doors."

"And they thought well enough of their general to deliver me my own bottle." He lifted the bottle towards Malcolm. "Here, have a drink."

"Thank you, sir. But I have a weak stomach for—"

"Anything else, Captain?"

"I believe we should stop the men from drinking to excess. They may be too...too lethargic for battle in Belvidere tomorrow."

The general took a generous swig from the bottle. "I worried a lot too when I was a young soldier like you."

Malcolm persisted. "I expect fierce resistance from the revolutionaries. Their morale may be boosted by the cannons they carried away from this post."

"Fear not, Captain. I am willing to bet a crown they abandoned the cannons along the way. The cowards in Belvidere will also flee as they did here in Gouyave." He took another swig and burped. "The men had a long day. Let them wear off the tension. They will be ready to end General Fédon's rebellion in the morning."

"Yes, sir."

The general handed him an envelope. "My situation report for St. George's. The enemy fled His Majesty's forces in Gouyave. Victory is at hand. Find your fastest rider to deliver it. Dismissed."

Malcolm found a militia rider at the post stables and ordered him to immediately deliver the report to the capital.

He also asked the man to leave a canteen of water and some bread for the one-armed woman, Lena, at the only shack left standing on Beauséjour Estate.

The man sped off into the dying sunset.

Malcolm mounted his horse and headed back down the hill. All along the sidewalks in the center of the town, British soldiers and militia engaged in rambunctious behavior and singing. Under lampposts lanterns, broken bottles glittered in open drains. A group crowded around an open barrel to refill their canteens with rum.

Malcolm dared not intervene to stop their unsoldierly conduct. General Lindsay would be displeased that Captain McDonald disobeyed his orders to let the men alone.

None of the soldiers acknowledged his presence as he rode past them towards Dr. Hay's house, his quarters for the night.

Later, Malcolm rolled out his blanket on the gallery floor. He tried to sleep, allowing the sound of waves and the sea breeze to wash General Lindsay's words with reassurance. All would be fine. In the face of overwhelming British force, the slaves would return to the plantations and resume their loyal servitude.

Or so Malcolm hoped.

He knew not what to expect in the morning, but he had a simple plan: capture Belvidere, free the prisoners, and seek help for Rosette. In that regard, Dr. Hay would be of immense value.

But what of General Fédon? If he surrendered, would the governor and the council show him mercy? They might exile him to Roatán, an island off the coast of Honduras as others were before. But given his stubborn character, he would never surrender.

Tomorrow seemed a long time away.

At that moment, he wanted only to think well of Rosette. The reason he chose to sleep on this spot in the gallery, where Dr. Hay and his associates signed Madame Fédon's Certificate of Freedom. Where Malcolm sat next to

Rosette, their knees touching in mutual fondness.

He wanted to fall asleep with Rosette alive in his dreams.

Yet, he pondered Lena's warning in Beauséjour.

"He go have big trouble in Belvidere," she had said about General Lindsay.

She seemed certain the British general would be in Belvidere. But the military plans approved by the council called for Malcolm to capture the estate, while the general held Gouyave. Of course, the general would eventually visit Belvidere—once Malcolm restored normalcy. So what trouble would the general face up there? And what would make the woman think General Lindsay, not Malcolm, would see trouble in Belvidere?

The crashing waves pulled Malcolm into a troubled sleep.

But soon, gunshots awakened him.

Chapter Thirty-Nine

Malcolm ran out of Dr. Hay's house and on to the courtyard, buttoning his vest and adjusting his sword. Rapid gunfire echoed from the south. Yells in the street. Galloping horses clopped the stone roads outside the courtyard walls.

A soldier rushed up to him in pale torchlight. "They are attacking to the south, sir!"

"Report to General Lindsay at the militia post immediately," Malcolm ordered, his heart pounding. "Tell him I am ordering all defenses around Gouyave to hold their positions, in case 'tis a decoy. Tell him I am on the way to the attack with some of my men."

"Yes, sir." The soldier saluted and sprinted away.

Malcolm barked orders at his platoon leaders awaiting him on the street. He gathered ten militia men with their horses and led them with carbines and swords drawn on a gallop towards the gunshots. The deserted coastal road, waves crashing on the right, hardly seemed a likely path to a battle. But fear tightened his stomach. In the dark distance, musket fire flashed against each other. Sweat rolled down his forehead.

They crossed a narrow bridge over a river and took a sharp left on a road that ascended towards estate grounds. The dreadful sounds of war increased—gunshots, yells, and screams.

Without warning, a horde of bareback men rose from the river bank and charged at Malcolm and his men with cutlasses and spikes.

Carbines blasted. Swords slashed. Men moaned and fell.

Malcolm fired into the mass. More men fell.

A man charged at Malcolm with a long spike. Malcolm's horse reared and snorted, its forelegs off the road.

Malcolm lost his footing in the stirrups. He fell on his back but held on to his carbine.

A big man rushed at him with a cutlass in one hand and a torch in the other.

Malcolm could not die now. Not here. Not this way. Not without seeing Rosette again.

He tightened his grip on the weapon and took aim.

The man kept coming, a battle roar flowing from deep in his gut.

Malcolm squeezed his trigger. Nothing. He squeezed once more. Again, nothing.

He scrambled for his sword. Gone.

More gunshots. Shrieks. The wails of dying men.

He struggled to stand but slipped in the mud. The bareback man stormed up to him in the glare of the torchlight, his black skin glistening with sweat. The man's eyes blazed with fury, his cutlass poised high and about to strike.

Malcolm raised his hands in defense. "Kojo, no."

Kojo swung his cutlass in full force at Malcolm's

head.

"We have to leave Grenada for our safety." Maman's words floated from her mouth and landed on Rosette's awareness with as little emotional impact as a handful of cotton falling on a stone road.

The fever seemed to have emptied her last teaspoon of care about almost everything—even life itself. She rolled in her bed, remembering how quickly her life and her world, had crumbled. When gushes of black fluids abandoned her body, the relief lasted just long enough for her fever to reignite and ravage her every nerve, her every joint. Even her skin cried out in agony for a merciful death.

Now she understood the peace on Lovely's face when she died.

Rosette sometimes wished for her end too. But as Dr. Hay prescribed, and as Maman insisted, Rosette forced down spoonsful of water and rosemary tea until her ailing body could stand it no more. Waves of fluid expulsions began with devastating misery. She leaned over the side of the bed and vomited another torrent of the *vomito negro*. In yellow lamp-light, it splattered green into the bedpan. The warm fluid burned her lips, cracked from dryness and swollen with painful sores. A bitter taste lingered in her mouth with such revulsion, she believed she had tasted her dying insides.

She could no longer smell it the way she had in Lovely's room, but she knew. A foul odor crawled out from her decaying body and filled the bedroom since the first day. It showed on the cringing faces of those who dared enter Rosette's room.

Maman patted Rosette's forehead with a damp rag. "Before Papa left with your Uncle Jean-Pierre and Kojo tonight, he said he wants us on the next ship to Guadalupe."

"Where did Papa take them?" Rosette's hoarse words crept past her heavy lips.

"They left with a big group. He never says where he goes anymore. He looked worried when they left. I am afraid one day he might not return. This has become a real war."

Rosette did not have to leave her bedroom to find evidence of war. Her window served as the eyes and ears to the human agony befalling Grenada. Each day, after skirmishes with British soldiers, returning warriors limped past her window. They shuffled by in reduced numbers and deflated exuberance from when they left hours earlier. Some moaned, dripped blood, and painted muddied footprints red.

Some died later.

Daily howls of grief blew through her window as more and more slaves died from wounds—or disease.

It mattered not what caused the deaths, the bawling sounded the same and seemed more numerous with each passing day.

Returning warriors also celebrated their victories. They spoke of British soldiers fleeing waves of brave Africans. They spoke of dead British soldiers, their previously white pantaloons so drenched with blood, they were as red as their uniform jackets.

None of it seemed to impact Rosette in her suffering. Even gunfire induced no fear in her. She did not care.

She simply wanted to die in her bed.

Maman pulled the filled bedpan aside and replaced it with a clean one. "Your Papa really hoped the British would have surrendered to avoid more bloodshed. But they might attack Belvidere any day now."

"Does Papa still believe Malcolm...Captain McDonald would lead an attack here?"

"I am afraid so. Kojo saw him with the British soldiers in Beauséjour on their way to Gouyave. Belvidere is next."

Rosette doubted the British could take Belvidere, protected by hundreds of armed men secure and battle-ready in hillside fortifications behind the house. Each day, huge trees came crashing down to be positioned as barriers against any British attack. And Papa had boasted that the two six-pounder cannons seized from the Gouyave militia post, now nested in strategic positions overlooking Belvidere, would turn British soldiers into chopped meat.

Any hope of seeing Malcolm again resided only in her youthful imagination. Despite that, would she ever forgive him, for first abandoning her, and then returning with the hated soldiers to attack the family's estate?

Even if by some miracle, she survived the fever and he survived a catastrophic attack on Belvidere, he would never recognize the face she saw in the mirror. Nor did she want him to see her bony cheeks, sunken eye sockets, and fat lips.

Why did God create such a nightmare for her?

Maman adjusted the pillow around Rosette's head. "Kojo also told me Captain McDonald visited a sick slave woman left behind in Beauséjour. She told Kojo the captain wanted to profess his love for you."

Rosette coughed. "Maman, are you making up stories to try to remedy my condition?"

"No, my dear. Kojo spoke to me in private before they left tonight. He said he wanted you to know the truth. In case he or the captain died tonight."

"Die, white man." Kojo knew exactly what he had to do with his cutlass hanging over Captain McDonald's head. He swung with all his might.

"Kojo, no." The captain's blue eyes, partially hidden behind his upheld hands, widened with fear in the torch light.

Kojo slammed the cutlass onto the dirt next to the captain's head and leaned over him. "Play dead. No move."

He left the British officer lying still in the darkness and ran back to the mayhem. Just then, wailing over the sounds of gunshots, clashing metal, and dying men, a conch shell blew from the hillside—General Fédon's signal to return to camp.

Kojo yelled. "Back to Belvidere."

He jumped over bodies on the road and bolted towards the bushes. One of his warriors crawled to his knees in difficulty. Kojo dropped the torch, lifted the man on to his shoulder, and raced into the hills with the surviving warriors.

Bullets raked the trees around them.

He stayed low and kept running with the man over his shoulder. A wetness, too thick to be sweat, dripped down Kojo's back. The firing ceased behind them, giving way to the crunch of scampering bare feet on fallen leaves and twigs. Men panted. Some moaned.

The man on Kojo's shoulder wheezed.

Kojo stopped and placed the man in a sitting position.

Simon.

"You are hurt, my brother," Kojo said.

"That officer shoot me." Simon coughed, and the discharge sprayed on Kojo's chest. "I see you take his head."

Captain McDonald?

Kojo never lied to his friend. Since the day they met on that brutal ship from Benin, in chains and in tears. They had remained trusted friends even after Simon became a free runaway in the mountains around Grand Étang, and Kojo continued to serve Massa Turnbull in practiced subservience.

When Kojo finally took his liberty from Massa, the day Venus and the baby died, Simon welcomed his friend into his community shacks and caves cleverly disguised in the jungle. Kojo's new family of runaways gave him comfort for his grief and protection from his fears.

In turn, Kojo gladly helped forge the alliance between the maroon community and General Fédon. He assured the general that the runaways under Simon's leadership could be valiant warriors in the rebellion against the British.

It pained Kojo that his parting gift to his warrior brother would be a lie.

But pain Kojo would nonetheless bear, if only to ensure Simon a joyous reunion with his ancestors. Killed heroically in battle.

Kojo had no time to explain that he knew the man who shot him.

"Yes," Kojo said. "I took care of the white captain that shoot you."

Simon smiled. "I going too, Brother." He held his chest and rolled into Kojo's arms.

This Kojo knew. If Simon had met the young captain who shot him, they would have exchanged mutual respect. Sometimes in war, good men kill good men. But it did not make the anguish any easier.

Kojo lifted his dead friend on his shoulder and continued up the hill. He would rectify the lie. Despite the weight, distance, and his sorrowful heart, he would carry Simon back to Belvidere for a respectful burial.

Kojo had repaid the debt he owed Captain McDonald for stopping Venus's whipping that day.

The captain would not be given a second chance.

Malcolm stood at attention in General Lindsay's office, his uniform muddy and bloody. "General, sir. I wish to plead the case for an immediate attack on Belvidere."

Malcolm believed a predawn march on Belvidere might force an early surrender, before General Fédon and his chiefs returned from their attack on Gouyave Estate. A quick victory meant less bloodshed, and improved chances of rescuing the prisoners. But also—this Malcolm could not tell the general—less of a chance the Fédons, especially Rosette, would be endangered.

Just as important now, he did not want to find himself in another faceoff with Kojo, the runaway slave who had just inexplicably spared his life.

British law in Grenada required runaways like Kojo to be hanged immediately.

Malcolm pressed on. "Sir, they came with about four hundred men on foot. They must climb mountains and valleys to get back to Belvidere. We have a road and horses. We can get there before them, before sunrise. Right now, Belvidere is under-protected."

General Lindsay scratched his bushy sideburns. "Captain, we just had a victory. I think we should consolidate and reinforce our positions in case the savages return. *We* could be under-protected."

"I understand, sir. But I do not think they will attack again tonight. I clearly heard one of their chiefs call for a return to Belvidere."

"It could be a ploy."

"Maybe. But I doubt it. They lost twelve dead and more than thirty wounded that we know of. Some left carrying others. It will be a slow hike for them. They took a beating from our brave soldiers."

The general held a steady gaze on him. "My decision is final. The men still need their rest. Prepare them to move out at dawn."

Malcolm rode back to Dr. Hay's house in bitter disappointment. General Lindsay's decision now gave the rebels ample time to return to Belvidere to prepare for the British attack.

General Fédon would be waiting.

Equally terrifying was Malcolm's cordial relationships with the enemy. He knew General Fédon. He loved Rosette. And complicating Malcolm's loyalty even more, he owed his life to Kojo, a runaway slave, and one of General Fédon's rebel chiefs.

Malcolm might encounter all three of them today.

His leadership classes did not prepare him for this. Did Father...Colonel McDonald, understand the noose he had set in motion for his own son?

Malcolm returned to Dr. Hay's gallery, hoping for

some sleep to calm his nerves. He tossed about on his blanket for about two hours before he fell asleep. But soon thereafter, a soldier awakened him with a message to meet with General Lindsay immediately.

Malcolm readied his uniform and weapons and rode up the dark hill to the militia post, guarded by half-asleep soldiers.

The general, looking rather dilapidated, handed him a dispatch from the council president, who acted as King George's chief executive in the absence of the governor. The letter spoke of heavy fighting to the east, where valiant British soldiers killed an estimated two hundred rebels. But the tone of the letter shifted, when it turned to the relatively lethargic report about Gouyave. The last part of the letter struck at Malcolm:

> *"I repeat to you, my positive order, that you immediately form as strong a detachment as possible of the effectives of two regiments, and of trusty armed negroes from the estates. And proceed without the smallest delay for the camp at Fédon's, there to support the general attack, by acting vigorously against the enemy as occasion may require.*
>
> *And I hold you answerable for every ill consequence, which may attend your further disobedience.*
>
> *Proceed immediately with what you have.*
>
> *I am, & C.*
>
> *"K. F. M'KENZIE"*
>
> *"Colonel McDonald"*

Malcolm recognized the stern tone of the dispatch as his father's. And the message was clearly meant more for

Malcolm than for General Lindsay.

Mr. McKenzie merely provided the signature.

Malcolm looked up from the letter and at the general. "Does that mean we march now?"

"Yes, captain. Prepare your men for victory at Belvidere."

Malcolm worried it might be too late.

Dr. Hay gazed out of the hut, expecting it to happen today. As soon as British soldiers from Gouyave attacked Belvidere, General Fédon would order the immediate execution of his fifty-one prisoners, including Governor Ninian Home, Mr. Turnbull, and Dr. Hay.

His certainty of his approaching demise started when General Fédon and his brother, Jean-Pierre, led a long trail of fatigued rebels out of the woods. Just as the first spear of sunlight pierced the misty dawn. Some of the rebels staggered with gaping wounds. Others carried dead comrades on their shoulders, limp arms swaying at their backs, like a hunting party returning with game. The rest of the men, a few hundred, collapsed in sighs and moans on a flat grassy area just down from the prison hut. Jean-Pierre directed several of the able-bodied to collect the wounded in an open shed with thatched roof, away from the others.

General Fédon, in bloodied clothes, panted his way up to the hut and roared. "Let Dr. Hay out. We have wounded below."

Dr. Hay hurried out of the doorway, and the guard handed him his medical satchel. They did not trust him to keep his surgical tools. The guards must have seen or heard how quickly he hacksawed mangled limbs and dug into live flesh with his clawed bullet extractor. Tools that could quickly become weapons in the hands of desperate men wanting to escape.

He had thought of escaping. But he knew a mad dash into the woods would quickly end at the hands of ferocious rebels. They had stronger motivation to see his blood than he had jungle skills to evade them. Even more consequential, the general had ordered the guards to kill all the prisoners if but one escaped.

The general faced the hut, his eyes in a cold gaze. "Tyrant Home, I know you can hear me in there. This is your last hour to surrender the island. Every day, more and more men die because of you. Your coward soldiers are on the way up here from Gouyave. One shot from them, and you all die."

Cries for mercy from the hut followed Dr. Hay down the hill to the wounded rebels.

The general must have been preparing for this day. He appeared distant in the last few days, even when Dr. Hay visited Rosette. The doctor wondered now if her failing health contributed to the general's increasingly sour mood.

"Keep your pleas for the devil," General Fédon hollered over the whimpering. "From today, I name this camp, *Camp de la Mort*. Camp of Death, for you English pigs."

The general's words floated over the quiet hillside, deflating the already melancholy Dr. Hay as he headed towards the first wounded rebel.

Kojo struggled up the muddy hill towards him with a body over his shoulder and a shovel in his hand. When they drew abreast of Dr. Hay, the dead man, upside down, his head bobbing against Kojo's back, looked remarkably like the man who chopped Lavallée to death. Tears streaked down Kojo's dusty face.

He stared past Dr. Hay without a word and turned down a trail into the woods.

Dr. Hay learned from the wounded men's conversations that they just returned from Gouyave, where both rebels and British soldiers lost lives. He amputated a boy's leg, the knee and tissue badly shattered by a musket ball. But the boy, not yet eighteen, soon died from loss of blood.

Disappointingly, the boy's passing found little empathy in Dr. Hay's dry soul. Father Pascal, in his thick robe and muddy sandals, kneeled at the boy's side and performed the last rites without acknowledging Dr. Hay. The priest, now a full sympathizer with the rebellion, probably expected he might soon have to perform the last rites on Dr. Hay as well.

Nonetheless, weakening from hunger and trembling in the cool morning, Dr. Hay quickly extracted bullets from a few rebels and cleaned up flesh wounds on others.

Now back in the hut, he surveyed General Fédon's preparations for the British attack. Most of the men who just returned from Gouyave slipped into the woods at the foot of the mountains, along the river bank and out of sight of any army choosing a direct attack on the estate. They carried cutlasses and eight-foot pikes.

Among a few Frenchmen with carbines and muskets accompanying the rebels, Dr. Hay thought he recognized Bourbon. In the distance, the Jean-Pierre's Chadeau Estate looked abandoned, probably because it was not as easily defended as Belvidere.

On the hills behind the Belvidere great house, the two six-pounder cannons, once in possession of Dr. Hay's Gouyave militia, sat hidden in batteries behind makeshift screens of branches and vines. Everywhere, smoke rose like fog from abandoned campsites, the women, children, and elderly having moved into wooded areas away from the potential battlegrounds. The bland aroma of boiled beef and dasheens lingered in the air even after the morning mist drifted away.

General Fédon's plans seemed obvious. When the unsuspecting British attacked head-on, the cannons would first blast into action, pounding devastation and confusion on the troops. On signal, the cannons would stop, and the rebels hiding in the ravine would emerge to attack the bewildered British from the side in a surprise flanking movement. The general would then rush from the heights with his men. The British would have little choice but to flee—or die.

Mercifully, Dr. Hay would not be alive to see the massacre. If General Fédon kept his word, his prisoners would be dead after the first British shot.

Deceptive quiet blanketed the camp—until General Fédon bellowed. "Here they come."

Dr. Hay could not see the approaching British soldiers, but from the distance, tapping drums and wailing bugles announced their arrival at Belvidere.

Cries rose in the hut.

Dr. Hay shut his eyes and said a silent prayer for his deceased parents, and for quick deliverance from a painful death.

Chapter Forty

At first light, Colonel McDonald paced his Fort George office, clutching General Lindsay's most recent situation report at his back. The uplifting news from Gouyave greeted him with a troubling mix of hope and apprehension after a long sleepless night.

Malcolm had at last been christened in battle for King George.

The news came after days of distressing news from around the island. Misguided slaves had abandoned their plantations by the thousands, burning fields and killing their masters in the most brutal and ungodly manner. The outnumbered eighty troops from the St. Andrew's and St. Patrick's regiments fled Grenville, marching to join General Lindsay's soldiers in Gouyave. The crucial Grenville port now lay in the hands of Fédon's rebels.

It pained the colonel that he could not spare any of the St. George's troops, many in the throes of the fever, to help hold Grenville. He had already assigned most of the St. George's militia to capture Gouyave and Belvidere. On the day the troops departed the capital, he stood in the market square to watch his son march off to battle. Militiamen waved tearful goodbyes to their wives and children, some shivering from fear and fever.

When Colonel McDonald met with the executive council the previous night, all the members vigorously warned of a calamity if the rebellion continued much longer. Plundered food stocks, burnt crops, fever spreading, and brutal killings blended in a cursed recipe for disaster. They pointed to the rising number of cancelled commercial shipments to the island. The key ports appeared staged to feed conflict, not human hunger.

St. George's in the southwest for British troops and weaponry. Now, Grenville port to the northeast for French revolutionary soldiers and weaponry for General Fédon.

Grenada sat in the middle, dying from bloodshed, shivering from fever, and weakening from hunger.

Soon, the island would not have enough agoutis and rats for the slaves to eat.

And only because a savage mulatto traitor sought to betray King George.

But the colonel held his grit. The snake resided in Belvidere. And Captain McDonald, the colonel's own son, was about to chop off its head.

The colonel read General Lindsay's note a third time.

> *Captain McDonald has availed himself proudly and bravely at the Gouyave Estate attack. The rebels were sent fleeing with great losses. So far, we have counted twelve dead on the spot and twice that number wounded. We lost three regulars dead and two wounded. Both regular and militia troops behaved*

*with great intrepidity, except for a
few drunks.*

*Invigorated from victory, Captain
McDonald has promptly departed
Gouyave to attack General Fédon's
camp at Belvidere. Captain
McDonald's leadership and courage
is a source of great optimism. By
sundown, Belvidere will be ours, the
prisoners will be freed, and the rebel
leaders dispatched with urgent
justice at the end of the ropes.*

The colonel salivated at the thought of sweet revenge
denied him since General Cornwallis surrendered His
Britannic Majesty's forces at Yorktown, fourteen years ago.
The wretched humiliation and physical depravation at the
hands of America traitors, French dogs, and African
barbarians sealed the colonel's purpose in life.

His greatest fulfillment came from sending to hell as
many of the King's enemies as God allowed.

And General Fédon embodied all the hog sewage one
might expect in such an enemy.

A Frenchman with African blood.

Colonel McDonald had but one final wish for General
Fédon: that Malcolm be the one to tighten the rope around
the mongrel's neck. It would sweeten the revenge, return
Belvidere Estate to the McDonald name, and restore the
colonel's faith in his son.

Yet, he tamed his excitement. If the day's events did
not go as planned, it would not be the first time his son
disappointed him.

But it could be the last.

⚔

"Looks like a trap." Surrounded by his platoon leaders on
the windy Chadeau heights, and under cloudy skies,

Malcolm gazed through his telescope at the Belvidere hillside defenses. He recalled Rosette standing on her Belvidere verandah and pointing at her Uncle Jean-Pierre's house on Chadeau, where Malcolm now stood. The Fédon brothers used to mock each other across the half-mile divide, a deep gorge blanketed by thick greenery. "They must have abandoned Chadeau to give us a clear path to Belvidere. 'Tis like an invitation."

An invitation to a rebel ambush.

Scattered groups of men with spikes and cutlasses occupied a few tactical positions across the mountain facing Chadeau. But their numbers seemed deceptively inadequate to defend the estate. By now, the estimated four hundred fighters would have returned from the previous night's attack in Gouyave.

Where were they?

Dying smoke drifted from cooking fires that must have fed thousands. And hundreds of deserted thatched-roof campsites blotched the landscape.

Many more rebels probably lay hidden in the woods, waiting to pounce on the unsuspecting British troops.

Malcolm pointed at a group of uniformed men high on the ridge behind the Great House. "French officers. I would bet my last shilling they have the cannons disguised in the foliage close by. See for yourselves."

He handed the telescope to one of his officers.

Malcolm hoped the show of disciplined British forces in their proud red and white uniform, armed with muskets and carbines, and marching to drum beats might lead the rebels to a quick surrender. He at least expected General Fédon to abandon Belvidere, like they had in Gouyave, maybe leaving behind just the women, children, and the sick—like Rosette.

This close to her now, he worried even more about her condition. He had witnessed how the Bulam fever mercilessly stewed the victims' minds and bodies to their last breath.

How did Rosette and he arrive here since he last saw her almost two years ago? Such a far cry from that sunset evening in St. George's. He had held her close and tasted her willing lips. The pure delight banished thoughts of war, fear, and hatred.

If God would but grant Malcolm two minutes with her, he would be eternally grateful. And it mattered not what Father, Mother, or anyone else had to say about the *unnatural* feelings he held for a mulatto girl.

But doubt clouded his thoughts.

If he saw her, would she reject him as an enemy? Or would she see them the way he did? She, a woman. He, a man. Stripped naked of the color, heritage, and religious barriers that separated their peoples. And left only with the bare humanity that sparked in each other's presence.

Today, he carried orders to attack her family's magnificent Belvidere estate to rescue the governor and put a halt to her father's rebellion. Did he have the resolve to order the assault?

God forbid if an attack hurt or killed any of the Fédons.

Malcolm recalled General Fédon saying that his brother Jean-Pierre was more valuable than fifty Englishmen. How many Englishmen was Rosette worth? Would General Fédon dare kill his prisoners like Dr. Hay and the British governor?

The grieving governor lost his wife, then his freedom, trading his Persian rugs and house staff on his Paxton House Estate for a muddy prison hut, guarded and threatened by his own slaves.

The burden of rescuing him now rested in Malcolm's hands.

Why would Father...Colonel McDonald, force Malcolm into such a predicament that poured anguish on his mind with the turbulence of a crashing waterfall?

Only God possessed the power to save Malcolm from this impending damnation. Only He could wish a peaceful surrender into existence.

Yet, no white flags appeared anywhere on the stubborn hillside. The rebels and their French allies seemed determined to fight.

One of Malcolm's officers peered through the telescope at the hillsides. "If the French are brazened enough to show up in uniform, greater numbers might be landing in Grenville in the coming days. 'Tis to our advantage to attack as soon as our soldiers are in position."

Another officer disagreed. "If we march straight up there, we might as well stick our heads in their cannons and wait for them to fire. We must fight on our terms, not theirs."

Malcolm thought for a moment. "I think it best we circle around to the top and attack from behind. We would get to the prisoners first and surprise the cannon squads. It might take longer to get there quietly, but less risky than a frontal assault."

The officers nodded in agreement.

"But we will need reinforcements and a few howitzers to keep the cannons busy," Malcolm said. "Send a team to see what the terrain looks like to get up there. In the meantime, I will notify General Lindsay of the plan."

"Yes, sir." The officers saluted and hurried away.

Just then, a tall, well-built mulatto man named Louis La Grenade, a captain from the St. George's militia, marched up. "Sir, we have a disturbing situation."

"Tell me," Malcolm said.

"A rumor has been spreading among our militiamen. They say a rebel force is moving towards St. George's. They say 'tis better to die defending their families in the capital than to die attacking Belvidere."

Malcolm snapped. "That is an abomination."

"I agree, sir. But if the rumor persists, we might have a mutiny on our hands."

"Pass this word immediately. Any man who abandons his post will be shot at once."

"Yes, sir."

Malcolm returned to Jean-Pierre's house and wrote a dispatch to General Lindsay in Gouyave.

Sir,

In the current situation, it is prudent that I put off the attack until I receive reinforcements and at least two howitzers you can afford to send with the greatest haste. My best estimate is that our men are outnumbered five to one and an ambush condition may exist. We have a plan, which I think best not to lay forth in this letter. I believe reinforcements will assure victory and lift the fighting morale of the men. They also perceive the situation as precarious. Captain Louis La Grenade has reported threats of desertions and mutiny among the militiamen. Much of the discord comes from the men drinking rum given to them by loyal slaves along the way here. I urge strict abstinence among any troops you send.

Respectfully yours,

Captain Malcolm McDonald

He assigned a fast rider with an escort team to deliver the message to General Lindsay.

A few hours later, after reviewing the plans with officers and inspecting the troops, Malcolm returned alone to the edge of the front yard facing Belvidere. Through his telescope, he scanned the defenses for any changes, but all indications suggested that General Fédon continued to expect a frontal attack.

Malcolm planned to leave enough men on Chadeau to make the rebels believe the British were still camped, while the main force circled around the rear for a surprise attack. If General Lindsay saw the wisdom of sending a few howitzers, those would keep Fédon's rebels occupied, and ensure the surprise.

Malcolm shifted the telescope towards the Great House and adjusted the lenses.

His heart thumped.

A girl stood peering through a telescope in his direction.

Rosette?

The height and feminine figure clearly belonged to Rosette. But she looked slenderer and more vulnerable than he remembered, especially in the thin dress blowing about her in the wind. He wished he could stretch out his hands and touch her.

He kept the telescope steady.

She stood frozen in his sight.

He had waited almost two years to see her again, but fate only granted him a distant image for his longing heart. It nonetheless warmed him enough to desire even more the sound of her voice, the smoothness of her skin, the pleasure of her kiss.

He needed more than a vision through a telescope. But how, and when?

A horse galloping towards him cut through his wishful thinking.

He recognized the rider as the one he assigned to deliver General Lindsay's first dispatch to St. George's the previous afternoon. The man Malcolm had asked to drop off bread and water to Lena at the Beauséjour slave village.

The horseman dismounted and hurried up to Malcolm.

"Captain." The man handed Malcolm a note. "I stopped off at Beauséjour, but there was no shack left standing, and no one around. Curious though, just one of the wreckage had red embers in the dark, like it had recently been burnt."

"Someone must have taken her. Thank you for

checking."

Malcolm read the note.

> *Captain,*
>
> *Stand your ground. The Quebec has landed with reinforcements, and more militiamen have arrived in Gouyave from St. Andrew's and St. Patrick's. I am on my way to Belvidere with them and cannons.*
>
> *Onward to victory,*
>
> *General Lindsay*

Almost as if in response to the note, a thick cloud darkened the sky and massive thunder shook the countryside.

When Malcolm pointed his telescope back towards the Great House, Rosette was gone.

But General Fédon now stood on the verandah, next to a stocky woman with a bright red headscarf. She held a rigid akimbo stance, her fists on her hips and her head upright like an alert hen. Malcolm felt certain she was one of the women who led the Shango dance the night he stayed in Belvidere.

Only then he recalled Lena's warning about General Lindsay.

He go have big trouble in Belvidere. How did she know General Lindsay would be in Belvidere?

If trouble headed their way, Malcolm knew exactly what to do to stop it before it began. And he had to do it now, before General Lindsay arrived.

Rosette thought her pillow must be as wet from her tears as the roof from the torrential rainfall soaking Belvidere. Physically, she felt stronger than she had in ten days. She had kept down the soup and cocoa Maman served her that morning. And with her increasing appetite, came a little more strength. Just enough strength to creep out of the bedroom an hour ago, and down to the verandah for a quick view of the British soldiers on Chadeau—without Papa's knowledge.

She wished she had a telescope to search for Malcolm among the soldiers. But the thunder and rain began to pound Belvidere before she could find one. She returned to her room in tears, wishing for sleep to rescue her.

But frantic yells from outside her window changed her mind. Footsteps sloshed up the verandah steps.

More shouts in the house. Papa's voice roared.

Had the attack begun? She heard no gunshots.

Just the distant tapping of a drum.

Papa must have received more bad news. "That young Englishman is a raging lunatic."

Rosette rolled off her bed and peered past the curtain.

Sheets of rain distorted two figures slowly climbing up the road to the house.

One looked like a British soldier holding a stick above his head. The stick carried a white flag, drenched and hanging limp. The other, a boy about twelve, tapped the drum in a slow, solemn beat. The soldier gestured the boy to stop.

The soldier held the flagstick high in the downpour and continued in a proud stride towards the house.

Malcolm.

Papa's bootsteps thundered onto the verandah. "What in God's name are you doing here? I can have your head."

"General Fédon, I come unarmed to propose an amicable truce."

"Did your father send you again to deceive me, like you did with the sale of this estate."

"I know not of what you speak, sir. I still appreciate your gracious hospitality."

"The hospitality you abused to treat my daughter like garbage?"

"Sir, with all due respect. My affection for Rosette is genuine and has only grown since our first meeting."

Rosette gasped, and her hands went up to her chest. *He does love me.*

"Enough of your nonsense." Papa shouted. "Englishmen only speak of truce when they have no way to win. You have neither the men nor the will to take these hills. Now be gone before I change my mind, and have you join the prisoners on the hill."

"When your emissaries enter St. George's with a flag of truce to deliver your demands, they are treated with honor and respect."

"You are testing me. Now say your piece and leave."

"British forces are closing in on Belvidere in overwhelming numbers. You have time to prevent any further bloodshed."

"You Englishmen and your tyrant governor are responsible for every drop of blood Grenada has suffered. For years you have treated us with disdain."

"We may one day have time to debate. For now, I propose you release all prisoners into my custody. And let me have any women, children, or sick who wish to be taken to safety. Such gestures of compassion may help assure safe passage—"

"Preposterous. No prisoners will leave Belvidere while I have a single breath in my body."

"Monsieur Fédon—"

"'Tis General Fédon!"

"General, I worry for the safety of you and your family. In a few hours, I will no longer have the authority to conduct this arrangement. At least Madame Fédon and Rosette can come with me. If she is not well, I promise you I will get her the best medical care we have."

"Captain." Papa's voice lowered to the tone he used when his verbal slashing gave way to physical reckoning. "Your naivete is exhausting. Leave."

Malcolm, please leave now.

"Just one more thing, General. Please convey my love to Rosette. My sudden departure from Grenada was none of my doing or my wish. I wanted to stay to be close—"

Papa stomped his boot. "Go."

Malcolm saluted, made a brisk about turn and marched off into the showers.

The drum began to tap again.

Rosette struggled out of the room, her hands reaching for the walls for support. She grasped the handrail of the staircase and headed down the wooden steps, each greeting her bare feet with jabs up her weakened legs.

The tapping of the drum faded.

She stumbled out onto the verandah.

Papa stood in a circle with Bourbon, Josephina in a white dress and red scarf, a French officer, and Zab.

Papa addressed Zab and Bourbon. "Ride immediately to Grenville and take the first boat to Guadalupe. The Commissars need to make haste with their supplies."

Rosette turned her attention to Malcolm and the drummer boy marching down the road towards the tree line.

She shouted with all the might her feeble lungs could muster. "Malcolm."

But a tremendous thunder shook the estate and grabbed his name from the air. The woods swallowed him up.

She knew now she would never see him again. It felt worse than impending death.

Just past midnight, Malcolm stood on one knee in the lantern light and pointed at the map spread out on the floor of Jean-Pierre Fédon's empty living room. "General Lindsay, sir. Even with the additional reinforcements you brought tonight, a frontal attack would be suicidal."

Rain pelted the roof, and gusts rattled the shutters. The general sat shivering on the floor, his hair and bushy sideburns still dripping from the rain after his overdue arrival from Gouyave. He held a musty blanket tightly wrapped around him. Besides his mud-splattered white pantaloons, the only other evidence he might be an officer—the highest-ranking officer in Grenada at that—was the grip of his Sharpe flintlock pistol peeking from below the blanket.

Malcolm wondered if the general's shivering was because of the cool rain, or an early bout of Bulam fever. Rosette might have recovered from her own episode. If so, why did she not come to the door, or acknowledge him from her window when he was talking to General Fédon?

"That was a brave move to face off with Fédon himself," General Lindsay said. "Too bad he did not accept your offer." He stared at the map in a daze. "Captain, you hinted at a plan in your note."

"The best approach was a surprise attack from above the ridge, here." Malcolm pointed at the map. "It would have achieved two objectives at the same time. Take the cannons and free the prisoners."

"Good. We move before daybreak."

"The rains changed everything, sir. The reconnaissance team reported that the climb would be bogged down in mudslides. 'Tis a total mess now. If detected on the climb, our men would be easy targets stuck in the mud. I am afraid all our options now face grave risks—"

Heavy banging on the door.

Malcolm glanced back. "Come in."

Captain La Grenade marched into the room with a wind gust, leaving a mud trail behind him. He saluted, and his wet sleeve tossed droplets onto the floor. "My apologies for interrupting, but my latest report might delay our plans for taking Belvidere."

"Get on with it." The general snapped.

"Sir, the main detachment of the St. George's militia abandoned camp and now headed back to the capital.

Rumors are spreading that General Fédon is keeping us bogged down here, so most of the rebels can attack the capital. I believe drunkenness added to their insubordination. Wish I had better news, sir."

"Thank you, Captain La Grenade. Dismissed."

When Captain La Grenade left, shutting the door behind him, General Lindsay turned to Malcolm in a solemn tone. "This battle is now in the hands of God. I will need to convey our dismal situation to St. George's. Please return in an hour to have it delivered."

When Malcolm returned, the general, looking more disheveled and distraught than an hour ago, handed Malcolm the letter.

"Please review it for accuracy," General Lindsay said.

Malcolm read it.

"Post before Belvidere, 21 March 1795.

"SIR

"Upwards of one half of the militia have left me, contrary to the most positive orders, and most likely on accord of a steady supply of rum from the negroes. I have been prevented from carrying my plans into execution. We face much hardship from the extreme badness of the weather, and our best plans are delayed until better conditions and more reinforcements. I am of the mind to grant leave to the men that remained behind so that they can return to St. George's to refresh themselves for two days. By then, conditions would be more favorable for operations.

"Further I beg leave to add, that the utmost exertion of every individual will be necessary to follow up this business; and it

is with much regret I hear, that there are many persons doing no duty at St George's, that might be of great use here.

"If our numbers should be reinforced, it will not be more than adequate to the service.

"I have the honor to be,

"COLIN LINDSAY"

Malcolm folded the letter and inserted it into a pouch. "This is precisely the situation, sir."

Still seated on the floor, the general extended his hand and shook Malcolm's. "Thank you, Captain. It has been a real honor to serve with you."

Malcolm had taken no more than a dozen steps into the rain when a gunshot shook the house. He rushed back and pushed open the door.

General Lindsay lay on the floor, a pistol in his hand, and his bushy sideburns dripping red.

Chapter Forty-One

8 April 1795

Two days after General Lindsay shot himself, Colonel McDonald leaped off his horse, stormed into Dr. Hay's house chewing a spit-soaked cigar stub, and accosted Malcolm.

"No son of mine will allow himself to be defeated by a mixed-race mongrel." Colonel McDonald's barks rumbled through the seaside house like thunder rolling over Belvidere. "Your retreat from Chadeau to Gouyave without firing a shot, even after General Lindsay's sacrifice, will go down in history as cowardice."

General Lindsay's death still shook Malcolm. He could only guess that the general had an early onset of the fever. When mixed with anxieties over the bad weather and widespread desertions among the militia, it must have led him to suffer exceedingly in his mind. But rumors persisted among the loyal negroes in the militia that General Fédon had a Shango woman working on his behalf. They said she willed the rain showers, dispirited the militia, and blew winds of hopelessness at General Lindsay.

Malcolm held little accommodations for such superstitions. But he also resisted Colonel McDonald's attempts to dump the dreadful consequences of the past two days on his shoulders.

"Sir," Malcolm protested. "General Lindsay recommended in his dispatch to withdraw—"

"General Lindsay is dead. I am now in full command. We are not going to sit here until these drunkards are refreshed. We will attack Belvidere today."

"With due respect, sir, the insurgents have us terribly outnumbered. They have cannons on advantageous grounds, and the muddy conditions might—"

"Conditions? Rubbish. There are no perfect conditions in war. As long as General Fédon is alive, we have a war to fight."

Malcolm knew when his father's capacity for reason had been reduced to naught. Obviously, General Lindsay's caution about a potential trap had but little sway on Colonel McDonald. He seemed steadfast with his decision to launch a reckless attack on General Fédon's stronghold.

Colonel McDonald continued. "Today you will learn a valuable lesson in leadership. I met the deserters on their way back to St. George's and turned them around. I set a few examples for them to get the message. They are back and ready to fight."

Even before Colonel McDonald arrived in Gouyave, the lead riders reported to Malcolm that Colonel McDonald ordered the executions of the three militia leaders who abandoned the camp in Chadeau. He left their bodies hanging from trees in the Beauséjour slave village.

Malcolm snapped to attention. "I await your orders, sir."

"We march to Belvidere in an hour."

This time, Malcolm did not need a one-armed woman to tell him that big trouble awaited him and Colonel McDonald in Belvidere, as it did for General Lindsay.

Through gaps in the wooden wall, Dr. Hay peered at General Fédon and his rebels in their frantic preparations for war on the muddy Belvidere hills. So much had changed in the past two days. First, rumors of General Lindsay's death and the British soldiers' unexpected withdrawal from Chadeau spawned celebrations across the estate. General Fédon sang and danced with the negro rebels. Even the birds seemed to chirp louder, and the rushing river sounded invigorated by a spirit of victory.

But a sense of dread darkened the mood among the prisoners.

General Fédon yelled at the prison hut. "You tyrants in there. Did you see that? Your soldiers have come to their senses. Governor, time to give up your forts in St. George's."

By all appearances, the British had abandoned the fight, and maybe about to surrender the island like they did sixteen years earlier.

Dr. Hay was aware of the heavy price the British Empire paid to control its sugar-rich islands from rebelling slaves and warring French. The last report he saw estimated that, just in the past year, the British buried about twelve thousand men killed in action in the islands. Many thousands more died from fever. Grenada was but one of many fires the British struggled to put out.

Governor Home also knew the diminishing odds for the island. As his courage waned, it infected the other prisoners. One of them whispered to Dr. Hay that he would rather welcome death than suffer another day of distress.

But everything changed that morning, soon after Dr. Hay had been called to the Fédons' estate house to treat several rebels wounded in overnight action. Two horsemen galloped their horses up the hill to the house and summoned General Fédon with bad news. British soldiers were on their way back to Belvidere—led by Colonel McDonald.

General Fédon exploded.

For once, Dr. Hay felt thankful to be quickly escorted back to the hut, where he relayed the news to his fellow prisoners. Their reactions ranged from excitement that finally they might be rescued, to dismay that General Fédon might have them all killed at the first shot.

For now, the general and his brother seemed more occupied with ambushing Colonel McDonald, than with killing prisoners.

Malcolm trotted his horse next to Colonel McDonald, afraid any attempt at conversation might lead to more verbal stabs from his father. Malcolm struggled to recall the last time he and the colonel held respectful regard for each other, as father and son. It must have been the sunny day Father said farewell in St. George's harbor, as he embarked on his journey to England. The day he assigned Malcolm to meet Monsieur Fédon, with a hate-filled warning:

I would rather split open that mongrel's skull like a coconut before I shake his hand like a gentleman.

How mockingly fate must have planned Malcolm's life from the morning he left St. George's on his first ride to Belvidere. First, the head wound from Mr. Turnbull delivered Malcolm into Mrs. Turnbull's—Charlotte's—compassionate arms. But she did more than pleasure him.

She opened his eyes.

She pulled back the curtains that hid Kojo's anger, Lovely's pain, and Venus's despair. Slaves screamed in the hands of brutes like Mr. Turnbull, and in crushing sugar mill rollers. They bled from whippings, they heard their own bones crack on the wheel, they saw their own legs chopped for a fleeting taste of freedom.

Charlotte exposed Malcolm to the true cost of sugar, and the true price for the luxury English mansions owned by sugar barons like Governor Home—now a prisoner to his own slaves, in a mud hut without roasted turkey, Persian rugs, and Galbiani paintings.

Only fate had the cunning to plan this day.

Malcolm understood Father's rage about Malcolm's indiscretion with Charlotte. Father probably had no more strength than Malcolm—or Dr. Hay, to resist her feminine inducements.

Fate had also ushered the Fédons and Rosette into his heart. But why would Father punish Malcolm for exchanging civility with the Fédons even before the rebellion? Maybe the path to this day began with Father's capture and imprisonment at Yorktown. He returned to England with fiery repugnance towards all things American, French, and African.

Fourteen years later, his fire raged on. And it scorched anyone in his way. Even Malcolm, for daring to befriend the Fédons, fornicate with Charlotte, and to cower in the face of the King's enemies.

Malcolm's separation from Father seemed as final as the separation of a head by a guillotine in Paris.

Malcolm regretted his weaknesses. They fractured the bond between son and father and led to the loss of Father's respect and admiration. He wished his father never knew his secrets.

Father knew them all—but one.

He falsely believed Malcolm's exile to Liverpool had cured him of Rosette.

He rounded the muddy trail under the midday sun, and the Belvidere great house took shape in the green smoky distance.

At that moment, Malcolm realized his future lingered on a tightrope between loyalty for his father and love for Rosette.

He had to choose, today.

Rosette leaned against Maman to catch her breath. From the hill above Belvidere Estate, she gazed down on cannon batteries, felled trees, defensive ditches filled with fighters, and the tightly shut prison cabin. When Papa ordered the great house evacuated for fear the British would attack it, the house slaves offered to carry her up the muddy hill. But even though still weak from the fever, she refused to be treated like a cripple. People were about to die for their freedom today. Climbing a hill would be her only contribution.

Moreover, she worried what the day held in store for them. Despite Papa's vociferous poundings that the British could never take Belvidere, he had been wrong before. Two days ago, after Malcolm marched his soldiers back to Gouyave in the wake of General Lindsay's suicide, Papa expressed his confidence that they would never return. That too had been proven wrong. They were on the way back—in larger numbers.

And probably with Malcolm as one of their commanders.

She worried about his safety. She worried about her family. She worried about the fighters. She worried about Grenada.

Rosette felt numb with worry. And it seemed to tighten around her stomach in a rope of dismay.

Someone blew a conch shell from higher ground behind her. The mournful sounds rose over Belvidere, as if grief oozed out of the very land itself.

"Here they come." Papa's voice roared from the hilltop.

Drums began to beat. The plantation bell, used to summon the slaves to work, now rang aloud to prepare them for war. War songs drifted in breeze still flavored with boiled beef and dasheen. Back and forth across Belvidere Estate, drumming, singing, bell ringing.

In the distance, men in red and white uniforms

marched onto Uncle Jean-Pierre's Chadeau property.

Rosette felt a chill and hoped the fever had not returned. She held her mother tightly.

"They have two of our men," a man yelled. "A white and a black."

Without a telescope, Rosette could only make out two figures held together in the open yard facing Belvidere.

"They are throwing ropes over that tree," a Frenchman announced close by.

"That devil better not tempt me," Papa shouted. "I have more prisoners than he does."

Within minutes the two men were hanging from the tree by their necks, their legs trashing about.

Rosette cried out. Darkness rescued her. She fainted in Maman's arms.

Malcolm never expected the rancid-smelling drunkard, whom he first encountered in the St. George's tavern a few years ago, would be a French spy. When British troops captured Bourbon and Zab on their way to board a French ship in Grenville, Bourbon carried letters and documents from General Fédon to the French Commissar in Guadalupe. Letters thanking the French for supplies recently delivered: forty thousand ball cartridges, four barrels of gunpowder, five hundred firearms, and another five hundred pikes.

For years, Bourbon had drifted around the island, an eyesore to the British, a homeless vagabond earning rum money as a dishonest guide and messenger on a miserable horse. No one noticed how he chose to sleep off his drinking under trees within view of militia posts. Through unsightly teeth, he confessed to Colonel McDonald and demanded the clemency due to a white French officer captured in war.

Bourbon made no such plea for his fellow prisoner. Zab stood tall and strangely at peace with his fate. Malcolm recalled the man's distant aura the day he accompanied Rosette and Malcolm to the St. George's shoreline. The day Malcolm kissed her for the first time.

Today looked like Zab's last.

With cold glee, Colonel McDonald reminded Bourbon that he had taken the oath of loyalty to King George. As a resident of his Majesty's colony, Bourbon had committed treason, punishable by death. Zab, a mere slave in open defiance against his Majesty, also faced immediate hanging.

"Colonel," Malcolm addressed his father. "I believe these men should be spared. They will be more valuable to us alive—"

"They are criminals," the colonel shouted. "Outcasts and scourges of society. Their destiny is at the ends of those ropes. For everyone on Belvidere to see."

The disturbing vision of Bourbon's boots and Zab's bare feet twitching accompanied Malcolm to the base of Belvidere Estate with his soldiers.

On Colonel McDonald's orders, Captain McDonald led the attack on Belvidere Estate.

In a frenzy of gunshots and the roars of men at war, the soldiers charged up Belvidere. A rushing wave of red, white, leather, and metal.

Cannons boomed. Malcolm flinched.

Tree limbs and human parts shot skyward.

The British soldiers pressed forward into the mayhem of exploding fire, smoke and blood.

As they approached the great house, men climbed out of trenches and stormed down the hill towards them with cutlasses and pikes.

Malcolm shot and slashed men, not because he knew them or hated them.

He did so because if he did not, he would die.

The rebels kept coming and kept dying. Screams.

White men. Black men. Brown men.

In the madness, a brown man fell to his right. He

looked like General Fédon's brother, Jean-Pierre.

Another quick glance up at the house to the left. Rosette's window opened. A white man leaned out and aimed a musket.

Malcolm fired.

The man's head sprayed blood against her curtains.

Malcolm wanted to feel regret for soiling her room. But he had no time to feel. The sickening orgy of death consumed his humanity.

All that mattered was to live. To see Rosette again, he had to kill.

A bareback man charged with a raised cutlass. Malcolm slashed. The man's scream died in a gurgle.

Then the moment Malcolm feared.

From the right and behind them, a groundswell of black fighters. The hundreds Malcolm suspected lay in wait to attack the British flank. The surprise about which he had warned both General Lindsay and Colonel McDonald. The rebels poured out of the woods with deafening bellows that hurt Malcolm's ears and gripped him with panic.

The panic must have also seized the other British soldiers.

When Malcolm glanced back at his men, all he saw were their backs and the weapons they dropped on the ground as they fled Belvidere, leaving behind their dead and dying comrades, including the drummer boy.

"The prisoners are to be put to death."

General Fédon's words pierced Dr. Hay's heart with trepidation. He had heard the general's threats before. But everything changed when Kojo struggled up the hill with Jean-Pierre's body and stretched him out at the general's boots.

The general stood over his brother's body, smoking a cigar, as the defeated British soldiers dismantled their last tent on Chadeau and rode away. On a mound, a short distance from the prison hut, Rosette and Madame Fédon sat in a sobbing embrace.

"Mercy." Some prisoners cried out to the general. Others fell to their knees in prayer.

The door flung open. Two men entered with hammers to remove prisoners held in stocks.

"Out," they ordered those not in stocks.

Dr. Hay stepped into the sunlight.

"Dr. Hay," General Fédon called out from about twenty yards away. "Come this way."

Unsure of the general's intent, Dr. Hay plodded through the mud towards him.

"*Feu.*" The general ordered.

A gunshot blasted behind Dr. Hay. He glanced back.

One of the prisoners stumbled two steps and fell facedown. He laid still.

"General," Dr. Hay screamed. "Please show mercy on the innocent."

"Your soldiers show no mercy to my men below or to my brother," General Fédon hollered from where he stood next to Kojo. "*Feu.*"

Another shot drowned out Dr. Hay's pleas. Another man fell.

One of Dr. Hay's medical colleagues, Dr. Francis Carruthers, made a frantic dash to escape. He made it fifty yards before being shot.

Next, the guards dragged out the twelve-year-old boy, Matthew Atkinson, whose courage Dr. Hay had grown to admire. Surely General Fédon, a father himself, would spare the weeping lad.

"*Feu.*"

In horror, Dr. Hay watched the boy fall lifeless. Governor Ninian Home met his end next. Then Mr. Alexander Campbell and Mr. Turnbull.

"*Feu.*"

The general must have barked the orders forty-eight times, for when he stopped, just three of the fifty-one prisoners remained standing: Dr. Hay, Father McMahon, and Mr. Kerr.

"Mr. Turnbull still moving," one of the guards yelled from the heap of dead and dying.

"He is mine," Kojo shouted.

Kojo grabbed a pike and hurried over to the writhing bodies.

"Mercy, Kojo." The wind carried Mr. Turnbull's broken voice out of the horrid pile. "Mercy."

"You get same mercy you give my brothers and sisters."

Kojo drove the pike into Mr. Turnbull's skull.

Chapter Forty-Two

22 October 1795

Malcolm had no doubt. Father wished him dead. After the bloody defeat in Belvidere, the colonel assigned him to Fort Frederick, where men came to die of the Bulam fever. Malcolm had already survived two spells of the miserable disease, and doubted he had the stamina left to win a third.

The desire to see Rosette kept him alive. It reminded him to climb the steps to the high walls each day. There, he would breathe in the clean island air, free from the coughing in the stuffy barracks below. Free from the sporadic fighting he heard about but no longer participated in since his new assignment. Free from the barricaded St. George's down the hill. The city hid behind musket-ball proof barriers and deep entrenchments, for fear of full-scale rebel attacks and sneaky attempts to set fires.

A few times in the past months, small pockets of

rebels approached the city, but the intimidating booms of deadly cannons scattered them. Maybe Rosette had shared with General Fédon the details of the inland-facing cannon power that protected St. George's. Details Malcolm hoped would discourage any full-scale attacks on the city. Throughout the rebellion so far, the general had not attacked St. George's in the manner he attacked Gouyave and Grenville.

Ironically, the very ring of forts the French began after their 1779 victory, now kept the French and rebels away. But from the high walls of Fort Frederick, the breath-taking view of the port and the sea kept alive Malcolm's memories of Rosette and the day their hearts became one in a golden sunset.

Just twelve miles away over the mountains, he imagined Belvidere still wept from the brutality and death it had witnessed six months ago. Rosette probably slept in a room scarred by musket balls and stained by the blood of the Frenchman he had shot in her window.

The estate doubtlessly still throbbed with General Fédon's rebellious spirit. He sparked an uprising with noble intentions. But now, he captained a rebellion like a ship lost in strange seas, clouded by barbarity, sinking in disease, its compass in disarray.

A ship Rosette would never abandon.

She visited Malcolm's mind daily, but no one visited him in person. No one visited the fort, except when Colonel McDonald and his staff officers made unannounced inspections of the external fortifications. Even when Malcolm sighted them from the walls, the colonel kept his distance from the garrisoned soldiers and never requested to see Malcolm.

The vision of British soldiers, his son among them, fleeing an army of bareback slaves in Belvidere probably still haunted him. On that day, he also lost the governor, close friends, and the last sprinklings of pride in his son.

Seeing Malcolm again might just revive the colonel's

nightmares.

So, one October morning, when a soldier notified Malcolm in the mess hall that he had a visitor, he received the news with much elation—and confusion. He gobbled his meagre breakfast of eggs and salt fish and rushed down to the barricaded gate.

"Dr. Hay." Malcolm shook the doctor's hand with much exaltation. "I could not imagine who on earth would want to visit me here."

They sat on a sheltered bench in the drill yard where Dr. Hay recounted how General Fédon spared his life on that bloody day and sent him on a French ship to Guadalupe. He remained in a French prison on that island until an exchange of prisoners returned him under the British flag in Martinique. He arrived in Grenada in July, and immediately returned to Gouyave, where lifelong friends greeted him with much applause, especially the Africans.

Dr. Hay adjusted his glasses with shaky hands. "A negro of my own, at first seeing me, laid hold of my hand with both his and after looking steadfastly in my face, burst into a flood of tears. We evacuated Gouyave a week ago when it looked like Fédon was planning another attack. He now has a reward out for my head."

"I heard the revolutionaries took over the town and set up a guillotine."

"True," Dr. Hay said. "In one day, they guillotined eight negroes for eating a mule. Hunger." He gazed around the fort. "The rebels could never take this place. We have only to outlast them until we receive reinforcements, maybe in six months."

Malcolm nodded. "'Everyone says that. But how much more disease, fear, and hunger can the island withstand? We have lost several food ships lately. One stolen right out of the harbor in a brazen attack by rebels in canoes."

"The tide is turning. The French are dismayed by the Belvidere executions. They had just sent a ship to take the prisoners safely to Guadalupe. Now, they are distancing themselves from Fédon. Many slaves are returning to our side. Many are half starved. We now have a battalion of loyal black rangers, more than five hundred. They behave themselves uncommonly well. They will help us restore peace and tranquility."

Malcolm wanted to ask for whom the peace and tranquility would be restored. But he held his tongue, not wanting to insult the only visitor he had in six months. How blinded the English people had become to the fury that burned beneath the skin of the enslaved, even during peaceful and tranquil times.

Laid bare, without color, without religious walls, the rich passions of men—and women looked the same. For was it not the same discovery he made beneath Rosette's dark skin?

And once discovered and embraced, it vitalized his own life beyond words. It sustained him in his isolation from his family and heritage, it strengthened him in battle and gave him hope in sickness.

He felt alone in his discovery. But not lonely.

As long as he had Rosette, he would never be lonely.

Dr. Hay adjusted his glasses. "I must be going. But I know you have a question for me."

"I do?"

"Rosette."

"She occupies much of my thoughts."

"You in hers as well," Dr. Hay said. "Your name frequently came up in her feverish rants."

"I am confounded by all that befell the island because of her father."

"He too might be confounded. A child who plays with a spark would be dumbfounded by the blaze it can exert."

"Do we judge the child by the spark or the blaze?"

Dr. Hay slammed his fist on the bench. "He is no child! For God's sake, I pleaded with him to show mercy."

"You did what you could."

Dr. Hay calmed. "Through it all, a most memorable thing happened. Jean-Pierre's wife, a free black woman, was sitting where her husband was stretched out dead. She saw I had no more clothes after all my belongings were stolen from the prison hut. She pressed me to accept a shirt and a pair of stockings, which I did."

"And Rosette?"

"She watched from afar with Madame Fédon, like unfeeling spectators."

"In shock maybe? Grief and shame? She cannot be blamed for the actions of her father."

"True, he made those choices. And he will pay the consequences." Dr. Hay adjusted his glasses. "Your father will soon be promoted to general. Left to him, all of General Fédon's family and friends will be executed."

"That is preposterous. These are women with no sway on General Fédon. You have got to talk to him."

Dr. Hay shook his head from side to side. "I did, to no avail. He even has Father Pascal Mandel listed for hanging. And Josephina the Shango woman, but the fever already took her away. Madame Fédon fell ill and moved to Trinidad."

"And Rosette?"

"She steadfastly refuses to leave her father's side. When our reinforcements arrive, they could be hanging from a tree."

*

In blistering sunshine, Malcolm watched Delilah struggle through the Fort Frederick gate with food provisions. He had seen her several times before, the big brown woman who owned the tavern at the port. Her famous rum punch gave him much solace during his first year on the island. He now wished for some to sedate his growing fears for Rosette.

He doubted Delilah remembered him, one of hundreds, even thousands of white sun-blotched faces to pass through her tavern doors. She no longer carried a full girth, but her mannish ways with her young black helpers persisted. After the guards searched her bags on the dusty ground, she barked directions to her helpers and watched them carry her goods towards the mess hall.

She abruptly turned and marched up to Malcolm. "Captain McDonald?"

"I am surprised you remember me."

She remained serious and whispered. "You see mountains behind me, *oui*?"

"Yes?"

"A girl live over there."

"Rosette?"

She glanced around. "I say no name. I know no name." She reached into her sweaty cleavage and retrieved a small paper-wrapped package. "Sorry, it wet. If guards find sweets when they search, them thief it."

She handed it to him, and he opened it—coconut snacks. The kind Rosette and Madame Fédon made him in Belvidere.

Delilah turned to leave. "When you in she mind, she pillow wet."

His eyes too were wet. Rosette's coconut snacks, even delivered in a sweaty package, never tasted so good.

Whatever befell them in the coming months, all Malcolm prayed for now was to taste Rosette's lips again.

Even for one last time.

Chapter Forty-Three

Six months later, 19 June 1796

"The day has finally arrived." General McDonald's voice boomed over the soldiers at the Gouyave market square. "We have waited many months for this day of retribution. We shall no longer spare the rod."

Each hour, each day for the fifteen months since the Belvidere defeat, had been anguish-filled for him. All his pleas for massive reinforcements came back with the same bleak message: His Majesty's forces fought many battles along the Caribbean islands. Grenada's turn will come.

Soon.

The waiting dragged on. But gradually, the general's own efforts began to payoff. The blockades of the island ports diminished General Fédon's food and weapons from the French revolutionaries. Back in April, more than three hundred rebels were killed in one day. Rumors spread that

General Fédon had been injured. Slaves ran away from Belvidere to join the British militias. And French soldiers, dismayed by the executions and sensing defeat, began to surrender.

General McDonald's son dishonored him. But he gained a coveted prize, the promotion to general. It crowned his lifelong loyalty to King George. Today, General McDonald, with his new rank and power, would restore his Majesty's colony under the British flag.

With a wave of his hat and three loud cheers, he led the march of soldiers to Belvidere.

Later that day, victorious bellows resounded in the hilltop jungle as General McDonald's soldiers captured negroes too wounded or fatigued to flee. The echoes of cannons, the clash of metal, and the moans of the dying faded with the Belvidere sunset. The general marched towards the stone hut that served as Fédon's headquarters, his boots sloshing in the reddish mud, odorous from fresh blood. He paused beside a flaming torch at the doorway to the windowless hut.

His shadow stretched across the mud floor, past a ghastly stack of blood-stained machetes shimmering in the yellow light. On a table ahead, a bottle beckoned him amidst hand-scrawled maps and rumpled tricolor flags of the French Revolutionary Army. He marched up to the table, sniffed the bottle for signs of poison, and took a swig. The sugarcane rum burned its way down his throat, its fumes chasing away the stench of death that choked the room and soiled his breath.

Urgent winds howled outside. A gust blew through the open doorway, scattering paper maps to the floor and reminding him he needed to write a dispatch to the new governor before nightfall. He pulled up a creaky chair to the table, unfurled a blank sheet of paper from his red coat, and began to write with pen and ink left on the table.

"Your Excellency,

We are yet to capture the traitor Fédon, but it is with great satisfaction that I acquaint you with news of victory. We have crushed the rebellion that pained the King's colony of Grenada these past months. It will afford your Excellency no small measure of pride to behold the courage of the militia and their gallant officers, with their resolute determination to defeat the savagery of these misguided Negroes and their Free Coloured leaders.

On reaching the camp an hour ago, a most distressing spectacle awaited us: upwards of twenty British prisoners, stripped, with their hands tied behind their backs, having but recently been murdered in the most barbarous manner. The wretches held prisoner on this summit tonight will suffer the same fate to send a clear message across this island.

There is no Godly way for Fédon to escape. We have this peak surrounded with enough lead and dry powder to render his carcass unfit for animal consumption.

Given at Mount Qua Qua this nineteenth day of June, in the year of our Lord one thousand seven hundred and ninety-six and in the thirty-sixth year of Our Reign.

God save the King,

General Hector McDonald
Brigadier-General of the Twenty-Fifth Regiment."

When he finished the letter, General McDonald called in his colonel, a tall officer in a red coat and white blood-spattered pantaloons.

"Assign our fastest rider to deliver this message forthwith to Governor Houston in St. George's." He handed the sealed letter to the colonel. "He needs to know of our victory tonight."

"Immediately, sir."

"Any sign of Captain McDonald and his search party yet?"

"They should return any time now, General."

"If we do not find Fédon, find his daughter. We will make her talk, even if we must remove her insides."

"Search patrol reporting back, sir." Captain Malcolm McDonald snapped to attention at the doorway of the hut, sweat dripping off his face and onto his muddy red coat.

General McDonald's blue eyes held an intensity that bored through Malcolm with stinging displeasure. "Captain, did you find Fédon?"

"No, sir. He is not with the dead we found at the foot of the cliffs. He must still be up here amongst the prisoners."

Malcolm had spent the last hour frantically searching among the dead, the dying, and the suffering.

No sign of Rosette or General Fédon.

"Maybe the prisoners know his whereabouts." General McDonald stood and adjusted his red waistcoat, crossed at the chest with white leather belts. Gold epaulettes hung at the shoulders. His black top boots crunched on the dirt floor as he headed for the doorway. He pointed to the stack of bloody machetes. "Bring along one of those. The sharpest you can find."

Malcolm hesitated.

"On with it, Captain. This is not over until we find Fédon."

Malcolm picked up a machete and followed the general into the murky twilight. Steady winds howled past. Beneath a nearby tree, about thirty rebel prisoners lay huddled in a pile of human misery. Loyal Black Rangers, barefooted Africans in red coats and blue trousers, stood guard with fixed bayonets.

The general pointed at a young rebel prisoner, no more than sixteen, wearing only a tattered pair of trousers, his hands bound at his back.

"Bring me that boy."

Dried blood caked one side of his head, and his sweaty black skin gleamed in the light of flaming torches.

An African ranger walked over and prodded the young prisoner with his bayonet.

The boy struggled to his feet and limped ahead of the guard towards the general. He lowered his head and fixed his gaze on General McDonald's boots.

The general barked. "Where is Fédon?"

The boy held his slumped posture in silence.

"Tell me where your leader is hiding, and you are all free to be slaves again."

The boy looked up slowly and nodded at the remaining prisoners. "They go free too, *oui*?"

"Yes," the general shouted. "But speak before I change my mind."

The boy glanced back and forth at the general and Malcolm with a meek grin. "You look father and son, *oui*."

The general stomped his boot and hissed. "I am losing my patience, boy."

"Winds." The boy stared up in wide-eyed wonder at the cluster of swaying trees. "Winds...winds take Fédon. Fédon fly in wind."

"What in the name of King George is this savage mumbling about?"

"Sir," Malcolm said. "They have all been saying that, about Fédon disappearing in the winds."

"What African superstitious rubbish. I have heard

enough. Off with his head, Captain."

"But you said—"

"Just do as you are ordered."

"But sir, must I act contrary to my passions when victory is already ours?"

"Your only passions are to King and Country, son."

The guard slammed the butt of his musket on the young rebel's back and knocked him to his knees in front of the general.

Tears streamed down the boy's cheeks. "You lie. Fédon punish all of you."

The general stepped back three paces. "Captain, he either dies a quick death at your hands. Or a slow death with mine. Off with his head."

Malcolm held the machete stiffly at his leg. "But Father, you—"

"Captain," the general yelled. "This is your last chance. Off with his head, now."

The boy stared up at Malcolm. "Fédon will pain you and your father many years. Winds come back with Fédon–"

Malcolm stepped forward with a full swing of the machete. The boy's torso tumbled over in a spray of blood, and the severed head rolled to a stop at the general's boots.

Malcolm's hands shook in their grip on the machete.

"Control your nerves, son. We have a long night ahead. Continue searching for General Fédon and his daughter." General McDonald turned to the guard. "Bring me another prisoner."

Relieved he did not have to partake further in General McDonald's bloody vendetta, Malcolm plodded down the muddy hill from Fédon's camp to where he left his horse overlooking the smoldering great house. His hands still shook from the beheading that saved the young rebel from an even more agonizing death. What evil had befallen the island, that Malcolm had to take the boy's life to spare him from torture? War drove men mad. The madness consumed Father in the same manner it did General Fédon.

Malcolm held a steady resolve. He had to find Rosette.

And he knew exactly what he would do when he found her.

But where could she be?

No one could have survived the fire that razed the great house during the bloody fighting. Those who ran out to escape the flames were either cut down instantly or taken prisoner.

Neither General Fédon nor Rosette among them.

Malcolm dismounted in front of the burning house, where he first met Rosette and shook her innocent hand. It seemed a faraway place and time now. The heat and stench of death reminded him of the fate that awaited her if captured. The fire crackled, and smoke burned his eyes. He felt lost and helpless in the chaos around him. British soldiers marched prisoners up the hill in the gray light. In the front yard, a bloodied leg, barefoot, without a body. A body without legs, face down on scorched grass. Moans of the wounded and dying tugged at him, but he had to keep looking for Rosette.

Even with the rebellion over, an emptiness ached in Malcolm that only she could fill.

Only the distant sound of the river calmed his thoughts.

The river.

He recalled how she pointed him to the river for his bath, cautioning him about the slippery rocks, and encouraging him to enjoy the refreshingly cool water. She knew the river very well.

Might she be hiding there?

He led his horse away from the anarchy, past felled trees used as defenses, and down the steep embankment. The chaos faded behind him, and the river invited him with its bubbly solace.

He found the worn trail in the fading light and followed it to the water's edge.

He held his pistol cocked, just in case.

Where vines and tree branches hung over the river, shadows danced. Water splashed white against rocks. On the far side, water circled in a calm pool prodded with upright reeds.

In the twilight, he scanned the banks, the rocks, the reeds.

No one.

A reed moved awkwardly away from the others.

Bubbles trailed it.

Then a head surfaced. And the figure of a young woman emerged from the water, her smooth dark skin glisteningly wet.

"Kojo, I am not leaving this Godforsaken island without my daughter." General Fédon's croaky voice lacked the power it carried when the rebellion started. "She never abandoned me, and I will not abandon her tonight."

It saddened Kojo to see the injured general on his back along the shoreline, his eyes in a tired glare at the moonlight.

Kojo glanced at the two canoes he and a few trusted slaves painstakingly crafted deep in the Westerhall Bay mangrove swamp over the past six months, in case the general had to make an escape.

Defeat at the hands of *L'Anglais* came fast and bloody. But Kojo's ancestors wanted their warrior son to fight another day. If he had a breath left in his body, his longing for freedom would endure. He and the general had only to board the canoes and slip away into the night.

They had rehearsed their death-defying leap off the hill as the British closed in on them that afternoon. Kojo knew where the thickest net of vines grew. So thick, it shut out sunlight and rain like a cave would. The vines cushioned Kojo's fall better than the general's. Kojo had to carry the moaning general for hours to get to the bay.

"Miss Rosette go find us. I show her many places to hide on the way."

The general coughed. "She knows south, past Mt. Sinai, to Westerhall Bay, would bring me deliverance. Go look for her. Take what weapons you can. If any British soldier comes within view of her, kill them."

In full moonlight, Malcolm held his blanket tight around shivering Rosette. She sat in his embrace on the horse as they rode south, away from the mayhem. Away from British search parties with lanterns and swords.

Away from Belvidere.

She slipped her hand from beneath the blanket and held his.

Despite the silence between them, he never felt more complete, rewarded.

He feared if he squeezed her any tighter, she would vanish and turn this moment into a dream.

Clouds drifted across the face of the moon. The path ahead darkened. Malcolm slowed the horse. A broken horse leg now would endanger their plans.

Thunder rolled. Raindrops splattered on leaves overhead. The night closed in around them.

"We should find shelter," she whispered. "We do not want to get lost in the dark. Kojo showed me a cave up ahead to the right where the maroons used to hide."

Malcolm dismounted. He led the horse on a narrow trail between the rocks and a thick wall of vines and shrub. He pushed his way forward until a sheer cliff blocked the way.

He could see no cave in the darkness.

Rosette slid off. "Leave the horse here."

He led the horse under a tree with dense canopy and looped its rein on a branch. He knew the mount, which had carried him confidently in the storm from Gouyave to **Beauséjour Estate,** would hold its place quietly and not betray their position.

Rosette held his hand. "Come with me."

He followed her along the face of the cliff, parting shrubs as they went.

Past another huge rock, a room-size hollow opened in the cliff.

They crawled in, on to a surface layered with dry leaves and old cloth abandoned by the maroons.

In the darkness, their lips met with unabashed desire.

Oh, how long the aching months of waiting to see Rosette again. The tumultuous upheavals he endured with his father. The vicious, inhumane battles. And the agonizing journey he travelled to expel his British pretenses, to make a safe room in his heart for Rosette. They all came roaring out of him in a moment of pure longing no mountain could stop.

She must have also felt the same. Did she not also have her innocence battered in a storm of war, brutality, and subjugation? And her will to live tested in the throes of the fever, like he had? And to see her father fall from the unconquerable hero in her eyes to a defeated fugitive, hunted like an animal in the land he loved so much. Rosette must have craved release as much as Malcolm did.

She locked her arm around his neck and pushed her hips against him with a strength he never thought could exist in her slender body.

He kicked off his boots and tore off his uniform. In a flareup of repressed passion, he lifted off her thin wet dress over her head.

His hands tingled on her smooth skin and feminine curves. He lowered her to the soft floor.

She pulled him on top of her and held his head to her breast, still damp with river water.

He took her breast in his mouth and mounted her.

His erection met her. She gasped and pushed against

him.

With gentle persuasion from his manhood, her warmth welcomed him deep inside her.

They gyrated against each other. Their rhythms grew faster and harder. Their moans grew louder. He pushed harder and deeper—until a mountain of delight rose in his groin and exploded in tremors of ecstasy he felt would never end.

She cried out and dug her nails into his back, her hips shuddering in a hard press against his.

He collapsed into her arms, and their moans slowed into heavy breathing.

War be damned. Hatred be damned. Bigotry be damned.

The rain softened outside, pitapatting with the chirping chorus of awakened insects. A mist of silver moonlight filtered through the trees and pushed away the darkness in the cave.

Her smooth dark face glowed, and her eyes searched his.

If fate took her away from him again, he wanted to preserve this moment forever.

He kissed her. "I missed you so much, my love."

"I love you," she whispered.

"I love you too." He rested his head on her chest and listened to her rapid heartbeat. "Your heart seems to be saying the same thing."

She sighed. "I am happy Delilah risked carrying our messages these past months. Without her, I would have thought you no longer desired me."

"I enjoyed all your baked sweets as well."

"'Tis all I had," she said. "Such horrid times. War turns good men into beasts. I do not recognize Papa anymore."

"I too have a father in name only."

"We are dreamers." She kissed him. "When we are alone, we are perfect for each other."

Moonlight retreated. Darkness rushed in again. Thunder rumbled. The trees cried rain.

She turned away from him and grew quiet.

He knew the bliss had ended. Harsh reality returned.

He understood. They lived in times unfit for them to be one. She and her father could no longer stay in Grenada. Malcolm had to help them escape.

He would lose her if he kept her in Grenada. He would lose her if she escaped.

He kissed her cheek and tasted tears.

Just then, a big hand grabbed him by the shoulder and ripped him violently away from Rosette.

She screamed. "Kojo, no!"

"General Fédon wait for Miss Rosette," Kojo said. "I take her—alone."

Malcolm pulled on his boots, his shoulder still hurting from Kojo's iron-clawed grasp. Had it not been for Rosette's scream, Kojo might have removed Malcolm's head with one stroke of his raised cutlass. He now stood with his back to the cave while Malcolm and Rosette finished dressing.

"You will need me," Malcolm said, "to get past any British patrols."

Kojo glanced back with a suspicious scowl in the moonlight.

Rosette placed her hand on Kojo's shoulder. "We can trust Captain McDonald."

They walked in silence to the horse.

Kojo led the way holding the harness while Malcolm and Rosette rode the horse behind him. They headed south in the shadowy moonlight, she in Malcolm's tight embrace. Chirping insects and residual raindrops from the trees shared the night sounds with the slosh of the horseshoes on the muddy trail.

About an hour later, they reached a roadway.

Kojo halted the horse on the trail. "We cross here."

Malcolm quietly dismounted and crouched up to a narrow break in the wet undergrowth. To his right, fifty yards down the moonlit coastal road, a group of British soldiers stood talking.

He returned to the horse and helped Rosette off. "Stay here with Kojo."

"Be careful," she whispered.

Malcolm climbed onto the horse, silently entered the road, and galloped towards the soldiers. They turned to him with muskets at the ready. His chest pounded. Fortunately, none of the five wore ranks higher than sergeant.

"What are you doing here?" Malcolm hollered when he pulled up. "You are in the wrong location."

The men snapped to attention and saluted.

The sergeant marched up to him. "Sir, we were ordered by the St. David's militia commander to be on the lookout here for rebels fleeing Belvidere."

"You are correct, but not here." He pointed down the road, around the corner and away from where Kojo and Rosette hid. "We found maps showing they might use a trail a mile that way. I have my men at another trail a mile the other way. You must make haste."

The sergeant hesitated. "But Captain—"

"We are wasting precious time, soldier. I shall explain to your commander later. Get going now."

"Yes, sir."

The sergeant saluted and led his team on a mad foot-scramble away from Westerhall Bay.

General Fédon's withered appearance shocked Malcolm. The ravages of war had drained the man to a fraction of the robust frame and defiant demeanor that confronted Malcolm at Belvidere a year ago. The day the general chased away Malcolm and the drummer boy in the rainstorm. But now, the general's hands trembled, not like the powerful handshake Malcolm recalled from their last greeting at the burial for Rosette's grandmother, almost two years past. The funeral service Pastor Mandel Pascal conducted.

How times had changed for both priest and rebel leader.

Today, they both faced a hangman's noose if captured.

Even General Fédon's raspy voice seemed too weak to scare a bird. "I was hoping for the head of one more white man, either a British pig or a French coward. Did not expect God to send you."

"Papa," Rosette snapped. "He got us safely past the British soldiers. We must hurry."

The general growled. "Your father will hang you from a tree as fast as he will hang me."

He was right. Malcolm had now joined General Fédon in his plight.

Did the general now consider him a traitor to the British, or a young soldier enamored by his daughter's love, forced to make choices of life and death?

The general probably agonized over similar thoughts about himself, having broken his oath of loyalty to the British, and ordered helpless prisoners executed. A decision that tarnished his reputation with the French, dried up their support, and contributed to the demise of his rebellion. Now he lay on the bare ground between the two canoes, hurt, preparing to escape to God-knows-where.

Without his rebellion, without his plantation, and without a future, he seemed a shell of the intimidating bear Malcolm first met on Belvidere.

Malcolm doubted General Fédon's decision to kill the prisoners came at a moment of calm deliberation. The general had faced years of persecution and social rejection, treated like an outcast, his wife treated like a slave, and his Belvidere purchase from Father seemed like an attempt to defraud him. It did not help that Fédon thought Malcolm, a British soldier, had abused his hospitality and his daughter's sentiments. Already simmering from real and perceived injustices, General Fédon had ordered the executions in the presence of his beloved brother's body.

But did not the British, and Father, also break their obedience to God's words, that all men were created in His image? Worthy of the dignity God intended for all His children?

In the maddening clash between them, the line that separated good men from bad men blurred beyond distinction.

Malcolm's remaining sense of loyalty was to his conscience, and for the girl whose dignity and love opened doors to his soul and gave him reason to live.

He stood ready to bid farewell to Rosette, knowing it would be the last.

She stood knee deep in the moonlit water, steadying the canoe while Malcolm and Kojo lifted General Fédon into it and covered him with a blanket.

A bullfrog bellowed nearby.

Kojo faced Malcolm. "I think all English soldiers enemies. I never meet one like you."

"And I never met a warrior like you." Malcolm held Kojo's big rough hands in a strong handshake. "Thank you for saving my life."

Kojo nodded and returned his attention to the canoes. He held onto the floating canoe with one hand and, in the other, a rope leading to the smaller canoe on the shore.

Rosette and Malcolm sloshed back to shore. Standing across from her with the empty canoe between them, he avoided looking into her eyes for fear he might lose control.

Instead, he kept his sights on a compass fastened to the middle seat of the canoe.

Obviously, if they had two canoes and a compass, the general and Kojo had prepared well in advance, and knew where they headed—a destination Rosette could never share with Malcolm.

Should Malcolm forsake everything and go with

Rosette?

No. The general certainly would have none of it.

But in his feeble state, would he have the force to resist if Malcolm decided to join them? Wherever they might end up, a British soldier surely would not be received kindly.

Rosette was right. She and he were dreamers. The world was not ready for them.

They pushed the canoe into the water, and Kojo roped it closer to the first.

He turned to Rosette. "We must reach horizon before sun come up."

Malcolm worried that Kojo and Rosette might not row the canoe fast enough to clear the horizon before sunrise, especially with the spare canoe in tow. Now that the new governor had posted a five-hundred-pound reward on Fédon's head, British ships patrolling Grenada's waters would surely be on the lookout for him.

Malcolm held Rosette's hand. She collapsed against him in sobs.

He held her face in his hands, the moon glowing in her eyes. "I will always love you." He kissed her.

She cried. "My heart bleeds for us."

General Fédon coughed with impatience.

At least, Rosette had her father.

Malcolm had to return to his, a stranger, a British commander bent on exacting unforgiving punishment on all who dared to help Fédon. If General McDonald ever discovered his son lifted Fédon into the canoe that took him to freedom, Malcolm would hang for sure.

How might Malcolm return to Belvidere and justify his overnight absence from his soldiers? And suppose the soldiers on the road later recognized him as the captain who ordered them away from Westerhall Bay, miles from Belvidere and a likely escape point for Fédon? He had no way to explain his ruse, that he also had soldiers searching the coastal road.

Malcolm had dug himself a hole too deep from which to climb.

Mosquitoes buzzed past his ears, as if warning of the dangers that awaited him in Belvidere.

Rosette released him abruptly and entered the water. Kojo helped her into the canoe, and he climbed in.

They pulled oars and dug them into the water.

At that moment, whatever clouds misted the sky slipped away, and the naked moon gazed down on them in full splendor. The night looked like noon.

Without warning, a massive thunder shook the ground and winds roared through the trees with frantic urgency. Just as quickly, a mystifying stillness returned to the bay.

Malcolm glanced up at the lit sky, puzzled.

When he looked back at the canoes floating on the glazed sea, Rosette and Kojo also stared at the moon, with mesmerized expressions, like those of Shango dancers in torchlight.

The decision struck Malcolm with the speed of lightning.

May Father and all he stood for be damned.

Malcolm raced into the water and waddled up to the canoe. He climbed in and took the oar from Rosette.

"Hurry, Kojo," he shouted. "We have to make it to the horizon before dawn.

Epilogue

Julien Fédon vanished from Grenada, but not from the minds of the Grenada people. A few days after he disappeared, a washed-up canoe was discovered with a compass nailed to the floor. Since it was nailed, it no longer functioned. So, what was its purpose? In his essay, *African Symbolism in Fédon's Rebellion,* historian Dr. Curtis Jacobs explains that the compass was a message from Fédon to the slaves, most born in Africa and still deeply embedded with their spiritual traditions. To these Kongo people, the circumference of the compass assured that the righteous person who presented it would reincarnate one day.

Fédon wanted them to know he would return.

A hundred and fifty years later, a union leader named Eric Gairy led plantation laborers on months of strikes and fires. Many asked if Fédon had returned. The governor at the time, Sir Robert Arundell, telegraphed the British government about Gairy. "He has, I am reliably informed, been hailed as the reincarnation of Fédon."

For his efforts to lift their working conditions, the Grenada people rewarded Gairy with political leadership of the island for the next thirty years. However, ironically, his increasingly oppressive regime was overthrown in the 1979 Grenada revolution led by Maurice Bishop, a descendant of Captain Louis La Grenade, the French Mulatto who fought against Fédon.

Yet again, Fédon, in name and in spirit, rose to prominence. The revolutionaries named a military base Camp Fédon. The government press was named Fédon Publishers. They even named a military exercise designed to resist an American invasion, the Fédon Maneuver.

But like the Fédon Rebellion, the Grenada Revolution was short lived. The Fédon rebellion lasted sixteen months. The Bishop revolution lasted less than five years.

Like the 1795 rebellion, the 1979 revolution ended in catastrophe: a sharp division within the revolutionary ranks in 1983 led to bloodshed and executions, including that of its leader, Maurice Bishop.

As with Julien Fédon, the whereabouts of Bishop's body is still a mystery.

The Fédon rebellion ended with the invasion by British troops.

The Bishop revolution ended with the invasion by American troops.

An estimated seven thousand people died during the Fédon rebellion, about twenty-five percent of the population then. Many lost their lives in the fighting, but a significant number died from the diseases, fevers, and malnutrition that accompanied the island's physical devastation.

No memorial commemorates the slaves who died, but the Grenada Anglican Church has a wooden plaque that lists the forty-eight prisoners that Fédon executed.

Those executed include:

Lieutenant-Governor Ninian Home—His Paxton House mansion in England survives today. It holds a remarkable collection of paintings, books, and furnishings, and regularly grants public tours. In 2007, the Paxton Trust invited a Grenadian cultural group to perform at the mansion in celebration of the bicentenary of the abolition of the slave trade. The group's name is Descendants.

Alexander Campbell—Former Speaker of the Grenada Assembly and a close friend of Governor Home.

Neill Campbell—Signed the Belvidere Estate sale documents from James Campbell to Julien Fédon. Other documents raise questions about the validity of the transaction. No genealogical links exit between those Campbells and the Campbells of Grenada today.

Matthew Atkinson—The twelve-year-old boy was the only one of the forty-eight to cry for mercy, in vain.

The three prisoners Fédon spared included:

Dr. Hay—Witnessed the executions on Belvidere and wrote an account of the event, describing Fédon's daughter and wife as 'unfeeling spectators.' He also cited multiple other occasions when the Fédons treated him and others with unexpected compassion and generosity. He penned Madame Fédon's Certificate of Freedom. Dr. Hay died in Gouyave in 1803 at age fifty-seven, seven years after the demise of the Fédon Rebellion.

Other personalities in the story included:

Father Mandel Pascal—French Roman Catholic priest, who wore the uniform of the French Revolutionaries at the onset of the rebellion. Captured and executed by the British.

Jean-Pierre Fédon—Julien Fédon's brother, killed in the failed British attack on Belvidere April 8, 1795, the day Fédon ordered the executions. Jean-Pierre's wife, even in her grief, offered clothes to the desperate Dr. Hay, which he accepted.

Charles Nogues—Husband to Fédon's sister. Once a tailor in St. George's. Captured and executed by the British.

Lavallée— A fervent revolutionary, was chopped to death in a fight with other rebels in Fédon's presence.

Captain Louis La Grenade—French mulatto, who like Fédon, swore an oath of loyalty to the British. He served with the British, commanding his own detachment of black and mulatto troops against Fédon. In 2013, Cecile La Grenade, one of his descendants became the first female Governor-General of Grenada.

Others who participated in the campaign against Fédon:

General Colin Lindsay—His suicide on March 22, 1795, dealt a severe blow to the British forces and raised the hopes of Fédon and his rebels.

Colonel McDonald and Captain McDonald—Served in Grenada during the Fédon rebellion. It is unknown if they were father and son.

Captain Philip Gurdon (not in the story)—Ordered to attack Belvidere on March 5, 1795. In a puzzling series of decisions that bordered on disobedience and described as shameful, he resisted the orders and withdrew to Gouyave without firing a shot. Desertions and near mutiny followed. However, in other locations, he fought bravely and gallantly and was eventually killed in battle in Grenville. If he knew the Fédons, there is no evidence of it.

Several soldiers defected from the British and joined the Fédon rebellion.

In 1814, the governor of Grenada wrote the authorities in Cuba to follow up on rumors that Fédon was sighted in Havana. No known documents explain what happened next. To this day, Julien Fédon's disappearance remains a mystery.

Lightning Source UK Ltd.
Milton Keynes UK
UKHW021113020619
343725UK00005B/232/P